DOUBLEDAY
CELEBRATES
100 YEARS OF
EXCELLENCE

Kiddo
Boss
The Man Who Died Laughing
The Man Who Lived by Night
The Man Who Would Be F. Scott Fitzgerald
The Woman Who Fell from Grace
The Boy Who Never Grew Up
The Man Who Cancelled Himself
The Girl Who Ran Off with Daddy

David Handler

The Man Who Loved Women to Death

A Stewart "Hoagy" Hoag Mystery

D O U B L E D A Y
New York London Toronto Sydney Auckland

PUBLISHED BY DOUBLEDAY
a division of Bantam Doubleday Dell Publishing Group, Inc.
1540 Broadway, New York, New York 10036

DOUBLEDAY and the portrayal of an anchor with a dolphin are
trademarks of Doubleday, a division of Bantam Doubleday Dell
Publishing Group, Inc.

Library of Congress Cataloging-in-Publication Data

Handler, David, 1952–
The man who loved women to death: A Stewart "Hoagy" Hoag mystery/
David Handler—1st ed.
p.   cm.
I. Title.
PS3558.A4637M295   1997
813'.54–dc20   96-31440
CIP

ISBN 0-385-48052-0
Copyright © 1997 by David Handler
All Rights Reserved
Printed in the United States of America
May 1997
First Edition

10   9   8   7   6   5   4   3   2   1

For William Goldman,
the master, from a grateful apprentice

The Man Who Loved Women to Death

One

Dear Hoagy,

You don't mind me being so familiar, do you? I hope not. I feel like I know you, having read and enjoyed your work so much. And "Mr. Hoag" just seems so stiff, somehow.

I'm enclosing the first chapter of what I'm hoping, with your generous assistance, to develop into a novel. It's about a character who I believe has the potential to make as big a name for himself in modern American fiction as Holden Caulfield. I've structured it in the form of letters to a friend, much like Ring Lardner did with the letters Jack Keefe wrote to Friend Al in "You Know Me Al," a work I freely admit has influenced me greatly. Maybe even too much. I don't know. I'm not a professional writer. At least not yet.

But I do feel this is a VERY commercial project. I need advice and help. I need a collaborator. I need YOU. Once we find a publisher I can promise you your usual fee and royalties, including a nominal share of the film rights. This is a natural for a film, by the way.

I have gone ahead and written the first chapter on my own as a sample. I am told I pretty much have to do this. I hope you can spare the time to read it. And can advise me what I should do next. I really look forward to meeting you. I'm a real fan.

Yours truly,
the answer man

I WAS AT THE COUNTER of the Oyster Bar in Grand Central that day showing Tracy the proper way to eat a bluepoint. I figured it was important that she learn about these things from me. Who else was going to teach her? Some pimply little weasel named Gunnar or Doogie? What the hell would *he* know about raw oysters? He'd probably tell her to order a dozen. Wrong. The correct number is nine. He'd probably tell her to drown them all in lemon juice. Wrong again. You squirt each oyster individually, and only when you are just about to eat it. Add a dash of Tabasco, then swallow whole. That's how you eat an oyster.

Tony, who'd been there behind the raw bar since VJ Day, certainly concurred. As for Lulu, my noted nose bowl champ, she merely grunted peevishly. She'd been in a sour mood ever since her annual physical exam, when her doctor remarked that she was becoming a trifle, well, jowly. It didn't matter that she was in tip-top health otherwise—sinuses clear as a bell, figure svelte, gums as gingivitis-free as those of a basset hound half her age. Lulu was steamed—her looks mean a lot to her. Plus Tony was taking his sweet time with her oyster pan roast, mostly because he kept stopping to make funny faces at Tracy, who kept responding with gales of laughter from her perch there next to me. At eighteen months, Tracy remained a sunny, happy baby. Clearly, the Hoagy genes hadn't kicked in yet. They would. I wasn't at all concerned. Or at all looking forward to it.

Still, no complaints from this end. It used to be that

spending the better part of an afternoon on a stool in the belly of Grand Central terminal slurping up oysters was called loafing. Now, thanks to Tracy and the sober responsibilities of fatherhood, it was called quality time.

Afterward, we meandered over to Fifth Avenue to take in the annual Christmas display in the windows of Lord and Taylor, Tracy swaddled in her periwinkle-blue snug suit and cashmere ducky blanket. It was a bright, frosty early December day, the best kind of day in the best time of year in the best city on earth. New York comes to life between Thanksgiving and Christmas. The air is as bracing as a sharp whiff of ammonia. The chestnuts are roasting. People have a bounce in their stride and an unfamiliar bit of color in their cheeks. A few of them even smile. At least they smiled at us as we walked along. It was Tracy, chiefly. Not that Lulu wasn't lookin' buff in her Fair Isle sweater vest, prancing along beside her baby sister's stroller. Not that I was looking too terrible myself in my shearling greatcoat from Milan, which I wore over the barley-colored Donegal tweed suit from Strickland's, a cream and blue tattersall shirt of Italian wool and a knit tie of rose-colored silk. No, it was Tracy. Her emerald-green eyes, chiefly. Merilee's eyes. And those luxuriant blond tresses that spilled out from under the knitted cap that was perched on her somewhat largish head. She was an uncommonly beautiful baby. People always lit up when they saw her. Especially when she was with Merilee. The two of them made quite some pair. In fact, I was becoming deathly afraid they'd soon be asked to appear in one of those vomitous celebrity mother-daughter fashion spreads in *Vanity Fair.*

I'd be damned if any daughter of mine would be exploited that way. Especially without me.

From Lord and Taylor's we strolled down to the Old Print Shop on Lex, me limping slightly. The limp had nothing to do with age and everything to do with that damned play Merilee was rehearsing. I picked out the frame for Merilee's

Christmas present, an etching that Levon West did in the early thirties of a busy New York street on a rainy day. Merilee had much admired it—looking at it, you can practically hear the car horns and the Gershwin in the background—but she was way too much of a frugal Yankee puritan to spring for it. That made one of us. For Tracy I had bought one good book. I'd decided to buy her one good book every year for Christmas—each a signed first edition. This particular Christmas, her second, she was getting *The Sun Also Rises*. From there we worked our way back up Madison to Worth & Worth, where I had my Statler reblocked while I studied how I looked in a homburg. Distinguished, I decided. I also decided I could wait another ten years to look distinguished. Lulu's new district check wool cap had come in. She tried it on in the three-way mirror, snuffling happily. Shopping always cheers her up. Something she got from me. That and an aversion to any film starring Meg Ryan. Afterward, we took in the tree at Rockefeller Center, a seventy-five-foot Norway spruce that had been donated by two nuns in Mendham, New Jersey. We watched the ice skaters. We stopped at the St. Regis, where Sal Fodera trimmed my hair. It doesn't take him as long as it used to, but Sal is courtly enough never to point this out. Mary at the front desk fussed like crazy over Tracy. Lulu took a nap, which is one of the things she is best at.

Yes, we made a real father-daughter-basset hound day of it. It was a happy day, a day I had earned. After all, I had at long last finished Novel No. 3. It's true, I'd done it. Seventeen years after *The New York Times Book Review* had labeled me "the first major new literary voice of the 1980s," six years after they'd called my second novel "the most embarrassing act of public self-flagellation since Richard Nixon's Checkers speech," I'd finally done it. Not that I had a publisher for it yet, mind you. It was not exactly an easy sell, seeing as how it was a prime example of what's known in publishing as a male menopause novel, a category that made it only slightly less commercial than, say, *My Life and High Times* by Neon Leon Spinks. Right now, it was making the rounds. Which meant I was having lunches with a lot of editors. Which is what they get paid to do and writers do not. Mostly, I was sorry to discover, they wanted to talk to me about my other, decidedly less distinguished career—the Claude Rains thing. When it comes to ghosting, I am The Man. The best of what's around. Five number-one bestselling memoirs and someone else's number-one bestselling novel to my noncredit. So I heard all about the basketball star who had just flunked his third drug test and his fourth reading test. The U.S. senator with presidential aspirations. Or perspirations. The actress who was finally ready to tell the world who she had and had not given the skin to—now that there was no one left alive in the world who cared. I certainly didn't. None of that celebrity rubbernecking crap for me. No more. I was Stewart Stafford Hoag, novelist. I had slain my personal white whale. Someone in power would agree with me any day now. It would happen. It would sell. I knew it was good. I was not going to worry. I was going to enjoy the city, enjoy my daughter, enjoy my life. Life was good. Repeat after me: Life is good.

Then again, maybe Joseph Wood Krutch was right. Maybe we moralists are never satisfied. Pay no attention to me. I'm just trying to give you an idea where my head was that day the first chapter came, okay?

It came, as do seeds from Burpee and bad news from the Internal Revenue Service, in a plain manila envelope. But inside was not the makings of Better Boy tomatoes or news that my deductions for home-office expenses had once again been disallowed. Inside was a manuscript, eight pages in length, and a very polite cover letter. Both had been typed on an old manual typewriter, which you don't see much of anymore, not unless you get a letter or a manuscript from me.

I stood in the somewhat grand lobby of our building on

Central Park West and read the letter under the suspicious gaze of Mario, the daytime doorman, who had never liked me and was liking me even less now that I'd taken to opening my mail down there before I went upstairs. Mario was positive that I was corresponding with some mystery woman. For the record, I wasn't. For the record, I'd never liked Mario either. And Lulu liked him even less than I did. When it comes to hating petty authority figures, we always stick together.

Like most authors who've had their names in the papers, I get my share of oddball mail. I get letters from droolers who are genuinely convinced they were captured by an alien or Elvis or Nicole Brown Simpson and need someone (me) to help them tell and sell their miraculous story. I get inquiries from dog lovers who are thinking of adopting a basset hound and wonder if they are easy to train. (You don't train them— they train you.) And, yes, I get submissions from would-be novelists who want my advice. (Generally, I suggest going to dental school, which qualifies you to stick sharp objects in people's mouths and hurt them and get paid a lot of money for it.) Some of these letters are forwarded to me by my agent or by the different publishers I've worked for through the years. Some of them, like this particular one, find their way directly to my home. I don't know how these people get my address. They just do. I get *Prison Life* magazine every month, for instance, and I have no idea why or how. Aside from the fact that so many of the celebrities I've worked for are presently doing time.

What I'm trying to say is there was nothing out of the ordinary about this letter. Except for one thing: There was no name on it—unless you count "the answer man." Not so much as a clue as to who this budding author might be. Not on the letter, which was typed on plain white typing paper—no letterhead, no watermark. Not on the title page of the manuscript. Not on the nine-by-twelve manila envelope it came in. There was no return address on the envelope either. Just my name and address typed onto a stick-on label, the kind that come twenty to a sheet. Same typewriter. There were four 32-cent stamps affixed to it. It had been postmarked the day before somewhere in New York City, which is to say Manhattan, not Brooklyn or Queens or any of those other boroughs.

Somewhat strange. But not so strange as to intrigue me. I just dismissed it as terminal shyness or forgetfulness or any one of the other million endearing little tics that tend to take root in authors, would-be and otherwise. I tucked the chapter back in its envelope. I stuck it under my arm with the rest of that day's mail. I rode the elevator up to our floor with Tracy and Lulu.

Merilee was home from rehearsal. I knew this because I walked through the door into utter and complete blackness, the kind of darkness that can be achieved in New York City only if you install Levolor blinds in every window and then cloak these behind heavy floor-to-ceiling blackout drapery. This, in case you were wondering, is why I'd taken to opening my mail downstairs. This, in case you were wondering, is what it means to have an ex-wife who is an actress.

Mine was deep into rehearsing the role of Susy Hendrix for a revival of *Wait Until Dark,* the Broadway stage thriller by Frederick Knott. Lee Remick had originated the role on stage thirty years back. Audrey Hepburn had played it on film. And now it was Merilee Nash's turn. She and her semi-notable co-star in the role of the heavy, Harry Roat. Susy, as you may recall, is blind. Merilee, so as to get into character, had turned our world into Susy's world. She spent hours every day stumbling around in the dark, eyes wide open, seeing nothing. Occasionally, she even moved the furniture around so as to make it that much harder. All of which was fine for her but hard on me. I kept bumping into our heavy Stickley originals, leaving me with welts on my knees and shins—hence the limp. It was also hard on Lulu, who had been recruited for much-hated doggie-on-a-string detail so Merilee could try walking down the street without benefit of sight. She wore a mask over her eyes for that. Merilee, that is. I voted that she wear one inside, too, so that the rest of us could enjoy the healthy benefits of light. Not to mention our million-dollar view of Central Park. No sir. Merilee was Susy now, and Susy's world was a dark one. Plus she claimed that practicing this way was sharpening her other senses.

My own sense of smell as I stood there, blind, in the entry hall, told me that Pamela, our silver-haired British housekeeper, had made Daube à la Niçoise for dinner. For dessert she had baked a walnut loaf made with black walnuts from our own tree in Lyme. My own sense of hearing told me that my stomach was growling.

She heard us come in, Pam did, and started down the long, dark hallway toward us from The Safe Zone, her brightly lit kitchen. She had a Petzl zoom headlamp strapped to her head, and looked somewhat like a cheery, pink-cheeked coal miner. Lulu stayed put in between my feet, whimpering mournfully. She's afraid of the dark. Only dog I know of who is. Tracy, she didn't seem to care much one way or the other.

"Yes, yes, here we are, Miss Lulu," Pam called to her soothingly from under the light beam. "Help is on the way. Here we come. Here we are. Did we all have a lovely day? Of course we did. Now we'll see that Miss Tracy has a proper bath and to bed, won't we?"

"Where is the divine Lady M?" I asked, handing over Tracy.

"Off wandering somewhere in the living room." Pam lowered her voice discreetly. "Poor dear's gone and moved the settee again."

And with that we heard a loud thud from somewhere off in the blackness. Followed by "Oh, sugar! Shirley Temple! Succotash!" And then a hurried "I'm all right, Pam! It wasn't an important toe! I'm all right!"

"Fine, dear!" Pam called back to her. Clucking, she

turned her headbeam on the entry closet so I could hang up my coat. "Poor girl's positively covered with bruises. The sacrifices she makes for her art. Unless, that is, you've been hitting her."

"I have not. Besides, how would that explain all of *my* bruises?"

"She's been hitting you back," Pam sniffed. "High time, if you ask me. Victor wanted words with you." Victor being Vic Early, celebrity bodyguard extraordinaire, who doubled as caretaker of our Connecticut farm. "Did he get hold of you?"

"No, he didn't. What's it about?"

"I really couldn't say, dear boy," she replied airily, heading back to her clean, well-lit kitchen with Tracy in her arms and a grateful Lulu on her heel. And leaving me there in the total dark.

"Honey, I'm home!" I called out, groping my way blindly toward the living room. *Wham.* That was me colliding with the umbrella stand. *Wham.* That was the door to the powder room. "Merilee?" *Wham.* That was the umbrella stand again. Cursing, I moved forward, arms waving wildly at my sides. I felt like I was playing the childhood game of Dare. Which I suppose is as good a description of my on–again, off–again nonrelationship with Merilee Gilbert Nash as any other. "Merilee, are you there?"

"Darling, in here," she whispered urgently from the blackness, her hand grabbing me by the wrist and tugging me toward the powder room. *Into* the powder room. She locked the door behind us. "Oh, God, Hoagy, you smell so good," she murmured in my ear.

"That's Floris, Merilee. I've been wearing it forever."

"But my other senses are so keen now. So *aroused.*" She let out a startled gasp. "I want you, Hoagy." Her lips were on mine now, her breath hot on my face. I heard the slithering of her silk dressing gown as it fell to the floor. Her hands took deadly aim at my belt, my zipper. "I want you this instant!"

"But Pam is right in the other—"

"Now, Hoagy!" she cried, flinging herself against me. She was brazen. She was wild. She was not wearing a stitch under that dressing gown. And, well, there was no talking her out of it. Not that I tried, mind you.

Hmmm . . . I suppose I should explain this recent and somewhat lubricious phenomenon. Or try to. I didn't know if it was Merilee's fortysomething hormones or some really interesting form of postpartum depression or just this role she was rehearsing—but something about being in the darkness had unleashed her untamed side. No sooner would I hang up my coat then she'd whisper, *"Psst,* over here, darling!" and faster than you can say Charlie Sheen we'd be locked in just this sort of feverish, teeth-clanking embrace. I never knew where or when the mood would strike her. I only knew that to date we'd consecrated the entry hall floor, the dining table and the coat closet. All of this made for quite some departure from Merilee's usual prim-and-proper Miss Porter's School self. But I'd decided not to ask why. And to just go along with it for as long as I could keep it up, as it were.

Afterward, I made us a pitcher of dry martinis, heavy on the olives, and made straight for a steaming bubble bath in the vast master bathroom tub, where I collapsed, limp in every known sense of the word. Merilee's Oscar could be found in there, mounted ceremoniously over the toilet tank. Lulu could be found in there, too, sprawled out on her back under the sink with her tongue lolling out of the side of her mouth. She likes the steam. More than I like sharing it with her, being that she will eat only that which swims or scuttles or inhabits the ocean floor. For dinner she'd just enjoyed some of her 9-Lives canned mackerel for cats and culinarily challenged dogs. Sharing steam with Lulu is like hanging out in the kitchen of a fish house.

Merilee came bustling in for her hairbrush, humming gaily to herself, her green eyes bright and animated, a healthy glow to her patrician features. They really are the stronger sex, you know. She had slipped into the black velvet Ralph Lauren for dinner, the one that makes her look willowy as a schoolgirl. This had to do with a certain pact we'd made. No nightshirts or jammies at the dinner table. No *Jeopardy* on the TV. None of those things that boring married couples do. We dress. We light candles. We use the good silver and the linen napkins. We are not a boring married couple. Repeat after me: We are not a boring married couple.

She remained there in the doorway, brushing out her shimmering waist-length golden hair. That's a sight I will never, ever grow tired of. "Demi turned down the new Brad Pitt. They've offered it to me."

"Congratulations, Merilee."

"Not so fast, darling. There's a problem with it. Rather large one. There's, well, this nude scene . . ."

"You and Brad?"

"That's right."

"You and Brad in bed together?"

"In an abandoned root cellar, actually." She tossed her hair back, a gesture that has always quickened my pulse, and stood there with her hip thrown out. "I've never believed in them, you know."

"Abandoned root cellars?"

"Nude scenes. I've always said no. But there's no getting around this one. It's pivotal to the story."

"Wait, what about that nude scene you did in *Romeo and Juliet* for Papp?"

"That was different, darling."

"Why, because it was Art?"

"No, because I was twenty-three when I played Juliet. Or, more specifically, my thighs were."

"Merilee, your thighs are lovely."

She took a sip of her martini, her forehead creasing fretfully. "I don't know what to do."

"Why don't you just do what every other actress your age does?"

"What, go in for tumescent liposculpture?"

"No, silly. Use a body double. Some twenty-year-old who's six-feet-three and works out on a Stairmaster fourteen hours a day. I'll sit in on the casting sessions, if you like. That way we'll be sure she's got a butt just like—" Somehow, her hairbrush bounced off my left ear. "Ow, that hurt!"

"It was supposed to, mister. A body double's out of the question."

"I don't see why. You used a stunt double when you jumped out of that helicopter in the Bruce Willis picture."

"Because I'm an actress, not a paratrooper. This is different."

"Why?"

"Because I'm *forty,* that's why. I know it, the audience knows it and Mr. Gravity sure as sugar knows it. Let's face it, darling, from the neck down I'm starting to resemble one of those cute baby elephants you see at the circus, the ones they dress up in little pink pinafores."

"I believe it's the monkeys they do that with."

"I'll know it's not me. *Everyone* will know it's not me. It's cheating. It's fake. It's—"

"It's a *movie,* Merilee."

"Oh, beans, I'm sorry I even mentioned it. Forget it, I'm not doing it. Let Sharon do it. What am I saying? She's probably turned it down already." She sighed grandly, tragically. "Oh God, I hate this business."

"Merilee," I said, reaching for her hand, "you're still one of the most beautiful women in the world." Which she is. Not that she's conventionally pretty. Never has been. Her jaw is too strong. Her nose too long. Her forehead too high. But on her it all adds up to beautiful. She was beautiful at twenty-five. She was beautiful at forty. And she would be beautiful at sixty.

"Bless you for that, darling. But you and I both know that I'm getting to be a card-carrying grown-up, and they don't believe in those out there. Not if you happen to be a she." She came over to freshen my martini from the pitcher. Two is my limit these days. After that I become incoherent, unless there is a language where the phrase "oot-groot" is considered intelligent conversation. "Did Vic get hold of you, by the way?"

"Pam asked me that, too. What's this all about?"

"Heavens, I wouldn't know. He phoned from the country this afternoon. I assumed it was to do with the furnace or the roof or something."

"Ah, a guy matter."

"Well, you are a guy, darling." From the doorway, she gave me her up-from-under look. "At least you were the last time I looked."

"Looking isn't all you did, Miss Nash."

That one drove her back out to the bedroom, where she started tearing at the mail I'd left on the bed. "My brother has invited us out to Aspen for Christmas," she announced gravely. "Please tell me we can't go."

I lay back in the tub with my martini, groaning comfortably. "Merilee . . ."

"Yes, darling?" she said, voice breathless with anticipation.

"We can't go to Aspen."

"Oh, what a relief. I hate that place. Especially over the holidays, when it's overrun by Sly and Barbra and all of those horrid sweaty men from CAA and their snarly, muscular little wives. Darling, let's spend it at the farm with our own little tree and Grandmother's decorations and a stuffed goose and Tracy and Lulu. We'll stuff a goose. We'll—"

"I'd prefer a large one."

"A large one, darling?"

"The tree. I want a large one."

"Oh, I see. And I suppose just because you want a large one we have to have a large one. Gosh, you're a brute. I'm so glad I didn't marry you."

"But you did marry me."

"I did? Oh, dear, I did. But then that means that Tracy is—"

"Ours, Merilee. But don't worry. She was conceived after our divorce."

"Whew, that's a relief. For a second there I thought we were becoming one of those stable, normal American families that the politicians keep talking about. Hoagy, promise me we'll never become stable and normal."

"I can't imagine that will ever be a problem in our case."

"Promise me!" she insisted.

"I so promise," I said solemnly, raising my glass.

She reappeared in the doorway. "What's this?" she wondered, meaning the nine-by-twelve manila envelope.

"First chapter of the next great American novel. Here, hand it over. We could be facing a historic moment in the annals of contemporary literature."

She did. I got comfortable. We have a pillow for that. I sipped my martini. I ate my olive. I ignored the prevailing aroma of fish in the air, or at least I tried.

I read.

1. the answer man hits town
New York City, November 30

Friend E: Well, old pal, I guess you've heard that the Big Apple has claimed me once more. Whoop-de-damn-do, as Derrick Coleman, basketball's most overpaid dog, likes to say. Not that I ever thought I'd end up back here. Just seems like I'm not happy nowhere else. Found myself a semi-decent jack rack in the shadow of G.T. Not much view, but the hot plate's brand new. So here I am.

Mostly I've been riding the subway. Been riding it for hours at a time, fact is. Just watching the people. So many different kinds of people from so many different parts of the world living and working and scratching and clawing here. All of them crammed together, noses buried in their newspapers, ears buried in their sounds. All of them going somewhere. I've been watching them, Friend E. Watching them and wondering: How do they do it? How do they brush their teeth, eat their breakfast, go to work, stand there on that platform waiting for a train . . . knowing that none of it means shit? I mean, they're all gonna die anyway, right? And they know this, right? So how do they do it? How do they not hurl themselves right in front of the oncoming downtown No. 1 local, making all stops to South Ferry?! Makes me wonder, Friend E. I truly wonder.

I mean, what in the hell ARE they thinking about?

Me, I think about what I always think about. And that's not money, as you damned well know for sure. Though if you could spare me fifty I would greatly appreciate it and will pay you back for sure just as soon as I find me some paying work. Tomorrow I'm gonna see about getting me my old job back at the restaurant, where the boss is pretty fair and don't seem to mind I sometimes can't deal with shit.

Wait til you hear about this girl I got over on. A real honey. Blows me away just how many honeys there are here, E, all of them lonely, all of them desperate to take a chance on some guy, any guy. Not that I'm any guy, but you know me.

THEY sure don't. The doctors, I mean. Or they wouldn't have let me out.

I searched for her for three days, riding the subway uptown, downtown, all around the town, day and night. Finally caught sight of her half-past nine one morning, standing there on the platform, waiting, locked into her own little space capsule, Walkman over her ears, her eyes deep into some book.

One look at her and right away I knew my day just got booked solid.

She was a little thing, five-feet-four tops, and slender. Couldn't have weighed more than a hundred pounds. Had nice blue eyes and real nice blond hair long and shiny. Good teeth, too, with just a slight overbite, which I've always had this thing for. Don't know why, I just do. She looked to be maybe 28. Wore a leather jacket with a small backpack over it, baggy jeans and those big heavy motorcycle boots they've all taken to wearing. Which I don't understand, since I think a woman's slender ankle and foot are among the sexiest things they got working for them. She was looking real tough and together, the way the honeys do in New York when they are standing around somewhere in public.

I knew better, of course.

When the downtown local came I got on the same car with her. She took a seat and got into her book, some damn thing about a housecat who went to Paris, France. Whoop-de-damn-do. I stood there with my back to the door and my eyes on her. She looked up once, when we stopped at Columbus Circle, her eyes sweeping across the different faces in the car. They locked onto mine for a second, but kept right on going. The expression on her face told me nothing. My heart was pounding. But I was cool. I was so very cool.

She got off at Times Square and started walking through the station toward the Grand Central shuttle. I did the same, eyeballing the clenching and unclenching of that terrific little butt inside those jeans. I stayed a safe twenty feet back, feeling loose and light on my feet, feeling good. She caught the shuttle, then came up in the Graybar Building on 41st Street and started walking downtown on Lex. I stayed right on her. Damned noisy in that part of town during the morning rush. People screaming, horns honking, ambulances with their sirens blaring. Somebody's car alarm went off, sounded like they just won the jackpot on one of those TV game shows you and me used to watch together when we were good boys. She paid no attention to any of it. Just kept right on walking. Went into a Korean grocery on the corner of 32nd Street and bought a bunch of flowers. Then she started toward Third on 32nd. Halfway down the block she stopped at a pet food store and got buzzed in. I waited across the street five minutes. When she didn't come out I figured this must be where she worked.

I crossed the street. I got myself buzzed in.

It was a small place, seemed to be about health food for dogs and cats. Stuff like organic kibble, if you can believe that, Friend E. There was some homey worked there, bringing big bags of stuff up from the basement. And there was her, standing behind the counter bossing him around. She ran the place. She smiled at me real nice. Didn't recognize me from the subway. Or if she did she didn't let on. She asked if she could help me. Her voice caught me by surprise. It was so unbelievably chirpy and high-pitched I almost lost it. Was damned glad I wasn't on any of the major hallucinogens. Or anything else. Which, as you know, is not too typical for me.

I said It must be nice. She frowned and said What must be nice? I said Being so sure of yourself—you seem like a person who never has any self-doubts, and I envy that.

Well, this pretty much got her attention, Friend E. Which, in case you are taking notes at home, is that Much Desired First Step. I said I'm looking for kibble for my new puppy and I want it to be free of chemicals and preservatives. She said What kind of dog is it. I said A golden retriever, eight weeks old. And she said They are soooo adorable when they are that age. I admitted as how he'd stolen my heart, which was not so very hard since I'd just gone through a really messy breakup and was trying to start over fresh.

This was me baiting the hook, E. Any honey who runs a pet food store and reads cat books is bound to melt for a human stray. Friend E, it's vitally important that you become who they want you to become. Guys are all the time asking me what my secret is, and that is it, nothing more.

Be who they want you to be.

She told me she herself had two cats, Fred and Ethel. I told her I'd named my dog Victor. And she said Like Victor Potamkin, the old guy who used to sell Cadillacs on TV? And I said No, like the RCA Victor dog. And she said You mean Nipper, don't you? And I said No, I mean the RCA Victor dog. And she said Right, the RCA Victor dog's name is Nipper. And I said Well, my dog's name is Victor. And we both laughed and that's when she said I looked really familiar. Which, as you know, I hear a lot. I said I just have an ordinary face. She said Well, I guess you must. She was playing with me now. I shot a look at the clock, suddenly in a big rush to get to work. I asked her how late they'd be open. She said Six. I said I'd be back. She said Cool.

Found a Greek coffeeshop around the corner and sat there drinking coffee with ten, twelve spoons of sugar in it. Only they wouldn't let me smoke in there. Why won't they let you smoke in coffeeshops

*anymore? I don't get it. So I walked and smoked. Then I realized I
hadn't eaten anything since yesterday so I went in a bar, where it
turns out they WILL let you smoke, and had me a double order of
french fries. I drank more coffee. I sat and stared at the clock. My
chest felt so tight I almost couldn't breathe. After five o'clock the
place started filling up with these loud, obnoxious Young Urban
Shitheads in fancy suits ordering brands of beer I'd never heard of.
Weird thing about this city, Friend E. They won't let you smoke a
cigarette in a coffeeshop but it's okay to be an asshole anywhere you
want.*

*She was waiting for me. I could tell by the way she looked up
from the counter when I buzzed. And the way she smiled. She had
a real nice smile, E. After some discussion I bought a 20 lb. bag of
kibble that had brown rice and free-range-chicken bonemeal and a
bunch of other ingredients in it you wouldn't believe. You wouldn't
believe the price neither. I hung around while she was closing.
Asked her if she had a long trip home. She said Not really. Told me
where she lived, which turned out to be less than two blocks from
where I was staying. I said Would you mind if I ride uptown with
you? She said No, not at all. I didn't try asking her out for a drink
yet, sensing she'd go cautious on me if I did that.*

*I told her my name while we walked to the subway. Hers was
Diane. While we were riding home Diane asked me the usual,
which was what I did for work. I told her I was employed by the
City of New York as a social worker specializing in helping young
inner-city fathers take responsibility for themselves both as providers
and as parents. It is my personal belief, I told her, that the only way
you can heal this city is one family at a time.*

*Which is total bullshit, as you and I both know, E. But let me
tell you, it was the perfect approach with Diane. Her big blue eyes
got bigger and bluer. Her lips got softer and fuller. She wanted me,
E. I could FEEL how she wanted me.*

I was in and I knew it. We both did.

*We were right near my place when we got off the train. I said
Hey, Diane, want to come up and meet Victor? She said I'd like
that. Just like I knew she would. She even let me hold her hand in
the elevator. It was real small, but firm and dry. I warned her that*

my place wasn't much. She told me it didn't matter, she wasn't into appearances. We walked in the door and I put down the bag of kibble, which was damned heavy, and turned on a light. I said See? I told you it wasn't much. She looked around and said Don't be silly. It's fine. Only, where's Victor? Is he asleep? I ducked my head, really sheepish, and said Actually, I don't own a dog. Now she was totally confused. I don't get it, she said. Why did you buy the kibble? And I said Because I wanted to meet you. And she said Why? And I said Because I am the answer to your prayers, Diane. And she said What prayers?

And then she didn't say anything more because she KNEW. Only it was too late now. I had her. She was mine, all mine.

This is the moment I live for, E. The moment when they KNOW. That's when I love them the most. I guess because they're so alone and miserable, so desperate to find someone. I AM that someone. They just don't know it, the poor things. So I have to show them. And I have to move fast, before they give in to their fears. So I did move fast. Grabbed the nearest thing, a table lamp. My only one. Came with the room. I hit Diane on the side of the head with it. Hit her hard. That relaxed her. Then I wrapped the lamp cord around her throat and I did it. I did what I'd been wanting to do to her since I first spotted her on the subway platform that morning. I did it fast and I did it sure.

I performed an act of kindness. A random act of kindness.

What is it if not kindness? I had nothing but love in my heart for her. And she returned my love. It was good for her. I know this, I'm telling you this. I answered her prayers, E. I made her happy.

When it was over I put my mark on her. You know what I'm talking about, E. You always know.

Damn, it's so good to be back in town.

Your pal, T

p.s. If you can get me that fifty I'd be much obliged

I set the pages aside and drained my martini. I have to tell you, I was stunned. I almost never make it all the way through an unsolicited manuscript. Ninety-nine times out of a hundred, the talent's just not there and that's painfully obvious by page two and there's no point in reading any further. This one was different. There was talent here. There was the germ of a major confessional novel. This guy had taken Lardner's boastful bush-leaguer, Jack Keefe, and made him over into someone entirely new and predatory and of our time—someone living on the edge, someone *with* an edge, someone lean and mean and deeply disturbed. He certainly disturbed me. Oh, sure, I had some misgivings. I thought the ending was a bit over the top. But that was minor. *That* we could talk about. Because this guy was worth talking to. This guy was the real thing.

Only, who the hell was he? Why hadn't he shared his name and his address with me? Would I ever hear from him again? I hoped I would.

For now, I had my life to lead. And E. B. White was right—no one should come to New York to live unless he is willing to be lucky. I showered and dressed—the double-breasted dinner jacket with peaked lapels, the matching trousers, ten-pleat bib-front shirt with wing collar. Black silk bow tie. Grandfather's pearl cuff links and studs. I enjoyed Pam's daube and a half bottle of a very nice Côtes du Rhone while I savored what Louis Armstrong did to "West End Blues" and what the candlelight did to Merilee's big green eyes across the hexagonal dining table from me. After dessert, we bundled up and walked arm in arm through the park in the crisp cold night while Lulu paid dutiful visits to some of her favorite haunts. There was a sliver of moon out over the Sherry Netherlands, and it was so clear we could see stars. It has to be very clear for that. We stopped off at Café des Artistes for a calvados and were home, snug in our bed, by eleven. Merilee was reading Alan Bennett's essays on his life in the theater. I was working my way through a collection of short stories by B. Traven, which is something I do every few years just to remind myself what good writing is. By

twelve all lights were out and all were fast asleep, Merilee
with her hip resting against mine, Lulu with her tail on my
head, Tracy snoozing peacefully in her crib in the nursery
next door to us. She had taken to sleeping all the way
through the night without waking us. I had taken to being
very grateful. Almost as grateful as Merilee.

I slept late the next morning. Merilee had already left for
rehearsal when I got up and padded into the bathroom and
got busy stropping Grandfather's razor. I turned on the radio
so I could catch the weather forecast. I caught the news as
well. That's when I found out that the body of a young
woman had been found early that morning by a jogger in
Riverside Park. She had been strangled. The victim had
worked as the manager of an organic pet food store on East
Thirty-second. Her hair was blond, her eyes were blue. Her
name was Diane Shavelson.

TWO

I MET ROMAINE VERY at Barney Greengrass the Sturgeon King, that noted Amsterdam Avenue landmark where they've been purveying smoked fish since before the outbreak of the First World War. And where they haven't changed the wallpaper in the restaurant since—well, I don't think they've ever changed the wallpaper in the restaurant of Barney Greengrass. I drank coffee at a Formica table while I waited for Very to show. Lulu, who regards the place as her personal cathedral, mooched choice morsels of sturgeon from the countermen.

Already, the murder was getting major play on the radio. Murders were supposed to be down in the city. The mayor did a lot of preening about this. A body found in the park, especially a young woman's body, was big news. WINS news radio had a bit more detail as I was going out the door. Diane Shavelson was thirty-one and single and a native of Rhinebeck, New York. She had lived at 343 West Ninety-seventh Street. Her body had been found in the brush about fifty feet from Grant's Tomb. A jogger had stumbled upon it shortly before dawn.

They had a bit more, like I said. But they didn't have much. They didn't have cause of death. Or whether the police had a lead or a motive or any damned thing. My guess was they didn't. My guess was I was the only one who did. That was why I'd called Very.

I almost didn't recognize Detective Lieutenant Romaine Very, hip-hop cop, when he came in the door. He'd gone hep cat on me. Buzz-cut his thick, wavy black hair down to an early Jerry Lewis, lost the earring, added a narrow tuft of beard under his lower lip and a pair of Ray-Ban wraparounds, all of which made him look vaguely like someone who might have sat in on tenor sax with Miles, Diz and Bird. Of course, it was easy to be deceived by Very's look. The first time I met him I thought this short, muscular street kid was a bicycle messenger, as opposed to a crack NYPD homicide detective with a degree in Romance Languages from Columbia. I'd also thought he was the single most wired individual I'd ever met. This was a man who couldn't stop nodding to his own personal beat. This was a man who'd given himself an ulcer by the time he was twenty-six. This was a man whose middle name was Try the Decaf.

Although *this* Romaine Very, the new Romaine Very, didn't come strutting across the restaurant toward me, chin thrust defiantly in the air, like the old one would have. This Romaine Very oozed in slowly and sluggishly. There was a grayish pallor to his skin. And, when the shades came off, there were dark circles under his eyes. His fingers fumbled clumsily, endlessly, at the belt of his old, worn leather trench before he finally got it undone and shrugged himself out of it. He wore a baggy, shapeless avocado-green sweater underneath, a black T-shirt, jeans and Timberland boots. He motioned to the waiter for coffee, then slumped heavily into the chair across from me, groaning like an old man in serious

need of disc surgery or an enema or both. Like I said, I
almost didn't recognize this Very.

Lulu sure did. She's always liked him. She thinks he's cute.
Plus he carries a gun, which I don't. She whooped and
thumped her tail until he patted her and said hello.

I said, "No offense, Lieutenant, but you look like shit."

"No offense, dude, but I ain't up for you right now," he
shot back, knuckling his bleary eyes. "So this better be
good."

"Oh, I wouldn't call it *good,* Lieutenant. *Good* is about the
last thing I'd call it."

"Whatever." He yawned deeply and poured some milk
into his coffee, glancing over at the pages of the answer
man's letter and first chapter. I'd laid them out on the table
next to us so Very could read them without having to touch
them. No sense adding his fingerprints, too. He flicked a
curious look at me, but didn't bother to prod me. Just drank
his coffee, loudly. The lieutenant was used to my ways by
now, just as I was used to his. We'd been around the bases
three times, most recently when Clethra Feingold ran off
with Thor Gibbs, her famous stepfather. Maybe you read
about it. I had grown rather fond of Very through the years.
We would even have been friends except for one small detail—he believed I'd been brought into this world strictly so
as to irritate, annoy and otherwise mess up his life.

We all three ordered lox and onions and eggs. Our waiter
refilled our cups.

"How's Tracy?" Very grunted. This was him being
friendly.

"Not terrible. But give her time—she's young. And you,
Lieutenant? How are you?" This was me being concerned.
"What have you been doing, pulling a double shift?"

Very made a face at me. "Pulling my pud is more like it.
Night after night I'm out there, dude, doing what I gotta do,
working at it, trying . . ." He sighed glumly. "Only, it just
ain't happening. Maybe I should just give up, y'know?"

Lulu and I exchanged a look. I told her to let me handle it. "Give up *what,* Lieutenant?"

He looked at me blankly. "Women, what else?"

I winced. "Hold it. This sounds like a personal problem."

"Check it out; what I've decided is I focus way too much energy on my career and not enough on *me,*" Very went on, undeterred. "Which means I get my self-esteem from my job instead of from my home life. Which, like, I don't even have. Which is really fucked up. So—"

"So you're trying to meet someone," I suggested, to hurry him up.

"And it ain't easy, let me tell ya."

"Lieutenant, I—"

"The shift I'm on these days I don't get off until midnight. So I'm out cruising the after-hours clubs until four, five o'clock in the morning. I get home at dawn, mondo wired. Takes me hours to chill. And then, just when my head hits the pillow . . ." he scowled at me ". . . the goddamned phone rings."

"I apologize for waking you, Lieutenant. But you won't be sorry. Well, actually, you will be sorry. But you won't be. Sorry that I called, I mean."

"Dude, don't do this on me. I don't get you on a *clear* head." Very shook his head, as if to loosen the cobwebs. "Don't know why I can't hook up, either. Ain't like I'm fronting 'em or nothing. I'm being *me.* But I'm just not getting anywhere."

"Maybe it's the haircut. Have you thought about the haircut?"

"I've chatted up some dope ladies, too. I'm talking phat— beautiful, smart, nice. I buy 'em a drink. They buy me a drink. It's decent. And then, *phhtt.*"

I tried to resist. Really, I did. But I couldn't. *"Phhtt?"*

"I don't finish off the play. Ain't up for it. I ain't buggin' or nothing. Only, there's no spark. And if there's no spark, I walk—home to another chorus of 'Randy Rides Alone.' "

He drank some more of his coffee. "Sure wish I could meet someone like Merilee."

"There's only one Merilee, that's for sure."

Our food arrived. We dug in.

"She have any friends?"

"None that are sane."

"How about you, dude?"

"Me, Lieutenant?"

"You must know a shitload of interesting women. Writers, editors—"

"I thought you wanted to meet someone interesting."

"Would you fix me up with one of 'em?"

"No."

He stared across the table at me, startled and offended. "Why not?"

I bit into my bagel and said, "I have my reasons."

"Because I'm a cop, is that it? Not good enough for them?"

"I have my reasons," I repeated. "And they have nothing to do with you. Let's just leave it at that, okay? Now can we please talk about *me?*"

"All right, all right. What you got, dude?"

"You tell me," I said, gesturing to the pages. "Don't touch. Just read."

He read. I ate, watching the people go by on Amsterdam through the window. Most of them in that neighborhood at that time of day are elderly, the city's survivors, still sharp, still tough, still New York. Lulu ate, too, though she had eyes only for her plate. When she had sanded it clean with her tongue she curled up on my foot with a satisfied grunt and went to sleep. Her world is a lot simpler than the one I live in.

I could tell when the lieutenant got to the first mention of the organic pet food store. He froze, his face hardening. He looked up at me. I looked back at him. He shifted his chair in closer to the table. He read on.

When he was done reading he said, "Yo, when did you get this?"

"Yesterday."

"Who else has touched it?"

"Merilee, by the upper left-hand corner of the envelope. No one else."

"Any idea who he is?"

"None."

"Any idea how to reach him?"

"None."

"Why'd he pick you?"

"You know as much as I do."

He tugged thoughtfully at his little tuft of chin spinach. "We may need a sample of your prints."

"You already have them on file."

"What, we busted you?"

"During my black hole days."

Lulu let out a low growl. She remembered those days only too well.

"For what, dude?"

"I'll let that come as a surprise to you."

The waiter took away our empty plates. He came back and refilled our cups. Very sat there staring at the pages. His head had started nodding to his own personal beat. He was not sleepy anymore.

"Well, Lieutenant? Is he for real? Do I have myself a killer?"

"You know as much as I do." He got to his feet. "Stay with me."

He went and used the phone. When he returned he was slapping a small notepad against his thigh. He sat, staring down at the notepad. He cleared his throat uneasily. "Dude, it's my unhappy duty to inform you that the answer is yes, the man's for real."

My stomach muscles tightened. "How do you know?"

"Because of what *he* knows. She was strangled. Side of her

head was bashed in with a heavy object. Plus," he added darkly, "she was branded."

"Branded how?"

"He put a question mark on her forehead with lipstick. Orange lipstick."

I frowned. "Why would he do that?"

"He's the answer man. Maybe it's about that." Very puffed out his cheeks. "Fuck, I don't know."

"When was she killed?"

"Two, three days ago. They're not sure yet."

"How come the body wasn't found until this morning?"

"Most likely on account of he didn't dump it there until last night."

"Today's Thursday. I got this in the mail yesterday. It's a local letter, mailed from somewhere in Manhattan, postmarked on Tuesday. So let's say he killed Diane Monday night . . . Christ, that means he held on to the body for two whole days. Why would he do that?"

"Because he's a sick fuck, that's why."

"Didn't anyone notice she was missing?"

"If they did they didn't contact us."

"She lived alone?"

"Unless you count two cats as roommates."

"What about the kid who worked at the store with her? Didn't *he* notice when she didn't show up for work?"

"Good question. I don't know the answer."

"Was she sexually assaulted?"

"Good question. I don't know the answer to that one either."

"You're starting to sound like a politician, Lieutenant."

"Fuck you, too, dude," he snapped. "We haven't got that information yet, okay? All I know is she was found fully clothed and stuffed inside a large, zippered canvas wardrobe bag." He glanced down at his notepad. "Garment bag was blue, to go with the color of her face."

"I didn't need to hear that, Lieutenant."

"Sorry. Sometimes I forget you're a civilian."

"I'll do my best to remind you from now on. How was she identified?"

"Pocketbook. It was right there in the garment bag with her. Contained her driver's license, credit cards, a hundred and twenty dollars in cash."

I tugged at my left ear. "Somewhat odd, isn't it?"

"Mucho odd. It was like he wanted her to be identified. Could say the same about where he dumped her—it was like he wanted her to be found. Dig, it's not like nobody happens by Grant's Tomb."

That gave me a thought. "Grant's Tomb, Lieutenant. *G.T.* He says, 'Found myself a semi-decent jack rack in the shadow of *G.T.*' He could be referring to Grant's Tomb."

"Could be," he agreed.

"She didn't live that far from there, did she?"

"She lived next to the river on Ninety-seventh. The tomb's at Riverside and One-hundred-and-twenty-second. Not mondo far. But not walking distance either, not carrying a body." He hesitated, thumbing his chin thoughtfully. "I, uh, schooled 'em to our thing. So I'm on this case. I wasn't but now I am."

"I'm glad you are, Lieutenant. I feel a lot better with you on my side."

"Save it, dude. I ain't up for your sarcasm."

"Okay, fine. I tried for a warm moment. It didn't happen. We'll move on."

"Who else knows about this?" he asked. "Who have you spoken to?"

"Well, I called Geraldo first thing, naturally."

He glowered at me.

"No one, Lieutenant. Not a soul."

"Good. I want this kept under wraps until we got all the facts. In the immortal words of Rickey Henderson, I don't need no pub right now. That means you talk to me and to nobody else. None of your grandstanding to the press. Keep

that shit off my wave. Last thing I want is someone like
Cassandra Dee breathing down the back of my neck."

"She's much better at breathing down the fronts of trousers, actually."

He sat back in his chair, a dreamy smile on his face.
"Woo."

"Woo?"

"*She's* someone I wouldn't mind getting with. Most bonus babe on television, except for maybe Cokie Roberts."

"I don't think I want to hear any more about this, Lieutenant."

"Dig, you *know* her, am I right?"

"Cokie Roberts?"

"Cassandra Dee."

"We've tangled," I said, groaning inwardly. Because she
was the sleaziest of the sleazy. We ghosted dueling memoirs
back when Cassandra was fresh from the *Enquirer*. She wasn't
ghosting anymore. Now she had her own red-hot nightly
tabloid news show, *Face to Face* or *Cheek to Jowl* or whatever
the hell it was called. Now she was a megastar. "And I never
grandstand, Lieutenant. At least, not without a celebrity."

"You got one, dude. You just haven't met him yet."

That one I left alone. Didn't want to go anywhere near it.

He peered at the letter again, frowning. "Weird how retro
this all is, don't you think? I mean, we are talking serious
low-tech here—manual typewriter, snail mail, *paper* . . .''

"Oh, God, you're not going to bring up the *I*-word, are
you?"

"Well, yeah. Everyone's on it," he said, meaning the Internet. "They're using E-mail, voice mail, faxes . . . Nobody uses the U.S. Postal Service anymore."

"I do."

"That's not the point, dude."

"On the contrary, Lieutenant, it most definitely is the
point."

"Oh, I dig. You're thinking we're dealing with an older
person like yourself."

"Thank you. Yes. Another troglodyte like myself." Although perhaps not as well dressed.

"All I'm saying," Very went on, "is no one under thirty would use these methods."

"You made your point. Now shut up about it."

He shut up about it, his eyes scanning Chapter One again. "What do you think of it?"

"Think of it?"

"He an educated fool? He got talent? What kind of gee is he? School me on him."

"He can write, there's no doubt in my mind about that. He has the tools. That doesn't have to mean he's college-educated, but given his use of the language, I'd have to say that he is. As far as what kind of person he is, that's much harder to say. This could be his confession, a blow-by-blow account of what went down. Or he could be a member of the frequent liar club. He *is* claiming that it's a novel. That would make his letter writer, T, a fictional creation, which is to say someone not to be confused with *him*. Holden Caulfield *wasn't* J. D. Salinger, after all."

"Yeah, but check it out, dude—chick's *really* dead."

"Trust me, I didn't forget that part, Lieutenant."

"You okay with this?"

"Why, don't I look okay?"

He didn't answer me. I gathered by his silence that I didn't.

I sipped my cold coffee. Under the table, Lulu stirred in her sleep, dreaming of epic battles with baby squirrels long since won and lost. Mostly lost. "What happens now?"

"We talk to Diane's friends, find out who she was giving it to. Could be she's got an ex-boyfriend who's a crazed, frustrated author."

"Is there any other kind?"

"She seemed to recognize him," Very mentioned, scanning the pages. "He says he gets a lot of that. What's up with that?"

"I don't know. I wondered about it myself."

Very shook his head in amazement. "Damned thing's full of chewy little morsels. Makes me want to scream. Like this G.T. thing of yours. And the mention of the hot plate. That tells us SRO hotel. Used to be a whole bunch of 'em in the low hundreds, west of Broadway, until the developers moved in. There's still a few. And look at this—he's buggin' here on the no-smoking laws. Those kicked in April of ninety-five. Where's he been? Was he in jail? Was he in a drug treatment facility? He *sounds* like a recovering addict, way he dumps all of that sugar in his coffee. Or maybe he's just plain wiggy. He's got this business here about the doctors letting him out. Could be he was just released from a psychiatric hospital. Could be he *escaped*. We got the Manhattan Psychiatric Center sitting right out there on Ward's Island with all kinds of security problems. Guy walked right out of there a while back and shoved a grandmother under a train at Herald Square. We got Kingsboro in Brooklyn, Creedmoor in Queens. Maybe he was in one of them. He and Friend E both. Who *is* Friend E? Does he exist? We got to check all of this shit out. Every goddamned morsel. Each one's a potential lead. Could be he works in a restaurant. Could be he's a social worker for the city—"

"Could be none of the above," I interrupted. "Could be it's all a product of his imagination—planted there so as to drive you off the scent. Or crazy."

Very shuddered. "Fuck me, this is strange."

"Very."

"Yeah, dude?"

"It's very strange."

"You got that right." The lieutenant's eyes were still on the pages. "He's got this here reference to the Young Urban Shitheads. Why does that sound so familiar?"

"It's an expression of mine. You've probably heard me use it."

Very looked up at me suspiciously. "You coined it?"

"Naturally."

"Like it's your trademark or something?"

"Or something."

"So how did he pick it up?"

"Read it somewhere, I imagine. He says in the letter that he's a fan of mine. I do have a few, you know. Some that aren't even related to me."

Very got to his feet and went over to the counterman and asked him for a clean pair of tweezers. There's nothing better than tweezers for removing the small bones from a fish—or for gathering up the pages of a manuscript you don't want to touch. Very worked the pages back inside the envelope and then dropped it in a shopping bag.

I picked up the check. Least I could do for getting him out of bed.

"What happened to you?" he asked, noticing my limp as we headed out.

"Ran into a Stickley."

"A what?"

"Never mind."

Outside on Amsterdam Avenue, a cold, Canadian wind had picked up. Trash swirled in the gutter. Shivers shot up and down my spine. And I noticed now just how frail and frightened those elderly people looked as they fought their way down the block, narrow shoulders hunched against the Arctic blast. And suddenly I wasn't feeling so good about the coming of Christmas. I was feeling gloomy and depressed. Much of New York life is like that, fleeting personal moods held together by the flimsiest of illusions, easily shattered and strewn. The city can turn on you in an instant. Not that *it* changes. It doesn't. Your perception does, the details your brain picks up and how it processes them. In a New York instant, pleasant anticipation becomes dark foreboding. Positive energy turns into frenzied, pointless desperation. Contentment gives way to a powerful desire to be someone, anyone, else. In a New York instant the air that was brisk and invigorating can freeze you to the marrow of your bones.

The city will do that to you, especially when a killer who calls himself the answer man has written you for literary advice.

Very stood there next to me on the sidewalk with the collar of his old leather trench turned up against the wind, looking like a hipster spy. He popped a piece of gum in his mouth, his jaw working it. He was chewing Beeman's that season. "Sure you're okay, dude?"

"Why do you keep asking me that?"

"Because I know you. Shit like this goes down, you get just like a dog with a bone."

Lulu snuffled at this in protest. Not that she's much for bones. Prefers strips of salmon jerky. We have them shipped to us from Alaska. Write for details.

"I'm fine, Lieutenant."

"Just don't get stupid on me, okay? I don't want to see you outlined in chalk somewhere."

"I wouldn't think of it. What *do* I do?"

"Hope we get lucky."

"Lucky how?"

"Lucky like the answer man contacts you again. Tells you how you can reach him back."

"I see." I pulled my coat tighter and my hat down. "I hate to break it to you, Lieutenant, but that's not my idea of lucky."

I spent a lot of time that afternoon sitting in front of plates of food listening to people who had been born after the Tet Offensive tell me what was wrong with my novel. I suppose there was a time, long ago, when the prospect of logging serious face time with two genuine New York editors would have been cause for jubilation. But back then those people were grown-ups. Where *did* all of the grown-ups in publishing go, anyway? Did they die off? Or are they merely in hiding? If so, who could blame them? Not me. All I know is I was not in the mood for this. I was not in the mood for

Michael's, a large, airy eatery on West Fifty-fifth Street where the walls are lined with unimpressive paintings and even less impressive mid-level editors, which is to say editors who are on their way up or down or nowhere. This one seemed to be on his way up, judging by his ponytail, his roster of snotty, overrated baby writers and his frequent use of the word "bullshit." My novel was "totally bitchen," he assured me, but I still had to turn it into "something a six-teen-year-old boy will buy, enjoy and pass on to a friend." "What, you mean like a joint?" I said. "It needs *urgency,*" he said. I said, "What, you mean like moving it to the bridge of a nuclear submarine that's about to blow up and take half the world with it?" I didn't hear a word he said after that. His lips moved, but all I could hear was the roar of a No. 1 train hurtling by. A small blond woman with a nice smile was on board, reading a book about a cat, unaware that she was about to be strangled and stuffed into a garment bag.

From there it was on to the lobby of the Algonquin, which was crowded with English Christmas shoppers who had flown over to take advantage of the weak dollar and to complain about how crass and money-conscious we Ameri-cans are. Frank, our waiter, brought Lulu her usual plate of pickled herring and raw onion, which she devoured while I listened to another editor explain how hard it would be to position me on their list now that I was no longer an "enfant terrible." When I suggested she try on "idiot savant" for size, she responded with a blank stare. Followed by "I just have two little words for you: Robert James Waller." I drank my tea and shivered, chilled to the bone. What I really wanted to do was take two aspirin, gargle and get under a nice warm bed.

What I did was walk uptown to Osners with my hands in my pockets and my mood foul, Lulu trailing a step behind me, nose, ears and tummy to the ground. Something had started to gnaw me about the answer man. Something about the way he wrote—his tone, his style, his voice. It wasn't anything I could put my finger on. It was just a vague itch.

But I don't like vague itches. They frequently lead to scratching, followed by excessive bleeding.

Who was he? Why had he chosen me? Why *me?*

Osners, which is on the corner of Seventy-ninth and Amsterdam, is one of my vital lifelines. If they ever close their doors I'll probably have to give up writing altogether. Because there's nobody else left anymore who can keep a fifties vintage Olympia solid-steel manual portable up and running and in serious enough shape to pound out a book. Just Osners, where the old manual typewriters are stacked on shelves to the rafters and the whole place smells of lubricating oil and ink, pungent scents of a bygone era. Stanley Adelman's widow, Mary, runs the place with an air of aristocratic, old-world dignity. Three full-time repairmen work the bench, taking apart two dozen antique machines a week, piece by piece, giving them chemical baths in vats down in the cellar, lubricating them, reassembling them. Parts are hard to come by. Some they have to make themselves. I bring them my Olympia twice a year. They keep it for a week. When I get it back it is like a new machine. A new machine that is forty years old.

If you want to know anything about a typewriter you ask Mrs. Adelman.

"I have a lovely Olympia just in, Mr. Hoag," she informed me crisply. Mrs. Adelman was always looking to sell me a backup. "Same vintage as yours. Excellent condition. It's a Scandinavian model, with accents, but it would serve you quite well. Just ignore what you don't understand."

"That's certainly gotten me through life so far," I said, grinning at her.

"You should do that more often, Mr. Hoag."

"Do what, Mrs. Adelman?"

"Smile. You have a very nice smile."

"I had them bleached."

"Bleached, Mr. Hoag?"

"My teeth."

"Ah," she said doubtfully. "I see."

I unbuttoned my coat and got out my copy of the answer man's cover letter. I hadn't told Very I'd made a Xerox of the whole thing. I saw no reason to. Besides, it wasn't as if he'd be surprised. I laid the page out on the counter and said, "What can you tell me about the machine that typed this? They're thinking of selling."

Mrs. Adelman reached for a magnifying glass and examined the page carefully. "It's a pica machine, Mr. Hoag. Not in good condition. The letters need cleaning. Also realignment. They're not striking evenly. No doubt needs a new roller, too. I can only imagine the condition the carriage is in. I'd say a complete overhaul is called for. We'd be honored to do it for you, but it would run you at least a hundred-fifty, plus parts."

"Do you know the machine?"

"I should say not. It wouldn't be in such sad condition if I did."

"What kind is it?"

"Why, it's an Olivetti Studio 44, of course."

Her reply shot through me from head to toe. So that explained the itch.

"You can tell by the graceful quality of the characters," Mrs. Adelman explained. "The lower-case *A* in particular. See the way it curls in upon itself? There's not another machine like it. The vintage is early sixties. I would guess sixty-two, but I would not swear to it. It's a steel machine. One of their more handsome designs. Sleek, streamlined profile. Pale green body with black keys. Flip-down return handle. Red leather case with brass hardware. An exquisite machine, really. Not as sturdy as your Olympia, but a classic nonetheless."

"What can you tell me about the person who typed this?"

"They have excellent taste."

"What else?"

She pursed her lips in thought. "Strong hands. It would

take someone with strong hands to produce a legible letter on a machine that is in such dreadful condition." She raised an eyebrow at me. "You are trying to track down a secret admirer, perhaps?"

"Something like that."

"Does Miss Nash know about this?"

"It's not that kind of secret admirer."

"I see," she said, with a shrug. Mrs. Adelman was used to responses that made little or no sense. She'd dealt with a lot of writers in her day. "Do let me know if I may be of service. If they wish to sell, I can find them a buyer in a second."

"Thank you, Mrs. Adelman." I pocketed the letter and turned for the door. "Oh, Mrs. Adelman? In case anyone asks, not that they will . . ."

"Yes, Mr. Hoag?"

"I was never here."

"Yes, Mr. Hoag."

There was light. I could see. This meant Merilee was still at rehearsal.

Voices and laughter came from the kitchen, where I found Pam giving Vic Early a baking lesson under Tracy's watchful gaze. Somehow she had gotten flour all over her nose. Tracy, that is. Pam seemed semi-frazzled, which was most unusual for her, but then, she wasn't used to having a hulking, sandy-haired giant in her kitchen, especially one who wore a frilly apron over his knit shirt and slacks. They were building a lemon cake together, step by step. Vic likes to cook but has always been intimidated by desserts. Right now he was intently creaming his butter. I could think of no better candidate for the job of beating a bowl of butter into submission. Vic Early was six-feet-six, 250 and all muscle. Once, he had anchored the UCLA Bruins offensive line. Would have been a first-round NFL draft pick, too, if he hadn't come back from Nam with a steel plate in his head. I first met him out in Los Angeles when he was bodyguarding Sonny Day, the comic. Vic could still work on either coast whenever he wanted to. He remained, at age forty-five, one of the best celebrity shadows. But he cared for that life less and less. And for the life on our farm more and more. He wasn't the only one.

I hoisted Tracy into my arms and wiped the flour from her nose. She seemed happy to see me. She'd noticed that I'd been gone all day. Sure, she had.

"Lieutenant Very rang up for you, dear boy," Pam announced, swiping at a tuft of silver hair that had fallen in front of her eyes. "His number is there on the counter."

"Thank you, Pam." To Vic I said, "Could you stick around for a few days? Things may start getting a bit weird around here. Or, I should say, weirder."

Vic's manner changed instantly. He was on alert now. "Be happy to, Hoag," he said in that droning monotone of his. "Anything in particular I should watch out for?"

"As a matter of fact there is. It seems I have myself a new pen pal. He's a murderer. If you get any unusual calls or letters or packages, if someone comes up to you on the street—anything out of the so-called ordinary—call Lieutenant Very immediately. I'll fill you in when I know more, okay?"

They exchanged a look. Pam seemed frightened. That was a first. Pam was normally the most unflappable person I'd ever come in contact with. Perhaps it was because we had the baby around now.

"No problem, Hoag," Vic said calmly. "I'll look after things here."

"Thank you." I put Tracy back down and started for the bedroom. Lulu stayed put. She smelled lemon. The smell of lemon often meant fish. I stopped and said, "I forgot, was there something you wanted to talk to me about, Vic?"

Vic hesitated, suddenly very uncomfortable. "Uh, yeah. There was. There is."

"Is it to do with the house?"

"Not exactly," he replied, scuffing at the kitchen floor with his size 15 EEE brogan. "It's, uh, a personal matter. But it can wait."

I frowned at him. "Are you sure?"

"Quite sure. But thanks for asking."

I went in the bedroom and closed the door. I called Very back. "Any news, Lieutenant?"

"A ton, dude. I been ultrabusy. For starters, I tracked down Diane Shavelson's ex-boyfriend. Turns out *he* dumped *her*—about three months ago. Married another girl and moved to Seattle."

"Him and everyone else."

"He's some kind of consultant."

"Him and everyone else."

"Now, dig, I just got off the phone with her sister in Rochester. She knows a lot."

"If she knew a lot she wouldn't be living in Rochester."

"Yo, I meant about Diane. Two of 'em were tight."

"Oh."

"The sister says Diane hadn't been out on a single date since the breakup. Not one. I'm talking zero contact with men."

"Hmm . . ."

"What's that, dude?"

"Nothing, just 'hmm.' "

"No evidence of a guy being around her place neither. I spent the afternoon there looking through her stuff. Seemed like a real quality person. Good heart. Cared about animals. Her sister's taking the cats." He sighed unhappily. "Damn, I never get used to this shit."

"I wouldn't like you if you did, Lieutenant."

"Oh, hey, I hipped your doorman to keep his eyes open."

"That'll be quite some change for Mario."

"I also have a man parked across the street, just in case."

I parted the curtains next to my desk and looked down at the street. "I don't see him. Where is he?"

"Look up, dude. See that gee in the tree?"

I could just make him out in the twilight, strapped in about thirty feet up, wearing a green parks department uniform. "Yeah . . . ?"

"He's on the job."

"He's a cop?"

"What I just said."

"I hope he knows what he's doing to that maple."

"Shit, yeah. Has a degree in forestry. Wanted to be a park ranger out west until he found out they get shot at by the crazies. Likes the odds better here. Dig, he was wondering why most of your windows are blacked out."

"You don't want to know. What else have you found out?"

"For starters, our time frame plays. They're guessing she was strangled sometime late Monday. The body was kept indoors, then dumped in the park shortly before it was found—she wasn't cold enough to have been out there for long. They didn't find any rope burns or lacerations on her neck, which means he did her with something smooth."

"Like a lamp cord?"

"Like a lamp cord. You with me so far, dude?"

"I'm with you, Lieutenant."

"Good, now dig on this—she was not, repeat *not* sexually assaulted. No seminal fluid in her vaginal vault or in her mouth. Even if he was ultracareful and wore a hat, which some of your career rapists have taken to doing, we'd still find vaginal secretions, bruises, abrasions, something. . . . We found bupkes. No bites. No scratches. No tissue or blood under her nails. No fingerprints on her skin. They iodine-fumed her head to toe, Magna-brushed her, Kromekoted her, nothing. No evidence of human contact, period. Man didn't lay a hand on her."

"Is that typical?"

"No way. When it's a pretty girl, and it's violent, it's almost always sexual. Although, come to think of it, David Berkowitz never laid a finger on 'em."

"I was really hoping you wouldn't do that, Lieutenant."

"Do what, dude?"

"Mention David Berkowitz." Better known as Son of Sam.

"Just thinking out loud."

"Next time you feel like thinking out loud, shut up."

"We did ID the lipstick on her forehead. It's Revlon Orange Luminesque. Available at any drugstore. Otherwise, we got zero to work with. No hairs, no carpet fibers. This gee's either a neat freak or a former crime scene technician. I mean, that girl's body is sanitary."

"Hmm . . ."

"What's that, dude?"

"Nothing. I just said, 'Hmm . . .' "

"What, again?"

"Have you had your hearing checked lately, Lieutenant?"

"Same goes for those pages he sent you. Man must have been wearing latex gloves when he handled 'em. Which leads me to believe he has a record. We could make him in thirty minutes if he was in our database—like, for example, you are."

"Told you."

"Those were some big-time black hole days you had yourself, dude. For damned sure. Drag-racing a member of the New York Mets up Second Avenue at three in the morning, doing ninety miles per."

"That wasn't such a big deal."

"Second Avenue runs *downtown,* dude."

"We felt otherwise."

"You also threw a barstool through the front window of Pete's Tavern."

"So?"

"So there was a person on the stool at the time."

"It was my stool and he wouldn't get off."

"And here all along I thought you were civilized."

"Well, now you know better."

"I'm liking you more and more, dude."

"Down, Lieutenant. I'm taken."

"The typewriter's an old Olivetti. Tracked that down at a place called Osners. Old lady there is major pissed at you, by the way."

I cleared my throat. "She is?"

"Said you used to be one of her best customers. Haven't been around in ages."

"I suppose I am overdue for a lube." Good old Mrs. Adelman.

Very paused a moment. "You're slipping, dude."

"Am I?"

"Aren't you going to ask me about the ink?"

"What about the ink, Lieutenant?"

"Came off a ribbon made by General Ribbon Corporation of Chatsworth, California. It's their universal ribbon, works on every manual typewriter known to man or woman. Their biggest customer is Staples. It's like their house brand."

"So we're talking dead end, in other words."

"You got that right."

"How about the envelope? Was that any help?"

"Prints galore on it. Half the fucking postal service touched it. No one who matches anyone in our database, though."

"Well, that's comforting to know."

"Postmark tells us zilch about where he mailed it from. You have it stamped and mailed at the counter of your post office, yes, they put a zip code on it. You stamp it yourself and drop it in a box somewhere like he did, no. All we know is it was mailed somewhere in Manhattan."

"What about saliva?"

"Saliva?"

"If he licked the envelope shut, wouldn't there be traces of his saliva on it?"

"What, you think it'll turn out he just ate some rare kind of salami that's only sold in one deli on the Lower East Side?"

"Actually, I was thinking more of a DNA test."

"See? That's the O.J. thing again. I hate that."

"The O.J. thing, Lieutenant?"

"Before O.J. you never heard about DNA evidence in normal conversation."

"Trust me, Lieutenant, this is not my idea of normal conversation."

"Suddenly everybody's an expert on blood evidence and how long it takes a cup of ice cream to melt."

"How long does it take?"

"In answer to your question, dude, our perp sealed the envelope with a moist sponge. And the stamps were self-adhesive. This gee is thorough and he's careful."

"Very."

"What's that, dude?"

"How about the garment bag?"

"Came from Hold Everything. They got two stores in the city, one out on the Island, two in Jersey, two more in Connecticut. Plus they got a catalog. We'll be tracking down any credit card sales of that particular item. The only problem is it retails for twenty-eight and change."

"Meaning he could have paid cash for it."

"Uh-huh. I also spent some face time with the kid who worked with Diane in the store. Malik Washington, age seventeen. According to Malik, Diane worked late on Monday. Said she had some orders to place. He offered to stick around but she told him to go on home. He left at a few minutes after six. Was home in Brooklyn by seven, according to his grandmother. He don't remember any gee stopping by just before closing time to buy kibble. Or any particular gee coming in that morning either, although he was down in the basement a lot stacking stuff. As for your next question, why didn't he report her missing, he claims Diane kept talking for weeks about taking a ski trip with her sister. When she didn't show for work on Tuesday he figured that's where she was, and either she forgot to tell him or she *did* tell him and *he* forgot."

"Any chance Malik's the answer man?"

"Doubtful. He's a high school dropout, below average language skills. Plus he doesn't know how to type. Which is the same shit my computer keeps telling me. Like, I turned up a gee just got paroled in Pennsylvania after pulling seven years for stalking a chick, okay? Under occupation they list 'dishwasher.' I'm thinking, okay, maybe he's worth looking up. Trouble is, he can only read and write at a fourth-grade level. Our man's way smarter than that. He ain't no mumbling crackhead lives out of garbage cans. He's someone you'd go home with. *She* did."

"This being your so-called information age, I'm assuming that if a similar unsolved crime had taken place somewhere else in the country—"

"We'd be on it in a flash, dude. I didn't turn up a thing. The answer man is all ours."

"Lovely."

"Check this out," Very went on. "There's no Greek coffeeshop around the corner from the pet food store. Nearest one's way over on First and Thirtieth. Man behind the counter don't remember anybody camped out there drinking coffee with twelve sugars any time recently."

"How about the Yushie bar?"

"Several in the area, but so far he's ringing no bells. You ask me, he made a lot of that shit up. Which just makes our job harder."

"That may have been the whole idea, Lieutenant."

"You got that right, dude." He sighed grimly.

"So what now?"

"We canvas the people who ride the numero uno train same time she did every morning. Maybe somebody saw something. We check the welfare hotels for recent arrivals. We check the psychiatric hospitals for recent departures— addicts, sex offenders, gees who write kook letters, gees with a history of violence, gees with mommy hang-ups. We talk to social workers who work with young fathers. We talk to drug counselors. We work the restaurants, 'specially places that routinely take on parolees or mental outpatients. We dog the details, dude, every single goddamned one of 'em, no matter how many man hours that takes. Because, dig, that girl was found in the *park*. And that fucks with the people's heads. Scares 'em shitless." Romaine Very sounded serious. More serious than I'd ever heard him. "Now listen up—no one, but no one knows how you hook up to this thing. Just me and my immediate superior, and he's sworn to secrecy. So the press should not be on to you. They *get* on to you, let me know, okay?"

"Okay, Lieutenant."

"Everything cool?"

"I think I can safely report that everything is not cool."

"Are *you* cool?"

"I'm fine."

"Stay with me, dude," he said, and then he hung up.

But I wasn't fine. Merilee knew it as soon as she joined me in bed after supper, which had been late. Rehearsal had run long. Her director, a hot young filmmaker, had never done a play. In fact, Merilee was starting to think he had never *seen* a play.

"You look awfully pale, darling," she observed fretfully. She had on her red flannel nightshirt. She always wears that when work is going poorly. Comfort food for the limbs, she calls it. "Your feet are positively gelid. And you barely touched your dinner."

"I've never liked lamb shanks. Ask anyone."

She glanced down at Lulu, who was curled up between us. "Why, even Lulu looks glum."

"Lulu always looks glum. It's one of her charms."

Merilee was silent a moment. We both were. My mind was elsewhere. My mind was on that typewriter, an Olivetti Studio 44.

"They're always out there, darling," she said quietly. "The loons and freaks and oddballs. The stalkers with their

AK-47s. The mad bombers with their fertilizer and diesel fuel. But we mustn't give in to them. We mustn't let them rule our world. That's how they win."

"I know that, Merilee." I reached over and took her hand and squeezed it. "I'm fine. Everything is fine."

"Of course it is, darling."

But of course it wasn't. And I knew it. I knew it as soon as the phone woke me and I picked it up and I heard Romaine Very's voice on the other end. This was early on Monday morning.

"Put your pants on, dude," the lieutenant said heavily. "We got us another one."

Three

Dear Hoagy,

I've taken the liberty of enclosing the second chapter of my work in progress. I don't dare call it a novel yet, but it really does seem to be taking shape. More importantly, I think I'm starting to hear my character's voice. And that is very exciting. But you are the expert, of course, and your opinion means much more than mine does.

It occurs to me you don't know how to reach me. If you want, you can take out one of those little personal ads at the bottom of the front page of The New York Times. *Just address it to me. I'll keep my eyes open, like any good writer should. And I'll be sure to get back to you. By the way, do you think I'll need an agent? Can you recommend one? Or will you be my agent? Please advise. Anyway, I hope you like this. And thanks again for your time.*

Yours truly,
the answer man

p.s. Did I mention the movie rights? Make sure you hold on to them. We're talking millions here!

p.p.s. Glad to see you're a fan of Barney Greengrass. It's always been one of my favorites. Those people at Zabar's are so incredibly rude. Who was that short, muscular guy in the leather coat, a fellow author?

2. the answer man goes to school
New York City, December 4

Friend E—Thanks for that fifty dollars, man. Knew I could count on you. You are a true friend, not like all of these front artists out here who call you their friend but are strictly looking out for themselves. I'll pay you back soon as I can, not that you're asking. I'm needing to get back to work anyway. Not just because of the bucks, but because work is what holds you together when you're out. Your work is who you are. Take a man's work away from him and it's like you've stripped him naked in the middle of Times Square.

That was one of the cool things about being inside. Didn't matter who or what you were before you got there. All that mattered was HERE and TODAY. Because EVERYONE has been stripped naked. As I'm riding the subway I find myself eyeballing some sharp, together guy and wondering how he would do in there. Not too goddamned well, I think. Because all he knows about is his own unreal little universe. He doesn't know about being in the cage with us. He doesn't know about REAL.

It was her legs I noticed first, E.

I was standing there on the platform waiting for the downtown train, which not many people do at six in the evening. Most of them are heading back uptown for home. Suddenly she came striding on through the turnstile toward me, her and those legs of hers. They were long. They were bare. They were tanned, which is unusual in December. None of those big fat hiking boots neither. She wore a pair of low-cut moccasins that showed off her ankles to full advantage. Her stride was a man's stride, long and athletic and self-

assured. A tall girl, at least five-feet-ten, with short black hair that she parted on the side like a boy. She had on a short leather skirt and a torn denim jacket. Mostly it was her walk I got off on. Man, could that honey walk.

Where she was going, I was going.

I sat halfway down the car so she wouldn't notice me. She was reading Backstage, which is some kind of show business newspaper. An actress, maybe a dancer. She was certainly hot enough. I figured she'd get off at Times Square. Maybe was in some show that was running there. But she didn't. Kept right on going all the way down to 14th Street. We both got off.

I followed her up the stairs and due east toward Sixth Avenue, staying a safe twenty feet back. She moved with great purpose. This has always excited me in a honey, E. I don't like the ones who can't make up their minds. I like the ones who are going somewhere. And this one was going somewhere. I had to pick up my pace just to keep up with her. No way I was going to lose her though. She had a Band-Aid on her left heel. Following that was like tailing a car with a broken headlamp, which you and I both got pretty good at in our younger days. But enough about that sorry subject. I'd much rather talk about these here legs. They were something, E. I mean you could go three, four years and not see a pair of legs like hers, except maybe in a magazine. I just kept beaming on them, wondering how anyone on the street could so much as think about anything else. But they paid her no notice. Locked into their own empty little lives, just like always.

Turns out she was heading to this place called The New School on West 12th Street. You know the place, E? They teach all of these bullshit classes there on how to write poetry and paint still lifes, like anybody who's teaching a class there has a fucking idea about how to do anything except scam people out of their money and their time. No way I was going inside, so before she went in the door I stopped her and said I just wanted to say thank you. She said For what? And I said It was just such an incredible pleasure following you down the street. You light up the whole neighborhood. She thanked me, E. And she smiled. She had a great big smile. You know the kind I mean. Then she went on inside.

I waited outside, smoking cigarettes. Waited a couple of hours. It was getting windy and cold, but I didn't care. She was with a small group when she finally came back out, all of them talking excitedly. When she saw me she stopped, frowning at me, and said What do you want? I said I thought we could get a cup of coffee. She didn't say yes. She didn't say no.

She just started walking with me.

It was really turning chilly. I kept wondering if her legs were cold, being bare. I finally asked her. She told me that the cold was no problem for her, since she was originally from Minnesota and it had to be something like thirty below zero for her to even feel it. I mentioned how confident and athletic her stride seemed, and she said Well, I was a real tomboy growing up. Played basketball and soccer and I still ski whenever I get a chance. I said Where did you get that tan? And she said I was just down in Miami with my boyfriend. He was down there on a photo shoot. Turned out her boyfriend was a model and so was she, but what she really wanted to do was act which was why she was taking this course at The New School on the history of the cinema from this guy who she said was brilliant. Mostly, she'd done a lot of modeling for the catalogs, although she had just landed a nonspeaking role in a Lipton Tea commercial which she was really pumped about. Laurie London was her name. I told her I was in the business myself, kind of. As a casting director for motion pictures. And if I could ever do anything to help her out it would be my pleasure.

She showed me her smile again.

It's like I told you before, Friend E: Be who they want you to be. That's my secret. Hey, I ought to write a book about it someday.

Hey, maybe I am.

Laurie said You know, I thought you looked familiar—I bet I've read for you. You probably have, I said. And she said Do you know Bonnie Timmerman? And I said Are you kidding? We're having breakfast together tomorrow morning. Which Laurie seemed to think was way cool. Right away she wanted to know what I was working on. I told her the new De Niro movie, which seemed safe, right? Isn't there always a new De Niro movie? And don't they always suck? I said In fact, Laurie, there's a part that would be perfect for you. She said Hey, I'd love to read for you. I said That might be difficult. I said I'm heading out to L.A. right after my breakfast with Bonnie. I said Too bad you don't have any pictures I could take a look at. She said Would you like to look at my book? My apartment's not far from here.

I said Well, okay. But I can only stay a minute.

Friend E, it flat out amazes me just how needy and desperate these New York women are. Even the beautiful ones. I mean, here I am walking along in Greenwich Village with this gorgeous honey and here she is all excited because she's thinking I'm the answer to her prayers. And all I'm thinking is Oh, baby, sweet baby—I am.

By the way, E, if you have the slightest fucking idea who this Bonnie bitch is, please advise.

Laurie lived on the other side of Washington Square on Sullivan Street in a not very nice building. Looked like it had once been a tenement. One big room that had a loft bed built in, a ladder going up to it. There was another bed in front of the window. Place was filthy, E. Heaps of clothes everywhere, dirty dishes piled up in the sink. I cannot believe what pigs so many of them are. I mean, people have this belief that women are so neat and we are such slobs. Not true. Can't live in a tiny cage if you're messy, as you and me know only too well. I said Do you have a roommate? And she said Yes, I live with a girl from home who's here in New York to get into modeling, like me, only right now she waits tables. I said Is that where she is now? And she said Yeah, until midnight. Laurie did apologize for the mess, E. Said lots of their girlfriends from wherever ended up crashing there on their way through New York and it could be a real zoo sometimes.

She got her photo album to show me. Cleared space on the sofa and we sat there together looking at them, our knees touching. There were pictures of her in all sorts of different poses. They were real professional-looking and she looked fine in them. Particularly the ones for panty hose. Man, those legs. Only she also looked, I don't know . . . hungry. Like she really, really wanted to please you. Like she really, really needed a gig, any gig, and fast. I could see something in these photographs that I couldn't see just from being with her, E. She wasn't ever going to get there. She didn't have it. I mean, no way. This honey was a loser. A born victim. Someone to be blewed and tattooed by every front artist in the business. Best she could ever hope for in life was to trade in those legs for some security—marry some nice guy with bucks who'd be good to her. And we both know how many of those there are in this world, E. I'll tell you, it almost brought a tear to my eye when I realized just how right this all was, me showing up now in her life. Just think how much heartache and pain I'd be saving her from by performing my one little random act of kindness. Laurie would never have to deal with that shit ever again.

Laurie would be free.

The night was young, E. Lots of time until midnight. But all of that talk of girlfriends coming and going was making me edgy. You know me, I got to keep moving. I asked her would she mind if I undid my necktie. She said No, of course not. So I did. And then I went ahead and told her I wasn't any casting agent. In fact, I wasn't even entirely sure what a casting agent did. And she said I don't understand—who are you, what are you? And I said Laurie, I am the answer to your prayers. And then she DID understand, because she gave me that look, the one where they KNOW. You know the one I mean. Only by now it was too late. I was doing my thing with my tie. She was a strong girl, no question. But I was too fast and strong for her. And too certain of my goal. And how right it was.

When it was over I helped myself to what I'd been wanting ever since I first laid eyes on her. I left my mark on her, too. Because she was mine now. All mine.

Thanks again for that fifty, E. I'll get it back to you when I can.

Your pal, T

p.s. Just think how much fun I'd be having if I didn't have to work

Four

"WHEN WAS Laurie killed, Lieutenant?"

"We're guessing Friday night, dude. Roommate found her this morning."

"That plays. He must have stuck this in the mail on Saturday."

I had called Very back just as soon as Chapter Two showed up in Monday morning's mail. I had read him the letter. Also assorted choice highlights. Now we were seated over steaming bowls of seafood soba in one of those Japanese noodle houses that were popping up around town almost as fast as Starbuck's coffee bars were. This one was down on Bleecker, not far from the murder scene. Very had on a hooded blue New York Giants sweatshirt and gray sweatpants. He looked wired and fierce.

Lulu was lapping up a bowl of soba herself. She was not quiet about it. In fact, she sounded very much as if she were in the john helping herself to a tall cold one from out of the you-know-what.

The pages of the answer man's second chapter were spread

out on the table next to us. This time I had handled them with tweezers, too.

I said, "If he murdered her on Friday, why didn't her roommate find her until today?"

"On account of she went to Sag Harbor for the weekend with some gee. Totally unplanned. They just hopped in the car and went. She called and left a message on the phone machine Saturday morning to let Laurie know where she was. You know, in case Laurie was worried. Which she wasn't, dig, on account of she was dead. We played back the message. It checks."

"And the details of Chapter Two? Do they check?"

He nodded glumly. "Laurie was right there on the sofa, her photos laid out in front of her on the coffee table. Most bonus-looking chick I've seen in my life. A stone fox. She was strangled with something that might have been a neck-tie, not that he left it behind. Branded her same as Diane— the question marks on the forehead. Appears to be—"

"Wait, did you say *marks?* As in more than one?"

Something flickered in Very's eyes. What, I didn't know. "The bastard's numbering 'em, dude," he said between grit-ted teeth. "Appears to be the same lipstick. Same color, anyway." He paused to slurp some noodles. "No sign of a struggle. No sign of sexual assault. No sign of a break-in. Place is a real mess, that's for damned sure. I never seen so much clothing and clutter and dust in my life. You'd think they never heard of a vacuum cleaner."

"You and the answer man seem to have a lot in common, Lieutenant. You don't harbor a secret desire to write, do you?"

"He strikes quick, dude." Very said it sharply. "He strikes quick and strong and clean. I'm betting we turn up bupkes there in the way of evidence."

I glanced at the end of the chapter. "He says here 'I helped myself to what I'd been wanting ever since I first laid eyes on her.' What did he mean by that?"

"The Band-Aid. One that was on her heel, remember?"

I stared at him. Lulu raised her large black nose from her bowl and did the same. "What, he took the Band-Aid?"

Very shrugged his shoulders. "It's gone, dude. Not on her heel. Not in the trash. Not nowhere. All that's left are some traces of adhesive. She had a blister there. Her boyfriend told me she got it down in Miami from a new pair of sandals. She's also got a bite mark—on her butt. Which *would* be major promising if our man did it. Only, the boyfriend says *he* gave her that a few days back when they were doing the wild thing." Very's lips pulled back from his own teeth in distaste. Or maybe it was envy. "We're taking an impression of his teeth to see if there's a match. According to the roommate, Laurie was crazy about this guy, only they were all the time fighting because he hosed around on her. Damn, how a guy could go out on that one. . . ." He shook his head, disgusted. "School me, why do they always fall for jerks?"

"Because that's all that's out there, Lieutenant."

"Name's Tibor Farkas. He's a model. Does beer commercials, shit like that. One of those tall, cut-up gees with white teeth and no waist that women are all the time giving some to. I hate him. Although he *was* pretty broken up when he got the news."

"Where was he Friday night?"

"You mean, could he be the answer man?"

"They do keep saying our man looks familiar. And Tibor *is* a model."

"Claims he was out bar-hopping that night," said Very. "Gave us a bunch of places and names to check out. Plus he's offered to take a lie detector test."

"Is that typical in this kind of case?"

"Dude, there's no such thing as typical in this kind of case."

I stared down at the remains of my lunch. I had lost interest in it. Our waiter came to take our bowls away. We ordered tea.

Very said, "We're keeping Tibor under surveillance. If he

is our man we got to connect him up with Diane Shavelson, who he says he never heard of. We're looking for some way they might have hooked up. Like did they ever go to the same eye doctor or bank at the same bank. We look for a link. Any link."

"And if there isn't one?"

"We try to link up the two victims. What did *they* have in common? We break down their address books, their credit card records. We talk to their neighbors, their families, their friends. Like, say this film class at The New School Laurie was in. That's for real. I just spoke to the guy who teaches it—big claim to fame is he did a book on latent homoeroticism in the films of Laurel and Hardy. What a dickhead."

"What a surprise."

"He gave me a list of her classmates. A dozen people. We check to see if one of them is a hello."

"A hello?"

"Y'know, like one of them pops up in Diane's address book—*hello*. Or one of them recently bought a big blue garment bag from Hold Everything—*hello.*"

"And if there's no hello? If the answer man kills totally at random? What then?"

Very didn't answer me. He didn't want to. His eyes turned to the letter. "I can't believe he was watching us at Barney Greengrass. That's twisted."

"Twisted."

"Kind of makes you wonder if he's watching us right now." He shot a glance over his shoulder.

"Kind of."

"But this is good that he wants you to contact him. This we can do something with. Only, a fucking *personal* ad. That is so retro."

I said nothing.

Very peered at me suspiciously. "Why'd you suddenly go quiet on me?"

"I wasn't aware that I had."

"Dude, you wouldn't hold out on me, would you?"

"Why would you say that, Lieutenant?"

"The fact that you always do, for starters."

"Believe me, if I knew anything I'd tell you."

He stared at me doubtfully a moment, then gave a short nod and sat back in his chair. "Me, I keep thinking this guy's got himself some serious chops. Check it out, these two women were both lookers, the kind who get hit on all the time. They weren't naive. They weren't dumb. Yet they both fell for his line. Diane went home with him. Laurie invited him up—even though he was a total stranger. You know any women who would do that? I don't. They'd be a helluva lot more careful. That means we're talking about someone who can really play the game. He's got to be charming. He's got to be good-looking—"

"Not necessarily good-looking. Laurie was a would-be actress, don't forget."

"So?"

"So she'd invite a two-hundred-pound dung beetle into her home if she thought he could help her career."

"Who *is* this guy, dude?"

"He's someone who can be whomever they want him to be, Lieutenant." Our tea came. I sipped mine, wrapping my icy hands around the cup. I still felt chilled to the bone. It was a feeling I couldn't seem to shake. "So tell me, does the answer man qualify as a serial killer now?"

Very's eyes widened with alarm. "Ssh, not so loud!"

Not that anyone else had heard me. We had the place practically to ourselves. There were three women busy talking over near the door. There was a guy with white hair going one-on-one with the *Daily News* crossword puzzle. There was us.

Very leaned toward me. "Officially, the FBI won't consider him a multiple until we have three confirmed strikes."

"How comforting."

"And for your information, dude, we're giving the press next to nothing about Laurie."

"I didn't know that was possible anymore."

"It's possible if you're waiting on next of kin to fly in from Minnesota. It's important we keep a lid on Laurie's murder. We don't want 'em to link it up with the Shavelson killing. They do that, they'll turn this place into fear city."

"They won't exactly be wrong."

"Hey, we're handling it. As of today, there's thirty men working this case around the clock. We're talking full-fledged task force, under the personal direction of Inspector Dante Feldman, who doesn't believe in waiting for three strikes."

I tugged at my left ear. "Dante Feldman? Isn't he the one who they call the Human Hemorrhoid?"

Very drew his breath in—a pained look crossing his face. "Not on the job, we don't."

"Sure, sure. I've read all about him in the newspaper. He's the one who they say makes George Steinbrenner look like Chuckles the Clown."

"He's my boss of bosses," Very said stiffly. "Commanding officer of all Manhattan homicide detectives. Made his rep on Son of Sam."

"I asked you not to mention him, Lieutenant."

"He wants to meet you."

"Isn't he still locked away in Attica?"

"Feldman, I mean."

"I can't wait."

"That's good, because you don't have to."

"Meaning?"

"Looking at him, dude," Very said uncomfortably.

It was the white-haired guy, the one who'd been doing the crossword puzzle. He was on his way over to us.

Very half-rose from his seat. "Inspector Feldman," he said, his manner turning vastly more formal and respectful than I'd ever seen it, "I'd like to introduce Stewart Hoag."

Feldman just stood there glaring down his long, narrow beak of a nose at me. It was a penetrating glare. It was an intimidating glare. It was the glare of a man who knew my every vice and weakness and human failing. He didn't, of course, but he wanted me to think he did. Then again, maybe he just didn't like being called a hemorrhoid.

"Mr. Hoag," he finally growled, by way of greeting. "What do your friends call you?"

"Haven't got any."

"This doesn't surprise me."

Okay, fine. Now he had Lulu's attention.

"Make it Hoagy," I said.

"As in Carmichael?" There was a trace of Brooklyn in Feldman's voice. Not much.

"As in the sandwich."

"A fan. I'm a huge one."

"Why, thank you."

"Of your wife, I meant. Merilee Nash."

"She's my ex-wife."

A faint smile crossed his thin lips. "Sorry. My mistake."

"No, I believe this one's on me."

Dante Feldman was in his fifties, tall and taut and sinewy, with a carefully combed snowy-white pompadour, pale lips and hooded black eyes that never seemed to blink. He was a sharp dresser for a cop, which meant a navy-blue Ungaro knockoff, pale blue broadcloth shirt with contrasting white collar and cuffs, a Hermès tie. And he was a preener. Standing there, he kept shooting his cuffs and smoothing his pompadour, shooting his cuffs and smoothing his pompadour. It was, I would discover, a thing he did. Somewhat like a tic. "I like to get a feel for an individual when his guard isn't up," he told me. "That's why I've been observing you without your knowledge. I hope you don't mind."

"Would it matter if I did?"

"Mind if I join you?"

"Would it matter if I did?"

Feldman glanced severely at Very, who looked away, coloring. Then the inspector pulled up a chair and sat, being careful not to kick Lulu under the table. The waiter brought him a teacup. He filled it and drank, swishing the tea around in his mouth like Listerine. He swallowed it. He sat back. "I would have preferred meeting with you alone."

"You can say anything in front of Lulu you would say in front of me, Inspector. She has my complete confidence."

"I was referring to Lieutenant Very here."

"Oh."

"But he insisted on sitting in. He felt I'd need a . . . what was it you called it, Lieutenant?"

"Interpreter," Very said quietly.

"Actually, what he said was that you have no license to practice but you'd try to operate on my head."

"He said that?"

"I didn't know what he meant at first, but now I do. You see, I am on to you, my friend," Feldman informed me with a smug, self-satisfied smile.

I don't do well around smug. Never have. "On to me, Inspector?"

"It has been my experience that most people are one shade or another of gray," he said. Actually, he didn't so much speak as deliver weighty, carefully worded proclamations. It was as if he were standing outside on the curb giving a press conference of nationwide import. "You are what I call Kodachrome Brash."

I glanced down at Lulu. She didn't particularly want to touch that one, so I tried Very. "Was I just dissed?"

Very didn't reply. He was like a different person around the inspector. Loyal. Obedient. Silent. I had never seen him in toady mode before. I didn't much care for it.

"The lieutenant was telling me about how you helped crack the Son of Sam case, Inspector," I said. What the hell, I was going to have to hear about it eventually. Might as well get it over with.

Feldman took another gulp of his tea and sat back, his hands gripping the narrow arms of the chair like huge claws, his hooded eyes flicking from one side of the restaurant to the other. He reminded me of a hawk perched there waiting for some unsuspecting prey to come out of its burrow so he could swoop down and snatch it in his powerful jaws and fly off with it, its tiny limbs flailing helplessly in midair. "That was the Omega Task Force," he recalled, his voice booming. "Largest manhunt in department history. We had seventy-five detectives and two hundred and twenty-five uniforms working around the clock in all five boroughs of the city of New York. Cost the city almost a hundred thousand dollars a day in overtime. Ended up costing over two million. At one point, we were getting as many as four phone-in tips a minute, people who were sure they'd spotted him. We checked them all out. Every single one. We investigated more than three thousand suspects. We consulted shrinks, hypnotists, numerologists, astrologers, biorhythm specialists. . . ." He paused to swallow more tea. "Dave Berkowitz attacked eight times in fourteen months. Stabbed two, shot six. Six of the eight died. And do you know how we got him in the end? On a parking ticket. The man parked too close to a fire plug." Abruptly, he turned his penetrating glare back on me. "How do I know *you're* not the answer man?" he demanded harshly.

"You don't," I replied. "For that matter, I don't either. Maybe I have a split personality. Maybe I slip out in the night and kill these women myself. That would certainly explain why I wake up so tired in the morning."

He let out a derisive snort, Lulu staring up at him curiously. He took note of her. "What's *she* doing?"

"Trying to make up her mind about you."

"What about me?"

"You'll have to ask her that. She doesn't tell me everything."

Now Feldman's eyes flicked over to the pages laid out on the table beside us. "What I want to know is why he picked you."

"I have no idea, as I've already told the lieutenant."

"But he seems to *know* you."

"He knows my work. A lot of people do. There are still plenty of readers out there for good, serious fiction. And when they run out of that they turn to me."

"Quite the little comic, aren't you?" Feldman snapped.

"I'm well over six feet tall."

"Well, do me a favor and cut the comedy. Now isn't the time."

"On the contrary, now *is* the time—or I run right out of here screaming at the top of my lungs in Swedish. And, Inspector, I don't speak Swedish."

"What it is, Inspector," Very affirmed. "Either you put up with it or you sedate him."

"That's the best idea you've had all afternoon, Lieutenant," Feldman said.

We sat there in brittle silence a moment. Something told me we three weren't going to be hanging out together when this was over. If it was ever over.

"Well, I guess you do have a certain rep," Feldman grumbled at me. "By that I mean you spend a lot of your life on the gossip pages. If you call that a life."

"I really don't need to hear this just now, Inspector."

"Hear what?" he demanded.

"That I brought this whole thing on myself. That I somehow made it happen."

Feldman's eyes narrowed. I doubt this man ever lost a no-blinking contest. "Okay, what *do* you need to hear?"

"How you plan to catch this lunatic would be nice."

"Fine," he agreed, rubbing his hands together. "That happens to be something I know a little bit about."

"The inspector teaches a course on serial killers at John Jay College of Criminal Justice," Very said, which explained why the guy reminded me of a professor I once hated.

"I've helped dozens of departments set up task forces of their own," Feldman said proudly. "I've lectured on the subject in seven different countries. And I have to tell you, I've

been sitting there listening to you two chowderheads helicopter over this thing until I'm about ready to puke."

Lulu promptly got to her feet and started across the restaurant to the back.

"Where's she going?" Feldman asked, watching her.

"She's showing you where the men's room is."

"A figure of speech," he protested. "It was a figure of
speech."

"She's very literal-minded." Also a charter member of the
upchuck-averse. Has real problems with Sadie, our barn cat,
over that whole furball thing.

Lulu returned and sat next to me, curling her lip at Feldman. She'd made up her mind. She didn't like him.

Very, he just sat there sipping his tea in tight silence, his
eyes avoiding mine.

"For starters," the inspector lectured, "we strike early.
Early on, *we* have the edge. He's still new to this. Hasn't
perfected his methods yet. Maybe he's even a little bit nervous. There's still a chance he'll trip over his own dick. The
longer this goes on, the more he kills, the better he'll get at
it. So we hit the ground running. Okay, what does this
mean? It means getting a system of procedures in place right
away. For preserving the crime scenes. For ensuring that
quality-control procedures are in place. Organization is critical. How we interface with the lab and the medical examiner. How we review and investigate outside tips. We have to
establish good, working lines of intradepartmental and inter-
departmental communication so that nothing, but *nothing*
slips through the cracks. We harness our best minds, and I'm
not just talking homicide. We want a team of shrinks working over these chapters. We want sex crimes to analyze his
every—"

"But I thought there hadn't been any sex," I interjected.

"He hasn't *raped* them," Feldman countered. "He hasn't
left them with their blood-soaked panties stuffed in their
mouths or their vaginas sealed shut with Krazy Glue. But his

victims are young, they're single and they're pretty. He is sexually involved with them. He is exerting power over them. Don't kid yourself, Hoagy—"

"But that's one of the things I'm best at."

"—these *are* sex crimes." He paused to drink, then resumed. Like any veteran lecturer, he could pick up precisely where he left off. "We have to control and coordinate the flow of information to the public. Because, more than anything else, a serial killer on the loose in New York City, especially a serial killer who is stalking attractive single women, is a public relations nightmare for this department."

"Pretty hard for the victims and their families, too," I said.

Very let out a small groan, barely audible.

"Okay, I don't need your smart remarks," Feldman said to me coldly.

"Sorry. I'll just share my stupid ones with you from now on."

The inspector heaved his chest, exasperated. "So what's the deal? You and me just going to tangle all afternoon?"

"That all depends."

"On what?"

"On whether you're planning to continue this on into the evening as well."

We stared across the table at each other in charged silence. Until, abruptly, he decided to let it slide. "How much do you know about the serial killer, Hoagy? As a species, I mean?"

"As little as possible."

"First thing I want you to do is forget the standard psychobabble. He doesn't want to be caught or helped or any of that shit. If he did, he'd turn himself in. What he wants is attention. That's why he's contacted you. Christ, Dave Berkowitz left us letters at the scene. Even wrote to that fat fuck at the *Daily News,* Breslin. Your boy, the answer man, is what I call a water walker. He's walking on water.

Making us plotz while we wait for his next move. He's playing games with us, my friend. He's playing God." Feldman sat back, his eyes examining the ceiling. "We are not dealing with an ordinary criminal here, Hoagy. It's vital to understand that going in. He's a unique animal. A cunning and utterly sociopathic animal. A roving killing machine. A shark. Whereas in more than half of your common murder cases the victim was killed by someone they knew, ninety percent of the time your serial killer goes after a total stranger. Serial killers do not view their victims as human beings. They view them as prey. If he were to kill someone he knew it would spoil it for him. He has no remorse. None. And I choose the word 'he' carefully. Invariably they are men, with the rare exception of women who go after elderly nursing home patients for their life insurance money. For all practical purposes, there is no such thing as a woman serial killer."

"Yo, what about that one down in Daytona Beach in eighty-nine, Inspector?" Very spoke up like an eager pupil. "They had her for doing seven guys, remember? She posed as a hitchhiker. She'd offer 'em sex for money and then she'd *do* 'em. What was her name again? Wuornos? Aileen Wuornos?"

"There is no such thing as a woman serial killer," Feldman repeated, raising his voice insistently. He did not dignify the lieutenant's comment with any other response. I didn't like the way he treated Very. He treated him like he was a grease spot on the floor.

Very clearly didn't care for it either. His ears were burning and one knee was quaking. The table shook.

The lecture resumed.

"Most of our common murderers, statistically speaking, are aged eighteen to twenty-four. They are below average in intelligence. They also tend to be poor, and therefore more likely than not to be black. Your serial killer is white, he is above average in intelligence and he is typically a more mature individual, in his thirties or even forties. His crimes are not spontaneous. They are well planned. He cleans up after himself. We seldom find anything. We search, naturally. We look for a matchup from one crime scene to the next—a latent print, a hair, a fiber. But he is careful. And he is clever. Some are so clever they deliberately change their method of operation so as to confuse us. Albert DeSalvo, the Boston Strangler, murdered thirteen women. Some he stabbed, some he smashed in the head with a pipe. Five more he raped but didn't kill. Christopher Wilder, the so-called Beauty Queen Killer of the mid-eighties, killed some by suffocation, some by stabbing. One he shot. Often, we find that these guys are consummate con men. Wilder posed as a fashion photographer, Ted Bundy as a police detective. A number of them, like Bundy and Wilder and John Collins, the Michigan Coed Killer, were charming, engaging, clean-cut guys who possessed a magical touch with women. In that sense, your answer man is a classic. He's the boy next door. He's Jekyll and Hyde . . .''

Okay, now he'd done it—he'd succeeded in scaring Lulu, the big bully. She was cowering between my legs, shaking. I reached down and gave her a reassuring pat. I just wished someone would give me one.

''That's why they fascinate and horrify the public to the degree that they do,'' Feldman went on. ''Let's face it, there's something inherently disturbing about a man who is capable of killing yet is also capable of functioning success-fully in polite society. Wilder ran a business. So did John Wayne Gacy. Collins was a few credits short of getting his bachelor's degree. Bundy was a law student. More than any-thing, these guys are clever. That's what the answer man is— clever. Making us think he's an addict. Making us think he's just out of jail. Making us think he's someone who washes dishes for a living.''

''You think he's none of the above?'' I asked.

Feldman sniffed. ''He's playing games with us. This is someone bright. My guess is he works in publishing.''

''I thought you just said he was someone bright.''

The inspector let that one slide by. He was thinking out loud now. "Sure, sure—he's an editor or a proofreader. Maybe some guy who works in the mailroom, thinks he should be a famous author."

"That's half the people in publishing, Inspector."

"He's frustrated. He's bitter. He's angry."

"That's the other half."

"I like this angle, Lieutenant," Feldman concluded, pleased, as if someone else had raised it. "I want you to work it. Discreetly, so you don't set off any alarm bells."

"We have been, Inspector." Very spoke up in his own defense. "We been checking the publishing houses to see if anyone remembers getting a submission that matches up even slightly. Also working the literary agencies. Maybe he shopped it to an agent first."

"I'd focus your efforts on the smaller, independent agents, Lieutenant," I said. "Most of the big agencies don't read stuff that comes in over the transom anymore."

Very made a note of this in his pad. Then he scratched his buzz-cut head reflectively. "Weird that he's so polite, don't you think? In his letters, I mean."

"You haven't been listening to me, Lieutenant," Feldman huffed impatiently. "Just because he's psychotic doesn't mean he's ill bred." Now the hooded eyes turned back my way. "Which reminds me, we're shortstopping your mail at the post office from now on. Before your carrier delivers it. That way, if you get another installment we'll get a jump of several hours. We'll make sure you get a copy, so you're kept abreast."

"What about this personal ad I'm supposed to place in the *Times?*"

"All taken care of," Feldman answered brusquely.

"Meaning what, exactly?"

"Meaning exactly what it sounds like. It's taken care of. It'll run in tomorrow's paper, bottom of page one, just like he asked."

"And what does it say?"

"It says, 'Answer man—Have promising news. Let's meet at Barney Greengrass at ten.' "

Lulu let out a cough.

He frowned down at her. *"Now* what's her problem?"

"Well, it could use some tweaking."

"Tweaking? What's that mean?"

"It means," Very translated, "he thinks it sucks."

"I usually write my own material, Inspector. I really wish you had consulted me."

Feldman shot a cold, hard look at me. *"Consulted* you? What do *you* know about it? You ever been on a task force?"

"I've worked with seriously disturbed individuals a number of times. We just don't call them disturbed; we call them celebrities. In my experience, it's vital that I gain his trust. He and I have to get a dialogue going. That's the only way he'll reveal himself to me. For starters, he has to believe I wrote that ad myself."

The inspector shook his head, disgusted. "Christ, I've heard about you writers and your egos—"

"This has nothing to do with my ego. It has to do with right and wrong. I'm right and you're wrong."

Feldman turned to Very, incredulous. "You *believe* this guy?"

"Welcome to my nightmare, sir."

"Pull your ad, Inspector. Pull it and let me write my own."

"I know what I'm doing, Hoagy." Feldman was speaking with exaggerated patience now, as if he were trying to placate a shrill, annoying old lady whose petunias had gotten trampled by some little boys. "I been through this kind of thing before. Just let me do my job, okay?"

"Fine, but he won't show. He'll know it's a trap. He's not stupid. You said so yourself."

"Maybe he won't," Feldman allowed. "But we have to try it, don't we? We have to try everything. You never know— just because he's clever doesn't mean he's smart."

"Maybe you should let me write your material, too."

"I picked Barney Greengrass because he's already observed you there. It's a familiar location. He'll feel at ease."

"That'll make one of us."

"You just start showing up there every morning at ten, starting tomorrow, until he makes contact."

"He won't," I insisted.

"I'll be the one behind the counter slicing sturgeon, dude," Very informed me. It didn't sound to me like his heart was in it, but I may have imagined that.

I tugged at my left ear. "Is that wise, Lieutenant?"

"Hey, I worked at a deli all through high school."

"But he's *seen* you."

"That's the whole idea," explained Feldman. Clearly, it was his plan, not that I ever had any doubt. "We *want* him to walk in and make the lieutenant. That's how we'll know he's our man."

"I'll go in real early, dude. He won't make me—not until it's too late."

"And he won't get away," Feldman vowed. "Once he reacts, he's ours."

"What if he resists?"

"We'll put him down. Sharpshooters stationed across the avenue and at neighboring tables."

"I don't like this."

"Now, there's no reason to feel concerned," Feldman said reassuringly. "We're very good at this sort of thing."

I said it again, louder. "I don't like this."

"We'll even outfit you with a bulletproof vest," added the inspector.

"Thank you, no. Kevlar doesn't do a thing for me."

"Hey, it's not like appearances are a priority," he said scornfully.

Which drew another cough from Lulu.

And another look from Feldman. "Now what is she . . . ?"

"She doesn't know how to laugh," I explained. "May I ask you a stupid question, Inspector?"

"Of course."

"Will the answer man strike again?"

He considered this a moment, his claws gripping the arms of his chair tightly. "I hope not. I fear yes. Once this kind of shark gets a taste for blood he usually comes back for more."

"Can I ask you another stupid question?"

"You can ask me any question you want."

"Are you going to catch him?"

"Of course we will," he replied, totally confident. "Two things have to happen, that's all."

I leaned forward anxiously. "What are they? What are those two things?"

Feldman shot his cuffs. He smoothed his white pompadour. He said, "The first is, we have to be lucky."

"And what's the second?"

"He has to fuck up."

But the answer man wasn't going to fuck up—he wasn't stupid. I knew this. I knew this because Feldman had said he wasn't. And I knew this because way down deep inside, where the great big ugly black snakes and the three-headed toads and the cackling rats lived, I had a feeling I knew who the answer man was.

Oh, yeah, I had me a feeling.

I had parked the Jag out front, my beloved red 1958 XK 150 drophead with its 60-spoke wire wheels, every inch of it original. I got in with Lulu next to me and started it up and cranked up the heat as high as it would go, which isn't real high. Especially when you're already feeling frozen.

Very and Feldman stood there at the curb watching me, Feldman muttering something sour at him, Very's jaw muscles clenching and unclenching. I watched them watching me. Then I got out of there fast.

I headed uptown to my personal crumple zone, my drafty old fifth-floor walk-up on West Ninety-third, which I'd had since I first moved to New York and which I still kept as an office. This is where I go to brood and to pace and to think my nondeep thoughts. It's not much. A small, dingy living room. A smaller, dingier bedroom. But it's my refuge, my treehouse, my fort—no girls or babies allowed. Not that they ever came knocking. Merilee loathed the place and Tracy was forbidden to go there. Too many germs.

The only bad part was the climb. My landlord wasn't making it any easier—he kept adding another flight of steps every couple of years so as to drive me out. Even Lulu was starting to notice it. She slowed up herself when we reached the fourth-floor landing. Only, she wasn't out of breath. She wasn't so much as panting.

She was stalking, her large black nose aquiver.

Slowly, quietly, she resumed climbing. Until halfway up the steps to the top floor she froze, her hackles rising, a low, menacing growl coming from her throat . . .

My apartment door was open. Maybe an inch.

Someone was in there. I could hear a drawer being opened, then closed. Footsteps. I stood there on the stairs, wheezing, weighing my options. I thought about tiptoeing back downstairs to call the police, only, Lulu had other ideas. She does that sometimes—freelances. This was one of those times.

She charged the door, teeth bared, a savage roar coming from her throat. Made straight for the bedroom, her nails clacketing, clacketing on the parquet floor. I heard a scream. A bloodcurdling woman's scream. Followed by a voice I would know anywhere:

"GEEZ, HOAGY, GET HER THE HELL AWFFA ME, WILL YA?!"

I relaxed at once. Because there was only one person in the whole wide world who actually was afraid of Lulu and that person was Cassandra Dee, star of *Face to Face* or *Cheek to Jowl* or whatever the hell it was called.

She was standing on a chair inside my bedroom closet, the better to go through the personal papers that were stored up on the top shelf. Lulu was circling the chair, barking up at her furiously. She had the poor woman treed.

"How did you get in, Cassandra?" I asked, standing there in the bedroom doorway.

"I shmeared the super, okay?" she cried in her nasal Bensonhurst bray. "Now w-will ya—?"

"No kidding, I have a super?"

"C-Call her off, will ya!" Cassandra was approaching hysteria.

"Not until you tell me what you were looking for."

"Okay, okay. The answer man's letters, okay? I f-figured maybe you'd hide 'em here. C'mon, Hoagy, will ya?"

I called Lulu off. She snarfled victoriously and went swaggering off to the living room to patrol there for other enemy invaders and to gloat.

Cassandra immediately leaped off the chair into my arms. "Gawd, cookie, I missed ya!" She kissed me hard on the mouth. "Chew my tights off," she commanded me. "I'm yours."

Cassandra Dee hadn't changed all that much since the last time I'd seen her. She was still tall and willowy, still young, still attractive in a vampy, campy sort of way. I always thought she came off looking like a mime done up as Betty Boop. Chiefly because of her eyes, which were permanently goggly, and her brows, which she plucked and penciled into high, exaggerated arches. Her skin was a vivid milk-white, her lips and nails a vivid crimson, her hair an abundantly curly mane of black. She wore an oversized, fuzzy gray sweater-coat-kimono thing with a big shiny leather belt around it, black leggings and a pair of those stupid race-car-driver moccasins with the bumps on the sole that everyone was wearing. A camelhair steamer coat was tossed carelessly on my bed.

"There you go again, Cassandra. Playing hard to get."

"I ain't playing at nothing, cookie. I'm doin' it. I'm schmokin'."

Indeed she was. Because Cassandra Dee, short for
D'Amico, *had* changed. Or maybe I should say the world
had changed around her. She was still what she always had
been—a bare-knuckle Brooklyn street fighter, a relentless
tabloid reporter with no ethics, no regrets and no conscience
whatsoever. In ghosting circles, she was known as the mis-
tress of the slash-and-burn. Until she got out of the printed
word altogether. Went to work for *Hard Copy* and never
looked back. The pack ate her dust on Joey and Amy, on
Nancy and Tonya, on John and Lorena Bobbitt. The O. J.
Simpson trial, the story that forever blurred the distinction
between tabloid and so-called respectable news, had landed
her on the cover of *People*. The headline read: CAN'T ANYONE
STOP DIS GOIL? No one could. Because Cassandra was, quite
simply, a bad idea whose time had come. She ran her own
half-hour tabloid news show now. She ran it, she owned it,
she *was* it. On the air, Cassandra was equal parts sleaze mon-
ger, sensationalist, sob sister and shill. And she was fast becoming one of the biggest stars on television. Not as big as
Oprah but getting there. Her audience adored her. Her col-
leagues hated her. Me, I'd always been somewhat fond of
her. Maybe because she never pretended to be anything
other than what she was. Maybe because she had always
looked up to me. I never quite knew why.

"C'mon, already," she pleaded, tugging at the sleeves of
my coat. "Lemme see his letters, will ya?"

"I have no idea what you're talking about, Cassandra."

She let out a shriek. "Cookie, this is *me* you're talking to,
not some uptight politically correct *Times* know-nothing
bimbo. I'm on to him, okay? I know that he's writing you. I
know that he's already struck twice. And I know that he's
the next Son of Sam. I'm calling him 'The Man Who Loves
Women to Death.' Whaddaya think? . . . Okay, okay.
You're right. It sucks. I'll work on it. Trouble is, the department won't confoim. They're too freaked, on account of this
is the kind of story keeps the German tourists away and the
locals from heading out after dark. But I'm breaking it on

tonight's show no matter how hard they lean on me. You lean on me, I bust ya in the fucking chops, baby. First blood, y'know what I'm saying?" She shot a hurried glance at her watch. "Look, I got a car and driver outside. I tape in a hour. So let's not dick around, huh? Talk to me, Marine to Marine . . ." Now she froze, staring at me with her protuberant eyes. "What, why are you looking at me that way?"

"I enjoy listening to you work. I can't help it."

"You mean you missed me?"

"Something like that."

"Gawd, Hoagy, I'm getting shivers down my backbone. You wreck me, you know that?"

"That's me, all right. A head-on collision."

"Promise me you won't laugh—what am I saying, you never laugh—I missed you, too. Wanna know why? You got class. Not fake class, like Ralph Lauren or Martha Stewart or me. You're the real thing. And, Gawd, you look gorgeous. That jacket you got on, what is that?"

"It's called houndstooth."

"Can I try it on?"

"You may not. Guys don't do that."

I moved into the living room. She had gone through my desk before she tried the closet. The drawers were open, the contents tossed. She followed me in there, eyeing Lulu, who was now totally focused on the door of the refrigerator. She was waiting for an anchovy reward. I went and got her one.

"How much you pay for this place, anyway?" Cassandra asked, checking out the walls and ceiling, which hadn't been painted in twenty years.

"Three hundred a month."

"You're getting hosed. I've heard of downscale chic but this is over the top." She hugged herself with her arms. "And did they ever hear of a little thing called heat? I can see my breath."

"Have a seat, Cassandra."

She looked around. "Where?"

I cleared the piles of newspapers and magazines from the

loveseat. She sat. Lulu came over to sniff her legs and to scare her. Then she curled up in my easy chair, tail thumping happily. It isn't often she gets to intimidate anyone.

Cassandra immediately went back into action: "So tell me what you're not telling me, cookie." Her patented phrase. She stole it from me, actually. Except for the "cookie" part.

I sat in my desk chair, an old captain's chair that swiveled. "I have nothing to say, Cassandra."

"Yeah, yeah, shewa. You wanna deal, we'll deal. You are talking to Domino's—I deliver . . . I want ya exclusive, okay? I'll pay you twenty-five grand a week to appear on my show every night until the answer man is caught. All you gotta do is tell the audience in your own words what's happening. Two minutes tops. If the trial gets huge, we can renegotiate, okay? Whaddaya say? You don't know what to say, am I right? You're dumbstruck. You cannot believe how phat this is gonna be, you and me together in fifty million homes every night. We will go through the fucking roof."

"Tried it. Got one monstrous headache."

"Hoagy, read my lips: I can turn you into the thinking man's Kato Kaelin."

Lulu let out a low growl.

Cassandra eyed her warily. "What, what did I say?"

"She's just confused about the particulars. Do I or do I not have to bite the heads off live chickens?"

Cassandra heaved her chest at me. "Okay, you're doing an elitist number on me. Cookie, honey, sweetie, it's time to wake up and smell the coffee. For as long as there has been civilization, people have gone to the circus. Now, thanks to the miracle of modern technology, the circus comes to them."

"On every channel, twenty-four hours a day."

"No one makes them watch."

"I don't agree. I think there's an evil spirit out there, the same one that makes them eat Egg McMuffins and shop at Wal-Mart."

"As if. They watch because they want to watch. And who are we to say they shouldn't? Besides which, and I don't mean to be critical, but you make it sound like you haven't been a major player yourself. You're the champ. That's why you're my idol."

"Still? I figured you would have moved on to Barbara Wawa by now."

"Uh-uh. That's not how it works. When somebody's your idol they're your idol for life, like pigeons mating. Except you know what your problem is, Hoagy? You can't enjoy the one thing in life that you're best at."

"Oh, that. It's a blood thing. Merely goes back six or seven generations."

"They got a name for it?"

"In some circles it's called being gentile."

"Gawd, I have this dream that someday I'll wake up and understand everything you say."

"That's amazing. I have that same dream, too."

"What, that I'll understand what you say?"

"No, that *I* will. Problem is, I keep waking up in the middle of it with leg cramps. Do you think I need more potassium in my diet?"

"You'll get a huge book out of it," she pointed out. "Enough to put over your new novel."

"How did you know I have a new novel?"

"Like I don't follow your every move? Like I don't pitcha us two riding off into the sunset together someday? Tell me what you want and it's yours. You want my help selling the novel? Because, cookie, you are sitting on top of a major buzz ploy here. Just say the woid and I can put you on the bestseller list."

"Why settle for mainstream success when you can enjoy the comforts of a small, nongrowing cult?"

"I give up," she said wearily. "What *do* you want? Talk to me."

"I want you to tell me how you found out."

"That's easy." She got up and went over to the window, not that it's far. She got a good view of the courtyard, not that it's much. "It got leaked."

"By who?"

"I got my sources at One Police Plaza."

"Feldman?"

She turned to face me. "The Human Hemorrhoid? Yech, no way. He's too busy telling everyone what a fucking genius he is. Nah, some deputy commish. Cost me a lousy hand job in his car. And he didn't even deliver his payload, the old fat fuck. All he—"

"I don't need to hear this part."

"And now they are *sooo* desperate to keep a lid on it," she went on, her eyes bright with excitement. "I mean, you wouldn't believe the 'tude I got from some butthead named Romaine Very on the phone this morning."

"Yes, I would."

"This guy was nasty. He even accused me of making the whole thing up just to further my career, that scumbag, that dick, that—"

"The lieutenant's a huge fan of yours, Cassandra. In fact, he thinks you're the second-best-looking woman on television."

"Who's better looking?" she demanded angrily. "Little Courteney Fucking Cox? *Who?*"

"You don't want to know."

She softened slightly. "Is he cute?"

"Very."

"That's who I'm talking about. Is he?"

"In my opinion, he's a stud muffin."

"Will you introduce me?"

"No."

"Why not? You ashamed of me?"

"I have my reasons."

She heaved a huge sigh. "Gawd, I'd give anything to get with someone."

"Hold it. This sounds like a personal problem."

"Night after night I rattle around in my house . . . Did I tell you I got my own friggin' brownstone on West Tenth?"

"That must be nice."

"It sucks. I'm so lonesome I'm ready to go out the window. I ain't asking for the moon anymore, either. I've lowered my sights. All I ask is he's got a fresh, unused brain and a good sense of direction."

"Direction?"

"As in he knows the southern route," she explained, with a flirty glint in her eyes.

Lulu grunted sourly. Cassandra's a bit unrefined for her.

Now Cassandra came over and stood before me, rested her hands on my shoulders, which got a low growl from Lulu. She removed them. "Talk to me, Hoagy. Who is he? Who is the answer man?"

"I don't know, Cassandra."

"Okay, okay, how about this: Do you deny receiving two detailed accounts of his murders from the answer man? I'm talking on the record now."

"I have no comment."

She rolled her eyes. "But I thought we were going to deal."

"We did. You told me how you found out, in exchange for which I'm not going to call Lieutenant Very and have him arrest you for breaking and entering."

She peered down at me. "You've changed, y'know that? You've gotten . . . respectable."

"That would be this whole fatherhood thing. Do you see me in a homburg?"

"Honey, I see you naked on my kitchen floor, slathered in peanut butter."

"Smooth or crunchy?"

She ran her finger along my chin. "So, what, you're a family man now?"

"I'm a family man. Me and Charlie Manson."

"Gonna show me a baby pitcha or you gonna make me beg?"

"Do I honestly look like one of those boring fathers who carries around baby pictures?"

She just stared at me.

"Well, if you're going to insist . . ." I pulled out my wallet and opened it for her.

"Geez, you got a whole friggin' portfolio here." She started leafing through it. "Ain't her head a little large?"

"It is not." I snatched it back from her.

"You and that green-eyed goody-goody still getting along?"

"If by that you mean Merilee, the answer is yes."

"Me, I keep thinking one day you'll wake up and realize you want a real woman. Somebody with Mediterranean blood coursing through her veins. Somebody who'd throw herself in front of a moving car for you. *Me,* in case I ain't making myself clear." Again she sighed. "But you're wearing me out, Hoagy. I'm getting tired of waiting for ya." She went and got her coat from the bed. She had a small black Ghurka card case in one of the pockets. She opened it and handed me a card. "In case you change your mind, all my numbers are on there—E-mail, voice mail, fax, the woiks." I helped her on with her coat. She looked good in it, and she knew it. "I'm gonna reel the answer man in, Hoagy. You just watch me."

"I want you to watch yourself."

"Yeah, yeah, shewa. Egg me on."

"I mean it, Cassandra. This guy is a cold-blooded killer. Be careful."

"Careful's my middle name. Actually, it's not. It's Apollonia. But I always hated it." She kissed me again, on the cheek this time. Lulu watched her sternly. "You don't fool me, y'know," Cassandra said coyly. "I know why you won't introduce me to Very."

"You do?"

"Shewa. You're saving me for yourself. You know it and I know it. And one of these days, cookie, I am gonna rock your world."

Okay, that was enough for Lulu. One toke over the line, happy-home-wise. She bared her fangs and charged, chasing Cassandra Dee screaming out the door. Barked *"And stay out!"* after her and harrumphed and made all sorts of territorial she-gal noises. Me, I locked the door and put the chain on. Also some Garner.

Then I stood there staring at the framed photograph that was hanging over the loveseat.

It was a photograph of three college track stars in uniform. How proud we three looked, squinting at the bright sun and the even brighter future that lay ahead of us. How sure. How ready. Each of us with our hands clasped before us like good little schoolboys in a class picture. Each of us with a crooked thumb sticking out of the bottom of our track shorts in a most X-rated manner. I was the one on the left, the third best javelin thrower in the entire Ivy League, looking tall and gangly and awful damned cocky. On the right, in the wire-rimmed glasses, was Ezra Spooner, looking like he was twenty going on forty. He was already balding. In between us, with his huge sloping shoulders and his wavy blond hair and his lopsided grin, was Tuttle Cash. We made quite some trio, we did—the angry young author, the unassuming numbers wonk and the Greek god.

I stared at the photograph for another long moment, Lulu watching me curiously from the doorway. Then I went hunting.

Cassandra had moved around a lot of the stuff on the top shelf of the bedroom closet. The storage boxes full of my tax returns and records. My book contracts and royalty statements. My journals, which to date no major or minor university libraries were clamoring for. I dug past those. I was looking for letters. Not the letters Cassandra was looking for. These were from long ago. These were letters from a friend.

I found them tucked inside a shoebox way in the back, wrapped tightly in rubber bands. Fat, square overseas envelopes covered with exotic stamps from all over the world. I had saved them, figuring they'd one day be a mother lode of source material for biographers. Ah, the arrogance of youth. Although it hadn't seemed like arrogance at the time. Not in the case of Tuttle Cash. Because there wasn't a soul on campus who didn't remark to themselves when they saw him striding across the historic Yard, the walk slightly pigeon-toed, the right shoulder always held a bit higher than the left: "There goes a future president of the United States." So I had saved Tuttle's letters from Oxford, where he had served out his Rhodes scholarship. And from Ghana, where he had gone to dig trenches. And from all over Europe, where he had pedaled his bicycle. I had saved the observations and ramblings and wit and wisdom of the man who was without a doubt the most extraordinary and gifted and miserable person I'd ever known. Of course I had.

Not that I'd looked at them in fifteen years. Not that I wanted to look at them now. I was too afraid of what I'd find.

I took them back into the living room and sat in my easy chair, holding them. I sat there, staring at that lopsided grin over my loveseat . . .

There had been Pittsburgh steel money behind his family at one time. One of his grandfathers had even been a United States senator. But by the time Tuttle arrived on campus there was little left. Just the Cash name. His father taught math at Choate, which was where Tuttle prepped. And where his legend was born. The kid, you see, could do some things with a football. He was offered full athletic scholarships to Syracuse, Penn State, USC, UCLA, Michigan, Nebraska, Stanford. He turned them all down. He wanted an Ivy League education. He paid for it with an academic scholarship. Seems he had done some promising research work in molecular biology his junior year at Choate. Besides, he could still play football if he felt like it. And he did.

The Ivy League has produced more than its share of U.S. presidents and way too many lawyers and economists and literary critics. But its list of athletic heroes is short. We're talking a scant few. There's Hobey Baker, the legendary football and hockey star who never made it back from World War I. There's Larrupin' Lou Gehrig and Dollar Bill Bradley. And there's Tuttle Cash.

King Tut.

He was the most graceful open field runner anyone had ever seen, six feet tall, two hundred pounds, with blazing speed and remarkable balance and even more remarkable peripheral vision. Tuttle Cash, the saying went, didn't have eyes—he had antennae. And an uncommon flair for the dramatic. In his very first game he ran a punt back eighty-two yards in a driving snowstorm with time running out to beat Cornell for the Ivy League title. That same week, at age nineteen, he sold his first poem to *The New Yorker*. He called it "As the Crowd Roars."

King Tut averaged 173 yards per game his senior year, nearly eight yards every time he touched the ball. That was the year he won his Heisman Trophy. Not that he was destined for NFL stardom like the big-time college players he edged out. No, he was more of a sentimental choice. Those were the dark, bitter days of Vietnam and Watergate. And Tuttle Cash, he was the exemplar of a vanishing breed—the gallant schoolboy hero. Modest in victory, gracious in defeat, a straight-A student, a generous teammate and classmate. He was, as Red Smith put it, "a throwback, a symbol of a bygone era when scholar-athletes were honored for sustaining the amateur tradition of sport for sport's sake."

Of course, Red Smith didn't know that King Tut, the golden boy, played the last game of his college career high on two hits of windowpane acid. Not many people know that. Not many people knew him. Not really.

For those of us who did, he was just Tuttle—down-to-earth, easygoing, funny, crazy. A regular guy, no different from anyone else, except for the small fact that he happened to have won the lottery when he was born, the one that made him smarter, stronger and handsomer than everyone else, teeth whiter, hair blonder, eyes bluer, body impervious to pain and fatigue, heart impervious to fear. Every woman who met him fell in love with him. Every guy who met him wanted to *be* him. Everyone, no matter who they were, wanted to stand close to him, hoping that if they stood there long enough some of the magic might rub off on them.

Spring semesters, he ran track to keep in shape. He was our best sprinter at 100 or 220 yards, even with his heavy football muscles. In fact, he could outperform most of us at our own specialties with almost no effort. He high-jumped six feet the first time he ever tried clearing a bar. Threw the javelin three feet farther than I ever could the first time he picked one up. I'm quite certain he could have been an Olympic decathlete if he'd wanted. The only thing that held him back was the impossibly high standard he set for himself. I was with Tuttle the first time he picked up a set of golf clubs. This was at Shinnecock Hills in Southhampton, where the U.S. Open has been played twice. He shot an 85 that day. Within a month he could shoot par. I saw him do it. I was there. And in the clubhouse afterward, he abruptly announced he was never going to pick up a golf club again. When I asked him why he replied, "I'm not good enough."

Much of track is rigor and drudgery. Sprints. Laps. More sprints. More laps. We fell in together. I never knew why. He could have chosen anyone to be his friend. He chose me. Me and Ezra Spooner, an earnest plugger of a kid from Nashua, New Hampshire, a so-so miler who was very shy around women. Mostly, as we three worked our way around and around the track, we concocted wild, dirty stories about our coach, crusty old Augie Cuchinella, who had been there since something like 1921. Tuttle did a drop-dead imitation of Augie's gruff, hoarse voice, especially that way Augie would roar out, "Pick those feet up, bub!" when we'd jog past him. Tuttle was an excellent mimic, among his many other gifts. Evenings, we partied. Smoked dope, cruised the bars. Tuttle knew them all. What fun he was to be with. He was frisky. He was up for anything. He was a star. People bought him drinks. Women flocked to him—all he had to do was smile. Every night out with Tuttle was an adventure, a kick, an event. Life was more exciting when Tuttle was around. Life was good.

Tuttle Cash was, to use a quaint, old term, blessed. I certainly felt blessed to have him as my friend. Not because of who he was. No, it was much deeper than that. As the months went by, Tuttle and I developed a special kind of friendship, the kind where two people are forever raising the bar on one another, daring each other to greater heights. Maybe I would have written my first novel even if I'd never met him. But I seriously doubt it. Because I know, deep down inside, that I wrote it to prove something to him—that I was worthy of his friendship. Tuttle pushed me beyond what I believed I was capable of. Simply by being who he was.

After graduation, Ezra ended up in that zany, madcap world of tax law. Went to work for Price Waterhouse. Got married to a dull, rather plain girl from Hartford, had a couple of kids, moved to the burbs. I wasn't invited to the wedding. Neither was Tuttle. We'd pretty much lost touch with Ezra by then.

But not with each other. He didn't come back right away from Oxford. The pro football thing was hanging too heavy over him. Everyone wanted him to play. Especially the Dallas Cowboys, who had drafted him in the first round, Rhodes scholarship and all. But he wasn't sure he wanted to don the pads again. So he went to Ghana. And he toured Europe. And, for a while, he drove formula-one race cars for Ferrari. He was well suited to the task. He was fearless and he always did know how to hit the hole. Mostly, he wanted to write. Or so he told me. A novel perhaps. But he never quite got around to starting it.

Instead, he reported to Cowboys training camp at Cal Lutheran College in Thousand Oaks, California. Coach Landry and he did not exactly hit it off. Tuttle was a twenty-five-year-old rookie who hadn't touched a football in over three years. He was smart. He was defiant. He was not a Cowboy. He phoned me from a pay phone after his first scrimmage, deeply upset. A kid from Clemson had tackled him so hard that afternoon he'd had no feeling in his arms or legs for a full fifteen minutes. But that wasn't why he was so upset. "These guys are not in it for the fun, Doof," he said in amazement. He always called me that—Doof. He turned in his playbook after the first preseason game. Quit and walked away.

Writer Frank Deford was there in camp to chronicle Tuttle's experience for *Sports Illustrated*. His account of Tuttle's brief stint as a member of the Dallas Cowboys served as the basis for the Robert Redford movie *As the Crowd Roars,* a lean, taut tale of a thinking man who chafes at the regimentation and dehumanization of pro football. Directed by Sydney Pollack, *As the Crowd Roars* remains one of the best films ever made about the brutality of pro sports. Tuttle himself did the stunt work for Redford and had a bit role. He was offered more film work after that, but he turned it down.

A lot of those who knew Tuttle hoped he'd go into politics. Not me. Politics isn't a business for anyone who has an ounce of self-respect or principle. He did try law school, which should have been my first hint that he was in real trouble, but he dropped out halfway through the first semester. Wandered north of the border. Ended up on the Toronto Argonauts of the Canadian Football League. He played most of a season for them. Played damned well, really. Was leading the league in all-purpose yardage when he blew out his knee. That ended his playing days forever. Still, the Ivy League welcomed him back with open arms. Made him a roving goodwill ambassador for all Ivy League sports. It was an incredibly cushy setup. Paneled office. Unlimited expense account. Zero heavy lifting. Tuttle lasted less than a year. Officially, the parting was called mutual. The real story was that he got roaring drunk at a fund-raiser for the Special Olympics and proceeded to jump on a banquet table and perform a striptease in front of Eunice Shriver. Not just any striptease, either. It was his old impersonation of Ethel Merman singing "There's No Business Like Show Business," something he'd been doing at gridiron banquets for years, complete with bra, garter belt, wig and slash of purple lipstick. Everyone is known for something by his friends. Tuttle was known for his Ethel Merman. God knows where it came from. I never did. Each of us have places we go that no one else knows about. Or wants to know about. Eunice Shriver sure as hell didn't. And so he had to go.

He liked women, money and a good time. Inevitably, he ended up in New York. Inevitably, he landed on his feet. Because they made allowances for the Tuttle Cashes of the world in those days. Still do. Some of those alumni who had cheered him from the stands ran television networks. To them, he was King Tut and he always would be. One of the local affiliates took him on as sports anchor for their evening news. For a while, he was damned good at it, too. Opinionated, bright, funny—a TV star in the making. Until that night he showed up for his eleven o'clock broadcast coked to the gills. And called Knicks center Bill Cartwright "a big fat tub of shit" on the air, live. And then couldn't stop giggling. And there went his broadcasting career.

But he was still Tuttle Cash, the golden boy. Everyone was glad to see him, to drink with him, to bask in his glow. No one seemed to notice that he had no visible means of support. No one seemed to notice that he never paid back the money loaned him. No one seemed to care that most of it went up his nose. He was not alone there. These were the eighties, children. Mostly, he chased women. He had a positively magical touch with them. He was handsome. He was charming. He was a star. His conquests were all the same—

body by Nautilus, brain by Mattel. He didn't care. Not as long as they had good legs and a great, big fetching smile. Especially the smile. He went through women by the dozen, often three in the same day. But there was a grim, joyless quality to Tuttle's relentless pursuit of sexual satiation. He was, it seemed, searching for something, anything to replace the roar of the crowd. He was, it seemed, adrift.

But I was still his friend and I was still flattered that he was mine.

He was the first person I called when I sold the novel. And no one was happier for me than Tuttle was. We celebrated with a night on the town. Ezra joined us, for old times' sake. Ezra was plenty excited himself. Price Waterhouse had just made him a vice president, and he was madly in love with some girl—although not the one he had ended up marrying, if I remember right. We three hit every bar on the East Side. We toasted my genius. We toasted the one, the only Augie Cuchinella. We toasted how good and right life was. We got roaring drunk. I believe we even got thrown out of Elaine's—although I don't remember why. Actually, I remember very little about that night. Except that we lost Ezra at some point. He had to be at the office in the morning. And that for some reason Tuttle and I decided we absolutely, positively *had* to drive to some all-night diner way the hell out in Amagansett that served the best corned hash in America, in the world, in the universe. We went tearing out of town in my battered Morgan Plus-4, top down, armed with two fresh bottles of Dom Pérignon. We never made it. I flipped it on the Montauk Highway—don't ever try to pop the cork on a bottle of Dom Pérignon when you're behind the wheel of an open car doing 100 miles per hour. Tuttle ended up in a ditch, unhurt. You couldn't hurt that man. I ended up smeared all over the road. Fractured skull, two broken arms, a broken leg. Also a deep, deep gash in my neck that I was losing blood out of fast. Things didn't look too promising there for the first major new literary voice of the 1980s. It was four in the morning. There wasn't another car on the road. We were a million miles from nowhere. Or, I should say, ten. Because that's how many miles Tuttle *ran* with me on his back, his shirt wrapped around my neck. That man carried me ten miles to the hospital in Southhampton. No one else could have done that. No one else would have even tried. Only Tuttle Cash. He saved my life that night. The emergency room doctor said I would have been dead in another five minutes if they hadn't gotten some blood into me.

I owed Tuttle Cash my life. I only wished his own could have been happier after that. Because he was the rarest of individuals: someone who had it all. Someone who could have been anything. And what he ended up becoming was the lead character in his own personal Greek tragedy, someone who spent his days and nights stumbling around in a cloud, morose and haunted and confused.

A few months after the novel came out I met Merilee and my own life changed forever. I invited Ezra to the wedding but he didn't come. For some reason, he had decided to keep a safe distance from me and from Tuttle. As for my best man, he was drunk at my wedding. And he stayed drunk for months and months after that. There was a darkness, an ugliness building inside of him. More and more, it started to bubble to the surface. He grew bitter, hostile, difficult to be with. Until one morning he showed up at my door, filthy and disheveled and soaking wet. He'd spent the whole night at the grave of Hobey Baker, who was buried somewhere outside of Philadelphia, and he was smiling. Smiling like I hadn't seen him smile in years. Something had clicked, somehow. He had decided it was time to get his life in order. And he did. He checked himself into the Smithers Clinic. He joined AA. He took a job selling bonds for a brokerage house that was headed by an old classmate of ours. He did well at it, too. Worked hard, stayed sober. He was fun to be around again, like the Tuttle of old. Otherwise I wouldn't have done it. I swear I wouldn't.

I wouldn't have fixed him up with Tansy.

Tansy Smollet . . . She was Merilee's dearest friend. Had been since they were at Miss Porter's together. Tansy's father owned most of midtown Manhattan. She herself was raised on Park Avenue. She was tall. She was leggy. She was blond. She was beautiful. She was also smart and tough and independent. After Miss Porter's, the modeling agencies all wanted her. Tansy blew them off. Ended up getting a master's degree in landscape architecture at Cornell and opening up her own very successful practice in Tribeca. Only for some reason, she could never find the right guy. I couldn't understand why. I thought she was way cool. And if I hadn't met Merilee first . . . well, never mind about that. So I introduced her to Tuttle Cash. The two of them fell hard for each other. I was best man at his wedding, just as he had been at mine. And for a while, they were good together. Not long, though. He stopped showing up for work. Started drinking again. Started fucking around on her. And, when she objected to it, he started hitting her. Until one night he almost killed her. Tuttle broke so many bones in Tansy's face it took months and months of operations to put it back together again. Briefly, the story made the papers. She was a socialite and he was King Tut—wherever he went, people recognized him. But Tansy refused to press criminal charges. Just filed for a divorce and quietly went on with her life. And the story dried up and blew away.

By then, Merilee and I were in trouble, too. Those were my black hole days. Don't ask me how long they lasted. I didn't keep count. As for Tuttle, he stopped calling me. I didn't ask him to. I was his friend. I was there for him. But I was grateful for it. Because Tuttle never got any better. Because all he ever did was wring me dry. Because I had more than enough problems of my own. I bounced back from mine. Kind of. He did not bounce back from his. And he never would.

It had been a long time since I'd heard from Tuttle. But I knew where he was. I always knew.

And now I sat there with his bundle of old letters, Lulu curled up on the loveseat, dozing. I undid the rubber bands and glanced through them. Many were handwritten in his rather primitive scrawl. But a number were typed. Typed on that battered old Olivetti he'd taken to Europe with him back when he wanted to write a novel. One phrase in particular caught my eye: "Just think how much fun I'd be having if I didn't have to work." It was his trademark sign-off. He ended every letter that way. It was the exact same phrase the answer man had used to end Chapter Two. I turned on the bridge lamp next to my chair. I held one of Tuttle's old letters up to the light. I pulled my copy of the answer man's last letter from the breast pocket of my jacket, unfolded it and laid it directly over it. That characteristic lower-case *A,* the one that Mrs. Adelman mentioned, was exactly the same in both. A perfect match.

Of course it was. Was there ever any doubt? Tuttle Cash was the answer man and I knew it. What I didn't know was what the hell I was going to do about it.

King Tut's was the classiest and most tasteful of the jock bars to be found in the city that season, which is to say it had the best kitchen, the finest selection of single-malt scotches and no LeRoy Neimans hanging on the walls. Just old prints of bare-knuckle boxers. And, behind the bar, a certain old photograph of three young and obnoxious college track stars. The decor was mostly dark wood and aged leather, the menu, steaks and chops. Not a terrible Caesar salad. There was an antique pool table, a fireplace that burned real wood, a clubby and collegial atmosphere. Pro athletes were known to hang out there, as were league and network executives, high-end sportswriters, selected literati and the usual gang of Madison Avenue and Wall Street jock sniffers. There was always a chosen place like King Tut's around town. P. J. Clarke's had been it for a time, Oren & Aretsky, Jim Mc-

Mullen. For the past three years it had been King Tut's. Tuttle didn't own the place. Just fronted for it. Four wealthy former classmates, lawyers all of them, were the money men. It was located on the corner of Third Avenue and East Seventy-seventh Street. Dinner reservations recommended.

It was four in the afternoon when I got there. The lunch crowd had cleared out. The happy hour had yet to begin. A pair of supremely self-important Yushies in suspenders were shooting pool, badly. Otherwise it was deserted. A fire crackled in the fireplace.

Malachi Medvedev was behind the hand-carved walnut bar playing a game of solitaire, impeccably turned out in a crisp white shirt, black bow tie and black chalk-striped vest. Malachi was a well-known New York character in his own right. Mayoral candidates came pleading for his support every election year. Don Imus frequently phoned him for live interviews during his radio show. Malachi Medvedev was no mere bartender, after all. Malachi was the hub of the invisible wheel that held the city together. Among other things, he owned a fleet of cabs, a dozen or more newsstands and controlling interest in several racehorses and prizefighters. If you wanted to place a bet, you asked Malachi. If you needed two tickets to *Sunset Boulevard* or a good, clean used car, you asked Malachi. If you wanted your stolen watch found, or a city building inspector off your back, you asked Malachi. You knew you had arrived in this world if he asked you what your name was. Once you told him, he never forgot it. In appearance, Malachi was a cross between a teddy bear and a pumpkin. He was short and chubby and had a large round head and no real neck or legs to speak of. He had pink, clean-shaven cheeks, a squashed nose that seemed to disappear down into his upper lip, moist, brown eyes and brows that were like two strips of electrical tape. He wore his jet-black hair combed straight back from a razor-sharp Eddie Munster–style widow's peak. The widow's peak was real. The black was courtesy of Grecian Formula. Although, frankly, it was impossible to tell just how old Malachi was. Somewhere between thirty-eight and seventy-eight was my best guess.

"You can't do that, Mal," I said, taking a stool.

"Can't do what?" he growled, not looking up from his cards.

"Put a black eight on a black nine. It's against the rules."

"Says who?"

"Hoyle, for one."

"Who's playing this game, Hoyle or me?" he demanded, glancing up at me. His round face immediately broke into a smile. That was his usual expression. Malachi had to be the most cheerful man on the planet. "How the hell are you, Hoagy?"

"Older and dumber."

"What it's all about, m'boy."

"So I've come to realize. And you, Mal? How are you?"

"Fan-fucking-tastic," he replied, beaming at me.

"That's what I was waiting to hear." It was his trademark reply. I had never known him to say anything else. "Just between you and me, Mal, do you ever have a shitty day? Do you ever feel like saying life just plain sucks?"

"Well, sure," he replied. "But who wants to hear that? Besides, if I put a smile on somebody's face while they're in here, maybe they'll go put a smile on somebody else's face when they leave. It's contagious. What you call a random act of kindness."

I froze. "A what?"

"A random act of—"

"Did you make that phrase up?"

"Hell, no. Some shrink did. Heard it on *Oprah*." He peered across the bar at me, his brow furrowing. "You okay, Hoagy? You look like shit."

"It's nothing. I should be fine by the beginning of the century."

"You feel chilled to the bone? Hot head, cold feet?"

"Well, yes, now that you mention it."

He nodded. "Whole lot of that going around. Rangers' team doctor was in here last night. They all got it." He waggled a stubby finger at me. "Got just the cure." He went waddling back through the kitchen doors. My eyes followed him, roaming over to the closed door next to the pay phone, the one that was marked "Private." "Here you be, my friend," he said, returning after a moment with a steaming mug. He placed it before me on the bar. "Homemade chicken broth with eight garlic cloves in it. Drink that down as fast as you can, then chase it with a brandy. You'll feel like a new man."

"I'll certainly smell like one."

"Old country remedy," he insisted.

"Oh, really? Which old country is that, Mal?" No one had ever been able to figure out Malachi's ethnic origin. It was a subject of keen debate. Lupica of the *Daily News* had cast his vote for Lithuanian Druid.

"You wearing wool socks?" he asked, instead of answering me.

I sipped the broth. It was scalding. "Why, are you selling socks now?"

He reached for a brandy snifter. "No, but a lot of people forget and wear cotton. If your feet are cold, you're cold."

"They're cashmere. And make it a Macallan."

"The twelve-year-old or the eighteen?" He clapped himself on the forehead. "Forgive me. I forgot who I was talking to—don't sip that, *drink* it!"

I drank it, Lulu grunting at me unhappily from the floor. She hates the smell of garlic.

One of the crack pool players came up to the bar for a refill. Between the two of them they still hadn't cleared the table. Malachi drew a New Amsterdam for him and sent him on his way. Then he poured my scotch and set the snifter before me, looking Lulu over from nose to tail with keen interest. "What did she used to be, anyway?"

I downed some of the Macallan, feeling the warmth of it spread throughout my body. "She's always been a basset hound, as far as I know."

"No, no. I mean her breed. Before they were domesticated."

"She hunted down bunny wabbits. Why?"

"We got us a little problem down in the cellar. Thought maybe she was a ratter and could help me out."

Lulu's response was to let out a strangled yelp and to scramble up onto my lap and then onto the bar, where she crouched low, front paws close together, her eyes nervously scanning the floor. I patted her. She was shaking.

Malachi watched her. "I guess that answers my question, huh?"

"I guess it does," I said, grinning at him. His cure was working. I was already starting to feel better.

"You should do that more often, Hoagy."

"Do what, Mal?"

"Smile. You have a very nice smile."

"I had them bleached."

"No kidding. Who did it?"

"My dentist, why?"

"I know a guy out in Pelham Bay Park could have done you the mold at cost. Next time you run out of gel, let me know."

Suddenly, it was quiet in there, except for the hissing of the logs on the fire and the sound of the billiard balls clicking against each other.

My eyes were on the closed door again. "Is he here, Mal?"

"He's here," Malachi answered evenly, his eyes revealing nothing.

"How is he?"

Mal poured me a little more Macallan, plus a short one for himself. He took a sip, smacking his lips. "He's circling the drain, that's how he is."

I drank down my scotch, eased up off my stool and started back there toward the door.

"Hey, Hoagy?" Malachi Medvedev called after me.

"Yes, Mal?"

"Watch out or he'll stab you in the front."

I knocked and went in. Tuttle Cash was seated behind his desk wearing a coat and tie. He was the only person left in New York besides me who always wore a tie. But Malachi was wrong—Tuttle wasn't going to stab me. Why, the man didn't even have a knife in his hand. That was a gun he was clutching. Besides which, he wasn't even pointing it at me.

He was pointing it down his own mouth.

Five

I F YOU'RE SERIOUS about eating that," I said, leaning against the doorframe with my arms crossed, "I'd try some piccalilli or chow-chow on it. It'll go down a lot easier."

He didn't seem to hear me. His eyes were off somewhere else. Way gone. Good-bye gone.

My eyes were on his finger, the one that was squeezing the trigger. It was trembling, the knuckle white. Until, suddenly, it spasmed. And relaxed. And then, slowly, his eyes came back. All the way back to the room we were in.

It was a bare, drab little office. Just enough room for a desk, a filing cabinet, a couple of chairs and an exposed hot water pipe, which clanked. The rug was worn. The paint was peeling. The restaurant business is no different than show business—the show is all out front.

Tuttle blinked several times, started to say something but couldn't. Not with that gun barrel in his mouth. He removed it. "Hey, Doof," he said hoarsely. "Still picking those feet up?"

"Every chance I get." My eyes stayed on the gun. He was caressing his temple with it, almost lovingly. "Say, you're not actually going to use that thing, are you?"

He grinned at me mischievously. He often grinned that way when he was with me. It was as if we two shared a joke no one else was in on. "You know what they say—no brain, no pain." He lowered it, then stared at it there in his palm. It almost looked like a toy in his big hand. It was not a toy. It was a Smith & Wesson nine-millimeter semiautomatic pistol. "Tell me, Doof. Do you still believe in death after life?"

"No, Tuttle, I believe that once you're born into this world you just keep on living forever."

"You believe in hell, in other words."

"Exactly. Not a bad tie, by the way. Really picks up the red in your eyes." It was an old school tie. Our old school, actually. I found myself staring at it, wondering if it had been wrapped around Laurie London's throat. I found myself staring at *him*. It had been a while, and time had not been on his side. Not that Tuttle Cash was a terrible-looking man in middle age. But you had to know how good he once looked to know just how bad he looked now. His lean, hard body had grown fleshy and suety. His clean, handsome features were melting, like wax that someone was holding a match to. The narrow, chiseled nose had grown coarse and blotchy, the blond hair thin and dull. I suppose it was his eyes that bothered me the most. Not so much that they were puffy and bloodshot. It was the look in them. Where once there had been a spirited certainty, now there was only confusion and defeat. Everything Tuttle Cash did he had to do better than anyone else. Right now what he was doing was failing. His breath was sour there in the small, hot space, as if something was eating away at his insides. He wore a good shirt. A gentleman always does. It was a blue chambray with a tab collar, a bit snug at the neck. His jacket was a lush herringbone tweed. The suede vest he had on made for a jaunty, chesty appearance. He looked plenty prosperous and dapper.

That was his job. It was not his job to order the beef or get the napkins cleaned. It was his job to be Tuttle Cash, the great American golden boy. He nearly pulled it off, too. Provided you didn't know him.

He put the gun down on the desk. He reached for a bottle of pills in the top drawer. He popped two of them in his mouth and poured three fingers of Courvoisier into a snifter and chased them down.

I reached for the gun and hefted it. I'm always surprised at how heavy they are. I dropped it in my coat pocket and said, "Rather inconsiderate way to go, Tuttle. Just think of the mess."

"Oh, I was," he assured me, brightening. "They'd have to repaint, redo the plaster, the rug . . . and imagine the publicity."

"Who is this *they?*"

His eyes looked past me at the door. "The partners. Place is running in the red at the rate of seven thousand dollars a month. Pretty expensive little clubhouse, even for four really rich assholes. They're trying to decide whether to pull the plug on the whole damned place or just on me." He poured himself three more fingers of brandy. "They don't seem to feel I'm worth a whole hell of a lot anymore."

"Hell, I could have told them that."

He let out a short, jagged laugh. There was an edge of hysteria to it. I didn't know it. He held the bottle out to me. "Drink?"

"Had one, thanks."

He raised his eyebrows at me. "I don't remember you ever saying no."

"That puts you one up on me. I don't remember anything."

"They were right, you know."

"Who was?"

"The people who told us that all of those drugs would fry our brains."

"Well, of course. That was the whole idea, wasn't it?"

He caught my eyes flicking around the tiny space. "What are you looking for?"

"The computer. I thought all restaurants were computerized now."

"Oh, we are. It's out back—I won't use it. Turns out I'm something of a Luddite in addition to all of my other problems."

Lulu ambled in and nosed around briefly before she decided the bar was more fertile territory. I didn't blame her. I closed the door after her. I sat down.

"What's it been, Doof? Two years?"

"At least. You hear anything from Ezra?"

He let out that laugh again. "Not too much chance of that happening, is there?"

"Why not?"

He watched me curiously from across the desk. "You don't know?"

"I don't believe so, no."

"Yeah, you do," he insisted. "You just forgot. Ezra doesn't speak to me anymore, Doof. Goes back to that night you flipped your Morgan."

"It does?" I had no recollection of this fact. None. "What—?"

"I'll let him be the one to tell you about it." Tuttle crossed his arms in front of his chest, stretching his jacket so tight I thought the material would tear. "How is she, Doof?"

"Merilee's fine, thanks."

"Fuck Merilee," he said roughly.

"Oh, I do. And, lately, in the oddest places."

He glared at me in cold silence. He was waiting for an answer.

I gave him one. "I wouldn't know, Tuttle. We haven't heard from Tansy in quite a while."

"Have you tried calling her?"

"Merilee's left a million messages. She never calls back."

He raised his chin at me. "I'm surprised *you* haven't called her."

"Why would I do that?"

"You trying to tell me you never had a load in your pants for her?"

"I am. That was my wallet."

"Sure, Doof. Whatever you say." He sat back in his chair with his hands clasped across his thickening stomach, a wistful glow on his face. "Tansy and me . . . that was the best time in my life."

"You didn't say that then," I reminded him. "You said you felt like you were drowning."

"I didn't appreciate what I had."

"I suppose that explains why you slept around on her."

"I was wrong."

"And why you beat the crap out of her."

"Once. One time, that's all."

"Oh, cut the bullshit, Tuttle. You turned her into a punching bag. She'd walk into the Gotham Bar & Grill with a black eye and people would say, 'Oh, hi, Tansy. When did Tuttle get back into town?' It got to be a running joke. All that was missing was the humor."

"We loved each other, Doof," he said stubbornly.

"Maybe you did." And maybe I should have done more. I had tried to steer him into counseling. I had even offered to go with him. He wouldn't go. Maybe I should have taken a more active role. Maybe I should have taken a baseball bat to him. I'd wanted to.

"She won't answer any of my letters," he said. "Why won't she answer my letters?"

I frowned at him. "I thought the judge said you weren't supposed to contact her."

"The restraining order says I'm not supposed to phone her or approach her. It doesn't say anything about writing her."

"I see," I said, liking this less and less. And I hadn't started out real up about it. Already, I could feel myself getting sucked in.

"Why won't she forgive me, Doof?" he asked pleadingly. "Why won't she give me another chance? I made a mistake. I've paid for it. When convicts serve out their sentence, they get a second chance. Why can't *I* get a second chance? I still love her. That's all that matters, isn't it?"

"It's over, Tuttle. You have to accept that."

"I can't."

"You have to."

"She belongs to me."

"She does *not*. You don't own her. She's not a snowmobile." I was starting to raise my voice in frustration. A too-familiar response. I crossed my legs, smoothed the crease in my trousers. I lowered my voice. "I take it you haven't met anyone else?"

Before he could respond a buzzer sounded.

"You'll have to excuse me a second—duty calls." Tuttle got to his feet and squared his shoulders. Cleared his throat. Jutted his jaw manfully. Then he threw open the door and went striding through that doorway like it was a hole in the line of scrimmage and there was nothing between him and the goal line but daylight. He was King Tut now. And, outside, there were whoops and hearty hellos at the sight of him, jokes and laughter all around.

Briefly, I recalled with horror my trip out to the coast after the first novel got hot. An agent with a taste for kitsch took me for a drink to Alan Hale's Lobster Barrel on La Cienega. When the two of us walked in we found the burly, white-haired actor who'd played the Skipper on *Gilligan's Island* hunched over a drink at the bar, staring morosely into it. When he heard us he struggled heavily to his feet and gave us a grin and a hearty handshake, followed by a booming, "Ahoy, little buddies! Welcome to my restaurant!" Then he went back to staring morosely into his drink.

I suppose, in one way or another, we all end up as actors playing ourselves. I knew that then and I know it now. But that doesn't stop it from being sad. After all, I'd seen Tuttle when he was something swift and sure and beautiful out there.

Me, I searched the man's desk. Those pills in the top drawer were Valium. Vitamin V and Courvoisier—the unofficial adult Happy Meal. There were a couple of business cards in there. One belonged to an editor at *Sports Illustrated,* the other to an HBO executive. Both were women. I found no account books or receipts or anything that had to do with the running of a restaurant. I did find his address book, of worn tan leather. I searched through it quickly. There was no listing for a Laurie London. Or a Diane Shavelson. I kept hunting. I found a pair of bifocals, a sewing kit from the Sheraton, a shoe rag, an electric razor. I found pills, pills and more pills—Naprosyn for his knee, Zantac for his stomach, Urispas for his prostate, Prozac for his head.

His topcoat, a hooded navy-blue duffel coat, was tossed over the filing cabinet. I checked the pockets. Nothing but a package of condoms.

Then I heard voices and I sat back down and he returned.

"A couple of advertising execs from Chicago," he said, shutting the door behind him. And dropping the golden smile. "One of them was a year ahead of us." He made his way back behind the desk, limping slightly from the pain in his knee, and sat. "What were we saying?"

"Women. I was asking if you were holding up your end."

"Nobody special. The models who come in here want guys twenty years younger than us. The women our age want security, which I can't offer them. I have nothing to offer them, actually. Them or anybody else." His face tightened grimly. "The truth is, I can't even figure out who the fuck I am anymore."

"Oh, hell. If you're going to sit around feeling sorry for yourself, I'm going to leave." I started to get up.

"Please don't, Doof!" he begged, suddenly panicky.

I remembered the gun in my pocket, and what he'd been doing with it when I came in. I settled back down. There, I was good and sucked in now. "Who do you want to be, Tuttle?"

He didn't seem to hear that. He was lost in his thoughts now. "These guys, they come in here with their fancy jobs, their six-figure salaries, their stock options . . . and all they want to do is suck my dick because of some tackle I broke twenty fucking years ago against Dartmouth." He shook his head in befuddlement. "I've had to declare bankruptcy, Doof. I'm three months behind on my rent. I haven't bought a new suit in I don't know how long. I take all my meals here because they're free. I need another operation on my knee, only I got no health insurance. My only luxury is the health club, because I have to keep up appearances. And I'm not even doing a very good job at that." He reached for the bottle of Courvoisier and poured himself some more. "I feel like shit. I look like shit. I *am* shit."

"Try water if you want to sober up."

"Who wants to sober up?" he said harshly.

"Okay. Fine. Just checking." He'd gone through a quarter of the bottle just in the short time I'd been there. How many bottles in a whole day and night, I wondered. "How's the Triumph running?" I asked. It was a '79 Spitfire, dark blue. Nice car. Not much trunk space, but Diane Shavelson was small.

"I wouldn't know," he replied. "Sold it to some stockbroker last summer. Aren't you listening—I'm broke!"

"I can let you have a couple thousand to tide you over."

"I don't want your money, man."

"Good. It wasn't a sincere offer."

He let out a laugh, a real one, like the old days. And for a second there was a spark of life in his blue eyes. But then it flickered and went out. And he sat there slumped in his chair, quietly stewing in his own melancholy.

"Are you doing any writing these days?" I asked.

He gave me a puzzled look. "Why would I want to do that?"

"You were good at it. You got pleasure from it."

"I get no pleasure at being ordinary at anything in life."

"In that case, you must take no pleasure at being alive."

"My own sorry conclusion, before you so rudely interrupted me."

"Maybe I should just give this back to you," I said, taking the gun out of my pocket. Until I saw the way he was staring at it—like it was a T-bone steak, medium rare, with onion rings and creamed spinach. The man was practically salivating. I put it back in my pocket. I'm not a big believer in author–assisted suicides. At least, not this author. "My wheels are right outside, Tuttle. Maybe we should run you over to Smithers. Let them have a look under the hood."

"No, I don't think so, Doof."

"C'mon, it won't hurt a bit. There might even be a lollipop in it for you."

"No," he snapped, his jaw hardening. "I said *no!*"

"That's right. You did." We stared at each other across the desk. I swallowed. My heart, I discovered, was pounding. "Tuttle, are you sure you're not writing something?"

"Of course I'm sure." He sat back in his chair, flexing the bad knee gingerly. It made a nasty popping noise. "Why do you keep asking me that?"

"Someone's been sending me chapters of a novel they're writing. Anonymously. Quite good stuff, actually. I rather thought it was you."

"I wish. But it's not. I haven't written a thing in years."

"About that old Olivetti of yours . . ."

He furrowed his brow at me. "My typewriter?"

"Do you still have it?"

"Christ, no. Got rid of it years ago."

"You sold it?"

He shrugged his big shoulders. "I really don't remember.

No, wait . . . I do. I put it out on the street so some homeless guy could sell it, maybe make a couple of bucks. Why are you so fucking interested in my old typewriter?"

"Where were you last Monday night, Tuttle?"

"That's my night off. I was home."

"Doing what?"

"I watched the football game. Raiders–Chiefs. Good game for a change."

"What else?"

"I did my laundry."

"What else?"

"I folded my laundry," he replied, with growing impatience.

"Were you alone?"

"Does that sound like a hot date to you?"

"You still have the same place?"

"On East Sixty-fifth. Yeah."

"What about Friday?"

"What about it?"

"Where were you?"

"I was here."

"All evening?"

"Of course all evening. I was *working*. Ask Mal if you don't believe me." He'd had just about enough of this. A vein in his neck was beginning to throb. His eyes had turned to chilly blue slits. I knew this face well: This was his game face. "Why did you come here, Doof?" he said between gritted teeth. "What do you want?"

"This guy who is sending me chapters of his book—he's doing some pretty terrible things to beautiful young women."

"Like what?" Tuttle demanded.

"Like, they're dead."

"He's *killed* two women?" This stopped him cold. Or seemed to. "Whew, bad business."

"Couldn't be worse from their point of view," I said. "He

calls himself the answer man. He'll be all over the news tonight, in case you want the gory details. For now, the details that may be of interest to you are as follows: He's a master pick-up artist, recognized wherever he goes. He likes women with nice legs and nice smiles. He's a big fan of mine. Even uses some of my favorite expressions. He's not picky, though. He uses some of yours as well. He uses an Olivetti that is a dead ringer for your Olivetti—"

"I told you—I don't have it anymore."

"And he's a huge Ring Lardner fan. Help me out here— didn't you used to like Lardner?"

Tuttle didn't reply. I studied his face for a reaction. Something. Anything. He just sat there, thumbing his square jaw, listening. He wasn't about to make this easy for me. Not that I had expected him to.

"His novel-in-progress," I went on, "is an updated version of *You Know Me Al*. Except his correspondence is between E and T. As in, say, Ezra and Tuttle."

Now he shifted in his chair, sniffling. "I see . . . okay," he said slowly. "And, naturally, your first thought was to come see me. Especially after what I did to Tansy. I get where you're coming from, Doof. Only—"

"Only?"

His eyes met mine across the desk. There was pain in them. There was hurt. Or at least a pretty good imitation. "If I *were* this guy, this answer man, do you honestly think I'd be stupid enough to use my own first initial?"

"I don't know what to think, Tuttle."

"But you think it might be me, don't you?" he demanded.

"I don't know what to think," I repeated. "Help me."

He looked away, blinking rapidly. Outside, I heard hearty male voices. The buzzer went off again. He ignored it, ran a hand over his puffy face. "I—I guess this answers any questions I might have had about where I stand with you. Not that I ever doubted."

"Tuttle, I haven't said anything to the police yet."

"That was big of you," he said bitterly.

"I had to talk to you myself first. I had to ask, under the circumstances."

"Sure, sure," he conceded, turning gracious. Maybe a bit too gracious. "No offense taken. You've behaved admirably. You're a true friend, Doof. And as far as I'm concerned there's no need to shield me any longer. Go ahead and tell them everything you know. I don't care. Hell, what difference does it make? What difference does *any* of it make?" He stared down at the desk, pulled the top drawer open, then pushed it shut. Open, then shut. Open, then . . .

Then he grabbed a pair of scissors out of the drawer and dove across the desk at me with them. We went over the back of my chair together—me wedged against the door with him on top of me trying to stab me in the chest with those scissors, his breath hot and sour in my face. I fought him off, gripping his stabbing arm by the wrist, grappling with him, but he had his knee in my groin. And he was still so goddamned strong.

"You pimp," he spat. "You whore."

"Make up your mind which it is," I gasped, straining against him, "so I'll at least know how to dress."

"You squat to pee!"

"Well, that narrows it down some."

And then suddenly the door flew open and we went tumbling into the doorway and Malachi was pulling him off me, clucking at us. "Will you two lunatics cut it out? It's happy hour, for crissakes. You should be out front, Tuttle, not horsing around in here."

"You're right, Mal," Tuttle panted. "You're absolutely right."

Lulu wandered in now, too, speaking of hot and sour breath. She seemed totally unfazed. She was used to finding me sprawled out on various floors in various states of consciousness.

Tuttle got to his feet slowly, massaging his knee. He dropped the scissors on the desk. He straightened out his clothes, smoothed his hair. "It was good to see you again, Doof," he said, gazing down at me there on his worn office rug. "But don't ever bother coming back here." Then he went out front to play host.

Malachi helped me up from the floor. "Did he hurt you?"

"No, but you sure did save *his* butt. Another minute and I would have lost my cool."

He let out a laugh. "You? That I'd pay to see."

"Mal, did you just call me unfailingly cool or unfailingly wussy?"

"Don't say I didn't warn you," he pointed out, brushing carpet lint off my back.

"Okay, I won't." I took the gun out of my pocket. "Don't let him play with this anymore, all right?"

He eyed the Smith & Wesson with concern, his tongue flicking at his lips. "Sure thing." He stuffed it in the waistband of his slacks, under his vest. Then he stood the chair back up and started to straighten out the mess we'd made.

"Was he here Friday night, Mal?"

Malachi hesitated. "Dunno, that was my night off."

"He said you could vouch for him."

"He's confused."

"That's certainly one word for it. I understand he takes Mondays off."

"Sometimes."

"Sometimes?"

"Ain't as if he keeps to a regular schedule. What can I tell you—he's The King. He comes and goes as he pleases."

"Is that why the partners are . . . ?"

Malachi's face dropped. "Oh, he told you, huh?"

I nodded.

"All they want out of him is a good day's work for a good day's pay. That's not asking so much, is it?"

"I wouldn't know. My last steady job was delivering

newspapers door to door. What are his hours, Mal? When he shows up, I mean."

"Four until whenever. Usually one or two. Depends on the crowd."

"Will you call me if he takes off?"

"When?"

"Today. Tonight. Any time between now and two."

He stuck out his lower lip. "Why?"

"For old times' sake."

"Which old times are those?"

"His and mine. I need to know, Mal. It's important."

A smile creased his round pink face. "You're worried about him, huh?"

"Something like that."

"Okay, sure. I'll call you."

"Friday's a pretty busy night around here, isn't it?"

"Busiest night of the week."

"Since when do you take it off?"

"Since the kids have all moved out. The wife don't have nothing to do, nobody to talk to. She gets lonesome."

"You two have been together a long time."

"Twenty-seven fan-fucking-tastic years," he answered cheerfully.

"I meant you and Tuttle."

He got busy again straightening the top of the desk. "That's right. We have."

"I suppose you'd do just about anything for him."

"That's right. I would."

"Would you lie for him?"

Malachi didn't touch that one. Just kept on cleaning up. When he was all done he stood there rubbing his pudgy hands together. He glanced at the door. I was blocking it.

"Is Tuttle seeing anyone special these days?"

"Not really," he replied. "Not since Luz. She dances over at Ten's. Only that ended two, three months ago. He told me he broke it off with her so he could devote more time to his writing."

I tugged at my left ear. "Oh?"

"But I didn't buy it."

"What did you buy?"

"That she's the one broke it off—on account of Tuttle wasn't good enough for her. She got wise, that's all." He shot another glance at the door. He was getting anxious.

"Why don't *you* get wise, Mal?"

"Who would take care of him?"

"Maybe he'd have to take care of himself."

"Maybe you see more than is there, Hoagy. Ever think of that? Maybe his real problem is that he's the second smartest man in the whole wide world."

"Who's the smartest?"

Malachi winked at me. "Everyone else."

I let him go. Outside, the place was filling up. A gang of out-of-town sportswriters were in for the Heisman Trophy presentation. John Madden was seated at a table with a trio of network executives, regaling them with stories. Dave DeBusschere and Walt Frazier, two of the Knicks from their glory days, were deep in conversation together at the bar. Tuttle was over by the pool table with the two Yushies who'd been there when I came in, all three of them flushed with drink. All three of them laughing the forced, hearty laugh that men laugh when they are telling dirty jokes. I made my way through the crowd to the front door, Lulu on my heel. Something made me stop when I got there. Stop and turn around.

It was Tuttle. He was staring at me from across the restaurant, his eyes boring into me. I stared back at him, our eyes locking together. His expression was utterly blank, his face like stone, hard and unyielding.

Until he relaxed into that familiar, lopsided grin. "Hey, Doof, who's The King?" he called out to me.

This was a thing he'd taken to doing as he got older. He needed to hear the words out loud. Kind of sad, but as I'm sure you've figured out by now, there wasn't much about Tuttle Cash that wasn't sad.

I left it hanging there in the smoky air for a second. Just long enough for him to wonder if I wasn't going to respond. "You are, Tuttle!" I called back finally. Strictly for old times' sake. Then I went out the door as fast as my feet would take me.

The press thing had happened.

The sidewalk outside our building was jammed with reporters and cameramen, all of them shouting and shoving and jockeying for prime position. The local TV crews were there. The tabloid TV rat crews were there. The newspapers were there. Everybody was there—spilled out onto Central Park West, their vans double-parked up and down the block, cables snaking everywhere. I'm talking pandemonium. This was no mere cash-for-trash scandal, after all. This was a bona-fide serial killer on the loose in the streets of Manhattan, some nut who had killed two beautiful single women and branded their foreheads with orange lipstick and written me detailed accounts of his exploits.

Let's face it, this was a story with a huge upside.

The commotion was courtesy of Cassandra, of course. I had no doubt she'd already spread word that she'd be outing the answer man on her seven o'clock broadcast. One thing she is not bashful about is self-promotion. Now everyone wanted a statement from me for the six o'clock news. They wanted it live. They wanted it now.

"Is it true?"

"Has the killer contacted you?"

"Why does he call himself the answer man?"

"Why did he pick you?"

"Is it true?"

I fought my way through them, elbows flying. Made it to the blue police barricades that had been hastily set up on either side of the front doors. A cop in uniform was there to give me a hand. The only problem was I'd somehow lost

Lulu along the way. I found the little ham flirting shame-lessly with Channel 2's ace crime reporter. She'll do any-thing to get her big black nose on the air. I suggested she join me or else. She did, and the cop helped us inside. Mario the doorman was only too happy to help, too. And get his own ugly face on camera.

"Evening, Mr. Hoag," he said crisply, tipping his hat at me. "Quite some commotion out there this evening. Yes-sir."

Then again, maybe this was just him sucking up for his Christmas bonus. If he didn't watch out he was going to end up with a signed first edition of my second novel, which was presently fetching 99 cents down at The Strand.

I grumbled something surly at him and started for the elevator.

But the fawning clod just wouldn't be denied. "Oh, hey, Mr. Hoag? This got put in Mrs. Nussbaum's mailbox by mistake this morning. Her nurse just brought it down." He held it out to me.

I froze, staring at it. It was a nine-by-twelve manila enve-lope. My name and address had been typed onto a stick-on label. There was no return address.

Six

Dear Hoagy,

I hope I'm not imposing too much on your valuable time, but I've been so productive lately I thought I'd go ahead and send along another chapter. The stuff is just really starting to flow now. I can't wait to get to the typewriter every day. I feel I'm really getting to know our hero's character. In a weird sort of way it's almost like he's taking on a life of his own now. I can really hear his voice. It's almost like HE controls ME. I'm curious—is it like that for you sometimes when you really get into it?

I hope you're making progress from your end. I'll be checking the Times every day for word from you. I'm feeling real close to you as I write this, Hoagy. I'm told that a collaboration can be very intimate this way. I'm starting to feel like we've known each other forever. I know it's too much to expect, but I hope we can someday be friends.

Yours truly,
the answer man

p.s. You don't mind that I think of you as my partner now, do you?

3. the answer man takes a plunge
New York City, December 5

Friend E——Health clubs, man. One thing I've gotten hip to since I've been back here—talking to the people, riding the subway, doing the thing that I do—is that the women all hang in health clubs, hoping to tone up those thighs and maybe meet some guy who'll save them from the desperate loneliness of their pathetic, miserable lives. If your mission in this life is to perform a random act of kindness, then you can do no better than to go grazing at one of these clubs. They are just full of women in need.

I love them so much, E. And I hate to see them in pain. God, how I hate it. I wish I could help all of them.

A lot of these clubs are steep to get into, the better to keep out fools like you and me. But they've got all these trial memberships and complimentary first visits so it's really not very hard to front your way in for a workout. And fronting, as you well know, is not something either one of us has ever had much trouble doing. No, it's the straight life we can't handle. Why is that, Friend E? Did somebody drop us on our heads when we were born? Or did somebody drop everybody else in this world on their heads? Maybe that's it. Maybe they're all crazy and we're the together ones. Maybe we should be running things and they should all be locked up. Maybe they ARE locked up. Maybe their whole lives are prisons. Maybe that's why they are so fucked up, and we are so free.

I found her in the Manhattan Fitness Center on East 39th Street. They advertise a lot on TV. Have four or five locations around the city. Plenty elegant, too, for a place you go to to grunt and sweat. Man, there's carpeting and polished chrome and potted plants and a juice bar and no smell of anybody's armpits. The people who go there all look like executives or people who play executives in soap operas. Upstairs, there's a workout room with a bunch of those fancy machines. Also a room where they have aerobics classes, which are mostly for the big girls. They wear headbands and spandex leotards, and it is not a pretty sight at all, believe it. Disco never died here, I'm telling you. Or did Mr. Tom Jones rise up from the dead while I was inside? Because that man is back. And sounding as shitty as ever.

I tried out one of those Stairmaster things, E. What a joke, people paying good money for that. Why don't they just take the stairs to their apartment instead of the elevator and save themselves a thousand dollars a year in membership? I guess I know why. Because you don't meet the man of your dreams in a stairwell. Not unless you want to fuck a janitor.

Mostly, I rode a bicycle in place and scoped for honeys. And there were some. They came in two categories—them that wanted to be bothered and them that didn't. Them that did kept changing bikes, adjusting their seat, keeping busy. Them that didn't stayed put. Wore headphones and stared at magazines while they pedaled, this shield of paper and sound between them and everyone else. Like they're fooling me. Like they don't WANT to be saved from their pain. Like they aren't PRAYING for me to come to them. Poor things. They're just fronting, that's all. We're all just fronting.

I found her down in the pool swimming laps. Knew she was the one for me right away, E. Not that I could even tell a whole lot about how she looked. She had on a bathing cap and goggles and was facedown in the water. Didn't matter. She had the smoothest, easiest stroke. Cut through that water like a knife, all smooth and slick and shiny, her little pink feet making not so much as a ripple behind her. I just stood there in my own swimsuit watching her for a minute, transfixed. Then I dove in and splashed around some. There were maybe a half-dozen lanes in the pool, but we were the only two in it. A sign said there was a lifeguard on duty, but I didn't see one, not unless you count the Puerto Rican who was mopping the floor. I did a couple of laps in the lane next to hers, taking it slow.

She knew I had my eye on her. They always know. But she wasn't at all self-conscious about showing me her butt when she got *out. Based on my experience, E, that meant she was under 25. Not that she had any reason to be self-conscious. She was plenty slim and shapely, her butt taut and muscular, her legs fine. Outrageously good ankles. She had the tattoo of a heart on the inside of her left one. Plus she had more than a little up top. I'm talking zoomers, E. She wasn't hiding them either. She had on a string bikini, the kind they wear when they're advertising. She took off her goggles and her bathing cap and tossed her hair loose and I knew for sure this one was the one. She was a redhead, E, with wild curly hair and creamy skin and pillowy, pouty lips. She looked so fresh and clean and lovely standing there. I cried inside for her, E. I did. Because she was so hopelessly sad.*

And, yet, she was so lucky.

Because I was there for her now. I was there to answer her prayers.

She seemed to have water in her ear. Kept holding her head at a funny angle and whomping away on it. She went over to the whirlpool and got in. I did another lap and joined her. She flashed me a smile, great big one, and said Hi. Which a lot of your New York honeys won't do. I said Hi back. She was in there up to her chest with her titties sort of bobbing around on top of the bubbles. Very inviting. She was still trying to get that water out of her ear. Had her head tilted at a funny angle and was shaking it and craning her neck around and fussing and I guess what happened is one of the jets gave her a nudge because she suddenly lost her balance and started waving her arms around in the air and sure enough one of her tits, the right one, came popping right out of her top. No kidding, E. It popped out. There it was, just as perky and as mouthwatering as can be. She got bright red and stuffed it back in where it belonged, but not before I got myself some view. Right away, I said Well, I guess we have no secrets from each other now. And she laughed and said Not so fast—it's your turn now.

And just like that we got to talking, real nice and easy.

She told me her name was Bridget Healey and she was a secretary for one of the big law firms until the scumbags laid her off over Thanksgiving, which she thought was an incredibly shitty thing to do. Since her membership here at the club was paid up through the rest of the year she'd decided to come by and have a swim instead of working on her resume, which was so incredibly depressing. I said Tell me about it—I run an employment agency for executives who are looking to relocate. She said You mean you're like a headhunter? Right away, E, her eyes started sparkling. Man, she could practically see it—her on a private jet zipping off to Corfu with some zillionaire corporate guy who was great looking and single and needed a personal secretary to suck on his dick.

Dare I say it again, Friend E? Okay, I'll say it again: Be whoever they want you to be.

We agreed to go out for coffee after we got dressed. I had to wait for her outside on the sidewalk forever. It was cold but the cold felt good after the whirlpool. Bridget had put makeup on was what took her so long. It made her look older and somehow a bit more common. She wore a New Utrecht High Twirlers school jacket, tight jeans and little red cowboy boots. You would have loved those boots, E. We started walking over toward Third in search of a coffee place. She mentioned there was this nice country-western bar, El Rio Grande, downstairs in the Murray Hill Mews. She lived right across the street, so it was kind of her neighborhood place to hang. I said that would be cool.

Until I got a good look at the place. This Murray Hill Mews turned out to be a modern high-rise apartment building, lots of doormen. And El Rio Grande was way full of people doing the brunch thing in front of big picture windows that looked out over Third Avenue. I didn't like any of it. Too many people who might recognize me. So I said You know, I'd be happy to take a look at your resume and give you some advice on how to polish it. She let out this sort of a squeal, and said Oh, wow, would you really?!

And she invited me up to her place, just like that.

Man, she was desperate. I mean, you know me, E. Would you invite me up to your place just like that? No way. It was almost like she couldn't wait for it, know what I'm saying?

Bridget lived in a converted carriage barn on East 38th, half a block down from the Cuban embassy, where a cop sits out on the corner in a little booth day and night so as to discourage any anti-Castros from blowing up the place. I paid him no mind. I didn't have to walk by him. Just up three flights of steps. Rear apartment, fourth floor. Bars on the windows to keep out the undesirables.

Like we can't get in if we want to.

The apartment was nothing special at all. Just someplace small and dark and cramped to die in. She had to turn the lights on even during the day. But she kept it neat, I'll say that for her. She even had a tablecloth on the dining table. That almost broke my heart, E. That tablecloth. I don't know why. I guess because it was like she was trying to make it into a home, even though she was there all alone and there was no one. Damn. She put coffee on and told me to have a seat on the sofa, which I did. I said So what would you like to be when you grow up? And she let out a nervous laugh, said To be honest, I would enjoy the challenge of launching and running a business of my own.

Which practically blew me away, E. Her sounding just like she was a contestant on some TV game show. I was waiting to hear the guy say What do we have for our winners, Johnny . . . ?

She sat down next to me and started telling me all about some direct marketing thing some friend of hers had started and blah-blah-blah and that's when I decided to put her out of her misery sooner than later because she was really starting to bring me down. Friend E, I am usually a very up sort of person most of the time. But, damn, I could see her future laid out right there in front of her. A series of bullshit jobs filled with nothing but disappointment. A one-sided affair with a married man who would fuck her one or two nights a week after work and never leave his wife for her. Man, her whole life was THERE in her eyes. I could see it. And it was so totally fucking depressing. And she was BEGGING for me to save her from it.

And here I was. So the best thing to do was just take off my belt and get it over with fast.

Which I did. Only, it was different for me this time, E. It just plain wasn't as good. Not totally sure why. Maybe because I got nothing back from her. It was over so quick she never did realize what was happening. She didn't KNOW. There was no MO-MENT. It was more like . . . one minute she was there, next minute she was gone. She just sort of went away, snap, like some bug on the kitchen floor. Gave me nothing back, is what I'm saying. Just left me standing there all by my damned self. I was expecting something more. I NEEDED something more. I had come a long fucking way to answer that bitch's prayers! I needed a thank you. I needed some kind of fucking attention to be paid. I needed what I was due. Instead, I got shit. And felt empty inside. Felt starved deep down in my very soul. I thought I was going to scream or something, E.

Man, I went staggering out of there. I was so upset I even forgot to take her boots, which I was going to give to you next time I saw you. I am sorry about that, E. Ended up at that El Rio Grande after all. Had me a bottle of Rolling Rock. But that didn't help and I thought it was a crummy boring place full of Yushie scum so I walked. I walked for hours, E, trying to figure out why this one left me feeling so down. I guess because there are so many more Bridgets out there in the offices and health clubs and bars of New York, and I have so much more work ahead of me. I mean, I need to help them all. I HAVE to help them all. But I don't know if I can do it. I just don't know. I keep getting this feeling late at night, lying here in my jack rack, that there is no goodness left anymore in the world, only ugliness and pain, and maybe I'm too late. Maybe I'm wasting my time trying to perform my small service.

I don't usually need a reward, E. The sheer pleasure of doing the work I do is usually reward enough for me. This one was different. But, hey, I guess they can't all be fun, can they? Better luck next time.

Your pal, T

p.s. Really sorry about those boots
p.p.s. What DO we have for our contestants, Johnny?

Seven

VIC WAS ON THE TELEPHONE in the kitchen, sparring gruffly with some annoying reporter. I snatched the phone away from him and hung it up and called Very and got through to him.

"Was just going to call you, dude," the lieutenant said briskly. "We got more on that bite mark on Laurie London's butt. It was twenty-four to forty-eight hours old at time of death. Plus the impression we took of Tibor Farkas's teeth matches up."

"Lieutenant, I—"

"So it looks like his story plays. Plus he passed the polygraph, which is to say the examiner's ninety-five percent certain Tibor's telling us the truth when he says he's innocent."

"Lieutenant, I—"

"Check it out, we also talked to her classmates at the New School. Not a one of 'em remembers her going off with some guy after class. She just said good-night and headed off by herself. You think our friend made that part up or what?"

I took a deep breath and let it out slowly. "Lieutenant?"

"Yo, dude?"

"Bridget Healey. She lived in a converted carriage barn on East Thirty-eighth Street, halfway down the block from the Cuban embassy."

He was silent a moment. "I heard you say *lived*. Did you say *lived?*"

"I did."

"You sitting on another chapter?"

"I am."

"Stay where you are, dude."

"I will. Oh—Lieutenant? She has a tattoo of a heart on her left ankle." I hung up, staring down at the envelope in my hand. Something in this chapter had struck me as odd, left a prickly feeling in my scalp. What it was I couldn't say. But it was there, if only I could place it.

Vic was staring at me intently. I went away from his stare.

I went into the nursery. Pam was in there seeing to Tracy, who had just awakened from her nap and needed changing. Merilee was still at rehearsal—they were keeping her later and later now, what with preview performances before audiences of semi-alert humans only a few days off. I took over for Pam. There were times when I found changing Tracy's diapers strangely comforting. This was one of those times. Because, well, here was something I *could* do. A problem I *could* solve: cleaning my daughter's bumhole. Afterward, I sat there in the rocker with her in my lap. Something I'd been doing more and more of lately when I was tired and confused and searching for answers. I'd go into the nursery and sit with Tracy and ask her what the hell I should do. She'd gaze steadily up at me with those emerald-green eyes of hers, waiting patiently for me to figure it out. She knew that I would. She had total and complete faith in me. There was tremendous clarity in her eyes. She seemed such a wise child. She was not, of course. She didn't even know right from wrong. But, then, neither did I. I thought I did once, but not anymore. Not now. They keep changing the rules of the game now. Sometimes, I don't even understand the language they write them in anymore.

My oldest friend was drowning. He was angry. He was broke. He was suicidal. Was he a serial killer, too? Was he roaming the city at night like a wild animal, picking out a victim, killing her and then writing about it? Writing *me?* Was he totally and completely insane? Or was I totally and completely wrong? Was there the slightest chance, the tiniest chance that Tuttle Cash *wasn't* the answer man? What if I gave him over to Very and it turned out he was innocent? The publicity would finish him off for good. Is that how you repay a friend for saving your life? Ah, but what if he *was* the answer man? Then what? How far was I prepared to go to shield Tuttle Cash from the law? Where did my loyalty to him leave off? When did I tell Very about him?

Questions. So many questions. Here's one:

If Tuttle Cash wasn't the answer man, then who was?

That one I had no answer for. Actually, I had no answers for any of them. All I had were choices. Maybe in another life you won't have to make choices. That same life where no one goes hungry and everyone laughs at your jokes. But in this particular life you have to. And that sucks sometimes. And I'd just like to go on record as saying so.

Tracy shifted in my lap, gurgled and said one of her words. She knew two of them. I'd like to tell you they were "Momma" and "Dadda," but I'd be lying. Her first word was "yesss . . ." She picked that up from Marv Albert on the Knicks telecasts. Her second word was "cheeseboogers," which was her current favorite, and which Merilee was convinced somehow originated with me. Lulu ambled in and sat at my feet and licked her toes. Tracy's, not her own. This was her way of showing affection for her baby sister. Tracy giggled with delight. Someday, she would get smart and wonder why her feet smelled like dead fish. But for now it made both of them happy.

Vic appeared in the doorway, pawing at the floor with his size 15 EEE black brogan. "Sorry to interrupt your quality time, Hoag," he said in his droning monotone. "Pam wondered if you'll be joining us for dinner. She's doing a chicken pot pie. I made the crust all by myself."

"I don't think so, Vic. Thank you." He started lumbering away. I called him back. "Vic, what do you remember about Tuttle Cash?"

"Tuttle Cash . . ." Vic frowned, searching his memory. Sometimes it was remarkable. Sometimes it wasn't there at all. Had to do with that plate in his head. "Superior peripheral vision and balance. Above average footspeed. Decisive when he cut to the hole. Hard to bring down. Durable. Dominant player at the small-college level. Not an NFL talent. Not hungry enough. More of the rah-rah schoolboy-hero type. I guess that's why the sports writers and the Hollywood people romanticized him the way they did. Take it from me, Hoag, there's nothing romantic or heroic about professional football. It's just a bunch of guys clobbering the snot out of each other for pay. Half of them would be in jail if they hadn't found football."

"Ever play against him?"

"No, I was in Nam by the time he came along."

"What's your opinion of him now?" I asked. Vic always had one of those.

He hesitated. "Friend of yours, isn't he?"

"Go ahead. Please."

"I saw too many people lose their lives over there to have patience with people like him who throw theirs away," Vic replied softly. "He could be making sandwiches at a soup kitchen or coaching underprivileged kids. Instead, all he does is drink and chase puss and mooch a living off of his glory days."

"Would he know you from anywhere?"

"Know me?"

"Would he recognize you?"

We were interrupted by the buzzer in the kitchen. Mario the doorman was calling up from the lobby. Vic went and answered it. Then he came back and said, "Inspector Feldman and Lieutenant Very are on their way up."

I greeted them at the door, manila envelope in hand. They came inside and stood there in the marble-tiled entry hall, the Human Hemorrhoid shooting his cuffs and smoothing his snowy-white pompadour, shooting and smoothing, shooting and smoothing. "Goddamned reporters," he muttered angrily. "I hate their fucking guts. I wish they'd get cancer and die. Every single one of 'em."

Very wore an exceedingly retro porkpie hat and an exceedingly grim expression. The hat came off when I closed the door. The grim expression most definitely did not.

"She was a real nice-looking girl, dude," he said tightly. "Red hair. Shapely ankles. Tattoo of a heart on her left one, just like you said. Name was Bridget Colleen Healey. Profession, legal secretary. She would have been twenty-four years old next month."

"He sure knows his women," I said. "I'll give him that."

"Huh?" Feldman demanded, whipping off his topcoat. "What's that?"

"Never mind." I hung his coat in the closet. Very's spy coat and hat as well.

"She lived alone," the lieutenant continued. "We found her on the sofa. She was strangled. Don't know with what."

"His belt," I said. "He used his belt."

Feldman shot a look down at the envelope. Then up at me. He said nothing.

Very said, "She was recently laid off, according to the old lady across the hall. Who, by the way, saw bupkes and heard bupkes. Nice enough girl, she said. Quiet. Wasn't seeing anyone special. Had been going with someone from her office, an older man, but that ended a few months back."

Oh, yes, he knew his women. "Three question marks on her forehead?"

"He numbered her, all right," Very replied. "Same orange lipstick." He seemed uneasy all of a sudden.

"Something else, Lieutenant?"

He and Feldman exchanged a look.

"No, dude. Nothing else."

"This makes twice he's made contact in the East Thirties," I observed.

"Yeah, we know that," Feldman snapped impatiently.

"Is it significant?"

"Maybe yes, maybe no," he replied.

"Meaning what?"

"Meaning we don't know," Very translated.

Feldman glared at him. Candor was clearly not appreciated. "So, what, that goddamned thing's been sitting here since this morning?" he demanded, meaning the envelope.

"I'm afraid so. It was delivered to the wrong apartment by mistake."

The inspector made a face, disgusted. "Well, our system's in place now. This *won't* happen again."

"If you say so."

Now he turned his glare on me. "You pushing my buttons or something?"

"No, when I push your buttons you'll know it." I held the envelope out to him. "Would you care to . . . ?"

He put his hands up. "I don't even want to touch it. Just lay it out somewhere so we can read."

"Shall we try the living room?"

We tried the living room, which was in a state of Susy Hendrix darkness, thanks to Merilee's blackout drapes. I felt my way to the table lamp in between the matching pair of Morris armchairs and flicked it on. It was a Dirk Van Erp of copper and mica made in 1910 and stamped with the windmill insignia on the bottom of the base. It bathed the room in a sepia glow. There was a mammoth old bungalow floor lamp in one corner over by the windows. I turned it on, too. Very took a seat in one of the armchairs, which are as comfortable as they are beautiful. Lulu came in and stretched out on the leather settee, curling her lip at the inspector. When she doesn't like someone she just plain doesn't like them. Something she got from me.

Feldman lingered in the doorway, gazing at those heavy drapes over the windows. "Dave Berkowitz used to live in the dark this way. Only, he used blankets."

"Thank you for that comment, Inspector. Thank you very much."

"I like this furniture, though. What is it, maple?"

"It's oak."

"Yeah, that's a good tree, too." He cleared his throat uncomfortably. "Look, I apologize if I seem a little fried."

"I really hadn't noticed," I said.

Lulu coughed.

He flicked his hooded black eyes at her, then back at me. "Only this should never, ever have been leaked to the press. By tomorrow morning every attractive single woman in this city who sets foot outside her door will do so in fear."

"Not dissimilar from a day in general."

"Not that they fucking care," Feldman fumed. "God-damned press. It's just another headline for them. And now they expect us to wrap it all up in a nice happy bow by the evening news, and if we don't then they'll say we're fucking up. And so will the mayor, because if he doesn't he looks like he's soft on crime and won't get reelected. And so will the Manhattan DA, because if he doesn't he looks like he's soft on crime and won't get reelected. And so will the public, because they watch too goddamned much television—they don't *realize* how clever and careful these water walkers can be. They don't *realize* how many man hours go into this type of investigation. We got no witnesses, no physical evidence—"

"Bridget's apartment was clean?"

"Appears to be, dude," Very affirmed. "We did find a couple of joints in an ashtray, whatever that's worth."

"It wasn't my doing," Feldman persisted. "I'm not the yutz who leaked it. I wanted you to know that."

This surprised me a little. I couldn't imagine why the man they called the Human Hemorrhoid cared about what I thought of him. "I know you're not, Inspector."

"You do?" He scowled at me now. "How?"

I tugged at my left ear. "There's an old, old saying in ghosting circles. Goes all the way back to, well, *me*—If the police know, the public knows. Do sit down."

Feldman sat in the armchair next to Very, gingerly, as if he were afraid there was a whoopee cushion hidden in it.

I spread the cover letter and the pages of Chapter Three out on the coffee table with tweezers. "How long had Bridget been dead?"

Very glanced inquiringly over at Feldman, who gave him a slight nod.

"A couple of days at least," the lieutenant replied.

"If he killed Laurie on Friday night," I suggested, "then he must have killed Bridget Saturday morning. Afternoon at the latest. Then gone straight to the typewriter. Hmm . . . I guess that means you're right, Inspector."

"What about?" Feldman glowered down his long nose at me. I was doing the mambo in the middle of his investigation. He clearly didn't like this.

"He's developing a taste for it."

"You can put that one in the bank," he sniffed. "FDIC insured."

They leaned over the coffee table and began to read, the letter first. I sat down next to Lulu.

"Okay, this I don't like." Feldman stabbed at the air over the letter with his finger. " 'I can really hear his voice. It's almost like HE controls ME.' This is not good. Sounds like classic delusional ravings."

"Or classic writer ravings," I said.

"Explain," he commanded.

"You can hear that kind of bullshit just about any evening

around the dining table at Yaddo. Usually accompanied by the line 'More Beaujolais, anyone?' It's writer babble, Inspector."

Feldman dismissed this with a wave of his hand and moved on to Chapter Three. Very considered it a moment longer, jaw clenching and unclenching, before he, too, resumed reading.

When he was done Feldman let out a thoughtful sigh and sat back with his elbows up on the arms of the chair, hands pressed flat together, fingers forming a steeple to rest his chin on.

Very, he went right into attack mode. "We'll hit the health club right away, Inspector. Check the membership rolls, the guest list . . . also this bar, this El Rio Grande. See if anyone there—"

"He's playing with us again, Lieutenant," the inspector broke in, his voice turning sonorous. "The bastard's playing games with us. He wants us to think singles killer now, as opposed to subway stalker. And we have to play along. Because we have no choice. Because that's how it's done. And he knows that. You bet he knows that." He sat there in chilly silence a moment. "Okay, fine. We park some female officers around town at likely pick-up spots—the coffee bars, dance clubs, museums. We establish a presence. And we go with our hotline. It's time to include the public so that they feel like they're part of the process. And why not? Nearly two out of three serials are arrested because of information that comes in from eyewitnesses. That's how they got Bundy. That's what we do. We tell them what we know about the answer man."

"Which is what?" I ask.

"That he is a white male in, say, his late twenties or thirties," Feldman replied. "Average height and build, good-looking, a promising novelist, possibly new to the city—"

"That could refer to a hundred thousand guys," I pointed out. "Except for the good-looking part."

"Dig, Inspector, he might also be a promising screen-writer," Very said. "I mean, if you figure in the New School angle."

"Now you've got a hundred thousand more," I said. "Minus the promising part."

"And I wouldn't be so sure about how average his build is," Very said. "He's strong enough to overpower these women without a struggle."

"Okay, okay, Lieutenant," Feldman snarled impatiently. "We'll say that he's physically fit, all right?" He paused, shot his cuffs, smoothed his white pompadour. I wondered if he was even aware he was doing it. "Bastard keeps coming back to this 'Be whoever they want you to be' thing. That suggests chameleon to me. And when I think chameleon I think—"

"Actor," Very said eagerly.

"Not bad, Lieutenant," he reflected, as if Very had been the one who raised it. "Ties in with the familiar-face angle. I like that. I like that a lot." He glanced sharply at the lieutenant. "You'd better get this chapter to the shrinks right away."

Very promptly began gathering it up, using the tweezers.

"Tell them we have to have some kind of personality profile by morning. I don't care how preliminary it is. We have to feed the press something new tomorrow. Show the public we're making progress."

"Even if you're not?" I asked.

Feldman treated me to an icy glare. "Based on my experience, you're our weak link."

"How kind of you to point that out."

"A task force requires team players. There's no room on my team for wise guys or glory grabbers or—"

"Did you ever coach high school football, Inspector?"

"You're pushing my buttons, mister!"

"See, I told you you'd know when I did it."

"Chill out, dude," Very ordered me. "You sound like you're buggin'."

"Do I, Lieutenant? I think I'm holding up rather well under the circumstances."

"Look, this is a tense situation for everyone," Feldman conceded, his manner softening. "I appreciate the position you've been put in, Hoagy. I know it's not a comfortable one. If you feel the need for counseling I'll be happy to recommend someone."

"Thank you, Inspector. I have someone I can talk to."

She came waddling in now, as if on cue. Tracy did, after all, have acting in her blood. And she did waddle, somewhat like a drunken sailor on a slippery deck. She plopped down on the floor next to the settee and began to play with her Tiny Touch phone, which had numbered buttons that played different melodies. So far her overwhelming favorite seemed to be number three, "Twinkle, Twinkle Little Star," which I had begun to hate almost as much as I hate Glenn Close, the friend of Merilee's who'd sent it. I will pay that bitch back someday if it's the last thing I do.

Very sat there watching her with a goofy grin on his face. She does that to some people. The inspector acted as if she wasn't there at all, although the sound track was hard to ignore.

Vic came lumbering in to retrieve her. "Sorry, Hoag. She's really starting to motor. One minute she's there, next minute she's gone."

"She's fine," I said, pulling her up into my lap. And away from her baby boom box.

Feldman got to his feet, studying Vic in the doorway. "And you are . . . ?"

"Vic Early," I answered. "He helps out around here."

"Ever been on the job, Early?" Feldman asked, smelling pro on him.

"He's a celebrity bodyguard, Inspector," said Very, who had encountered Vic before. "Whazzup, Early?"

"Can't complain, Lieutenant," Vic replied.

I said, "May I ask you a stupid question, Inspector?"

"What is it, Hoagy?" Feldman asked wearily.

"He brought Diane home with him, but not Laurie or Bridget. Why?"

"Easier that way. He didn't have to worry about dumping their bodies. All he had to do was split."

"That makes you right again, I guess."

"How so?"

"He's getting better at it as he goes along."

No one particularly wanted to touch that one, so we started for the front door in silence, me cradling Tracy in my arms. Lulu voted for the comfort of the settee. She's partial to the oak tree herself, especially when it's been upholstered. They fetched their coats from the closet and pulled them on. I opened the front door and they went out in the hall and pushed the button for the elevator.

"Do we still do Barney Greengrass in the morning?" I asked.

"We do," Feldman said.

"Will I be wearing a wire?"

"The table will be wired. Do you need a dummy run?"

"Generally. But I'm prepared to make an exception in this case."

Feldman muttered something under his breath at Very. I'm probably better off that I didn't hear what it was. I'm certain that Tracy was. And then the elevator doors closed and they were gone.

I shut the front door and put Tracy down. I got my coat and hat and driving gloves out of the closet. "I have a job for you, Vic. It's Tuttle Cash. He'll be at King Tut's until around two. I want you to babysit him. Without him knowing it, of course."

"That's no problem," Vic assured me. "Plenty of old jocks hang out at the bar there. I'll fit right in."

"Take the Rover. If he leaves anytime before two, tail him. And keep me informed. I want to know every move he makes." We had cellular phones in every car now, even the battered old '62 Land Rover. They came with the baby, for some reason. "I'll take over for you after two. I should be free by then."

"What's this all about, Hoag?"

"I found him trying to eat a gun this afternoon."

Vic's face darkened. "If he's having that kind of problem, a supervised environment is what he needs."

"Tried that. He turned me down. This will have to do, okay?"

"Okay, Hoag," he said reluctantly. He suspected there was more to it than I was letting on, but didn't press it. "I'll get right on it."

"Good man." I put on my hat and started for the door.

"Oh, hey . . ." Vic glanced at his watch. "Cassandra is on. Want to see what she's got?"

I opened the door. "No." I closed the door. "Yes."

She was on the TV in the kitchen, where Pam was making a salad to go with the chicken pot pie, which sat bubbling and golden brown on top of the oven.

"Above all, Cassandra, we must not panic," the mayor was imploring her by live video remote from his office at city hall. "One man cannot hold this great city hostage."

"Shewa, that's easy for you to say, Mister Mayor," Cassandra fired back at him from behind her newsroom anchor desk, which was cluttered with papers and looked just like a real reporter's desk in a real newsroom. Except the newsroom was a studio, and the hard-working young reporters who were bustling around in the background were in fact hard-working young actors. "You got a full-time police escort and you ain't no single woman. I'm just a goil from Brooklyn. I'm working the phone. I'm hearing threepeat—he's just struck again. And that's confoimed . . ." Damn, she was a good reporter. "I'm living in Fear City here. What am I supposed to do, huh?"

"Show good common sense, Cassandra. If a man you don't know approaches you, walk away. If he follows you, go into a place of business and phone the police. Don't hesitate.

Do it. We have a state-of-the-art task force under the personal direction of Inspector Dante Feldman pursuing every possible avenue. We *will* catch the answer man. I can't say when, but we *will* catch him."

And now she was thanking the mayor very, very much for his time and he was thanking her very, very much for hers and then he went bye-bye and she turned her goggly eyes full on us. "Who is this answer man? When will he strike again? No one knows. No one except maybe his confidante . . . Stewart Hoag."

Up flashed my photograph. A particularly awful one that Dick Corkery of the *News* snapped of me at the height of Merilee's pregnancy flap. At the time, I was trying to smash his head in with my umbrella, my face drawn back in a tight grimace that resembled the death rictus. I looked like Vincent Price on a bad hair day.

"I spoke to Mr. Hoag, the one-time star novelist, late this afternoon at his luxurious Upper West Side office," Cassandra went on. "His response, and I quote was: 'I'm a family man. Me and Charlie Manson.' " She let out a heavy, dramatic sigh. Up swelled her heavy, dramatic sign-off music. "And on that upbeat note, I'm Cassandra Dee, and you're somethin' else. G'night, people."

Pamela flicked the TV off, clucking at the screen angrily. "Someone should give that girl a good, proper spanking."

"Nice sentiment, Pam," I said. "But I'm afraid she'd enjoy it way too much."

My first stop was Hell's Kitchen. Or I should say Clinton, which is what they call the Kitchen now, thanks to Yushification. I stopped off there because that's where the Cupcake Cafe is, and the Cupcake Cafe happens to be the best bakery in the city. I picked up a little something in chocolate in a size 40 long, then steered the Jag on over to the theater district, Lulu riding shotgun. Frozen rain had begun spittering down, melting as soon as it hit the pavement. I ditched the Jag outside the Belasco on West Forty-fourth and went in by way of the stage door. The geezer on the door had been there since Tallulah was an ingenue. He knew me from when Merilee played Desdemona there to Raul Julia's Othello. She was Joe Papp's newest, loveliest darling then. But that was another era, gone and forgotten. Papp was dead. Raul Julia was dead. Broadway was dead. These days, the Great White Way was nothing but Andrew Lloyd Webber musicals for the hearing-impaired and Disney spectacles for the young and the dim. Very few dramas opened anymore. Those that did tended to be revivals, most of them showcases for TV brand names in search of a weightier identity. In the case of *Wait Until Dark,* that brand name was Luke Perry, who was starring opposite Merilee as the malevolent villain Harry Roat, a part originated by Robert Duvall.

I sat up in the balcony with Lulu. I munched. I watched. They were rehearsing the climax, where the evil Roat has the blind Susy trapped in her apartment, defenseless. Roat torments her by pouring gasoline on the stairs and threatening to light it with a match. Susy evens the score by killing the lights on him. A terrifying game of cat-and-mouse ensues, much of it played out in utter darkness. I watched in awe. Not just because the last scene of *Wait Until Dark* happens to be one of the scariest in the history of modern theater, but because I knew Merilee. And yet I didn't know *this* Merilee at all. She was totally convincing now as Susy. Vulnerable and frightened in the light. Resourceful and brave in the dark. I don't think I'll ever get over how she can turn herself into someone else. It's like magic. Of course, as a wise old director once told me, that *is* why they call them actors.

A skinny kid in a T-shirt and jeans jumped on stage full of snide put-downs. A skinny kid in a T-shirt and jeans who I realized was the director. And then they were on a ten-minute break and Merilee disappeared backstage. I'd left word that I was there. A moment later she appeared in the aisle next to me, looking exhilarated but tired, her long golden hair tied back in a ponytail. She wore a baby-blue cashmere turtleneck that had once belonged to me, jeans and Tanino Crisci ankle boots. Lulu moaned, tail thumping. Her way of saying hello.

Merilee's way was to exclaim, "My Lord, darling. That's the gaudiest, most obscene-looking chocolate thing I've ever seen in my life." She flopped down in the seat beside mine. "Give me some."

I did better than that. I gave her her very own.

"How does it play?" she wondered, taking a starved, grateful bite.

It played a bit ragged, especially so close to previews. But she knew that—she didn't need to hear it from me. "Not terribly," I replied.

"Luke's growing into it," she said tactfully, draping her long legs over the seat in front of her.

"So what did you tell them, Merilee?"

"Tell who, darling?"

"The Brad Pitt movie."

"That I'll do their nude scene. And I will *not* use a body double. I want to make a statement. I want to show America that women who are forty *are* beautiful."

"I'm proud of you, Merilee. You're a pioneer."

"You bet your sweet patootie I am. Besides, darling, it's now or never. In another year there won't be a single person left on the planet who will even *want* to look at me naked, let alone pay eight dollars and fifty cents for the privilege. We start filming on location in the spring."

"Where?"

"The former Soviet Union."

"Which part?"

"Sarajevo."

"That should make for a nice, relaxing change of pace."

She finished off her chocolate thing, studying me with her shimmering green eyes. "You got another one, didn't you? He wrote you again."

"How did you know?"

"You only go to the Cupcake Cafe when you're extremely up or extremely down. I can see your face, darling. You're not extremely up."

"The press are on to it. And me. They're camped out in front of our building."

"Oh, dear."

"I may not be home for a day or two, Merilee. I wanted to let you know. Tracy's fine. She's with Pam."

"Any particular reason?"

"I didn't think I should take her with me."

"I meant you not being home for a day or two."

Down on stage, the prop men were moving everything back into position. The better to start all over again.

"Have you spoken to Tansy lately?"

Merilee furrowed her brow at me. "Why, no. Not for months and months. She's, you know, pulled away from people. And her work takes her out of the city a lot."

"She still living in the same place?"

"As far as I know." Merilee raised an eyebrow at me. "Why, are you planning to run off with her?"

"Who, Tansy?"

"You always said she was great-looking."

"I most certainly did not."

"Did, too. At our first New Year's party. I distinctly remember it."

"I said she was a great catch."

"You've never said that about any of my other friends."

"Your other friends are all actresses." Somehow, my left shoulder ran into her bunched fist. "Ow, that hurt."

"It was supposed to, mister."

"She *was* a great catch," I pointed out. "That was why I put the two of them together."

Merilee's mouth tightened. She said nothing. She did not like to discuss Tuttle with me. She was still too angry.

"I think he's our man, by the way."

"Our man, darling?"

"I think Tuttle is the answer man."

She stared at me. "Tuttle Cash? Now, that would surprise me."

"Would it? Why?"

"Because he hasn't the nerve to pull this off," she replied. "Or the discipline to cover his tracks. Or the talent to write about it so well. Face it, Hoagy, Tuttle Cash is a conceited, spoiled, self-indulgent pain in the Aunt Fanny. Plus he's a coward. Only a coward beats up a woman that way."

I let her have this. She wasn't wrong, after all.

"Why do you think he's the answer man?" Merilee wanted to know.

"I have my reasons. But I want to be sure. And until I am, well, I owe Tuttle that much. I do have a sample from his old typewriter—an expert would be able to tell in a flash if it matches the answer man's. But that would mean enlisting Very, and Very's got Feldman breathing down his neck."

"Feldman?"

"The inspector who's in charge. A fan. He's a huge one."

"Ah. And what is this huge fan like?"

"Professional. Competent. Hard-nosed."

"You don't like him."

"And here I thought I was hiding it so well." I glanced over at her. "I'm not a team player, by the way."

"Thank God for that. I wouldn't get weak in the knees every time you kiss me if you were. Darling, I'm going to get serious for a moment. You do value me for my truth telling, don't you?"

"Only when you tell me what I want to hear."

"As I'm sure you've noticed by now, I do not happen to have a penis . . ."

"I have noticed that, Merilee. I myself am not prejudiced, but I know this makes my parents very happy."

"Hush. As a consequence, I have never fully understood why you look up to Tuttle. Why you are so proud to be his friend. You have no big brother. Maybe he's like a big brother to you. I don't know. But what I do know is that you can't let your relationship cloud your judgment."

I pondered this a moment. "In other words, you think I should turn him in."

"No, I think you shouldn't. Because if he were any other celebrity you wouldn't. Not until you were *sure*. Believe me, I'd just as soon see Tuttle Cash put away for a long time in a small cell with a mean, mean cellmate. But, darling, you make your living these days working with celebrities. And when it comes to ghosting, you're *always* sure. That's why you're better at it than anyone else."

"What are you saying, Merilee?"

"I'm saying you should do what you always do—collaborate. Treat this like you would any other project. Because if you do, then you'll end up doing the right thing, and if you don't, you'll end up losing your way. Just promise me one thing."

"What's that, Merilee?"

"Promise me you won't try to be a hero."

"Heroism is not something I know much about."

"Promise me," she insisted.

"I so promise." I sat there gazing at her. "You're not the worst, Merilee."

"You say it but you don't show it," she said softly, her eyes twinkling at me.

"Why, Miss Nash, what *are* you getting at?"

Now she gave me her up-from-under look, the one that makes *my* knees weak.

"But Merilee, the cast and crew are right down there on stage. *Luke* is down there."

"I don't care," she said, running her hand up my thigh. "I want you this minute. *Now,* Hoagy."

And so we, well, we stopped talking for a while. I won't bother you with the details, except to tell you that what began in my seat ended up in the aisle, rows one through four, and that I ended up with some rather wicked second-degree rug burns on my knees. Lulu stood guard over us, aghast but loyal to the end.

Afterward, we lay there on the balcony floor.

"Merilee, what's gotten into you lately?"

"Why, whatever do you mean, darling?" she wondered, all wide-eyed innocence.

"I mean this new . . . amorousness."

"Merciful heavens, Hoagy, you make it sound like I belong on the cover of *Time*."

"I was thinking more along the lines of the *Guinness Book of World Records*."

"Bother you much?"

"Not even a little. In fact, I'm ready to stand up and salute you."

"I believe that's what you just did, sir."

The stage manager was calling for her now. "Miss Nash? We're ready for you onstage! *Miss Naaaash?*"

"Good gravy." She lunged for her jeans and did her best to wrestle them back on. I did my best to not help her. "Mr. Hoagy!" she objected primly. "Behave yourself. I have a show to rehearse."

And with that she gathered up her debauched self and marched out the exit for the stage, her chin held high.

Lulu, she stared at me with withering disapproval.

Me, I drove to Scarsdale.

Eight

I ONCE ASKED an old-time cab driver what was the fastest way to get out of Manhattan. He told me the fastest way to get out of Manhattan was whichever way out of Manhattan youse happened to be closest to. I happened to be closest to the West Side Highway. After a while they start calling it the Henry Hudson Parkway, and then you're in Yonkers, where I caught the Cross County, which merges into the Hutch, which runs through Pelham and then New Rochelle, where the Petries, Rob and Laura and Ritchie, once lived. From there it's on to Scarsdale, the buttoned-up little burb where the diet doctor Herman Tarnower used to live. Until Jean Harris murdered him, that is.

It was colder north of the city. The frozen rain was a steady snowfall, and there were patches of ice on the shoulder of the road. I kept the speedometer under 65 and my eyes peeled for those cretins who believe the TV commercials and actually think that their four-wheel-drive rolling cushioned shoeboxes make them invincible on slippery roads. They scare me, those people. They have children and the right to vote. Lulu shivered next to me under the ragtop. I wrapped my cashmere scarf around her. She snuggled into it gratefully. She likes cashmere. She likes being warm.

I listened to 1010 WINS news radio while I drove. They were giving out Bridget's identity now. They were comparing him with Son of Sam out loud now.

If you absolutely must live in a suburb, Scarsdale is not the absolutely worst around. It's less than an hour from the city. The homes are older and well built, the plantings mature. There's some semblance of a village. Yes, you can do quite well for yourself in Scarsdale if you have, say, $800,000. But as I worked the Jag through its tidy streets, the place still gave me the creeps. I always get them on those rare occasions when I find myself in a suburb. Any suburb. After the bright lights and the tumult of Gotham, the darkness and calm seem unnatural to me. It's as if everyone for miles around has just been wiped out by ethnic cleansing. I should also explain that I hold to the perfectly rational belief that people who move to the suburbs gradually grow old, lose their teeth and die. And people who live in the city don't do any of those things.

My cell phone beeped. It was Vic, checking in from King Tut's. "The party's still going on," he reported, which was his way of saying Tuttle was still in the house.

I thanked him and hung up. It immediately beeped again.

"Hiya, cookie," that familiar voice brayed in my ear. "How ya doing? Whattaya doing? *Who* are ya doing?"

"Hello, Cassandra. Fine. Nothing. Nobody."

"Oh yeah? Then why are you in Scarsdale?"

"How did you know I'm in—?"

"Hoagy, you got no secrets from me. C'mon, what's her name? She married? She swallow it?"

"Thank you large for the Charlie Manson quote. It made my day."

"Hey, you said it, not me."

"And what's with that 'one-time star novelist' thing? I *do* happen to have a manuscript going around."

"Like I didn't offer to help you. Gimme something and I'll plug it to death for you." She was wheeling and dealing now. And even more bare-knuckle than she used to be. The stakes were higher. "Gimme a taste—something, anything—and I'll have twenty publishers wet for it. So is it true what I hear?"

"I doubt it. Why, what do you hear?"

"That the police bungled the intercept of Chapter Three. That the Bridget Colleen Healey murder could have been prevented."

"No, that's not true. It couldn't have been prevented. At least, not by them."

"What's that mean?"

"It was just something to say."

"Honey, cookie, sweetie, you never say anything just to say it."

"You don't say."

"Can I get real here a sec?"

"Don't let me stop you."

"I *need* this story. My ratings have hit a wall."

"It happens to all of us, Cassandra."

"I need a Pulitzer, Hoagy."

"I need a new prostate gland. That doesn't mean I'm going to get one."

"Work with me, Hoagy. I need you. Say something."

"Okay, okay. Cassandra?"

"Yeah, cookie?" she said hopefully.

"Good-bye, Cassandra."

The Spooners, Ezra and Heidi, lived around the corner from a country club in a very large Tudor that was crowded onto a very small lot. It was a brand-new Tudor. In fact, it was a Tudor-in-progress. Piles of lumber, cement blocks and roofing tiles were still stacked there in the driveway. A blue tarp protected the part of the roof that wasn't finished yet. The grounds were as barren as a moonscape. No shrubs. No lawn. Just bare, frozen dirt crisscrossed with bulldozer treads. There were lights on in the house. And there was a "For Sale" sign at the curb.

Out back there was a garage with an office. Ezra had said I would find him there. I saw the blue glow of a TV downstairs in the house as I made my way back there. Upstairs, I could hear the *thud-thud-thud* of rap music.

It was a paneled office, with French doors overlooking the nongarden. I could see him in there, working away at one of those colossal Power Macs, his thick, wire-framed glasses perched on the end of his stubby nose. He had a peaceful, almost dreamy look on his face. Until I tapped at the door. Then he completely panicked.

"One second, hon!" he cried out, eyes wild with fear. "Just give me one second!" Hurriedly, he cleared the screen of whatever was on it, his fingers flying over the keyboard. Then he shut the thing down and took a deep breath and opened the door, an uneasy smile on his round face.

"Hey, Ez," I said.

"Oh, it's *you,* Hoagy." Ezra Spooner was decidedly tubbier than he was when I saw him last. One might even call him portly. He was also completely bald now, aside from some thin, see-through brown tufts that clung here and there around his head. Actually, Ezra's head looked a lot more like a scrotum than anyone's head ought to. He was wearing one of those fleecy polythermal pullovers that are popular with skiers, mountain climbers and middle-aged tax attorneys, a pair of baggy corduroys and Mephisto walking shoes. "I just saw your picture on the news. Some guy in the city who's wiping out single women and sending you all the gory details. Unreal."

"That's certainly one word for it. Am I interrupting something?"

"No, no. Not at all." He glanced over my shoulder at the house, lowered his voice. "I was just chatting with this divorced labor lawyer out in Eugene, Oregon. We talk every night. Heidi, uh, doesn't know about her."

I tugged at my left ear. "Say, is this one of those Internet things?"

"I've met a lot of interesting women on-line," he exclaimed, waving his arms in the air for emphasis, fingers aflutter. Ezra was forever doing that. Ezra had always reminded me of a little boy pretending to be a snowflake.

"Safe sex, huh?"

"Not so safe. You'd be surprised how degenerate some of these women are."

"I would not."

"You on-line yet, Hoagy?"

"I am not."

"You got to get on-line, man."

"I do not."

Ezra shook his head at me, grinning. "Same old Hoagy."

"It's true. I'm ageless, the Dick Clark of modern lit."

"Come on in. It's fucking freezing out there."

I went on in. A little Jack Russell was curled up by the heater. It immediately came over and tried to get familiar with Lulu. She showed it her teeth. She doesn't like twerps sniffing her privates. Ezra shooed the Jack Russell outside. Lulu took its place by the heater with a sour grunt. This was her telling me she'd much rather be in her nice warm bed than schlepping all the way out to some frozen burb.

Ezra had himself a full-fledged home office back there. A laser printer. A fax machine. A second computer. All sorts of phone lines and power cords and junction boxes. There were shelves crammed with discs, cartons crammed with papers. For decor he had his high school athletic trophies arrayed on top of a filing cabinet. He did not have the photograph of the three college track stars displayed anywhere.

There were two ergonomically correct desk chairs. I sat in one of them, my eyes taking in all of the equipment. "Ever use a plain old typewriter anymore, Ez?"

"Why would I want to do that? They're obsolete."

He sat back down in front of his computer, peering at me. His eyes behind those thick lenses had changed. They were frightened eyes, hopeless eyes. I could remember very clearly the last time I'd seen eyes like Ezra's—in Tuttle Cash's office. Tuttle had them, too. Did I have them as well? Maybe I did. Maybe I was just so used to looking at myself in the mirror every day that I didn't notice it.

Ezra fidgeted, reached for a paper clip, toyed with it. He seemed nervous and preoccupied. "Can I offer you a beer, Hoagy?"

"You can."

There was a small refrigerator under the worktable. He poked around inside of it. "Sure, sure, a beer . . . I'm in the Beer of the Month Club now, you know. Just got me a Full Sail Nut Brown in. Most amusing little bottle of ale." He popped two of them open and handed me one. "To days gone by," he said jovially. Though his joviality seemed forced. The eyes weren't playing along.

"To Augie," I said, feeling vaguely like we'd gone all the way back to the Fabulous Fifties, parked out here in Dad's rec room with his sports trophies and his New Age ham radio. Hell, all we needed was Chester A. Riley and his pal Jim Gillis and we'd have us some real laffs.

He rested his beer on his tummy. "I guess this is pretty much everything you hate, isn't it, Hoagy?"

"Looks like a very nice place, Ez."

"It's a dump," he said glumly. "Damned contractor won't come back and finish my roof, won't deliver my topsoil. Who the hell's going to buy a house that's got half a roof and no lawn? Get this—he claims I have to pay him more money to truck in the topsoil that used to be here until he took it away. First I paid him to haul it away. Now I got to pay him to haul it back. It was *my* topsoil!" He took a gulp of his beer. "Know who used to live right behind us?"

"I can't imagine."

"Frank Gifford. He lives in Greenwich now, the rich bastard."

"Yeah, but look at it this way—he has to wake up next to Kathie Lee every morning." I sipped my beer. "Why are you selling?"

He cleared his throat, reddening. "We're, uh, relocating out west. Kind of a sudden development. Heidi's flying on ahead to get us settled. I'll be driving cross-country with the kids and the dog." He mustered a sheepish grin. "I guess that sounds pretty horrible to you."

"You forget, Ezra. I change diapers now."

"Hey, that's right. Merilee's celebrated love child. Sure, I read all about that. Christ, who didn't. Got a picture?"

"Do I honestly look like the kind of boring father who carries around baby pictures?"

He just stared at me.

"Well, if you're going to insist." I took out my wallet and handed it over.

"Nice-looking baby, Hoagy," he said, inspecting her picture carefully. "Say, isn't her head kind of large?"

"It is not," I snapped, snatching it back from him.

"First thing I thought of when I saw you on the news tonight was that it must be another one of your publicity stunts. Like the baby was. You've always been one for the limelight, haven't you?"

"That's not something I plan, Ez." I had not realized until this moment just how thoroughly Ezra Spooner disapproved of me. "It just happens."

"Sure, sure. It happens. Stuff happens." He looked around at his office. "I know about that."

"I'm an innocent bystander. I don't know why the answer man chose me. Unless, that is, he knows me."

Ezra frowned at me. "Knows you? What do you mean, knows you?"

"Ez, there are certain references in the chapters I've received. References that lead me to believe that the answer man may be Tuttle."

"Tuttle?" Ezra didn't seem at all upset by this news. He seemed tickled. *"*No way!"

"Have you had any contact with him lately?"

"Who, me? Naw. We were never really that close. And then after he . . . well, no. I haven't heard from him in years."

"Tuttle says you despise him. I seem to be rather blank as to why."

Ezra opened the top drawer of his desk and pulled out two hand-rolled joints. Lulu perked right up—her mind, such as it is, on what Very had said he'd found in Bridget Healey's apartment. I told her to cool it.

"Want to get stoned?" Ezra asked me with a sly grin.

"Not right now, thanks."

"You didn't used to say no."

"I didn't used to be high on life. Since when do you . . . ?"

"This kid at the office got me back into it last summer," he answered wistfully. "Real cute kid. What a bod." He left the joints there on the desk and sat back, put his feet up. "It's true, I do hate Tuttle. Have ever since that night we celebrated your first book. Your best, in my opinion. Your second one missed the mark, not that it didn't have a few good scenes."

I nodded politely. People don't hesitate to casually slam an author's work to his face. This is not something they would do to their internist or their plumber, but for some reason they have no problem doing it to us. Is that because they don't realize how vulnerable we are? Or is it because they *do?*

He was looking at me. "Tuttle never told you what happened?"

"Tuttle never told me what happened."

"I guess because it was no big deal to him. That'll give you an idea just what kind of bastard he—" He broke off, took a drink of his beer. "I met up with you guys at Elaine's. I was with D-Dana."

"Dana?"

"Gorgeous girl. A nice girl. Always had a smile on her face. I met her at the office. She went to Barnard, came from a good family. I was serious about her. Until that bastard, h-he . . ."

"He stole her?"

Ezra sneered at me unpleasantly. *"Stole* her? Oh, no. Nothing that classy." He ran a soft, white hand over his face. "Christ, that was what, seventeen years ago? I can still remember every detail. . . . Ten minutes after we get there she gets up and goes to the ladies' room. Doesn't come back. Tuttle goes to the men's room. Doesn't come back. After, I don't know, half an hour I'm wondering what the hell's going on. So I go back there looking for them. Found him giving it to her in the ladies' room, his pants down around his ankles. Her tits were hanging out, lipstick smeared all over her face. I was going to *marry* her! And h-he just *took* her, Hoagy. Because he felt like it. Because he was Tuttle-fucking-Cash, the great big fucking football hero." He drained his beer, slamming the empty bottle down on the desk. "She chased after him for weeks after that. He wouldn't even call her back. She was just last week's quickie to him. One of a dozen. Dana . . ." He trailed off, lost in his memories of her. Until, abruptly, he shook them off. "Want another beer?"

"Thank you, no."

"He's no hero, Hoagy. Want to know what my definition of a hero is?"

"Yes, I would, Ez."

"A hero is someone who takes responsibility for himself and his family. A hero is somebody who pays his bills on time. A hero is somebody who tells the truth in business. A hero is somebody who doesn't screw other people. I'm starting to feel like I was brought up in a different world, Hoagy. I don't understand what's happening to people anymore. I can't believe how they have no scruples. How they think you're some kind of weakling if you do. I guess that's why I'm looking for a job now instead of sitting in a corner office billing people three hundred dollars an hour. They canned me last summer, you know."

"Price Waterhouse?"

"Oh, no, no. I haven't been with them for years. I was with Fine, Weinberger, one of the big law firms. Only, they said I wasn't lean and mean enough anymore. I got the news the day after we poured the foundation here. So now here I am," he reflected miserably, "trying to get out from under this place, trying to hook on somewhere. I have two kids who hate me. A wife who thinks I'm the loser of the century. I thought maybe if we could get a fresh start out west . . ."

From the house there came the sound of a door slamming, followed by footsteps on the hard dirt. Ezra quickly shoved the joints back in the desk. Then he held a finger to his lips. For one oddly nostalgic moment, I felt like we were two little boys hiding in their tree fort from the big, bad mommy.

The big, bad mommy was a drab, wrung-out dishrag of a woman with limp brown hair, a strand of it stuck to her forehead with Scotch tape. Heidi Spooner was thin but it was a wilted, unhealthy-looking thin. Her color was the color of bread dough left out on the counter too long. The expression on her face was sour. And she moved heavily, ploddingly, like a much bigger, much older woman. She wore a baggy gray sweatshirt, baggy gray sweatpants and a pair of fuzzy green slippers, the kind of fuzzy green slippers that are popular among chain-smoking grandmothers in Far Rockaway, Queens.

She stopped in the open doorway. "Oh, I didn't realize you had company." There was a dreary, forlorn quality to Heidi's voice. She sounded like she was out on the sidewalk in the cold, begging for spare change. Or maybe it was just the way her nose was running. She dabbed at it with a wadded tissue that she then proceeded to tuck, used and moist, into the wristband of her sweatshirt.

I found myself staring at it, knowing that I would remember that tissue for a long, long time. Just as I would remember how cheerless the air got when she walked in. It was the air of two people who don't love each other anymore and don't know what to do about it.

Ezra grinned up at her uneasily. "You, uh, you remember Hoagy, don't you, hon?"

"Yeah, I guess so." Not that she seemed too pleased to see me. Lulu she wouldn't even look at. "Jason thinks he's driving down to Daytona Beach for New Year's with his friend Jade instead of staying here and packing up his room."

Ezra considered this with a judicious frown. "Which one is Jade again?"

"The rabbi's daughter."

"The rabbi has a daughter named Jade?"

"Her real name is Tovah, but she hates it."

"So?"

"So he's sixteen years old and he's not going."

"So?"

"So *talk* to him, would you?"

"What, now?" he said sharply.

"What, now," she answered sharply.

He got up, muttering to himself. "Be right back, Hoagy."

Heidi started to go inside, too, but decided that would be too overtly rude. So she lingered there, sniffling. I offered her my linen handkerchief. She declined it. I didn't know Heidi well. I had met her only once. But about her I had no doubt—I *knew* she didn't approve of me.

"We saw Merilee in that musical last year, *Gilligan,*" she said blandly. "We went in for our anniversary. I didn't much care for it."

I nodded. Another critic. "Get into the city many evenings, Heidi?"

"No, I hardly ever do."

"How about Ez? Does he?"

"Well, yeah. Naturally." She looked at me oddly. "I thought . . . I figured he's been hanging around with *you.*"

"With me?"

Her eyes searched my face carefully. "What, you mean he's not?"

"No, he's not."

"Oh, that's great," she said defeatedly. "That's just great. I don't know where he is half the time anymore. He just gets in his car and he goes. Or he sits out here by himself, brooding. He's very upset about what the firm did to him. He's not like you, you know. He played by the rules."

"And I didn't?"

"You know what I mean."

"No, I'm afraid I don't."

"He's not talented. He's had to work within the system for everything he's gotten. He's a decent, hardworking family man from a good school. He did everything he was supposed to do and he got crapped on. He's on his ass, Hoagy. *We're* on our ass, and that's just not supposed to happen to people like us."

"Exactly who *is* it supposed to happen to?"

"We *just* built this place and now we have to pick up stakes and move."

"There's no other jobs in this area?"

"I don't even know if he looked. All he keeps saying is he wants to start over out west—Eugene, Oregon, of all places. What the hell's so special about Oregon?"

That one I left alone. Didn't want to touch it.

Ezra returned now, looking grim and unhappy.

"Did you take care of it?" she asked him.

"I told him he's not going," he answered irritably. "If that's taking care of it, then I took care of it, okay?"

"Well, you don't have to bite my head off, okay?"

"Well, I'm busy, okay?"

"Well, okay." She went scuffing out, slamming the door hard behind her.

Ezra stood there staring at the door in tight silence. "Did I ask you if you wanted another beer?"

"You did, and I didn't."

He nodded and sat back down in his chair.

"Whatever happened to Dana, Ez?"

"I have no idea, Hoagy. She couldn't face looking at me every day at the office so she quit. Moved to Chicago. That was years ago. I never heard from her again." He pulled one of those joints out of the desk and lit it. He drew on it deeply, holding the smoke in a moment before he slowly let it out. "Tuttle didn't remarry, did he? After the business with Tansy, I mean."

"Malachi told me he was seeing a stripper until recently."

Lulu got up and scratched at the door for me to let her out. I did. Marijuana smoke makes her gaack. Plus, for some strange reason she's very susceptible to a contact high. Trust me, you don't want to be around Lulu when she's stoned.

Ezra studied the joint in his hand. "And you really think Tuttle's the answer man?"

"Unless *you* are."

Ezra's eyes widened. *"Me?* Why would I do something crazy like that? I don't hate women."

"But you do hate Tuttle. His typewriter, his words. It's a helluva frame, Ez, and there aren't too many people around who could build it. There's me. There's you."

"Sure, sure," he conceded easily. "I hear you. Only, if I wanted to get even with Tuttle I wouldn't go to that much trouble. I'd just hire some guy to kill him." He smoked in silence a moment. "Is that why you came all the way out here in the snow? Because you think I'm some kind of crazed serial killer?"

"I came out here," I said, "because I'm trying to figure out what's going on."

"You want to know what's going on? I'll tell you what's

going on. Tuttle Cash has no respect for human life, that's what's going on." Ezra was waving his arms now. "Particularly if that human life happens to be female. He *uses* women. He *destroys* women. *Killing* them's not a whole lot of a stretch from what he did to Tansy, is it? Hell, that's just making it official. I hope they get him for this, Hoagy. I really do. And I know it isn't politically correct to say this, but I'm glad we have the death penalty in this state again. Because I hope to God they fry him."

"I believe they use lethal injection now. What do you do with yourself when you're in the city, Ez? Heidi said you go in a lot."

"I'm not porking anyone, which is what she thinks. I do *nothing,* Hoagy. I leave the car in a garage and I walk. Or I ride the subway, sometimes for hours at a time. The city has changed so much, but in a lot of ways it hasn't changed at all. I guess I'm . . ." He trailed off, reflecting on it. The marijuana was having its way now. "I'm just trying to get back the feeling of what it was like when I first moved there, y'know? The enthusiasm. The energy. The desire. That make any sense?"

"Yes, it does."

"I thought about calling you."

"Why didn't you?"

"I dunno. Figured you and she lead such a glamorous life."

"I change diapers, like I said."

He nodded. We were silent. We seemed to have run out of things to say. I got up and reached for my coat.

"Want me to do it for you, Hoagy?"

"Do what, Ez?"

"Turn him in. I know how hard this must be for you. You two were close. I'll make the call if you want me to."

"You'd do that?"

"In a flash," he said, reaching for one of his phones. He was more than happy to do it. Hell, he was eager to do it.

"No, no, wait," I said, stopping him. Why so eager? *Was* he building a frame? He *was* prowling the city alone. He *was* riding the subways. Was he the older man from the office who Bridget had been seeing? Why not? Why the hell not? "When it's time to do it, Ez, I'll be the one to do it."

"Suit yourself," he said, backing off. "And you don't have to worry. I'll keep this to myself. We teammates have to stick together, right?"

"Track's not really a team sport, Ez. It's just you against the competition."

"All the more reason to stick together. A man's got to have *somebody* watching his back." Ezra got up and stuck out his hand. "Good to see you again, Hoagy. I'll send you my new address."

"Do that," I said, shaking his hand.

Lulu was waiting outside for me on the cold hard ground, her teeth chattering. Heidi was in the kitchen, watching me through the window. I tapped on the back door quietly. She opened it.

"You haven't come across an old typewriter around here, have you? Packing up, I mean."

She looked at me curiously. "We still have my old one from college, but nobody uses it anymore. The kids have their own computers."

"Is it an Olivetti?"

"No, a Royal."

"Are you sure?"

"Of course I'm sure. It's a Royal Safari. I typed enough papers on it, okay?" She started to close the door.

"Ever shop at Hold Everything, Heidi?"

"Well, yeah. I've ordered from their catalog. Why?"

"Did you tell Ezra?"

"That I've ordered from Hold Everything?"

"That you don't want to move to Oregon."

She sniffled. "We don't talk about it much. He's afraid that he's become a failure in my eyes."

"Has he?"

"Christ, no! I don't care how much he makes. I just want him to be happy. I *told* him that."

"And what did he say?"

"He said he couldn't remember the last time he was happy."

"May I make a small suggestion? Take him to dinner and a show in New York. Broadway needs all the help it can get right now. And so does Ezra. Also get a new pair of slippers."

"For him?"

"For yourself."

She looked down at her fuzzy green feet. "These are brand new."

"Heidi, I hate to give Nike any credit but . . . Just Do It."

She stood there looking at me. "You're being a help."

"Don't sound so surprised. I like to spread a little joy wherever I go." I grinned at her.

She didn't say anything about how nice my teeth looked. She didn't say anything at all. Just closed the door on me.

I went back down the driveway to the street. She was watching me from a darkened front window now. I could see her outlined by a light behind her. She stayed there watching me as I got in the Jag and started it up. She was still watching me as I drove away into the night.

Tansy Smollet, The Garden Lady, lived and worked in an old yellow brick warehouse that she owned down in Tribeca where Duane Street meets Staple Street. It's a quiet neighborhood at eleven o'clock at night. The streets were deserted and slick, the skies clearing up above. The name Staple Street comes from when this was the city's chief marketplace for eggs, butter, etc. Her place had been a coffee warehouse. It was neo-Flemish in design, six stories high, with all sorts of gables and dormers and weathered copper details at the roof. At the street level there was a garage door situated in the middle, somewhat like a large, square mouth. The mouth was open. I had phoned ahead.

News radio was reporting one arrest by Feldman's undercover task force. A female officer had run in a shady character who'd tried to pick her up outside the White Horse Tavern. The suspect had been released after questioning when it turned out he was a rabbinical student at Yeshiva who truly *was* looking for the nearest subway station.

I pulled in, the steel door automatically lowering shut behind me, and nuzzled the Jag up alongside the car Tansy had driven for as long as I'd known her. It was a 1957 Porsche 356A Speedster, silver with a black top and black leather interior. She did most of the repair work on it herself. Spent a year in Germany learning how. That was Tansy. Her small fleet of Garden Lady panel trucks and pickup trucks was parked in there, too, a dump truck, a Chevy Suburban—all of them painted silver and bearing her garden fork insignia on their doors. Bags of manure and peat moss were piled everywhere, pallets of brick and bluestone, railroad ties, redwood two-by-fours, terra-cotta pots, hoses, garden tools. If you lived in a penthouse on Fifth or Park and you wanted a garden on your terrace, you called The Garden Lady. She did design, she did installation, she did maintenance. She also worked out of Bridgehampton, where she kept a cottage.

It was cool and damp in there, and it still smelled like coffee beans. In the center of the old warehouse there was a steel-caged freight elevator. This went up to her third-floor offices, where Tansy employed a dozen designers and project managers, and then on up past that to her loft. Tansy had taken the top three floors and blown out the walls and turned it into five thousand square feet of what the realtors would call highly dramatic living space. There was a center atrium fifty feet high, with a glass roof under which the living area, dining area and kitchen all flowed into each other. A pair of spiral staircases flanked the atrium. One led up to her bedroom loft, where she had a gymnasium, a sauna and a drop-dead view of the Hudson. The other led to her studio, where she designed gardens for people. There were no rugs in Tansy's apartment, no paintings and almost no furniture save for the precious handful of pieces her brother Curtis had made of native Vermont hardwoods, each a work of art in itself. All lighting was recessed, all counters granite, all floors polished cherry. There was no clutter, nothing but bare surfaces and light and tranquillity. It was not a home for a baby and a dog and laughter. Actually, Tansy's place was not a home at all. It was more like being inside a work of minimal art.

New Age music greeted me when the elevator door opened. Harps and flutes, tubular bells, sounds of waves breaking gently on the shore. And then Tansy came gliding across the room to meet me, tall and lean and lithe. I forced a big brave smile onto my face and kept it plastered there the way one does when visiting a terminally ill patient. Because the sight of her was so terribly unsettling. Not that they hadn't done a wonderful job on her face. They had. I can't remember whether it took eight or nine operations to put Tansy back together again. There had been endless bone grafts. Thirty titanium microscrews and seven titanium plates held her cheekbones in place. The incisions had been made inside her upper lip and her lower eyelids, so there were no scars. At least none that showed. She looked almost exactly as she had. The slightly uptilted blue eyes, delicate nose and jaw, those exquisite cheekbones that had the modeling agencies salivating when she was a kid. Tansy looked the same.

Except she didn't. Because the pale white skin was somehow drawn tighter across the bone and the eyes were sunk deeper and something had happened to the muscles or the nerves, because she couldn't move her mouth like she did before. Oh, they had given her nice new teeth and she could talk and chew solid food and all of those things so-called normal people could do. She could do everything but smile. Her face just wouldn't work that way anymore. Not that this was too much of a problem in her case. See, there had been internal injury as well. She'd blown a fuse somewhere—the one that powered her spirit. Tansy Smollet had been a lively, animated person before Tuttle Cash put her in the hospital. Now she was a subdued and somber one. There was a heartbreaking sadness about her, a deep and profound melancholy.

It didn't help that she'd cropped her lush, luxuriant blond hair so close that she looked like one of those French women who consorted with the Nazis.

"I hope I didn't wake you," I said.

"No, no . . . I was working," she said, her voice thin and halting.

"And how is that going?"

She considered her answer carefully. "Fine. I'm very busy. For some strange reason I seem to have cornered the market on rich gays with bad taste."

"I didn't know there was such a thing."

"It's a small, exclusive clientele. But my own."

"Why, Miss Smollet, I'd swear you're getting your sense of humor back."

"No, it's you—you've always brought out my zany side," she said, totally deadpan. Eternally deadpan. "God, Hoagy, it's so good to see you."

She put her cool, dry lips against my cheek and knelt to pat Lulu, who was circling her excitedly and whooping. Lulu adored Tansy, which I'd always found most surprising. She ordinarily detests any woman she regards as potential competition for Merilee. It was my personal belief that Merilee had once sat her down and told her that if she, Merilee, were ever killed in a plane crash, Tansy had a better than decent shot at being her new mommy. Or maybe Lulu just sensed this. Dogs generally do. And Lulu is one, whether she admits it or not.

"I like your new look, Tansy," I said, referring to her

sleeveless dress of brown wool. She was a Zoranian now, a
disciple of the minimalist Yugoslavian designer Zoran
Ladicorbic, who dressed the likes of Candice Bergen and
Lauren Hutton in monkish tunics and shapeless dresses that
ran in the many thousands. You bought into a whole look
when you went Zoranian. Tansy's haircut was all about that,
as were her absence of jewelry and makeup, her short, unpainted fingernails, her shoes that were plain and flat. She
was still an inch or so over six feet in them. Her arms were
bare and well muscled. Her long legs were bare, too, and
very white, which accentuated their nakedness. There were
some scratches on her hands from wrestling with something
thorny. There often were.

"I got tired of playing the victim," she said flatly. "I was a
classic fashion victim. Whatever they told me to do, I did. I
dressed in black, I dressed in white, I dressed in pumpkin. I
was a cowgirl, a Paris tart, a British aristocrat. I've just said
no to all of that. Enough. I mean, think of it, Hoagy—
people are actually wearing Hush Puppies again."

"No one we know, fortunately."

"I've made tea. Or would you rather have wine?"

"Tea would be fine."

"Is it still milk, no sugar?"

"It is."

"Go sit in front of the fire. I'll be right there."

There was seating for exactly one in front of the brick
fireplace—one graceful, perfect rocker. There was nothing
else in the vast space, unless you counted the cheery fire or
the cheery Eskimo death mask from Hooper Bay, Alaska,
that was mounted over the mantel. Lulu stretched out in
front of the fire. I took the chair. Tansy came in with two
mugs of tea and handed me one and curled up on the floor
at my feet, face to the fire, back resting against my knees.

Briefly, I felt that same tingle of excitement I'd always felt
when I was alone in a room with Tansy and close to her.
From the beginning, it had been there. For her, too. Every

once in a while over the years I'd catch her staring at me from across a dining table or a crowded room, wide-eyed, as if she'd just discovered something shocking about me. I'd meet her gaze, and she'd look away. Not that anything had ever happened between us. When Merilee and I split up that first time, she and Tuttle were in heaven. When she and Tuttle split, Merilee and I were, well, not in heaven but making it work. Our timing had always been off, Tansy's and mine. And I'm convinced that timing has as much to do with whether two people end up together as desire does. And if you were to say to me that timing is just another word for fate, then I'd say to you, okay, I guess I believe in fate.

We sat there gazing at the fire. Lulu decided Tansy's lap would be more comfortable than the floor, so she moseyed over and plopped down in it. Tansy petted her. Lulu responded by going to work on Tansy's long, lovely fingers with her long, unlovely pink tongue. Lulu licked and she licked. She licked with an intensity that bordered on the feverish. I told her to cut it out. She just kept on licking, as if Tansy's fingers were an ice cream cone about to melt in the hot sun.

"It must be my new hand cream," Tansy commented mildly. She didn't seem to mind this tongue towelette. "I just put some on."

"What's in it?"

"Nothing but organic ingredients. A farmer up in Maine makes it. There's rosemary verbenon, olive oil . . ."

"Keep going."

"Um, beeswax, sage leaves . . ."

"Keep going."

"Lemongrass—"

"Bingo. Good thing you don't moisturize your hands with tartar sauce or you'd be minus a finger right now."

She let out a laugh. Or at least it almost sounded like one. "Oh, God. I can't remember the last time I did that."

"You do happen to be in the presence of a charter member of the Soupy Sales Society. Very few people can keep a straight face around me."

She turned her straight face to me, her teeth digging into her lower lip. "How is he, Hoagy?"

"I don't see much of him anymore, Tansy."

"Is it true what I hear about him?"

"Only the bad stuff."

"All I hear is bad stuff."

"What do you hear?"

"That he may lose his restaurant."

"It's not his to lose." I sipped my tea. It was Irish Breakfast, strong and hot and good. "I understand he's been writing you."

Her sunken eyes went back to the fire. "He has," she acknowledged unhappily. "Almost every day."

"What does he say?"

"I wouldn't know. I tear them into little pieces and burn them." She stroked Lulu, who was drifting back into the land of Nod. "He's completely losing his grip, isn't he?"

I didn't respond, just looked at her.

"Okay, okay. Maybe I do read them before I burn them."

"What does he say?"

"That he feels it all slipping away. That he sees nothing ahead of him that is positive or good. That he w-wants me back. . . . I-I try to tell myself he's nothing more than what the Japanese housewives call a *nure-ochiba,* which, loosely translated, means a wet fallen leaf that sticks annoyingly to your leg, but—" She broke off. "I suppose you think I should give him another chance."

"Not even maybe. Are these letters he sends you typed or handwritten?"

"Handwritten."

"Whatever happened to that old Olivetti of his? Did he get rid of it?"

She had to think about this a moment. "Yes, I believe he did. He put it out on the street so some homeless person could take it and sell it. I remember him saying there was no point in having it around anymore because, unlike you, he had nothing to say. He always admired that about you, you know. He said you had courage."

"He's the one who drove a race car at two hundred miles per hour in heavy traffic. How can he say I'm the one with courage?"

"Because you're willing to risk humiliation."

"Hell, I risk that every time I open my mouth. That's no big deal."

"To him, it is. It's huge. I guess you can't understand that."

"I guess I can't."

"Tuttle hasn't the nerve to confront the scariest truth of all, Hoagy—himself. Driving a race car, that's just an escape from it, like drinking or chasing women or . . ."

Or walking on water? Holding an entire frightened city in your grip, waiting for your next move?

"Sometimes, I think he's following me," she said softly.

I stiffened. "When? Where?"

"It's more a feeling than anything else. I haven't actually seen him." She sipped her tea. "Maybe I'm just going insane."

"*Maybe* you should call the police."

"No, no. I want them out of my life."

"He's *not* a wet leaf, Tansy."

"No police," she insisted. "Besides, I know how to protect myself now." She climbed out from under Lulu and went to the elevator and came back with her shoulder bag, a scuffed old leather one. She reached inside. Out came a Ladysmith, the slim and trim .38 that Smith & Wesson tailors for a woman's hand and a woman's fears. "Tuttle comes near me again and, believe me, he'll be sorry. You think he's the answer man, don't you?"

I stared up at her. "Why would you say that?"

"Because I'm thinking it, too, that's why." She shoved the gun back in her bag and sat back down. Lulu moved back into her lap without hesitation. A contented grunt followed. "As soon as I heard it on Cassandra Dee's show to-night. What was it she called him—'The Man Who Loves Women to Death'? That's Tuttle. That's always been Tuttle. He hunts them down. He catches them. He takes whatever meat he chooses and he moves on, leaving the steaming carcass behind for others to deal with. He doesn't actually *want* them, you know."

"He wants you," I pointed out.

"No, he doesn't. He just thinks he does."

"May I ask you a personal question, Tansy?"

She cocked her head at me curiously. "Of course."

"Why did you drop the criminal charges against him?"

She shrugged her shoulders. "Because I couldn't win, that's why. His lawyer told my lawyer that they were planning to plead self-defense."

"Wait, *Tuttle* was planning to plead self-defense?"

"Uh-huh. By claiming I attacked him with a kitchen knife."

"Did you?"

"Of course not. But it would have been my word against his. And Tuttle Cash just happens to be the proverbial all-American boy. A sports hero. A star. Who do you think the jury would believe, him or me? Who do you think the police believed when they showed up? Christ . . ." Tears started forming in her eyes. She swallowed, fighting them back. "They f-figured he'd caught me fooling around, that's what they figured. They figured I was a no-good slut. They figured I *deserved* it."

"No one deserves that."

"Domestic violence is the number-one health risk in America for women ages fifteen to forty-four, Hoagy. Did you know that? But the only way we can get any attention from the police is to get killed. Otherwise, as far as they're concerned, men and women fight, and boys will be boys, and that's all there is to it." She trailed off into brittle silence, her eyes on the fire. "I knew I would lose. And it would be very public. And I would destroy my reputation and my business in the process. I couldn't risk that. I wouldn't risk that. So I filed for a divorce and I hobbled away. I just wish he'd stop writing me. God, how I wish he'd stop writing me."

"Are you seeing anyone these days?"

She shook her head. "I'm still not ready for that. Maybe I never will be. I have my work. I read a lot. I exercise every day, which keeps me feeling healthy and strong."

"It does more than that," I said, admiring the taut, toned line of her naked calves.

"Plus I counsel battered women over at a clinic on East Tenth Street."

"And who counsels you?"

Tansy swallowed, her eyes searching mine. "Hoagy, do you . . . ?"

"Do I what?"

"Do you remember that time we went to see *The White Sheik* together at the Thalia, just you and me? Tuttle was out of town. You had left Merilee."

"She threw me out, actually."

"Do you?"

"Vaguely. You wore a cream-colored turtleneck, faded jeans and black boots. Your hair smelled like Kiehl's chamomile shampoo. You had a bandage around the pinky finger of your left hand from where you'd cut yourself pruning a forsythia. We ordered moo-shoo pork at the Peking Duck House on Broadway afterward, and the waiter forgot to bring us our pancakes."

"Do you remember after that?" Her voice was almost a whisper. "When you kissed me good-night in the cab?"

"I remember," I said, my own voice turning husky.

"I was a fool."

I said nothing. She was the one doing the talking.

"I should have gone right upstairs and called him and told him that the wedding was off, Hoagy. I should have run to you and begged you to make love to me all night long."

"And I could have done it, too, in those days."

"Stop joking," she said crossly. "I'm being serious."

"I'm always at my most serious when I'm joking, Tansy."

"We would have been happy together, Hoagy. We would have made each other happy."

"No, we would have made each other miserable. Trust me, I was no prize. I was confused. I was angry. I was a mess."

"You're not anymore."

"I am, too. I've just gotten better at hiding it."

"I was a fool," she repeated.

"Okay, you were a fool," I said roughly. "He was no good and you should have known it. You were supposed to be smart. You weren't smart at all. You were stupid. How could you have been so stupid?"

Stung, she pulled back from me. "That wasn't a very nice thing to say."

"I'm not a very nice person."

"You try hard not to be, but you are."

"No, I'm not. You're kidding yourself."

"In that case, I've been kidding myself for an awfully long time."

"Not to worry. That's the new national pastime. Replaced baseball."

She let out a sigh and rested her head on my knee. "This is so nice, yammering with you in front of the fire like we used to." Her voice had turned small, like a child's. "Will you come back again some time? Talk to me like this?"

"Sure I will."

"I feel so safe. I may even be able to sleep tonight."

"Sure you will." Gently, I caressed her cheek with the back of my hand.

"I don't feel anything when you do that, Hoagy."

"Don't tell me I'm losing my touch."

"No, it's the nerves. The feeling never came back." She took my hand and held it. Hers was cold. "Merilee never calls me."

"She felt you pushed her away."

"I needed some time."

"It's been some time."

"I know it has," she admitted. "Hoagy?"

"Yes, Tansy?"

"You don't have to worry about Tuttle coming after me or anything. He won't. I realize that when I'm able to think about it clearly. Because, let's face it, if he really wanted to kill me he would have by now. That's not what he wants. Don't you see what it is he wants, Hoagy?"

"I'm afraid not, Tansy."

She held my hand up to her face, the one that didn't feel anything. "He wants something much, much worse than that. He wants me *alive.*"

It was one-thirty in the morning when I pulled up on Third Avenue across the street from King Tut's. There was still plenty of activity going on. Three Yushies in topcoats climbed out of a cab and went in, laughing and ruddy-faced. So did two members of the New York Rangers, Mark Messier and some other player I'm sure I would have recognized if I knew shit about hockey. A white stretch limo pulled up and out tumbled a gaggle of half-naked fashion models, impossibly young and giggly. I had a battered silver flask of calvados in the glovebox. I opened it and took a drink. I sat there, Lulu dozing next to me.

Vic Early came out a few minutes after two, big hands stuffed in the pockets of his overcoat, and clomped across the street toward us and got in, nudging Lulu into my lap. Vic smelled of cigarette smoke and beer. He looked miserable.

"How is everything?"

"Fan-fucking-tastic."

"Ah, you met Malachi."

"I met Malachi." He shifted in the seat next to me, wincing in pain.

"What's the matter?"

"Nothing. I just have to pee."

"They do have a men's room. You could have used it."

"No way. That's how I lost Sharon Stone."

"I believe she was found."

"Not by me, she wasn't." He yawned hugely and rubbed his eyes. "He's still in there, playing the charming host, Hoag. Telling old football stories. Downing shot after shot of brandy. He seems real jolly. Personally, I think he's depressing as hell. I guess I've just been around too many ex-jocks like him, guys no longer in the limelight, trying to hang on. He remarked upon my size. I told him I once played for the Bruins. He actually remembered my name."

"You *were* an all-American your junior and senior years, Vic. Did he make you for a friend of mine?"

"No chance. And he's been here all evening. I guarantee it."

"Thanks, Vic. I'll take over from here. Get some sleep."

"Don't mind if I do."

"I'll need you back on duty at eight."

"You got it, Hoag. When are *you* planning to sleep?"

I didn't have an answer for that one.

Tuttle came out the front door of his place just as Vic was reaching for the car door. The collar of The King's duffel coat was turned up and he was reeling slightly, either from the brandy or his bad knee. He started toward the corner of Seventy-seventh Street. I started up the Jag.

Vic watched him critically. "Be careful, Hoag. He's carrying."

"Carrying?"

"You can tell by his stride. And by the swing of his left arm. He's favoring a weight in his left coat pocket. There, see that? He just adjusted it with his left hand when he stepped off the curb."

"Damn, I can't believe Malachi gave him back his gun. What must he be thinking?"

"Oh, that reminds me—he cut out early."

"Malachi?"

"Yeah, about ten-thirty. Didn't come back." Vic glanced at me. He still wasn't sure what this was all about—although he had to have his suspicions. "Want me to find out where he went?"

"Yes, Vic. I believe I would."

Vic got out and hailed a cab. Lulu climbed gratefully back into his seat. Tuttle was making his way toward Lexington on Seventy-seventh. I backed up to the corner and went after him. Found him out in the middle of Lex searching for a cab. I wondered about this. Why hadn't he just grabbed one outside his restaurant? Was he afraid someone would overhear where he was going?

I pulled up in front of him and honked. He recognized my ride, of course, but wouldn't look at me. Just kept on scanning the avenue for a taxi, his jaw squared stubbornly. I rolled down the window and thumped the door with my gloved hand. "Hey, good-looking. Feel like taking a ride?"

He swiped at his nose with the back of his hand. "You going to offer me money to suck on your dick?"

"No, I'm going to offer you money not to."

Grudgingly, he got in, displacing Lulu, who was getting fed up with this whole up/down, up/down routine.

"You following me or something, Doof?" he said thickly. He was very drunk. Glazed drunk.

"I felt bad about what happened between us. Thought I'd stop by. They said you'd just gone out the door. You headed home?"

"No, down to Ten's. Girl I know named Luz dances there. Dead ringer for Julia Roberts."

"I thought Mal said she—"

"Mal said she *what?*" he demanded, his voice turning icy.

"Nothing. Never mind."

"Care to tag along?"

"Try and stop me."

We drove, Tuttle staring out the window, me thinking about what a thrill it had been, once upon a time, to have

Tuttle Cash, *the* Tuttle Cash, riding along next to me in my car. To know that Tuttle Cash was content to be in my company. That Tuttle Cash was my friend. God, it had made me so proud, I wanted the whole world to know about it. But that was then and this was now. Now Tuttle Cash was a suicidal, middle-aged alcoholic with a gun in his pocket. And some nut calling himself the answer man was answering to his description.

Now I didn't want anyone to know Tuttle Cash was in my car with me.

"You'll be happy to know, Doof, that I've decided to forgive you for thinking maybe I killed those girls." He waited for me to respond. When I didn't he continued. "It was on the eleven o'clock news. I had it on over the bar. There's three of them now, you know."

"I know."

"They said business was already down thirty percent to-night at a lot of movie theaters and restaurants. Women are scared to go out alone. Imagine one guy having that much power over the city. Incredible, huh?"

"Incredible."

He was watching me. "It's not me, Doof. You have to believe me."

"I don't have to do anything, Tuttle." I glanced at him curiously. "Why have you?"

"Why have I what?"

"Decided to forgive me."

He fished around in my glovebox for the silver flask and found it. "Because you can't help yourself, Doof. It's Tansy. You want her for yourself. I don't blame you. Really, I don't."

I sighed inwardly. "Tuttle, I'm with Merilee, remember?"

He ignored this. "Sure, you're looking to pin this thing on me so I'll be out of Tansy's life."

"Tuttle, you *are* out of her life!"

He ignored this, too. Just went back to staring out the window, his chest rising and falling.

We had reached midtown now, where there is always traffic on Lex, no matter the time. I cut over to Park, which was
quieter, and continued downtown.

"I saw her tonight, Tuttle."

"Oh, yeah?" He finished off my calvados and tossed the
empty flask back in the glovebox. "Did you fuck her?"

A ferocious growl came from the direction of my lap.
Followed by a yelp of the human variety.

"Jesus, Lulu *bit* me!"

"You don't say," I said mildly. "Where?"

"In the wrist," he moaned, holding up his torn cuff. "I'm
bleeding!"

"Atta girl."

"Shit, she's not rabid, is she?"

"Only in defense of the people she cares about."

A red light stopped me at Forty-sixth Street. The 230
Park Avenue building stood before us, ornate and gilded. In
days gone by, it was the New York Central Building, as in
the railroad. Now it belonged to the Helmsleys, as in Leona.
Looming over it was the Pan Am building, that ghastly up-
ended shoebox which in fact was now the Met Life building,
although no one called it that, just as no one called Sixth
Avenue the Avenue of the Americas or Phil Rizzuto anything but the Scooter.

"Are you stalking her, Tuttle?"

He didn't respond. The light turned green. I nosed the Jag
through the tunnel that went under 230 Park and then rose
up and around Grand Central Station.

"Well, are you?" I persisted.

"I hate that word," he answered softly. "It has such a
negative connotation. I'm watching over her, okay?"

"No, it's not okay. You're making her crazy, and she's in
a highly fragile state. Keep it up and she'll end up in the
hospital. And you'll end up in jail."

"That's exactly what you want, isn't it?" he said, sneering
at me.

"Damn it, Tuttle!" I hit the brakes, hard, stopping us cold

in the middle of the street. A cab swerved around us, honk-ing. "What I don't want is *this!*"

"What, Doof?" he asked dumbly.

"You and your miserable self-pity. You and your pointless, empty, upper-middle-class, white bullshit."

"I'm not upper-middle-class."

"Oh, fuck you, Tuttle."

He gaped at me in shock. "That . . . that was beneath you, Doof."

"Yeah, well, I've lowered my personal bar, okay?"

"You used to be a lot wittier."

"And I used to have a lot more hair and gum tissue and spermatozoons. So what? I used to be a lot of things. We both did."

He stuck his chin out at me. "I didn't ask for you to show up in my life again. It was all your idea, not mine. So why don't you just get lost, huh?"

Why indeed? For the same reason that I couldn't let him out of my sight until 8 A.M. Because I had too much riding on him, that's why. Because if Tuttle Cash's life was mean-ingless, then somehow, mine was, too. If he was nothing, then I was nothing. If he was a murderer of innocent women, then, well, I didn't want to think about what that made me. Later. When there was time to reflect. For now, I couldn't get lost. That much I knew.

I resumed driving. "Which health club do you belong to, anyway?"

"Manhattan Fitness Center. They've got a branch right around the corner from the restaurant."

"They have one on East Thirty-Ninth, too, don't they?"

"I believe so. Why?"

"I'm thinking about getting back in shape."

"Doof, you never were in shape."

"Tuttle, please. Leave me one of the few illusions I have left."

Ten's, formerly known as Stringfellows, was squeezed into

a soft spot on East Twenty-first Street in between the Orien-
tal rug district and Gramercy Park. There were double doors
of smoked glass and lots of shiny chrome out front. Also a
doorman in a tux. Cabs were lined up there, waiting for the
big tippers to come staggering out after their night on the
town. I parked down the block and in we went. There was a
cover charge of fifteen dollars each, and they made us check
our coats. The girl who took them didn't seem to notice the
extra weight in Tuttle's. Or maybe she just checked a lot of
coats with guns in them. She smiled at Tuttle. She knew
Tuttle. Everyone knew Tuttle.

Inside there was more shiny chrome and lots of mirrors
and strobe lights and women, women everywhere—women
in G-strings, spiked heels and nothing else. Unless you count
all the silicone they were wearing. Their breasts were so
inflated it was a wonder the poor girls didn't just lift right up
off the rug and float to the ceiling. I'm talking the Goodyear
Blimp *Columbia* here. Ten's was not Times Square by any
means. This was Hef the Ancient's glossy magazine come to
life, as upscale and respectable as a place full of nude women
and fully clothed men can be. Huge, too. I'm talking a veri-
table three-ring circus of perfumed flesh and lacquered hair.
Seventy-five women at least. Every type imaginable. Tall or
short, blonde or brunette, black or Asian. Everything except
flabby or flat-chested or old. There was a stage with a DJ,
and a stripper was working it to a pounding beat, all slither
and lubricious undulation. Disco was still alive here. Or at
least Tom Jones was . . . *Or did Mr. Tom Jones rise up from
the dead while I was inside? Because that man is back. And sounding as shitty as ever. . . .* There were four different bars
where eight-dollar beers and assorted light snacks could be
had. And then there was the sea of tables, most of them
taken. Here, for twenty bucks, lap dancers waved their hoot-
ers and their butts in the faces of businessmen in dark suits.
Some merely sat and talked with the women, which was
fine. You could talk to them. You could look at them. You

could do everything but touch them: the ultimate in safe sex. It was all very posh and clean and friendly. And yet it was all very grim and cheerless, too. Maybe it was the stony boredom in the women's eyes. Or the bouncers wearing tuxes and earplugs who were stationed every six feet, big as houses. Or the surveillance cameras up above, watching, watching.

Lulu took one look around and asked me if she could spend the rest of the evening in the car. I said no. We took a table. We tried to order a drink. We couldn't find a waitress.

Luz Santana turned out to be tawny and long-limbed and no more than twenty-three. She came with the preferred equipment package—the antigravity tits, fattened collagen lips, big Jersey hair dyed the color of butterscotch. Her lips and nails were bright orange, her G-string and spiked heels hot pink. Personally, I saw no resemblance to Julia Roberts whatsoever.

Luz was not in the least bit happy to see Tuttle. Passed right on by our table, flaring her nostrils at him. Not that this fazed Tuttle in the least.

He just grabbed her by the arm and said, "Join us."

"Like, ask someone else, okay?" Luz's voice was somewhat screechy. It was not her best feature.

"Aw, come on, baby," he pleaded. "I want you to meet my oldest friend in the universe."

"If he's anything like you I don't wanna have nothin' to do with him, okay? And I *ain't* your baby."

Tuttle climbed unsteadily to his feet. "I've missed you, Luz," he said, gazing deeply into her eyes. He could do this better than anyone, even drunk. Especially drunk. "I've missed what we had together."

Luz looked away uneasily. She suddenly seemed extremely young and very vulnerable. "Yeah, well, I didn't like where it was headed, okay?"

"You make it sound like the whole thing was my idea."

"Like, the handcuffs weren't exactly mine, okay?"

Lulu let out a low unhappy moan. Not her kind of conversation.

Tuttle looked hurt now. "What, you're saying it was no good for you?"

"No, that's not what I'm saying," Luz admitted, softening. "Like, I'm standing here talking to you and it's like my heart is beating so fucking fast. You got skills, honey. You got it going."

"You're the one's got it going." His eyes were feasting on her plump, golden-brown breasts, thighs, drumsticks. "My God, look at you."

"*No,* Tuttle! Just . . . no. It's over, okay?" She started away from him.

He grabbed her by the arm again, harder this time. "No, it's *not* okay!"

"Let go of me!" she cried, squirming in his grasp.

Instantly, a bouncer appeared.

"I'm afraid I'll have to ask you not to touch the ladies, sir," he informed Tuttle politely.

"Oh, really?" Tuttle tightened his grip on Luz's bare arm. Splotches formed beneath his fingers. "Well, I'm afraid I'll have to ask you to get out of my fucking face."

The bouncer moved in closer. He wasn't any taller than Tuttle, but he was a whole lot wider. And calm. Really calm. "We like for everyone to have a good time, sir. But you have to behave yourself. If you're going to bother the lady, you're out of here."

Another bouncer appeared behind him now. Backup.

"Tuttle, why don't you go get us a couple of drinks at the bar?" I suggested, playing Mr. Peacemaker.

"You get them, Doof. Me and Luz have to talk."

I tried it again, louder this time. "Go get us some drinks, Tuttle. Or we're leaving."

Tuttle scowled at me. He seemed dazed and confused all of a sudden, like he'd just been thrown to the turf by an onrushing linebacker. I found myself wondering just how many tabs of Vitamin V he'd taken. "Oh, okay, Doof," he said hollowly. "Sure. Whatever." He released Luz, straightened his tie with exaggerated care and started across the crowded club toward one of the bars, weaving on rubbery legs. The bouncers watched him carefully.

"Thanks, Eddie," Luz said to the first bouncer.

"Enjoy your evening, sir," Eddie said to me. Then he and his backup headed off into the crowd.

"May I have a moment of your time, Luz?"

She tossed her head at me, rather like a palomino. "Want me to dance for you?"

"Just talk."

She glanced longingly over her bare shoulder at the suits stacked four deep at the bar, then doubtfully down at Lulu, who was huddled between my feet. Finally, her eyes fell on the fifty in my hand, and that made her mind up, no problem.

She sat. "Are you like a friend of his?"

"We went to school together."

"You the one goes with Merilee Nash?"

"Why, yes."

She nodded. "Sure, he talks about you all the time. Your name's like Yogi or Bogie or—"

"Close enough," I said, my eyes getting used to the presence of her naked breasts across the table from me. And you do get used to them. Because you are so surrounded by them. And because it's all so impersonal. "What does he say about me?"

"That you was a very famous writer."

"It's true. I was."

"No, no," she said apologetically. "I don't talk so good sometimes. I wasn't saying you aren't one no more. Like, I'm sure you are."

"I guess you don't get many publishers in here."

A waitress appeared now. When a dancer sits they show. Luz ordered a cranberry juice and soda. I ordered a Rolling Rock. At the bar, Tuttle was still in line.

At my feet, Lulu started sneezing furiously from all of the perfume in the air. She's allergic to any number of them, especially anything musky or Calviny. I would regret this later. Her sinuses would clog up. She would sleep on my head. She would snore. Oh yes, I would regret this. I removed Grandfather's silver cigarette case from my inside jacket pocket and offered her one of her allergy pills. They are small. They are for her own good. Usually, she will take one without a fight. Not this time. Stubborn? Unless you've spent time around a basset hound you don't know the meaning of the word. I tried Plan B, the one where I pry her jaws apart, chuck the pill down her gullet and massage her throat until she swallows it. Nothing doing. She has an amazingly strong jaw. This called for Plan C—insert pill directly into right or left nostril of large black nose. Wait for her to schnarfle it back into my hand, relaxing her jaw in the process. Shoot pill down throat before she can clamp it tightly shut again.

And everyone thinks she's the brains of the outfit.

"You okay now, honey?" Luz arched an eyebrow at me.

"Oh, I wouldn't go that far."

"How come you got your little dog with you anyway?"

"She likes to party."

"I never heard of that. That's so cute."

"Believe me, it gets old fast."

Our waitress returned now with our drinks. Luz reached for hers and somehow managed to grip it—her orange fingernails were at least an inch long. She took a sip. At the table next to ours, a hardworking little blonde was earnestly air-humping a middle-aged guy's knee. She reminded me of a frisky cockapoo my parents had when I was a boy.

"What happened between you and Tuttle, Luz?"

She thought this over, running her tongue around the rim of her glass. "Like, we went out a few times, okay? And he seemed pretty nice and all, if you like older guys. Oh, hey, I'm not trying to insult you or nothing."

"I know you're not, Luz. That's the sad part."

"Huh?"

"You went out a few times . . ."

"Only I tol' him to stop calling me, on account of it got weird, okay? If it was just the handcuffs, that woulda been one thing. Only he wanted to get rough, too."

"Rough, how?"

She shifted uncomfortably in her chair. "You know, where you tie a stocking around your throat and pull it so tight you almost choke. Makes it like a more intense orgasm."

"His or yours?"

"Huh?"

"Throat. His or yours?"

"Mine, for damned sure." She fingered it. It was a lovely throat, creamy and unlined. "You ever know a guy who liked to do punishment to himself?"

"I guess you don't get many writers in here either."

The little blonde was done dancing now. She put her leg up on her customer's chair. He put a twenty in her garter. There were a lot of twenties stuffed in her garter. Up on the stage, another stripper was at work. Same disco beat.

"I tol' him no way, okay?" Luz went on. "Like, I ain't about that shit. And that's when he gave me a black eye. I had to call in sick for three nights. And now I just want he should leave me alone, only he *won't*. He keeps coming by, bothering me. He even . . ." She hesitated.

"He even what, Luz?"

"I feel like I'm being followed," she blurted out. "I mean, I *am*. Like, he's following me, okay?"

A cold chill went through me. "Are you sure it's Tuttle?"

"Well, yeah. Who else would it be?"

I looked around the room. It was crowded with restless men. Unhappy men. Salivating men. "Working in a place like this, I would think it could be just about anyone."

"Oh, no. Uh-uh. I'm real careful. We all are. You never tell him your last name. You never tell him where you live.

Uh-uh. No way. It's Tuttle. I know it is." She glanced over her bare shoulder again at the bar. He was still there, ordering now. She leaned across the table toward me, our drinks all but disappearing beneath her silicone wonders. "Look, you seem pretty okay. And he kind of listens to you. Can I be straight here?"

"You can."

"I've met someone else, okay? And he's nice and he's got a good job and it's pretty serious. So I'm thinking I wanna get out of this. Not that I been deceiving him. He knows I'm an entertainer and everything. And he says it's okay with him. Only, this life makes you kind of hard if you don't get out in time. I got nineteen thousand saved up. I want to go to college, become like a nurse." She looked across the table at me imploringly. "Y'know what I'm saying?"

The stripper up on the stage finished her dance now to a smattering of applause. The throbbing disco died. Briefly, there was quiet.

"Yes, Luz, I believe I do. You want Tuttle Cash out of your life."

"That's right," she said, relieved that I understood. "That's it."

"He often has that effect on people—particularly women."

He had made his score at the bar. Four shots of whiskey cradled carefully in one big hand, four bottles of Rolling Rock in the other. Slowly, he started his lurching journey back across the club toward us. Only, he wasn't going to manage it and he knew it, so he stopped to dispose of one of the shots. And then another one.

I turned back to Luz and her swollen orange lips. "What kind of lipstick is that you have on?"

"It's Solar Sunburst by Maybelline. I do my whole look myself, y'know, on account of I got a flair for design." She sipped her cranberry spritzer. "Why you asking?"

"It's most becoming." If you like orange. Only it was the

wrong brand of orange. The answer man was a Revlon man. What did that mean? What did any of it mean? Was Tuttle stalking her? Was she in danger?

I looked around for him but he seemed to have disappeared. Possibly under a table somewhere. I took a sip of my Rolling Rock. I glanced at the tab and was suitably outraged. I reached for my wallet. And then I heard it:

I heard Ethel Merman singing "There's No Business Like Show Business."

It's true, The King was up there on the stage of Ten's belting out his old dining hall showstopper at the top of his lungs. The man was singing it. The man was shaking it. The man was stripping it. Off came the jacket and tie, then the shirt. He flung them out into the audience.

Luz gasped in horror. I guess Tuttle hadn't shared all of his hidden talents with her. And you don't find a lot of Ethel Merman fans anymore among the young.

There were a few half-hearted snickers from the crowd. One guy called out, "Go for it, Tut!" Mostly, there was indifference. They had come to look at the babes, not some beefy ex-jock with too much booze in him. Mostly, Tuttle was just plain ignored.

Except by the bouncers, of course. Three of them were on him before he could get his pants off. One of them was Eddie, who'd come to Luz's rescue. They hustled him off the stage to our table. Tuttle was cackling with delight.

"I'm afraid I'll have to ask you gentlemen to leave," Eddie informed me while the other two tried to wrestle Tuttle back into his shirt and jacket. "I warned you, we can't tolerate any disturbances."

"I have no problem with that," I assured Eddie pleasantly. "We were just leaving, as it happens. Come on, Tuttle. Let's get out of here."

Tuttle stood his ground. He had that zonked, disoriented look on his face again. "What, you want to leave?"

"I want to leave."

"Oh, okay. Sure, Doof. Whatever you say." He was looking at Luz. He was smiling at her. She was not smiling back
at him.

Eddie grabbed his arm. "Okay, let's go."

Tuttle's eyes instantly turned to angry blue pinpoints.
"Get . . . your . . . hands off of me."

"I said let's go," Eddie persisted, steering Tuttle toward
the front door.

"And I said get your fucking hands off of me!" Tuttle
snarled. "Don't you know who I am? I am The King."

One of the bouncers snorted. "Fucker thinks he's Elvis."

"Actually, he is somebody," said the other. "Played ball, I
think."

Eddie moved in closer. "Let's talk about it outside, Mr.
Presley, okay? We don't want any trouble."

Tuttle nodded his head obediently. "Oh, okay. Why
didn't you say so? You don't want any trouble." To me he
said, "He doesn't want any trouble." To Luz he said, "Not a
problem. I understand completely."

I saw the punch coming from a mile away. I don't know
how Eddie didn't. Maybe good bouncers are hard to find
these days. All I know is that Tuttle's right caught Eddie
flush on the nose, staggering him. Blood spurted from Eddie's nose. A lot of blood. This made Eddie mad. A lot of
mad.

It certainly didn't help that Tuttle was standing there
laughing at him.

One of the other bouncers pinned Tuttle's arms back
while Eddie rammed a huge fist into his belly. An animal
groan came out of Tuttle. Then he went completely limp,
his face ashen. They hustled him toward the door, his feet
trailing along feebly behind him.

"Well, I guess we'll be leaving now, Luz," I said. "Real
nice meeting you."

"Nice meeting you, too, honey," she said. "You got man-
ners. You can come back anytime. I'll show you my moves."

I gave her my card in case she ever needed to reach me. Friends of Tuttle often needed to reach out to each other. Then I strolled out with Lulu prancing along ahead of me. She was downright jolly now. She loves to get thrown out of places. Gives her something to brag on to the other dogs in the elevator of our building. Most of them lead boring, predictable lives.

Tuttle was causing another scene at the front door. The man wanted his coat. They were having none of it. Just tossed him out onto the cold, wet sidewalk. They did it extra-rough, like he was a no-good, penniless, stinking bum.

"Was that absolutely necessary?" I asked Eddie.

"That crazy fucker *hit* me!" Eddie howled in response, fingering his bloody nose. He was big, but he wasn't tough. "Don't come back, mister. You aren't welcome here anymore."

"I'll try to mask my disappointment. May I have our coats?"

"Gimme the tabs. I'll have her bring 'em out."

Tuttle was on his hands and knees in the gutter, getting rid of his dinner. The cabbies who were standing around there waiting for fares were having a good, mean chuckle over it.

Yes, the crowd was roaring, all right. With laughter.

The girl who'd checked our coats came outside with them, Eddie standing watch in the doorway. I gave her a couple of bucks and put mine on. Then I helped Tuttle to his feet and she handed him his. My own turn to be stupid. I forgot what was in his coat pocket. He sure didn't—went right for the Smith & Wesson and took dead aim at Eddie with it. I dove for Tuttle just as he was about to fire, tackling him hard to the pavement. I didn't stop him from getting off the shot. But I did mess up his aim. Instead of taking out Eddie he took out one of the smoked-glass doors. Pebbled safety glass cascaded everywhere. A security alarm wailed.

I wrestled the gun away from him and pocketed it. And

then the two of us did the only thing that proper, well-bred gentlemen can do under such circumstances.

We ran, Tuttle limping noticeably on his bad knee. But the bastard was still faster than I was. And Lulu was faster than both of us. She was waiting for us at the Jag, Eddie and the other bouncer bringing up the rear by half a block, bellowing curses at us. We jumped in and sped off, Tuttle cackling again, happy as a clam.

"I cannot believe this," I said, when I'd caught my breath. "I tackled you to the ground. I actually brought Tuttle Cash down."

"Hey, put it back in your pants, rookie. I'm half the man I used to be."

"Don't be so hard on yourself, Tuttle. You're six tenths, easy."

"May I have my gun back now?"

"You may not." But I did give him my linen handkerchief to wipe his mouth with. "Did you pay for those drinks with a credit card?"

"No, I lost them all when I declared bankruptcy. Why?"

"They'll try to make you pay for that door, that's why."

"Let them try."

"They can sue you."

"They can get in line," he said, without apology or regret. For him, lawsuits were just one of those things you ended up with in life, like ingrown toenails.

A red light stopped us at Twenty-first and Broadway. The Flatiron Building sliced through the night sky overhead. I stifled a yawn and glanced at Grandfather's Rolex. It was three-thirty. Tuttle still didn't seem the least bit inclined to pack it in.

"I want meat," he declared lustily. "Meat and wine for my troops."

"Where does that come from, anyway? I've always wondered."

"My appetite?"

"Your Ethel Merman."

"I never told you?"

"You never told me."

He thumbed his chin thoughtfully. "Well, I guess I know you well enough by now . . ."

"I guess you do."

Tuttle winked at me. "I'm her illegitimate son, Doof."

And who's to say he wasn't.

I took us to Billy's, a crusty-old-workingman's steak house on Gansevoort and Ninth Avenue in the heart of the whole-sale meat packing district, where the streets are still cobbled and the stench of beef never leaves the air. Billy's stays open all night: In that neighborhood, there's always someone coming off work or going to work. There's sawdust on the floor, a tin ceiling, a battered mahogany bar. A pair of gnarled old citizens were perched on stools there, drinking up whiskey. A much younger couple sat at one of the tables, drinking up each other. He had on a tuxedo. She wore his topcoat over her formal gown. Both of them looked trembly and grave and sixteen.

We ordered T-bones and eggs and coffee. Tuttle asked for a shot of brandy to go with his coffee. Lulu elected to snooze in the car. It was well past her bedtime, and there was nothing on Billy's menu to interest her.

"Why are we doing this, Doof?" Tuttle said, attacking his food hungrily.

"I'm beginning to wonder about that myself," I said, chewing on my steak. "The meat here is a lot tougher than it used to be."

"I mean, why are you hanging around with me?"

"I'm beginning to wonder about that, too." I pushed my plate away. "Tuttle, why are you following Luz?"

"Luz?" He frowned at me, befuddled. "I'm not following Luz."

"She says you are."

"Well, she's wrong."

"Uh-huh."

He raised his chin at me. "That's all you have to say—'Uh-huh'?"

"What do you want me to say?"

"That you believe me would be nice."

"Uh-huh."

He shrugged his big shoulders and went back to work on his steak. Cleaned his plate, sat back with his coffee. "I know of an after-hours club on Eleventh Avenue that has a pool table. How about we head on over there? I'll kick your butt."

"And what will you kick it with? I understood you to be broke."

He mulled this over, poking at the bone on his plate with his steak knife. "Okay, I got it," he exclaimed, brandishing the knife and a devilish grin. "You lose, I get to cut off one of your pinkies." This was like out of the old days. Always, there was some crazy dare. Always, there was someone fool enough to take it. Me, usually.

"No chance."

"Don't tell me you're wimping out on me, Doof."

"Okay, I won't tell you."

"Chicken," he jeered. Honestly, the man hadn't matured one bit in twenty years. Not like me. "Pussy."

"That's me, all right. A great, big ten-fingered pussy."

And then suddenly his jaw went slack and he was off pursuing his post-graduate degree at Catatonic State again. It seemed to come and go with him, like a tide. "You don't have to worry about me, Doof." His voice was almost a whisper now, his eyes glassy. "I just wondered, that's all. What it would feel like to have your life in your hands. But I won't do it, honest. I'm fine."

"Sure you are, Tuttle. We're all fine."

"Hey, Doof?"

"Yes, Tuttle?"

He motioned for me to lean closer. I did. "Who's The King?"

I sighed inwardly. "You are, Tuttle. Come on, I'll run you home."

Tuttle Cash lived in the bottom two floors of a rose-colored-brick town house on East Sixty-fifth Street. For me, Tuttle's place had always been the ultimate New York bachelor apartment. There was a living room with a working fireplace and built-in bookcases and comfortable leather chairs. There was a gourmet kitchen, a snug dining room. Out back a private garden with a patio, a fountain, a shed for firewood and garden tools. Upstairs, there was a paneled study with more bookcases and floor-to-ceiling windows. The master bedroom suite overlooked the garden. Tuttle's place was exactly the sort of place I thought I'd live in when I came to New York to be a writer. Who knew that only in Hollywood movies did struggling young writers live this way. Who knew that the tab on a place like this was $4,500 a month, which explained why Tuttle was three months behind and on the verge of losing it.

"Care for a nightcap, Doof?" he asked when we pulled up out front. He seemed totally alert now.

"All right."

Lulu groused at me unhappily. She wanted to be home in her nice warm bed. I insisted she join us. We're a team. If I work, she works.

One wall of Tuttle's living room used to be nothing but his trophies and awards and magazine covers. No longer. The living room walls were completely bare now, except for a framed black-and-white photograph that hung over the fireplace. It was a portrait of Tansy standing against a rough fieldstone wall with her hands thrust deep into the pockets of a rakish tweed blazer. She was all cheekbones and attitude, a faintly mocking smile on her lips, her lush blond hair thrown carelessly over one shoulder. It reminded me very much of a

Hollywood portrait that the great George Hurrell took of
Carole Lombard in the late thirties. I had never seen this
picture before. It was superb.

"Who took it, Tuttle?"

"I did," he said offhandedly.

"I wasn't aware that you took photographs."

"I don't anymore."

"Let me guess—not good enough, right?"

He limped toward the kitchen. "What'll it be?"

"What do you have?"

"I have brandy," he said.

"What else?"

"I have brandy," he said again.

"Mmm . . . make it a brandy."

I heard him open a cupboard in there. Then I heard a
crash of broken glass, followed by a heavy thud. I looked
down at Lulu. Lulu was looking up at me. I sighed and went
into the kitchen. Tuttle was good and passed out on the
kitchen floor with his mouth open, a saliva bubble forming
between his lips. Tracy does that, too. There were two broken glasses on the floor. No sign of any brandy. I cleaned up
the broken glass and put it in the trash. I dragged him by his
feet into the living room, wrestled him up onto the sofa and
threw his coat over him. I stared at him. Lulu stared at me,
wondering if this meant we could go home now.

It meant we could search. For the old Olivetti. For a
supply of manila envelopes and stick-on address labels. For
bloodstains on a rug, on a table lamp, on a lamp cord. For a
sign, one clear sign, that Diane Shavelson's murder had taken
place here.

It meant I could find out for sure.

The living room was tidy. No dust bunnies along the
baseboards. No finger smudges on the glass coffee table.
Clearly, someone came in to clean up after the man. There
was a matched pair of table lamps for reading. They were
ceramic jar lamps, squat and heavy and difficult to wield

one-handed. The shades were of white linen. Neither one looked crumpled or damaged. Or brand new, for that matter. Each had been yellowed by sunlight and time. Neither cord looked as if it had been replaced recently.

I found his trophies stashed in the narrow coat closet underneath the staircase. Two whole cartons' worth. The stubby little bronze fellow with the leather helmet was all by himself on the closet floor, his right arm poised to deliver that famous stiff arm. I picked him up, surprised by just how heavy he was. A Heisman Trophy weighs thirty-five pounds, in case you're wondering. I examined him for blood, for hair, for any sign he had been used as a weapon. Nothing. I put him back.

We went upstairs. Lulu took the bedroom. I took the study, with its immense walnut desk, its worn leather loveseat, its bookshelves lined with Tuttle's library of first editions. Tuttle was an ardent fan of what today's literary scholars and critics dismiss as "the dead white men." It's true, they are dead and they were white males. But at least they could write, which is more than I can say for today's literary scholars and writers. Tuttle collected them. Tuttle read them. He read Jack London and Rudyard Kipling and James Fenimore Cooper. He read John Buchan and Geoffrey Household and Graham Greene. He read the Tarzan novels by Edgar Rice Burroughs—although I noticed he had parted company with his much-prized complete set of A. C. McClurg & Co. firsts. These Tarzans were A. L. Burt reprints, worth many fewer zeroes.

He read Ring Lardner. He even owned a signed first edition of *You Know Me Al.* This Tuttle still had. This Tuttle had not sold. The book was right there on the shelf with his other volumes of Lardner. He owned them all.

The piece of paper upon which he had hand-scrawled his poem "As the Crowd Roars" was under glass there on his desk. The Olivetti was not on the desk. Nothing was, except for a brass gooseneck lamp. I examined this for blood or hair.

It told me nothing. I sat in the desk chair and started going through the drawers. I found overdue notices from the phone company and from Con Ed. I found a registered letter from the Internal Revenue Service, dated the previous June, informing him that he still owed them $21,356. I found a lined stenographer's pad that contained an assortment of doodles and random thoughts. On one page he had written, "Subject for short story—Doof. How does he keep going? Doesn't he fucking KNOW?" I stared at this a long time, then kept looking. I found his passport. He hadn't left the country in three years. London had been his last stop. I found a passionate love letter from a woman in San Francisco with whom he'd apparently had a fling a year ago. He had also borrowed a thousand dollars from her and not paid her back. I found an invitation to a football team reunion that had come and gone in September. I found a set of blue Tiffany's boxes that contained bundles of oyster-gray note-cards with his name engraved across the top in peacock blue. There were matching envelopes, too. Very proper. Very tasteful. Possibly he'd had a fling with Miss Manners, too.

I found no manila envelopes, no stick-on address labels, no typing paper. I went to the closet and opened it. He had stashed his darkroom equipment in there: an enlarger, trays, chemicals. I found no typewriter. I closed the closet door and looked around the room. And that's when my eyes fell on the suitcase. It was a gallant, battered old leather one, big as a steamer trunk and covered with decals from the *Queen Mary,* The Excelsior in Florence, The Dorchester in London, the Ritz Tower in New York. Tuttle used it as a coffee table, laid flat before the loveseat. Heavy leather straps kept it shut. I undid them, my heartbeat quickening. I had a feeling I would find something in there.

I did. But it wasn't the Olivetti. It was a zippered black leather portfolio, the kind that artists and photographers carry around. Inside of it there was a photo album—more black-and-white photos that he'd taken of Tansy. These were nude shots. They were not pretty nude shots. They were shots of Tansy spread-eagled on a bed, masturbating, her lips pulled back from her teeth in a savage snarl. Tansy chained to a radiator with a black stocking wrapped tightly around her throat and her eyes bulging from her head. Tansy on her hands and knees with alligator clips on her nipples and a plastic bag over her head, her face underneath twisted in horror. Tansy's body was beautiful, long and graceful and supple. But it was also bruised around the hips and arms, and there were scratches on her stomach and her hair was messed up and her eye makeup smeared. She looked zonked and miserable. Tuttle appeared in some of the photos. Sometimes he was a face in the mirror. Sometimes all I saw was his foot. Or his fist.

Why had he done this to her? Why had she let him? Was this any of my business? Definitely not. There are certain things you never want to know about other people, especially your friends. I felt voyeuristic. I felt dirty. I zipped the portfolio shut and threw it back in the suitcase. And then Lulu came in and nudged me in the leg with her head. She'd found something. I belted the suitcase shut and followed her into Tuttle's bedroom.

This particular room was not tidy. The bed was unmade. Clothing was strewn all over the floor. Dirty glasses and coffee cups were heaped on the nightstand. It smelled bad in there. It smelled like a lonely man's room. I know about that. I know what a lonely man's room smells like. I threw open a window. There was a *New York Post* on the floor by the bed, open to the pro-football betting lines. Several games were circled in red pencil. But it wasn't the point spread on the Dolphins-Chiefs game Lulu was intent on showing me. It was something in the closet.

It was the garment bags. There were three of them. They were big and they were blue and they were from Hold Everything.

I told her she was a good girl. She agreed as how she was.

Then she waited for me to make my next move. I seemed nailed to the floor. Didn't know why. What was I expecting to find inside those zippered bags—more attractive single women with blue faces and nice smiles? . . . *What do we have for our contestants, Johnny . . . ?* I took a deep breath and unzipped one and flung it open.

It held Tuttle's summer wardrobe—his seersuckers and khakis. His tropical worsteds were in the next bag I opened, his linen slacks and shirts in the third. I zipped them all back up and closed the closet door and asked myself what the hell I was going to do now. Should I give Tuttle up? Okay, he belonged to the Manhattan Fitness Center. Okay, he was into rough sex. Okay, he owned some Hold Everything garment bags. Did this make him the answer man? Where was the typewriter? What about the fucking typewriter? And what if I was wrong? What if Tuttle Cash had nothing whatsoever to do with these deaths? Could he handle a police probe? How about the media crawling all over him, gnawing on him, devouring him? Christ, I'd found the man with his gun in his mouth. What if I pushed him over the edge?

How much more proof did I need? How much?

He was still snoring away on the sofa under his coat. Dawn was growing near. I could just about make out the shape of the fountain outside the sliding glass door. I kicked off my shoes and loosened my tie and sprawled out in one of the leather chairs. With a grunt, Lulu climbed into my lap. Briefly, I slept. In my dreams I kept seeing those awful photographs of Tansy. Only it was *Tracy's* face I was seeing, not hers. It was my baby with a plastic bag over her head. It was my baby with her eyes bugging out.

I awoke with a start. Tuttle and Lulu were snoring in stereo. A weak winter sun was slanting in the glass door. I glanced at Grandfather's Rolex. It was seven. Outside, they were picking up the trash. Horns were honking. Another day. I yawned and nudged Lulu. She woke up but wouldn't move. I nudged her again. She got down, grumbling. I got up, grumbling. My back ached, my knees ached, my eyes ached. Plus my left elbow was all swollen from tackling Tuttle to the pavement outside Ten's. Stiffly, I hobbled into the kitchen in search of coffee. I found some beans in the freezer. I was looking for the grinder, and not having any luck, when I heard a noise. Only, it wasn't Tuttle.

It was somebody trying to get in the front door.

Nine

THEY HAD a key.

Both keys. One to the Medeco deadbolt lock that was drilled into the door. The other to the lock that was in the doorknob, which was turning now. The door swung open. Lulu growled. I shushed her. Tuttle just kept on snoring.

"Hey-hey-hey!" a familiar voice called out. "If you got the java, I got the buns!"

It was Malachi Medvedev, all chipper and combed and cologned. He was an Aqua Velva man, in case you're interested. He carried a bakery bag and a package of shirts from the laundry. Also that morning's papers. I could make out the front page of the *Daily News,* which hadn't played up the answer man one bit. All they did was give over the entire front page to three giant black question marks.

"How are you, Mal?" I said to him from the kitchen doorway.

"Fan-fucking-tastic," he replied brightly, looking me up

and down. "Hoagy, you look like shit. What'd you do, try to keep up with The King?"

"Something like that."

"Bad idea. He can drink 'em all under the table. Even the ol' Mick himself back when the Mick still had it going." Malachi took off his coat and came bustling into the kitchen with his packages. He put them down on the counter and went right for the coffee grinder, which was in a cupboard over the refrigerator. I felt sure I would have found it within two hours. The only hard part would have been lifting either arm that high. He ground some beans and dumped them into a Melita filter. He put a kettle on to boil. He said, "I thought you two parted on bad terms."

"Who, me and Mickey Mantle?"

"You and Tuttle."

"We patched things up. Kind of."

Malachi nodded approvingly. "That's nice. I like to see that. Only, why didn't you go home? Wait, you had a fight with Merilee, am I right?" He wagged a pudgy finger at me. "You pulled a Hugh Grant on her, am I right?"

"You are not."

"Then what are you doing here at seven o'clock in the morning?"

"I was just about to ask you that, Mal."

"I keep an eye on him, like I told ya." He took the package of shirts into the hall and put them on a table next to the stairs. That's when he spotted Tuttle there on the sofa. "You didn't put him to bed? I always put him to bed."

"I considered it a major accomplishment to get him from the kitchen floor to the living room."

Malachi shook his head at me, clucking. "Man needs to sleep in his bed. Otherwise his back stiffens up."

"Poor baby," I said, arching my own back.

"Gimme a hand," he commanded. "C'mon, c'mon. Let's go."

Malachi grabbed Tuttle's feet. I took him by the shoulders, which meant I was the one who got to walk backward up the curving stairs lugging Tuttle and his two hundred-plus pounds of dead meat. But it was no problem at all. Really it wasn't. And Lulu made it so much easier by scampering up and down the stairs between us, barking incessantly. Just her own endearing way of saying thanks for keeping her out all night.

Tuttle, by the way, didn't so much as stir during any of this procedure. The man knew how to sleep, I'll give him that.

We tossed him onto his unmade bed. Malachi undid Tuttle's belt and pulled his pants off him, exposing his puffy, hideously scarred knee. He threw the covers over him, shooting a perturbed look at the window. "Who opened that? Man'll catch his death. He's very susceptible to colds." Malachi stormed over to the window and slammed it shut, clucking to himself some more. He was acting real fussy and territorial about me being there. His role as Tuttle's keeper was very important to him.

We went back downstairs. The water was boiling now. Malachi poured some over the grounds. While it dripped through he got a broom out and went to work on the kitchen floor. This scared Lulu away. She's deathly afraid of brooms. Don't ask me why. She's deathly afraid of many things.

There must have been something in the *Daily News* that wasn't about the answer man, but I sure couldn't find it. How he'd struck again, swiftly and brutally. How Inspector Dante Feldman and his special task force were toiling around the clock to catch him. How he, Feldman, was urging anyone who might have witnessed anything to come forward. They ran the number of the hotline. Also the profile of the answer man that Feldman had wanted to release—that this was a good-looking, intelligent white male in his twenties or thirties, physically fit, new to the city, interested in becoming a novelist or screenwriter. They ran choice snippets of the material that he'd been sending me. The most chilling was featured in raised type across the top of page three:

> There are so many more Bridgets out there in the offices and health clubs and bars of New York City, and I have so much more work ahead of me.

There was a nice, big story about me and how I was the killer's go-between. That's what they were calling me—his go-between. And Cassandra Dee got major play, too, for being out ahead of the pack, scoop after scoop. "It's just a whole lotta shoe leather and luck," she explained modestly. There was a story on Tibor Farkas, the boyfriend of Laurie London, and how he had passed a lie detector test and was no longer considered a suspect (but was being considered as a substitute host for *The Grind* on MTV). There were extensive profiles of the three victims, interviews with their families and friends. There were profiles of David Berkowitz, Ted Bundy, John Wayne Gacy, Jeffrey Dahmer. Interviews with the families and friends of their victims.

Most impressive, really. The entire staff of the paper must have worked all night on it. Not a surprise. About the only time print people show what they are capable of doing anymore is when they are handed a hurricane or a good, meaty serial killer. The rest of the time they just cruise on automatic pilot, living on handouts from the creeps, clowns and con men who pass for our leaders these days.

I was very interested in the name of the law firm where Bridget Healey had worked before she got laid off. The law firm where she had gotten herself involved with some older man. The *News* didn't have it. The *Post* did. It was Ryan, Angelico and Parks—not Fine, Weinberger. So much for that theory. Still . . .

In case you're wondering, *The New York Times* did run my personal ad at the bottom of page one in their usual tiny agate type. It was totally inconspicuous. I doubted anyone besides the answer man would even notice it.

I tossed the papers aside and said, "If you look out for him, Mal, then why did you give him his gun back?"

Malachi's moist brown eyes widened with surprise. "Jeez, I didn't. Left it under the bar with strict instructions to my backup, Tootie, not to give it to him."

"And?"

"I guess Tootie give it to him. Why, did he shoot somebody?"

"He tried to. Took out the front door at Ten's."

"That's my boy," exclaimed Malachi, chuckling merrily. "Ready for coffee?"

"Desperately."

He poured. We drank. There were Danish in the bakery bag. We helped ourselves. Malachi stayed on one side of the counter, I stayed on the other. He was a career bartender. It felt unnatural to talk to him any other way.

"You do this every morning, Mal?" I asked, glancing at the broom.

"Pretty much," he replied, munching. "Man used to have a Puerto Rican woman came in a couple, two-three times a week, only she stopped coming when he stopped paying her."

I sipped my coffee. "You must have to leave Queens before dawn to get here by seven."

Malachi didn't respond, unless you call blushing a response. The little man's whole head turned the color of a ripe tomato.

"I understand you left the bar early last night."

He stuck out his lower lip like a petulant child. "I didn't think he noticed."

"He didn't. I did."

"You was there? I didn't see you."

"Oddly enough, when I phoned your wife she said—"

"Muriel said what?" he demanded.

"Muriel said she didn't know when you'd be home." I hadn't actually called his wife, of course. But I'm often at my most devious on little or no sleep. "She said that a lot of nights you don't come home at all."

"Okay, you win, Hoagy." Malachi grinned at me sheepishly. "Got me a Filipino girl stashed in a place in the East Fifties. Nice, clean-cut young girl."

"How young, Mal?"

"She's twenty-three."

I stared at him.

He caved. "Okay, she's nineteen. At least, she *looks* nineteen. And Christ, Hoagy, when she sucks on my toes I just about—"

"I don't need to hear this part."

"I'm helping her get her green card," he said.

"And your wife?"

"No problem there. Muriel was born in this country."

"I meant—"

"Got that all covered. She thinks I'm sleeping over here with Tuttle. Y'know, keeping my eye on him. Which I am, as you can see. Only I'm also at my place with Coochie."

"Coochie?"

It's shockingly easy to make a middle-aged man blush when he's gone gaga over a teenager. Malachi reddened again. "What I call her. Yolanda's her real name."

"I see. And where is this place you and Coochie have together?"

"The East Fifties, like I told ya." He turned chilly on me. "Why are you asking me so many questions? What is all this?"

"I want to know where I can reach you if there's an emergency."

Now Malachi Medvedev got downright hostile. "Little bit late in the fourth quarter for this, isn't it?"

"For what?"

"You feeling guilty."

"Me feeling guilty for what?"

"Taking Tansy's side over his."

"I didn't take anyone's side, Mal."

"Didn't you?" he said angrily. Clearly, this had been on his mind for some time.

"No, I didn't. And believe me, that wasn't easy—*she's* the one who needed all of those operations, not Tuttle."

"If you didn't take sides, then tell me this, Hoagy. Where the hell you been these past couple of years when he needed you?"

"Taking care of myself."

We fell into sudden silence.

"Yeah, well, I guess that's what we all do," Malachi conceded. "Can't blame you for that. But why don't you do the man a favor now and butt out, huh? We're doing okay."

"If this is your idea of okay I'd sure hate to try on lousy for size."

"Some days are better than others. Time's all he needs."

"Time's running out, Mal. Which reminds me . . ." I went and got the gun out of my coat pocket and came back with it and laid it on the counter between us. It looked like a giant, dead bug there. "Like I said before, don't let him play with this anymore."

Malachi looked down at it, then back up at me. "He's down but he's not out, Hoagy. The King's a survivor, if that makes you feel any better."

"It doesn't, Mal. It doesn't make me feel any better at all."

It was clear and bright and frigid outside. The Land Rover was parked across the street in front of the Jag, Vic dozing behind the wheel. I unlocked the Jag and let Lulu in. Then I tapped on the Rover's windshield gently. You never want to startle someone who has a metal plate in his head, especially someone who is six-feet-six and very likely armed.

Vic opened his eyes slowly, peering out at me dumbly through the windshield. He didn't seem to remember where he was. Or even who he was. Briefly, this seemed to panic him. But then the panic subsided, and he rolled down the window, blinking at me. "All quiet, Hoag?"

"I don't know if I'd go that far." I filled him in on the night's activities and told him what I'd found out about Malachi's child concubine.

"I don't know what it is with these middle-aged guys and their lollipops," he droned at me disapprovingly. "Why would you want to spend your free time talking to some stupid teenager?"

"Call me crazy, Vic, but I don't think they spend a lot of their time talking. He got a little vague when I asked him exactly where it is he keeps her. Might be worth looking into."

Vic yawned. He rubbed his eyes. "I'll nose around at the bar tonight while I'm keeping an eye on Cash. See what I can find out."

"Good. You going to make it, Vic?"

"Sure, Hoag. You can count on me." His eyes examined my face with concern. "Are *you* okay?"

"Why do you ask?"

"I guess you haven't looked in a mirror lately."

I climbed in the Jag and started it up and got a good look at myself in the rearview mirror. I didn't look bad at all. I looked terrific for a guy who, say, had just been pulled out of a mine after having been buried alive for five days. I looked hollow-eyed and pasty, like my brains had been fried. I looked like I felt.

The apartment seemed uncommonly tranquil when I came in. The sounds of the morning traffic down on Central Park West were muted and far away. The loudest thing going on was the ticking of the tall clock in the entry hall. Pam wasn't up and about yet. Tracy was still sound asleep in the nursery, safe and snug. As for Merilee, a hand-lettered sign was taped to our bedroom door: To WHOM THIS MAY CONCERN—REHEARSED WITH LUKE UNTIL 5 A.M. AWAKEN ME BEFORE NOON UPON PENALTY OF DEATH.

I opened the door quietly and carried Lulu in so that the scrabbling of paws on parquet wouldn't awaken her. Of course, she was burrowed so deep under the down comforter you could barely tell she was even in there. This was not a positive sign. Merilee always sleeps like a mole when a show is going badly, her blond head rooted halfway down the bed—far, far away from her pillow, from her director, from her demanding public. Not to mention oxygen. I never could figure out how she breathed down there. Lulu curled up with a grateful grunt on her mommy's hip, or maybe it was her mommy's head. Poor girl was totally pooped from our latest, most excellent adventure. She wasn't even up for Barney Greengrass. And for Lulu, that is serious.

I was rummaging through the closet for clean clothes when I heard a snarfle of the noncanine variety, followed by a deep, slow intake of breath. The mound of covers rose and fell. "You smell of cigar smoke," intoned a voice from the great, muffled beyond. "Also beer. Gallons and gallons of beer."

"Imported or domestic?"

"And *perfume*. Cheap perfume, cheaper perfume, *still* cheaper perfume . . . My Lord, where have you two been all night? Wait, don't answer that."

"I wasn't planning to."

She groped her way out from her hidey-hole of flannel and goosedown. First I saw a hand, then an entire arm, then out came the tousled blond hair. She squinted up at me, eyes puffy from sleep. "Isn't it amazing, darling, how keen my other senses have grown?"

"Amazing." I sat down on the bed and took her in my arms and hugged her tightly.

She hugged me back, all snuggly and warm. "You've learned something disturbing, haven't you?"

"Have you also learned how to read minds, Miss Nash?"

"Yours is a snap. It's your eyes."

"What about them, are they hopeless?"

"Mournful is more like it. But that's only natural, what with all these years you've spent around Lulu."

One tuckered thump of the tail greeted this, nothing more.

Merilee gazed at me curiously, her forehead creasing. "What is it, darling?"

"Tuttle took nude pictures of Tansy. It was raw stuff, Merilee. Ugly stuff."

She looked away. "Yes, I know. She told me about them."

"She did? When?"

"Years ago. When they were doing it."

"What did she tell you?"

"That she found it *different.*" Merilee reached over and stroked Lulu thoughtfully. "Tansy was always the one to try new things, darling. She was the wild child at Miss Porter's. The first to take drugs, the first to go all the way with a boy. Anything for a laugh."

"She wasn't laughing in these pictures."

"I've always wondered . . ." Merilee hesitated, coloring slightly. "What I mean is, how does Tansy *look* in them, darling? Does she look pretty?"

"She looks like a sad little girl."

"She *is* a sad little girl. And he's a mean, sick, dirty man. He enjoyed hurting her."

"Did she enjoy being hurt?"

"No woman enjoys that. Some of us merely delude ourselves into believing we somehow deserve it." She yawned and plumped her pillows and sat back against them. "I assumed Tuttle would have bragged to you about them."

"Well, he didn't." I sat there on the edge of the bed, feeling used and lousy. "We really don't know them at all, do we?"

"Darling, no one knows anyone. Look at us. I'm an actress, you're a writer. We like to believe we understand other people, that we can shed light on them, ennoble them. It's how we earn our livings. But we're total frauds, Hoagy. The truth is that no one understands anyone. We are all strangers to one another, each of us frightened and alone, groping blindly in the darkness.''

I tugged at my left ear. "Trouble with the play, Merilee?"

She sighed grandly, tragically. "It's the absolute berries, Hoagy. I keep hoping and praying that we're getting closer. But every time it seems as if we are—*kerchunk*—it slips right through our fingers."

"Sounds familiar."

"It's somethin' arful."

"Want breakfast?"

"Sleep." She burrowed back into her warm, comfy cave. "I want *sleep.*"

I showered and stropped Grandfather's razor and used it. Dressed in the dark brown wide-wale corduroy suit over an ivory cashmere turtleneck. By now Pam had put on the coffee and started making her scones. Pam's always raring to go in the morning. I hope I'm that way when I get to be her age. Actually, I just hope I get to be her age.

I had a fistful of phone messages from the night before. Cassandra had called to double her offer to me. The other toxic tabloid shows called to see her offer and raise it by however many zeroes I chose. Each of the New York daily newspapers called. So had each of the network news shows, CNN, *Time* and *Newsweek*. My agent called twice. First to tell me that no less than five reputable publishers were interested in seeing the answer man's novel in progress. Then to tell me that one of those editors whom I'd had lunch with, the one with the ponytail, was also keenly interested in my idea for that submarine novel.

I stuffed them all in my pocket and poured myself some coffee.

"Wherever did Victor go off to so early?" Pam asked me.

"I have him on a job. Surveillance work."

"Yes, yes, I see. This would explain why he was out until two last night, I suppose."

"It would."

"It's not dangerous work, is it?"

"Not on his part, no."

"Good. Victor's no youngster anymore, Hoagy. He needs his rest."

I glanced at her. She seemed unduly concerned about him. "Pam, he's not sick or something, is he?"

"Why, no. Why do you ask that?"

"He wanted to talk to me about something personal. And now here you are acting all motherly."

"I am not acting motherly," she said frostily.

"What's wrong with him, Pam?"

"Nothing, dear boy. Not a thing." Abruptly, she changed the subject. "Can I get you anything? Stewed fruit, perhaps?"

"Never touch it."

"You might wish to reconsider." She raised an eyebrow at me tartly. "You look as if you could use it."

What I could use was a one-hour rubdown followed by ten solid hours in Merilee's burrow with her. What I got was a brisk walk over to Barney Greengrass all by my damned self. Although first I had to lose the media, who by now were crowded onto the sidewalk outside of our building, starved for their morning fix. Not a problem. I took the elevator down to the basement and ducked out by way of the service entrance. I was not spotted. A stiff wind had picked up, the kind that seems to blow in directly from wherever it is in Northern Canada that all of that pure bottled spring water and crystal-clear beer are supposed to come from. Me, I think they come from Weehawken, New Jersey. I turned up the collar of my greatcoat, turned down the brim of my hat, buried my chin in my scarf. I walked, people staring at me as I passed by them. I may have been muttering to myself. I can't be sure.

I have a new definition of the word "lame." "Lame" is me sitting all morning at a wired table in Barney Greengrass waiting for the answer man to show up when I damned well knew he wouldn't. "Lame" is Detective Lieutenant Romaine Very standing behind the counter in an apron and silly white paper hat pretending he actually knew how to slice smoked fish when there are maybe twelve men in all of New York City who do—and not one of them is named Romaine.

But I sat there, me and the fleet of oh-so-obvious unmarked vans that was parked oh-so-casually outside. I had my Nova and cream cheese on a toasted bagel. I had my glass of orange juice. I had no stewed fruit. I sat there. The phone rang a few times. Delivery orders. Two little old ladies toddled in and spent an entire hour talking to each other about their gall bladders. Otherwise the place was so quiet you could have stretched out and taken a nap in there. Or at least I could have.

Until eleven-thirty, when the door flew open and in barged Cassandra Dee. She marched right over to my table, stripped off her camel's hair coat and plopped down in the chair opposite me. She had a blue blazer on over a gray gym shirt and torn jeans. "No luck, huh, cookie? Yeah, yeah, shewa. Dumb, he ain't. Gawd, I'm *stawved.* Hey, honey!" she called out to Very, who was shooting his own starved looks at her. "Gimme a bagel and a shmear, will ya? And maybe a nice little smoked chubb on the side!" To me she added, "I wouldn't mind his nice little smoked chubb on the side. I mean, ow, that boy is cut up and twisted."

A waiter brought the coffeepot over. He poured.

I said, "Cassandra, what are you doing here?"

She batted her eyelashes at me. "Cookie, why do you keep doubting me? I heard all about this little circle-jerk of Feldman's last night from my source. Thought you could use the company. Besides, they got the best smoked fish in town here. I oughta know. I'm one-eighth Jewish on Grandma Trigiani's side."

"You don't say."

Very brought her food over and put it down in front of

her. Then he took off his apron and his silly paper hat and he joined us. He wore a yellow Henley shirt unbuttoned to the chest, heavy wool lumberjack pants and an anxious expression. She stared at him with her poached-egg eyes, waiting for him to say something. He was waiting for me to say something.

I said, "Cassandra Dee, allow me to introduce Detective Lieutenant Romaine Very, Columbia College class of . . . what year did you graduate, Lieutenant?"

"Major thrill to meet you, Miss Dee," Very exclaimed. "I'm just a total fan."

"Oh, that's so fucking sweet," Cassandra simpered, going into major meltdown mode. "How's your sense of direction, cookie?"

"Decent." Very frowned at her. "Why?"

Cassandra licked her lips. "On account of I just go bonkers for a man who knows the southern—"

"Cassandra, behave yourself," I interjected sternly. "This is a family-hour broadcast."

She shot him a look. "Is this table wired, Lieutenant? Are youse putzes recording me without my prior knowledge or consent?"

"I didn't ask you to sit here," Very pointed out.

"And you didn't ask me not to, neither. Honey, you don't want to tangle with me. Nuttin' will be left when I'm done with you—I eat the bones, the head, everything. So don't you try to play cute."

Very glowered at her a moment before he reached under the table and yanked the wire out of operation. "Satisfied?"

"Not yet," she said sweetly, running a long red fingernail along his cheek. "But I got a feeling I'm gonna be soon. Hoagy did not tell me you was such a raw dog. I mean, you can be my stuff anytime. You don't even have to call. Just come knocking on my door, day or night. I'll know it's you."

"There you go again, Cassandra," I said. "Playing hard to get."

"You down for that?" she asked him. Me, she ignored.

"I'm down for whatever," he said, ducking his head bashfully.

"Ooooh, I just got shivers." She took a giant bite out of her bagel. "I got me a plan, Hoagy," she announced with her mouth full. "Wanna run it by you on account of you're still the master and I'm still the lowly peasant girl in a ragged dress and bare feet." She stabbed at the chubb with her fork, came away with a smoked morsel. "I'm gonna pull a Breslin on tonight's show."

"Bad idea, Cassandra," I said. "Really bad idea."

"Why?" she demanded.

Very said, "Wait, what's a Breslin?"

"I'm gonna offer the answer man my platform," she explained to him. "I want him to toin himself in to me, live, on the air." She turned back to me, puzzled. "I thought you'd love it. It's proactive. It's confrontational—"

"It's a self-promotional stunt, Cassandra."

"Wait, you say that like it's a bad thing."

"It's also dangerous. This guy has killed three women. You don't want to mess with him."

"It's my kind of move, Hoagy." She stuffed the rest of her bagel in her mouth. "I need this. My ratings need this."

"Don't do it."

"I'm doing it."

"You wanted my advice, I'm giving you my advice: Don't do it."

"Okay, okay, I'm hearing you now," she huffed. "Yeah, yeah, shewa. This is like a turf thing with you, am I right? You want him all to yourself."

"Turf has nothing to do with it, Cassandra."

"I'm flattered, you wanna know the truth. This means you actually think of me as a *rival* now. Someone you *respect*. Gawd, you paid me a compliment and you don't even know it. I mean, I'm sitting in a puddle here." She drained her coffee and got up and put on her coat. "You can't stop me, Hoagy. It's not your story anymore. It belongs to the woild now. It belongs to all of us. It's *news.*" She let out a yelp. "Gawd, I always wanted to say that!" She pointed a taloned finger at Very. "If I don't see you again I'm gonna hurt myself."

"You'll see me," Very vowed, grinning after her as she went flying out the door.

She did not offer to pay her share of the check, in case you were wondering.

"Jump back," Very gasped. "She's even more *her* in person than she is on TV."

"That, she is."

He eyed me cagily. "You two really get after it."

"That, we do."

"She's not yours, is she?"

"Mine, Lieutenant?"

"You doinking her?"

"No, I have never had that privilege."

"So, there's no reason I couldn't call her?"

"None that I can think of. Provided you're up to the task, as it were."

"Oh, I'm up to it, all right. I been up to it for so many months I'm about ready to—"

"Hold it. This sounds like a personal problem."

Very took out a piece of gum and unwrapped it and popped it in his mouth. He narrowed his eyes at me, jaw working on the gum. "Don't say it, dude."

"Don't say what, Lieutenant?"

"Don't say, I told you the answer man wouldn't show."

"Okay, I won't."

He looked away uneasily. "It's Feldman's investigation. We do it his way."

"Just out of curiosity, Lieutenant, how do you put up with that man?"

"My job to," he said. "What it is. Besides, they come mucho worse than him. Man can throw down. Must have had every decent-looking babe in the whole department out there last night posing as targets. He blanketed Manhattan. Plus that hotline's already pulling in phone calls by the hundred. And we're checking 'em out, too. Every single goddamned one of 'em."

"Any luck so far?"

"None," he confessed glumly. "Not with any of it. Gee who mops up around the pool at the M.F.C. thinks he saw Bridget swimming laps. But he don't remember her talking to any guy. Oh, hey . . ." Very had some official-looking papers folded in the back pocket of his pants. He smoothed them out on the table. "Got our boy's psychiatric profile from the shrinks this morning, if you're up for that."

"I am."

He squinted down at the blocks of type, running a finger along the page. "Okay, what it is . . . Overall, they rate him in the bright range in terms of intellectual function. His common sense, his vocabulary and his social intelligence rate high. Likewise his ability to differentiate essential from nonessential environmental details, meaning he perceives reality well. Only, dig, he also appears to be delusional. Believes his victims are deeply unhappy and that he alone is making them happy by his actions—'By performing his random act of kindness he is transferring his own inner turmoil onto them. By "healing" them he is attempting to heal himself.' Blah-blah-blah, blah-blah-blah . . . okay, dude, now check this out: 'There are signs of pathological elevation regarding paranoia. He displays no true, meaningful insight into his own motivation, hence his intellect may be split off from the rest of his personality, leaving him free to function without the context of his moral and emotional self.' " Very read a little more to himself, then stopped, running a hand over his stubbly, rude boy hair. "They think he's a possible paranoid schizophrenic."

"Then again, he could simply be manipulating us into thinking that."

Very glanced down at the page, then back up at me.

"They say that, too. You ever thought of being a shrink, dude?"

"I've thought of going to one. Does that count?"

" 'His cunning and neatness are consistent with many serials we've studied,' " Very read on, " 'as is his burning desire to call attention to himself.' "

"What do they make of those question marks on the victims' foreheads?"

"Um . . ." Very scanned the report. "They don't."

"How about why he doesn't rape them?"

"Killing 'em is a substitute." He tapped the page with his finger. "The sexual force is what drives him to hunt for his prey. He wants 'em. He wants to achieve power over 'em. But at the moment when he could give 'em sexual pleasure, and get sexual pleasure in return, he freaks out. They can only speculate why—'. . . most likely some form of seriously distorted sexual development.' " He stopped reading. "All we know for sure is that violence takes over for his sexual aggression."

"The ultimate power," I said.

Very nodded grimly.

"I see. And they got all of that just from reading three chapters?"

"Plus his letters to you."

"I wonder what they'd get on me if they plowed through my novels."

"Why, you got something to hide?"

"Haven't we all?"

The phone rang. A counterman answered it and told Very it was for him. He got up and took it. I sat there looking out the window at the bright, cold morning. I was thinking about what Luz had told me about Tuttle and *his* sexual aggression. Thinking about Tansy and those photographs. I was thinking Merilee was right—I was a fraud.

Very returned. "Yo, it's Inspector Feldman—for you."

"I don't much feel like talking to him."

"That's what I said you'd say."

"Tell him to write me a letter."

"That's what *he* said you'd say." Very stood there waiting for me to get up. "Take the call, dude."

I took the call.

"Okay, so maybe you were semi-right about this one, Hoagy," the Human Hemorrhoid said grudgingly, his voice over the phone sounding strained and hoarse. "Maybe he does need to build up rapport with you. Get that trust thing going. You write the next ad yourself. Just clear it with me first."

"Thank you, Inspector. Anything else?"

"No . . ." He was silent. I could hear him breathing. "No, there isn't. Nothing."

"Fine. Good-bye, Inspector." I hung up the phone and went back to the table. I sat down. "Okay, Lieutenant, what aren't you telling me?"

Very looked at me blankly. "What do you mean?"

"Last night at my apartment I got the feeling you guys were holding out on me. I just got it again. What is it?"

He cleared his throat, his eyes avoiding mine. "There's nothing, dude. Nothing at all."

"Damnit, Lieutenant, I'm *in* this thing whether you like it or not. Whether you like *me* or not."

"This ain't about you and me," Very protested. "I ain't running this thing, remember? I just do what I'm told. Break it down. I'm saying I-I . . ." He took a gulp of air. "I been under strict orders to tell no one."

"Since when does no one include me?"

"Since Feldman was sitting right there eavesdropping on our lunch. Since he was by my side at your place last night. Since he—"

"You can't pick up the phone and call a person?"

"That works both ways," he snapped, glowering at me.

"Meaning what, exactly?"

"Meaning what aren't *you* telling *me?*" Very demanded.

"I know you, dude. You're not being straight with me. Feldman, he don't trust you. Me, I keep telling him, chill, I can
work with you. Okay, sure, you're egotistical. You're argu-
mentative. You're irritating. You're—"

"Feel free to pull this over to the curb anytime."

"But when it's crunch time you're good people, okay?
There's trust between us, okay? Only I don't see that happening here, dude. I see you fronting me, is what I see."

I sampled my coffee. It was cold. I said it again. "What
aren't you telling me, Lieutenant?"

He sat there a moment in tight silence, nodding to his
own internal rock 'n' roll beat. "All right, I'll tell you. Because you *are* in this and you deserve to know. But, fuck me,
if you dish to anyone . . ."

"I'll dish to no one." I found myself leaning forward
across the table. This one was deep and dark, so deep and
dark not even Cassandra's deputy commish had leaked it to
her. If he had she'd have gone with it, that's for damned
sure. Cassandra did not keep secrets. "What is it? Tell me."

Very tugged nervously at the tuft of beard under his lower
lip. "Those question marks he drew on Laurie London's
forehead . . ."

"The two question marks? What about them?"

Now he was the one leaning toward me. In a hushed,
urgent voice he said, "Yo, it wasn't two question marks. It
was three. And it wasn't three on Bridget Healey's forehead,
it was four. Understand?"

"No, wait, I don't understand. What happened to number two?"

"We don't fucking *know* what happened to number two!
All we know is there's another dead girl out there somewhere. You got it now?" Romaine Very's eyes met mine
across the table. "We're missing one, dude."

Ten

Dear Hoagy,

Funny, isn't it, how sometimes the work just erupts right out of you and other times you can't make it happen no matter how hard you try? I had no problem writing chapters two and three, for example. But this chapter I just couldn't seem to lick. I don't know why. I guess if I knew why then I would have been able to lick it, right? Boy, what a doof I am sometimes!

This chapter you are holding, chapter 4, was originally supposed to be chapter 2. I started it more than a week ago. When I ran into trouble with it I decided to set it aside for a few days. I remember you said once in an interview that it's important to keep on working, and so that's what I did. I wrote the next chapters out of order and changed the dates around. I hope this doesn't confuse you. I didn't think it would much matter. The main thing is that the problem worked itself out. At least I think it did. I'm still not a hundred percent sold on the way this one ends. It feels a tiny bit sudden to me. If you have any ideas for improving it, please advise. You are the master. I am an apprentice.

Which reminds me: In response to your personal ad, which I am absolutely positive you did not write yourself, I'd just as soon keep our relationship the way it is. Especially since it would appear that the police are running your life now. Which I have to tell you really pisses me off. And you do not want to be around me when I am pissed off. But I have decided to forgive you. You probably had no say in this matter. They run everyone's life, even yours. They were certainly all over the place at Barney Greengrass for our supposed meeting, weren't they?

Really, who do they think they are fooling?

I have to say, in all modesty, that I'm quite pleased with the progress we're making. Didn't I tell you this would be big? Your phone should start ringing with mega-dollar offers any second now. Why, the Daily News ran twelve whole pages just on ME yesterday! And last night I dropped into Pete's Tavern for a beer and I heard these three women going on and on about some guy and— guess what—they were talking about ME! What a trip! I guess you're used to that. Hearing strangers talking about you. But for me this was a first. It excited me.

What do you think of Keanu Reeves? For the movie, I mean. I was thinking he would make a really good me. Who do you see in the role of you? I was thinking about Kevin Costner, or is he too bland? How about Alec Baldwin? Too oily?

I'll be watching the Times every day for word from you on the offers that are coming in. I can't wait, Hoagy.

Yours truly,
the answer man

p.s. Johnny Depp as Lieutenant Very, am I right?

4. the answer man changes channels
New York City, December 7

Friend E——This particular one was sitting cross-legged on the carpet in the Meditations section of that big Barnes and Noble on

Broadway and West 82nd Street. Biggest damned bookstore you've ever seen, E. Not to mention one total female mosh pit. I'm talking motherlode here, thousands and thousands of square feet of hopelessly lonely career honeys searching for their white knight. Or their black knight. Or their brown or yellow knight. Or any color of knight at all. Just so long as he has a clean dick and doesn't sell drugs for a living. They have a coffee bar there even. No alcohol though, which I consider a big mistake. Without some Chardonnay going down, these honeys seemed all the more grim and desperate to me. At least the wine gives them, however briefly, the illusion that they are glad to be alive. These girls, whew, I could see the tombstones in their eyes.

She was reading some piece of shit called 14,000 Ways to Stay Happy. *I eased on over to her and said It would make a lot more sense if they wrote a book called* 14,000 Ways to Stay Unhappy, *don't you think? Presenting myself as some sad, lonely jerk in search of suckling at her breast.*

What's my motto, E? Do I have to say it again? Didn't think so.

And, besides, she did have herself a pair of them inside of that black sweater. She was a skinny little thing otherwise. Wore an oversized man's tweed jacket over her sweater, looked like it came from a secondhand store, black leggings and a pair of clogs. She was young, 23 tops. Had long, shiny black hair she wore in braids, freckles, a cute little turned-up nose, a big dimply smile. Said her name was Francie Sherman.

Right away, I knew what I wanted to do with Francie.

There was some kind of musical instrument case on the floor next to her. Also a zippered leather portfolio. I said Are you a musician? And Francie said Yes, in this life I am. And I said This life, what do you mean? And she said I am a very spiritual person. With the help of a channeler, I've been able to uncover a lot about my past lives. I did the cave thing, for instance, thousands and thousands of years ago. Then I was in Egypt in the time of the pharaohs. And, more recently, I was in the Mafia in Newark in 1952, when I killed my brother in a dispute over drug territory. I feel I've been brought back in this life to be a healer. I heal through my flute. So I said Oh really? I play the guitar some. Maybe we could try playing together. And she said Well, I really only play classical. I'm studying at Julliard. I also do art in my spare time.

Now she unzipped the portfolio on the floor so as to show me some of her art, E. Watercolors of flower petals, mostly. Weird-looking shit done with some kind of a sponge. Francie explained that they were in fact interpretations of her own vagina. You know me, E. I'm no genius. But if this shit was art then we both picked the wrong career.

This wasn't art. This was a cry for help.

Helluva nice-looking pussy on her, though. In this life, I mean.

She talked about us maybe getting a double espresso at the cafe. But as you know, Friend E, it is not advisable for me to be seen lingering in such places. In fact, we were already hanging maybe a little bit too long where we were, people walking back and forth. All I wanted to do was get her home so I could show her this stranger's kindness. My hands tingled at the prospect. My instrument burned a hole in my pocket. I told her I had to be heading on out. She said she was walking down to Lincoln Center for some recital. I said I was going in the same direction. We headed on out.

It was a clear evening, not too cold. Still pretty early. I suggested we stroll by way of Riverside Park, it being so peaceful down there by the 79th Street boat basin and everything. She said that would be fine. She felt safe with me. They all do, E. Have you noticed that? It's a gift I have, no question.

After walking a while we stopped and sat on a bench overlooking the Hudson, which smelled like, well, human shit. Am I the only one who seems to notice that? Do you stop noticing it after you've been in town for a few weeks or what? There were a few winterized houseboats with lights on in the boat basin not far from where we sat. That's pushing it, E. Living on a houseboat in New York in the winter. Got to be a little whacked to do that. But not in a good kind of way. Just in a stupid way. We saw a few joggers go by in the darkness, speaking of whacked. Mostly, we had the park to ourselves.

Francie didn't seem to be in any huge hurry to get to her recital. Which was just as well, E. Because, between you and me, she wasn't going to be making it tonight. She pulled her flute out and started playing on it for me, something real soft and slow and boring. It may have been some famous piece of classical music for all I know. You know me, E. My musical education begins and ends with The King. Would have wigged completely without him when I was in the cage. Three hots, a cot and Elvis to get me through my days and nights . . . Thank you. Thank you very much. Thank you.

And then she stopped playing and took hold of my hand and suddenly things turned real ugly. First she started telling me all about how I need to stop suppressing my true inner self. You may remember from group, E, how much I like to be talked to this particular way. Then she said You know, I'm not saying any of this to be critical, I just feel really close to you right now and I sense you're holding back.

And THEN she was all over me, E. I mean, this Francie went from zero to sixty in no time. Her tongue down my throat. Her fingers working my zipper. And just like that I had totally lost control of the situation. I hate that.

I really, really hate that.

I want to be the one who's running the moment. It's MY moment. That's my purpose. That's what I do. That's who I am, you know what I'm saying? Sure you do. But she didn't. Not even when I said No. She just came at me even harder there on that damned bench. Was all over me. Bitch would have raped me if I hadn't brained her with her flute, which surprised her more than it did anything else. Weird how they always end up surprised, isn't it?

Because they asked for me, didn't they?

They prayed for me, didn't they?

Now she got mad. Started calling me nasty names. Ruining it. Making it ugly and mean and awful, instead of the something beautiful that it was meant to be. It took a nice, big rock to shut her up. I hit her in the side of her head with it, hard. Then I got out my instrument and I put that poor miserable creature out of her misery.

But it was no good, E. It wasn't right. I was shaking with rage and this weird, animal cry was coming from my throat. This wasn't me. None of it. This play was busted. Besides which some jogger could come by any minute and see me.

Time to break for daylight, make something happen.

I hid her under a bunch of leaves. Prayed nobody came by walking their dog for a while. Went straight to my jack rack, got what I needed, stashed it in my long duffel. Waited until it was late and I was sure no one would be out. Then I went back there. She was right where I'd left her, undisturbed. I finished the job. Then I came back and showered and changed. Hit a couple of spots I know. Drank some shots and some beer and felt better. But not happy. I wasn't feeling happy, E. Because Francie ruined it. I tried to perform an act of kindness and goodness and she ruined it.

But, hey, there's always next time, right? I mean, you got to keep a positive attitude or you'll go crazy or something, right?

You hang in there, Friend E. I'm trying my best at this end. Sometimes they just make it kind of hard on a man, that's all.

Your pal, T

p.s. I don't know what this says about me but I really, really don't like to lose control of the situation

Eleven

I T TOOK TWENTY MEN two hours to find her.

Francie Sherman was buried in a grove of trees a hundred yards from the boat basin, two feet down, with dead leaves heaped over her crude grave. She had been down there in that cold ground for at least a week.

I waited on a bench overlooking the river while they searched, hands buried deep in the pockets of my greatcoat, Lulu curled between my feet. It was a gray, blustery day. The water was choppy and foul. Romaine Very was around, but he didn't bother to say anything to me. He knew I was there. He'd known Francie was there, too. Or somewhere. A Julliard classmate had reported her missing the same day as the failed rendezvous at Barney Greengrass. Said no one had seen or heard from her in days. Said she was slender and pretty and possessed a most fetching smile. But it wasn't until Chapter Four came in the mail two days later that Very or anyone else knew where to find the answer man's second victim.

There was no whoop of triumph when they did. Just a quickening of footsteps as they gathered around the grave. Followed by a ghastly silence. One young patrolman staggered over to a trash can and was sick in it.

She was missing her head and her hands. They'd been chopped clean off with an ax or a hatchet or something that did the job like an ax or a hatchet. The two question marks, in Revlon Orange Luminesque, were drawn on the inside of her right forearm.

They did keep searching. Must have turned over every leaf in Riverside Park. But Francie's head and hands were nowhere to be found. Her parents, who drove in at once from Cranston, Rhode Island, identified her by a birthmark on her right hip and an X ray of her left leg, which she had broken skiing in New Hampshire when she was twelve. The pin was still in there.

No one who worked or shopped at the Barnes and Noble on Broadway and West Eighty-second Street remembered seeing Francie Sherman sitting on the floor in the Meditations section reading a book called *14,000 Ways to Stay Happy*. Which does happen to be a real book. And which did enjoy a brisk upsurge in sales, thanks to all the free publicity. No one remembered her, period. It's a big store, lots of people coming and going. Plus, over a week had gone by. There was no reason anyone would remember seeing her sitting there. No reason at all. There had been nothing special about Francie Sherman in life. Only in death.

As for the answer man, this was something new and entirely disturbing. He hadn't mutilated a victim before. I suppose it was the savagery of it, the pure evil that this innocent victim's headless and handless corpse represented. I can't say for sure. All I know is that the story lifted right off after this, soaring up into that rare air where only the choicest few, like O.J. and Susan Smith and the Menendez brothers, Erik and Lyle, can live and breathe. The answer man became front-page news all over the world. And that meant every greasy lawyer and agent and bottom feeder in the business wanted their shot, their share, their piece of the action. And now.

Four major publishing houses were already right in the middle of it. Before Francie's headless body was found, the bidding had climbed to $2 million for what was, to date, less than forty pages of a work-in-progress by an unknown author. God, I love the book business sometimes. I said I would have to contact my "partner" to get his feedback. And I did. I placed a personal ad on the front page of the *Times,* duly cleared by Feldman, that read: "My hands are untied. I am talking to you. What is our price? And will we stop this if we get it?"

After Francie's body was found, the bidding for the book skyrocketed to $5 million instantly. If nothing else, the answer man knew how to run an auction. And we're still not even talking movie sale. What about the new-and-improved Son of Sam law, you're wondering? What about the question of whether this killer should or should not be allowed to profit from his crimes? None of the houses seemed too worried. Certainly not on ethical grounds—publishers have no ethics anymore. As for the law, hey, that's why they have lawyers.

One house even went so far as to hint that a contract for my own novel might be included as part of the deal. I was not, repeat not, the one who suggested this, as so many critics later claimed. That wasn't what I wanted out of this. I didn't want anything out of this, actually. I didn't even want to be in it. But no one believed that. A few editors and agents around town even started whispering that I was he— that I, Stewart Hoag, had fabricated this poison-pen pal of mine. That I was killing these women myself and mailing myself these chapters so as to revive my own, semicomatose literary career. A theory that was not, I should point out, totally dismissed by the New York City Police Department. In response to a question on *Larry King Live* about whether I was considered a suspect, Inspector Dante Feldman would say only that his task force was "considering everyone."

I did not consider this a ringing personal endorsement.

Cassandra Dee, in case you're wondering, did indeed go on the air with her appeal for the answer man to turn himself in to her, live and in stereo. "Call me, fax me, E-mail me, I'm yours" was what she said. It was very emotional, the way she said it. Also very nasal. She repeated it several times during the broadcast, only it didn't work. The answer man didn't turn himself in to Cassandra on the air. I guess he was too busy writing Chapter Four for me.

I sat there on that bench with my hands in my pockets staring out at the river for the longest time. Eventually, after they had taken the body away, Very made his way over to me and sat there staring out at it, too. He wore a hooded sweatshirt under his leather spy coat. His nose was red from the cold. He hadn't shaved in a couple of days. Or slept, by the look of him.

"Inspector Feldman was right, Lieutenant."

"How so, dude?"

"Serials do change their methods."

Very considered this a moment, nodding to himself. "Could be this was just him taking care of business."

I glanced at him. "Business? What business?"

"Check it out, he says he and Francie swapped some spit, am I right?"

"Right . . . ?"

"So maybe that freaked him out. Like he thought maybe we could score some of his DNA from her tongue or her lips. No telling what scientists can do now. Maybe he figured he better be careful and take the head with him."

"Could they actually do that, Lieutenant? Identify him from traces of his saliva left behind in her mouth?"

"That's hard to say, dude."

"How come?"

"We got no head, remember?"

"I assure you that didn't slip my mind. What about her hands?"

"Could be this one put up a fight. Scratched him some before he did her. She'd have his skin under her fingernails. A trace of his blood, even. Same story, him being careful. He's always being careful, that's for damned sure." Very swiped at his red nose with the back of his hand. "Something you want to get off your chest, dude?"

"I'm not the answer man, if that's what you're wondering."

"It's not," he said, scowling at me. "And don't you front me no more, because I ain't hearing that."

I studied him curiously. "Meaning?"

"Meaning give it up, will ya!" he pleaded, his voice abruptly cracking with emotion. "Whatever it is, *whoever* it is! Give it up, damn it!" Very was shaken. He was freaked. It was the horror of it, the pressure. Everyone has their limit. Very had reached his. He sat there in silence a moment, trying to calm himself. "You can't sit on it no more, dude," he said quietly. "You just can't."

I took a deep breath and let it out slowly. I reached into the inside pocket of my jacket and removed the slender, folded page of a letter that Tuttle Cash had sent me from Ghana twenty years ago. I didn't feel good about this. In fact, I felt real bad about it. But he was right—I had to do it. You see, I had reached my limit, too. I handed it to him and said, "See if this was typed on the same machine that the answer man's using. If it was, then I'll give him up."

Very stared at it, stunned, not making a move to take it. "Dude, how could you do this on me?"

"I had my reasons."

"Well, I hope they were *damned* good ones."

"They were. They are."

He pocketed the page, seething. "His name. C'mon, c'mon. What's his name?"

"I can't. Not yet."

"Fuck this shit!" Very grabbed me by the lapels of my coat. "What are you doing on me? I thought we was *friends!*"

"We are friends, Lieutenant. And I'm sorry. But it has to be this way. Because if there's one chance in a million that I'm wrong, well, I don't want to be wrong."

"Even if it costs another girl her life?"

"I have that under control."

"Oh yeah?" he snarled. *"How?!"* When I didn't respond, he released me. Shook his head at me, disgusted. "What is it—somebody you're tight with?"

"Something like that."

"Loyalty goes out the window when shit like this goes down."

"Correction, this is precisely when loyalty does not go out the window."

He tried a different approach. "How about we keep it between us two? You can trust me. I can keep his name under wraps."

"No, you can't."

"What are you saying, I'm a fuck-up?"

"I'm not accusing you of being a fuck-up."

He peered at me. "I see. So he's a celeb, huh? Somebody famous. Fuck me, this is getting wiggier by the day."

"And the night," I added. "Don't forget the night."

Very got up and strode over to the railing and gazed out at the water. Then he turned back to me, his head nodding to its own rock 'n' roll beat. This one was speed metal. "I can take you in for withholding evidence, you know. I can throw you in a holding cell with the worst kind of vermin on earth."

Lulu moaned at my feet, horrified.

"You can, but I still won't tell you his name."

"I'm hip to that," he admitted, puffing out his cheeks. "I go back with you long enough to believe it. Damn, you are one mondo pain in the ass, you know that?"

"It has been brought to my attention before, yes."

Romaine Very glowered at me. "It'll take me two hours, tops. Don't disappear."

"I'll try not to, Lieutenant."

It was two in the afternoon by the time I made it over to East Sixty-fifth Street. I did not take a direct route, figuring Very would put a tail on me. I took a cab from Riverside Park to Columbus Circle, then rode the A train downtown, watching the people's faces across from me just as He watched their faces . . . *What do we have for our winners, Johnny?* . . . Most of those faces were buried inside that morning's edition of the *New York Post,* which boasted an exclusive jailhouse interview with David Berkowitz. Son of Sam's take on the answer man was blasted across page one: SAM SEZ HE WANTS TO BE A STAR. At Fourteenth Street I caught a cab back uptown to Grand Central, where I picked up the No. 6 train. That took me to East Sixty-eighth. I walked the rest of the way. No one was on my tail. I was sure of it. Well, I wasn't but Lulu was. She knows about these things.

Vic was on duty behind the wheel of the Land Rover halfway down the block from Tuttle's building. He'd been on duty since 8 A.M., when he took over for me. I had spent my own night staked out across the street from King Tut's, waiting for The King. Tuttle had come staggering out of there at 3:29 A.M., drunk and alone, and had limped home in the cold. He had arrived there a few minutes before four. The lights went on. The lights stayed on. The lights were still on.

One thing Vic had managed to do over the past forty-eight hours was follow Malachi Medvedev to his little Coochie roost, which was on the corner of Second Avenue and East Fifty-eighth Street. According to the doorman, Malachi stopped by there several evenings a week to visit

Miss Ochoa. Had his own key. Vic couldn't get any more details out of the doorman. Maybe Malachi had shmeared the guy plenty not to give out anything more. Maybe there *was* nothing more. Maybe Malachi Medvedev slept over with his Coochie-coo like he'd said. Maybe he didn't.

"Malachi stopped by this morning at 8:35 with the newspapers and pastry," Vic reported to me through the Rover's open window. "He stayed one hour. Otherwise, all's quiet."

"It's all over, Vic," I announced to him in a low voice.

"What's all over, Hoag?"

"I've given Lieutenant Very a letter that will verify within the next couple of hours that Tuttle Cash is the answer man."

Vic's eyes widened a bit, but not much. Clearly, he had suspected what my interest in Tuttle was all about. But he hadn't said anything. And he didn't say anything now. Just sat there, grim-faced.

"I want to thank you for your help, Vic. I suppose I just needed time to accept this."

"Sure thing," he said gently. "You needed some time."

"But if I shield him any longer, I might cost another woman her life. And I couldn't live with that."

"Of course not, Hoag," he agreed. "Want me to stay here with you until you get the word?"

"That won't be necessary. You go ahead and catch a cab home."

Vic climbed out of the Rover slowly, groaning from the stiffness in his heavy limbs. Lulu hopped right in, anxious to claim dibs on his nice, preheated seat. I claimed it for myself. I'm the boss, and don't you let anyone tell you otherwise.

Vic lingered there by the open window. "Something, uh, I've been meaning to talk to you about, Hoag. Unless now isn't a good time . . ."

"No, no. Now's fine, Vic. What is it?"

"I, uh . . ." He cleared his throat uncomfortably. "I wondered if you'd be my best man. At the wedding, I mean."

"Why, Vic. You're getting married?"

"I am," he admitted, ducking his big, meaty head.

Lulu started thumping her tail. She loves weddings, although she has been known to sob uncontrollably at them. I had to carry her out of the Baldwin-Basinger nuptials because she was stealing the show.

"When is the happy occasion?" I asked.

"As soon as possible."

I raised an eyebrow at him. "You mean . . . ?"

"Shoot, no. It's nothing like that, Hoag. We're just anxious, that's all." He kicked at the pavement with his brogan. "We were thinking maybe over Christmas, if that's okay."

"Do I know the lucky girl?"

"Yes, you do."

"Well, don't keep me in suspense, Vic. Who is she?"

"Pam," he replied. A blissful smile softened his plain features. "And she's not the lucky one—I am."

"Pam who?"

"Pam, Hoag."

"Wait . . . *our* Pam?"

"We're in love."

Lulu started whooping now. I think she sensed flower girl honors.

"Since when, Vic?"

"The passion has been overtaking us for some time," he said dully.

"Vic, how can I put this delicately—Pam's old enough to be your grandmother."

"That's not so at all," he responded, flaring. "She's barely seventy."

"And you're barely forty."

"And she's intelligent and warm and we get along great. I've waited all my life to meet a woman like her."

"That shouldn't have been so hard. The nursing homes are full of them."

I felt a withering glare from the seat next to me.

Vic was glaring at me, too. "I'm really disappointed by

your reaction, Hoag. I didn't expect you to be so close-minded. You of all people."

"You're absolutely right, Vic. I was totally out of line. I apologize."

"Merilee was delighted when Pam told her. Delighted."

"I said I was sorry, didn't I?" I stuck my hand out to him through the window. "Congratulations. I'm happy for both of you. And I'll be honored to be your best man."

We shook on it, then he went lumbering off to catch a cab home, beaming happily. Me, I sat there drumming the steering wheel with my fingers, thinking once again about just how little I knew about people.

And then Malachi Medvedev came hurrying up the street in a trenchcoat with a worried look on his face. When he got to Tuttle's building he stopped on the sidewalk out front, squinting up at the big second-floor study windows, craning his neck for a better look inside. He waddled across the street and climbed the stoop to the brownstone opposite Tuttle's so as to get an even better look. Then, clucking to himself, he crossed back to Tuttle's building and went inside. Me, I waited all of three seconds before I got out of the Rover with Lulu and went in after him.

The apartment door was open, the keys still in the lock. Malachi stood there in the living room with his hands on his hips and his lower lip stuck out.

"What's up, Mal?" I asked him from the doorway.

"Man didn't show for work today, that's what's up," Malachi replied distractedly, running his hand over his face. "Ain't answering his phone neither. Help me look around, will you?"

We both helped him. Lulu checked out the bathrooms. Malachi took the bedroom. I checked out the study. There was no sign of Tuttle in there. Just an empty bottle of Courvoisier and a dirty glass on the desk. A wrinkled necktie was slung over the desk lamp.

Moving swiftly, I tore open the old leather suitcase, dug out that horrid X-rated photo album and tucked it inside my

coat under my arm. If the police were going to get involved,
I did not want them to find it, to paw through it, to smack
their big fat lips over it and maybe, just maybe, pocket the
odd picture and sell it to the likes of Cassandra. This much I
could do for Tansy. It was the right thing to do. I knew this.
But I still felt like some sleazy little man who cleaned up
after people, some bagman, some fixer. I didn't feel like *me*.
Or the me I liked to believe I was.

"Man ain't here," Malachi reported gravely when we met
up at the top of the stairs. "He's flown the coop."

Lulu concurred, based on her own exhaustive search. She
had even looked under the bed. I knew this because she had
a dust bunny on her nose.

"Not possible, Mal. He couldn't have left."

"Why not? Wait, don't tell me." Malachi shook a stubby
finger at me. "You been watching over him, am I right? You
had this place staked out."

I nodded.

"Thought so. I seen the same guy parked out front every
morning. Seen him in the bar every night. Big guy. At first,
I figured he was a private detective somebody's husband
hired—you know how The King is, always messing with
married women—until I seen *you* out there talking to him
the other morning. That's when I put two and two together." He smiled at me warmly. "Awful decent of you,
Hoagy."

"Decency has little or nothing to do with it."

"Man was real down on himself last night," Malachi went
on. "Saying how nobody gives a shit about him, nobody
loves him. I says to him, you are so full of it. You wanna
know how much your friend Hoagy cares about you?"

"Wait, you *told* him?"

"Well, yeah." Mal frowned at me. "Why not?"

I grabbed him by his soft shoulders, lifting the little man
practically up off the ground. "You idiot, don't you realize
what you've done?"

Malachi squirmed in my grasp, frightened. He didn't

know what he'd done. How could he? He hadn't done a thing. I was the one who had. I was the one who'd fucked up.

"How, Mal? How did he slip out?"

Malachi swallowed. "There's a b-back way. Over the garden wall, through the service entrance of the building around the corner on Sixty-sixth."

I released him and stormed out of the apartment with Lulu on my heel. Jumped back in the Land Rover. Slid the photo album under the seat. Pondered my next move. Hours. Tuttle could have been gone for hours. Should I call Very? Call him right now? I couldn't think clearly. One thought kept crowding its way to the front of my mind—If he kills again, I will never forgive myself.

If he kills again, I will never forgive myself.

My car phone beeped.

I answered it. I heard heavy breathing from the other end, someone gasping for air. Then I heard a faint whisper: "Help me, cookie. Help me . . . It's raining. R-raining . . ." A muffled thud. And then silence.

I had barely heard it at all. But I knew that voice. I'd know it anywhere. It was Cassandra Dee. And she was dying.

Twelve

I CALLED 911 while I floored it down to West Tenth Street, which is not an easy thing to do in midtown Manhattan while you're running red lights and trying to dodge cabs and messengers on bicycles and potholes the approximate breadth and depth of Ubehebe Crater. Lulu hugged her seat and howled when I took the corner of Thirty-fourth and Fifth Avenue on two wheels, nearly flipping the old Land Rover over onto its back like a turtle. But the stubby old beast righted itself and went bouncing and rattling on down the avenue.

I also left word for Very, who could not be reached.

Cassandra Dee lived a half-block west of Fifth in one of the nicest rows of houses to be found anywhere in the city, if not the whole world. I beat the ambulance there. Not a surprise. Double-parked and jumped out, dashed up the front stoop. There was no answer when I rang the bell. Not a surprise either.

The front door was of solid oak with an iron pry guard

around the lock and no sign that anyone had messed with it. There were decorative iron bars over the basement and ground-floor windows. Not so the elegant second-floor parlor windows, which were level with the front door. These were wired to a silent alarm by an armed security service. Fine, let them come—them and their arms both. A pair of big terra-cotta pots flanked the front door, each with some form of small, dead-looking tree in it. I picked up one of the pots and walked it over to the edge of the stoop, groaning, and hurled it through the window closest to me. Then I climbed out on the ledge, kicked in the rest of the window with my ankle boot and jumped inside, broken glass crunching underfoot.

Cassandra was sprawled out next to the phone on her plush white living room rug. She had that same startled expression on her face that she always wore. Only, she generally favored red lipstick, not orange, and she certainly never used to wear it on her forehead in the form of five question marks. Plus those protuberant eyes used to blink sometimes. And she was never, ever silent. How had that plea of hers gone? *Call me, fax me, E-mail me, I'm yours.*

Well, she wanted him and she got him.

There was no sign of a struggle in the room. No sign of a weapon. There would be no fingerprints. I knew this. I knew all of this by now.

The decor was cool and pale, with lots of low-slung suede things to lounge on, all of it as homey and inviting as a Paramus furniture showroom. Her living room walls were a full-fledged shrine, every square inch of them covered with framed photographs of her—on the cover of *People*, *TV Guide*, *Esquire*, *Vanity Fair*. On the set of *60 Minutes* with Mike Wallace. At Planet Hollywood with Arnold. Backstage with the rock star formerly known as Prince. With Stallone, with Cruise, with Cindy Crawford, with Jim Carrey. All of these photos were autographed. Many of the celebs had added personal messages as well. Sinatra had written,

"You're my kind of chick." Andre Agassi: "You can serve me anytime."

Me, I had written: "You keep me on my toes, girlfriend." It's true, there was even a picture of her standing with me at some big Hollywood movers-and-shakers bash a while back. I looked bored. Fabulous but bored. I had signed the picture as well as inscribed it. Except I hadn't done either of those things. It wasn't my handwriting. It wasn't even close. I stood there a moment, staring at this little forgery of hers. I looked around at the other signatures, wondering if they were all fakes, too. I wondered why she had done this. Was it to fool people? Which people? Her parents from Bensonhurst? Herself? I wondered how many people she had invited in to see this shrine, and who those people were. I thought about how sad this was. How very, very sad.

I shook myself and went to the front door to let Lulu in. First, she circled the entire downstairs of the house, briskly, nose to the floor. Then, slowly and warily, she approached Cassandra's body. She stopped cold in her tracks about a foot away from her. And then Lulu did something that was most unusual for her.

She raised up her head and started howling. Not just any howl either. This was a lonely, haunting howl. The kind of howl you hear in the mountains in the night when you're stuffed inside your sleeping bag out underneath the stars. It was a heartbreaking howl. And it was an unfamiliar howl. I'd certainly never heard such a sound come out of her and I've known Lulu since she was eight weeks old. I hadn't realized before just how much she cared about Cassandra. I guess there weren't very many people around who were afraid of Lulu. Just Cassandra.

I knelt beside my partner and stroked her, wondering if she would howl like this for me when I was dead, and wishing, wishing I were.

❑ ❑ ❑ ❑

"Is it the same typewriter, Lieutenant?"

"It's the same typewriter, dude."

We were seated out on Cassandra's front stoop waiting for the Human Hemorrhoid to show. The technicians were inside working the scene, not happy with me for tromping broken glass around in there and touching the doorknob and letting Lulu in. Like I cared. Very didn't seem at all angry, just subdued and down. Lulu had squeezed herself in between my feet, quiet now, but still looking sadder than I'd ever seen her.

"Same typist?"

"They can't tell about that." Very's eyes were on the row of houses across from us. Lucky people lived in those houses. Lucky, alive people. "Different qualities of paper. Plus the answer man's using a fresh ribbon. Ribbon on your letter was all worn out. He had to strike the keys a whole lot harder." He got a piece of gum out of his coat pocket, unwrapped it and stuck it in his mouth. "Tell it to me again, dude. What Cassandra said."

"She said, 'It's raining.' "

He looked up at the sky. The sky was gray, streaked here and there with blue. There was no rain. None. "I don't track it."

"I don't either."

"Must be she was delirious. People say the darnedest things when they're starting to go."

"Yes, I believe Art Linkletter did a book on that subject once."

He glanced at me curiously. "You cool, dude?"

"I think I can safely report that I am not cool, Lieutenant."

"He must not have realized she was still alive," Very said, thinking out loud. "When he split, I mean. Maybe she faked she was dead. Bought herself enough time to call you before she went for good."

"Maybe."

"Yo, she called you on your car phone. What's up with that?"

"I was in my car, that's what."

"But how'd she know that?"

"She always seemed to know where I was. She was a good reporter. A damned good reporter."

He sat there, jaw working his gum. "You dug her, am I right?"

"I was fond of her. She was smart. And honest, in her own way. So few people are either of those things anymore."

"I wanted to get to know her better," he confessed. "I was thinking maybe we'd freak it, her and me."

We fell silent. Behind us, the front door was open. I could hear the technicians in there yapping away at each other.

"Dude?"

"Yes, Lieutenant?"

"This isn't going to go down so good with the inspector. That I was running a test on your letter while Cassandra was getting herself done. That you wouldn't tell me who wrote it. That I let you have it your way. This isn't going to go down so good."

"I know that."

"You'll have to give it all up now."

"I know that, too. You have my full cooperation."

A dark blue sedan pulled up now with a screech. Out hopped Inspector Dante Feldman, shooting his cuffs and smoothing his white pompadour. Also sneaking worried looks over his shoulder. The press corps—they were a scant half-block behind him, van after van filled with reporters and cameramen and trouble racing down the block toward us. Feldman hurried up the steps and went inside without so much as looking at either of us. Very told me to stay put and went inside after him. I stayed put. I watched the rampage. It was free. It was some rampage.

Within seconds they had taken over the street. Shut it right down. The down-jacketed video guerrillas with their manic urgency and their box-out moves. The frozen-faced, frozen-haired TV reporters with their earnest topcoats and their empty notepads. The news radio boys with their battered black tape recorders and their problem dandruff. The print reporters with their small-time talents and their big-time egos. The photographers with their cameras and lenses hanging from them like so many water canteens. All of them crowding the sidewalk, surging toward Cassandra's stoop, jostling each other for position, shouting questions at me, at anyone. Three burly cops held them back. It was not easy. There were so many of them. And they were in such a dither. Because nothing, but nothing, gets the press more riled than losing one of their own in the line of so-called duty. Partly this arises out of a genuine sense of grief and loss. Mostly this arises out of a sense that here is a chance to make one of their own into a martyr— and thereby draw more attention to themselves, which is what the press is really and truly all about, in case nobody ever told you. I have been on both sides. I know this.

I felt a tap on my shoulder. It was Very, motioning for me to follow him inside. I followed him inside.

Feldman was waiting for me in the entry hall, away from the others, looking at me with what I can only describe as total and complete hate. "I w-want to know r-right now, Hoag!" he sputtered at me angrily. "I want to know just exactly h-how long you've known his identity!"

Now Lulu started to howl again.

I shushed her. "I haven't known anything, Inspector. I've suspected."

"Don't you split hairs with me, you grandstanding bastard!" His face was very close to mine, his breath reeking of pastrami and garlic pickles.

"I wasn't sure, Inspector. I had to be sure."

"Sure?" Feldman gaped at me in dumfounded amazement. "Oh, baby, I'll give you *sure*. You *sure* are the shit-

heel of the century! You *sure* are going down for this! Are you *insane* or do you just enjoy seeing hundreds and hundreds of good cops chasing around this city like fucking fools?"

"The latter, Inspector. You wouldn't believe how much fun I've been having. I just laugh and laugh. My sides ache from laughing so much."

Feldman glared at me with his hooded black eyes. "Get him the fuck away from me, Lieutenant. Throw him in a fucking dungeon somewhere."

"He's promised he'll cooperate fully, Inspector," Very spoke up in my defense. What a pal. "I have his word."

"I don't care what he fucking promised!" Feldman blustered. "You going to take him in or you want to make a midlife career change?"

Very panicked. "No, sir. I mean, sure thing—whatever you say."

"Tuttle Cash," I said. It was what they were waiting to hear. I said it. I said it again. "It's Tuttle Cash, okay? The answer man is Tuttle Cash."

Feldman's eyes widened; the color drained from his face. He shot a look at Very. Very was looking at me, his head bobbing up and down now like one of those dolls people put in the back window of their car.

"For the record, Hoagy," the inspector said between his teeth, "are we talking about *the* Tuttle Cash?"

"The one and only."

"Fuck me," he gasped. "This is . . . this is going to be like O.J. all over again. He's the white O.J. The white fucking O.J."

To Feldman's credit, this realization seemed to horrify rather than excite him. It is at moments like these that I tend to decide about people. Dante Feldman wasn't such a bad guy after all, I decided. Just a hard one.

"Now do you see why I had to be sure, Inspector?"

Feldman's tongue darted out of his mouth, nervously

wetting his lips. He breathed in and out a few times, composing himself. "You could have let us in on this. We'd have put him under surveillance."

"I did that."

"By professionals."

"I used a professional."

"You could have taken us into your confidence," he argued.

"No, I couldn't," I argued back. "Not with the likes of Cassandra circling around. Her top floor source would have blabbed it to her. And she would have put it on the air in a flash. And an innocent man, a public man, might have been ruined."

This much Feldman seemed willing to accept, although most grudgingly. "Where does the man live?"

I told him where. "But he's not home, Inspector. At least he wasn't a little while ago."

"Where is he, dude?"

"I don't know."

"I want his place sealed *now,* Lieutenant," Feldman barked.

"Done."

I said, "You won't find the typewriter there. I looked." Come to think of it, where *was* the typewriter?

"His restaurant, too," Feldman ordered. "And his car, if he's got one."

"He hasn't," I said. "He sold it."

"Proper paper every step of the way, Lieutenant. I will not be drop-kicked out of court on some bonehead technicality."

"Yessir."

Feldman turned back to me. "Sounds like you know King Tut pretty well. Who is he to you?"

I considered that for a long moment. I had so many answers to choose from. Tuttle Cash was my idol, my oldest friend, the best man at my wedding, the man who saved my life. He was all of these things. I could have said any one of them. Only, I didn't.

I said, "We were on the same team together once."

I drove around for awhile. I didn't much feel like going home. Didn't want to see anyone. Didn't want to talk to anyone. I just wanted to go someplace where I could curl up and feel lousy.

I ended up at my place on West Ninety-third Street. I took the X-rated photo album inside with me and stashed it deep in the bedroom closet. I didn't look at it. I didn't ever want to look at it. But I didn't want anyone else to, either. I took off my coat and put down some mackerel for Lulu. It was supper time, but she wouldn't so much as sniff at it. She was still too upset about Cassandra.

I put some Garner on the stereo and poured myself two fingers of the fifteen-year-old Dalwhinnie and sat in my chair. The Dalwhinnie didn't hurt one bit. It's an Upper Spey single malt, a bit fuller than the Macallan. But for some reason the Little Elf wasn't the ticket at all. He just made me feel sadder. I put on some Grateful Dead instead. Not the tie-dyed, flower-power Dead, but the old Dead, the real Dead, the marauding-huns-in-shitkicker-boots Dead. I turned them up loud and let them blast away. I sipped my scotch, trying not to look at that photo of the three young track stars hanging over the loveseat. Trying to forget that Cassandra had stood in this very room not too many days before telling me how much she looked up to me . . . *It's raining* . . . Trying to forget that the entire New York City Police Department was now hunting down Tuttle Cash so that they could arrest him for murdering five women. Trying to figure out why. Because it kept coming around to that— why? Why had he killed them? Why had he dragged me into it? Why had he turned the city of New York into a terror zone?

Why?

The phone rang next to me. I let it ring. Poured myself some more scotch, Lulu watching me carefully from her perch on the loveseat. She worries about me when I start drinking alone. She's afraid I'll jump the track again and go crashing back into my lost days and nights.

The phone kept on ringing. Damned thing wouldn't stop. I picked it up.

It was Very, sounding edgy and hyper. "Thought maybe I'd find you there. Housekeeper said that's where you hang when you want to be alone."

"It's nice to know I'm so unpredictable."

"There's no sign of him, dude. No one's seen him. No one's heard from him. He's flat-out disappeared. We figure he's on the run." Very paused, waiting for me to say something. When I didn't he said, "Listen, if you have the slightest idea where he might be heading . . ."

"I haven't, Lieutenant."

"Break it down, would you tell me if you did?"

"Yes, I would."

"Are you alone?"

"Yes, I am."

"No offense, but I gotta ask you—whose voice is that I hear in the background?"

"It's Jerry Garcia."

He considered this a moment in silence. "You cool, dude?"

"I'm fine, Lieutenant. Although I am getting really tired of you asking me that. Is there anything else?"

"Yeah. Phone home. Housekeeper wants to talk to you."

"What about?"

"What am I, your answering service? I'm trying to find a serial killer." He hung up on me.

I called the apartment.

Vic answered on the first ring. "I'm real glad you checked in, Hoag. I have news for you—the man called here."

"Very? I know. I just got off the phone with him."

"Not him, Tuttle Cash. He called."

I froze. "When, Vic?"

"About an hour ago. Pam spoke to him. I told her not to say anything to the lieutenant about it until she cleared it with you."

"Good thinking, Vic. Exactly what did Tuttle say to her?"

"It was a short conversation," Vic replied uncomfortably.

"Vic, what did he say?"

"Just three words: 'Tell Hoagy good-bye.' "

I thanked him and hung up the phone, my mind on what I'd found Tuttle doing when I walked in on him in his office that day. My chest suddenly felt heavy.

The phone rang again. I picked it up. This time it was a woman and she was screeching at me.

"Is this you, Hoagy? Because if it is you better tell me where the fuck it is and I mean *right* now! Because I don't take this shit from nobody! I don't care who the fuck he is, y'know what I'm saying?"

"It's nice to hear your voice again, Luz."

"Don't you start talking pretty at me. I ain't hearing that shit, man. I want it back and I want it back *right* now!"

"You want what back, Luz?"

"My baby, that's what. Your fucking friend stole my Miata from the fucking garage where I fucking keep it and he better—"

"When, Luz?" I leaned forward in my chair. "When?"

"Just now. Maybe half an hour ago. I called down to tell the guy to get it out for me and he's like, hey, your boyfriend's already on his way over with it. Motherfucker scammed 'em out of the keys and took off. I am going to cut him, man. I am going to make him so sorry he ever fucked with me. He ain't going to be worth dipshit when I'm through with him."

"Luz?"

"Like, *nobody* rips me off. He even had 'em fill the tank and charge it to my account."

"Luz!"

"What?"

"Your Miata—what color is it?"

"Red. Like his nose's gonna be after I hit him."

"Good-bye, Luz."

I turned off the stereo and threw on my greatcoat. I ran down the stairs with Lulu hot on my tail and jumped into the Land Rover. I stopped at my own garage, on Amsterdam, and traded the Rover in for the Jag. The Rover doesn't like to go over 55. The Jag doesn't like to go under 70.

Then I took off.

It's usually a five-hour drive. Six with traffic. Four with luck and a heavy foot. I needed to make it in three. Because he had a head start on me. Because I had to get there before he did.

I knew where he was going. Oh, yeah, I knew.

There are a couple of different ways you can get there. One is to work your way through the northern burbs on the Sawmill River Parkway until you hit the Mass Pike. The other is to hug the shoreline on I-95. I took the shoreline, doing 90, using the breakdown lane to pass any damned car or truck that got in my way. There's a shortcut I know, Route 395, which forks off the interstate at New London and shoots straight up through the barren desolation of eastern Connecticut into Massachusetts. You can go a half-hour on 395 and not see a single car. You can do 100. I did, Lulu dozing next to me with my scarf wrapped around her. There were patches of ice on the road when I hit the Mass Pike at Worcester. There always are, even in August. Worcester has to be one of the coldest places on earth. I don't know why. I don't care why. And then we were on the outskirts of Boston, where all roads converge at the tollbooths. I paid and went on through and we were there.

Cambridge. Home to the most pretentious, overrated Ivy League breeding ground of them all. You know which one I mean—I'm talking about the *H*-word. Those of us who went there never, ever mention it by name. We prefer to make people force it out of us, thereby drawing even more attention to ourselves. It was here where I achieved so-called higher learning. It was here where I would find Tuttle Cash. He would be here.

Most of the campus is found in Cambridge, on or near the banks of the Charles. Some of it is sited on the other side of the snaking river, across the Larz Anderson Bridge, which puts it in Boston, if you want to get picky. The much reviled Graduate School of Business Administration is across the river, for example. But I wasn't going to the business school.

I was going to the stadium. The one where they play football on Saturday afternoons in autumn.

There's a spiked iron fence all the way around it, a big iron gate at the main entrance. The gate was open. I eased the Jag on through it and crossed the empty parking lot, the horseshoe-shaped stadium looming overhead. There's a chain-link fence across the open end of the horseshoe. The red Miata with the New York license plates was parked there. I shut off the Jag's engine, dug the torch out of the glovebox and got out, Lulu joining me reluctantly. It was barely in the teens outside. My nose and ears felt it right away. I could hear cars off in the distance on Soldier's Field Road. Otherwise all was darkness and quiet. I took off one of my cashmere-lined deerskin gloves and felt the hood of the Miata. Still warm. It was just past two in the morning, according to Grandfather's Rolex. Three hours and fifteen minutes it had taken me. Fast. But was I fast enough?

Lulu took over from there. Followed his trail, black nose to the frozen ground, snarfling, breath rising from her nostrils like a plow horse's. She led me to the chain-link fence and stopped. I shone the light up at it. It was eight feet high. There was a torn shred of gray flannel caught in the top of it where we stood. From his trousers, no doubt. I pocketed the torch and started climbing. It had been a while since I'd scaled a fence. Only kids and thieves scale fences, and a thief is one thing I've never been. But muscle memory is a funny thing. My arms and legs remembered immediately how to get me over the top, trousers intact. I dropped down the last few feet to the ground on the other side and brushed myself off. Lulu came prancing up next to me, arfing triumphantly. She had found her own way in. She can do just about anything when she sets her pea brain to it.

I shone the light ahead of us. Together, we ventured out onto the field where Tuttle Cash was faster and stronger and better than anyone else. The field where nobody, but nobody could catch him.

The field where the crowd roared.

The best and the brightest chanted his name here on those crisp autumn afternoons with their cheeks pink and the band playing and the wind blowing. And it seemed, when he had that ball tucked under his arm, that he was the best and the brightest of them all. Someone blessed. Someone invincible. Maybe all of the Tuttle Cashes on all of the fields seem like invincible young gods on those Saturday afternoons when the wind is blowing. Maybe some of them even stay that way. I never met one who did.

Lulu led me to him. I thought I'd find him on the fifty-yard line—no man's land. I didn't. King Tut was in the end zone, under the goalpost, gone. I was too late. I had a feeling I would be. I also had a feeling that maybe it was best this way. Worse things could have happened. A trial could have happened. He had his duffel coat on, no gloves. The gun was still gripped in his right hand. It looked like the same gun I'd taken away from him twice before. I couldn't tell for sure. I didn't want to touch it. He'd fired up through his jaw. The bullet came out the top of his head. It was not a neat way to die but it was quick. One eye, the left one, was still open. I closed it. His left hand clutched a piece of paper. I took it from him. It was a lined sheet from a steno pad. On it, scrawled in his handwriting, were two words: *Sorry, Doof.*

I stood there a while on the hard, pale green December grass, shining the light down at him. Lulu sat there in between my feet, nose quivering. She didn't howl like she had for Cassandra. She just sat there, waiting for me to tell her what to do. I told her to stay put. She promised she would. Then I went back over the fence and called Very to tell him that it was all over.

The answer man had written his final chapter.

Thirteen

Dear Hoagy,

Message received. And I could tell this one was really from you, not Inspector Feldman. What kind of name is that anyway, Dante Feldman? And who does he think he is comparing me to David Berkowitz on Larry King's show? Berkowitz was a fat hairy slob, a pig. I am an artist. Doesn't Feldman realize that yet? Oh well, I guess it's like they always say—a bad review is better than no review at all. I'd better just get used to it, huh? Comes with the territory!

I don't know what my price is, in answer to your question. What's good money these days for a guaranteed No. 1 bestseller? I read the newspapers. If Newt Gingrich is worth $4.5 million and Colin Powell is worth $6 million then how much am I worth? What does John Grisham get? Not that I consider myself in Grisham's league yet, but this is exactly the kind of thing I need to know from you, Hoagy. That's why I brought you in. Also, what's included in this figure? As I hope I've already made clear to you, I *want to hold on to the movie rights. But what about the foreign rights? Would the publisher get those? How about the paperback rights? Audiocassettes? Help me out here, Hoagy. We're in this together, you know. It's you and me against the world.*

In response to your other question: Will I stop this when we get our deal? I can't answer that. I don't know. I only know that I am an artist, as you are, and that I have no control over my artistic impulses. They have a life of their own. I'm just along for the ride. Frankly, I have no idea when the book will be done or even how it will end. I do know that I'm feeling incredibly productive. I wake up every morning looking forward to my work. I'm having the most fun I've ever had in my life, Hoagy. I'm just so excited. When I don't feel that way anymore, when this just starts to feel like routine drudgery—I guess that's when I'll know it's over. And time to move on to a new project.

But I will need a good long rest first. This book has been a great strain on me, I don't mind telling you. I have to pay attention to every little detail. I have to concentrate, day in and day out, because one little slip and the whole thing will just fall apart. I guess I never really appreciated before just how hard it is to write a book. But I guess I don't have to tell you that, do I?

In the meantime, here's another chapter. I have to confess it's my favorite so far. I hope you don't find it too weird. I'm still experimenting. And, I hope, growing.

Yours truly,
the answer man

p.s. Is James Coburn too old to play Inspector Feldman?

5. the answer man goes uptown
New York City, December 12

Friend E——The Christmas shoppers are out in full force. You've got to see it to believe it. The pushing and shoving. The honking and cursing. The flat-out craziness. And for what, to buy a bunch of stupid shit nobody needs and won't use? One good look at Christmas in New York, E, and I've got this to say—the wrong people in this world got all of the money.

And you would not believe the women. Especially if you move on up Madison Avenue into the 60s and 70s, where the Park Avenue rich bitches shop, all of them so slim and sophisticated, noses stuck up in the air, shoulders thrown back, hips swinging. It's hard to believe, looking at them, that they are just as miserable as all the rest. Maybe even more so. Because, damn, they got what every woman wants—great looks, great bod, some rich guy who's fool enough to give her every cent he's got. They got it all, right? Only, it ain't working, E. I can see it in their eyes. I can see how lonely they are. How starved. How desperate for someone to come along and save them from their pointless lives.

And that someone is me. They don't know it. But I do.

I was on Madison in the low 60s when I saw her coming out of this Italian shoe store, looking tall and lean. Looking like she was going somewhere that mattered. She had on a camel coat, black leggings and a pair of moccasins. I had to use my imagination a little this time, E, because she wasn't doing the makeup thing and her frizzy black hair was tied back and she had on these big, ugly horn-rimmed glasses. But there could be no doubt about it—this was a major honey. My major honey.

I followed her down Madison. A big black limo followed her, too. She stopped to throw a couple of shopping bags in back and say something to the driver. When she got to 57th Street she hung a left and went into the Ghurka leather store. I didn't much like the feel of it. Too small. I waited outside. She wasn't in there for long, and she came out empty-handed. Headed over to Fifth, where the cabs jammed the intersection, riding their horns, and the people were shoulder to shoulder on the sidewalk and some guy was roasting chestnuts and another guy was ringing a bell for the Salvation Army and another guy was selling flowers. I bought a bunch from him, cost me five bucks. I thought maybe she was going into Tiffany's but she crossed over to the other side of Fifth and went in Bergdorf Goodman. A prime-time ladies' clothing store, nothing but the fancy designer stuff, floor after floor of it. Standing just inside the front door was this little sugar-lipped Chinese honey offering free perfume samples to the folks. What a little cutie. Making, what, six dollars an hour to come all the way here from Queens during Christmas season to spray that bad-smelling shit on people? Little honey would be better off dead.

Another time, Friend E. Not today. I already had business today.

I followed my own honey up the escalator to the second floor. I didn't exactly blend in there, as you can well imagine, but the flowers helped me out some. I just looked like one of those messengers you see around town, making another delivery, trying to keep it together.

She ended up in this shop with stuff by one of those Italian designers that got only one name. She was checking out a navy blue suit. There were a few other women beaming on stuff. One clerk. But nobody was standing too close to her.

Until I was.

I said That's a crime against nature, you know. She looked me up and down, cold as cold gets, and said What is? I said Pulling your hair back that way. It's much too beautiful. Well thanks, she said, trying to act like she wasn't interested. But she was. She was a woman like all of the rest, E. Desperate to be saved. I said These flowers are for you. She said As if, I couldn't take them. I said Yes you could. She took them. Sure she did. I asked her what her name was. She said it was Cassandra. I said Wait, don't I know you? Because she did look familiar, like maybe I saw her once in a movie. She said Well, I am on television sometimes. I said That can't be it. I don't own a television. She said Geez, how do you stay in touch with what's happening? I said From life. She said Get outta here, that's a totally nothing magazine now, Jurassic fucking Park. I said Not the magazine, life itself. Then I launched into this whole bullshit argument about how too many people experience life second-hand from their lounge chairs instead of getting out there and talking to the people. I made it all up on the spot, but she was real intrigued. Hooked, you might even say.

I'm telling you, it's a gift I have, Friend E. I am blessed.

She was staring at me now. Had these weird eyes, like great big saucers of cream. She said Y'know, I'd swear you look familiar, too. Where do I know you from? I said You don't, but I hear that a lot. She said Listen, let's go someplace. I said Where to? She said My place. I wanna hear some more about your ideas on television and society—ties in with a story I'm doing. I said You're a writer? No way, so am I. And she said Get outta here, that's so cool. And out the door we went.

Me thinking this one's going to be like a hot knife going through butter.

That limo of hers was waiting out front for her. Right away she started to get in. Right away I said No way. Didn't want any driver remembering me, E. She said C'mon, what's your problem, cookie? I said Nothing, I just don't believe in limos. She said What, you wanna take a cab? And I said No, the subway. And she said What are you, weird? And I said Hey, maybe some other time. And she said Yeah, yeah, shewa. We'll take the subway.

We took the N train down to 14th Street, her acting real tense and paranoid the whole way, like she thought somebody was going to mug her. My guess was she hadn't been down below with the people in ten years. One old lady sitting across from us seemed to recognize her. But she didn't say nothing. Nobody did.

Cassandra lived alone on West Tenth Street. Owned the whole damned building. Not what I'd do with my money but, hey, it's a free country. Or so I've been told. There were a million pictures of her with famous people plastered all over the walls. Man, this honey knew everybody. Didn't matter one bit, though. She was still praying for me to come along. She needed me, E. Maybe even more than the others did. Because this one, this Cassandra, she had the looks, the money, the career . . . And yet she was alone and miserable and she knew it. I sure knew it. The pain in her eyes was enough to make me cry. But I would make that pain go away now. I would make it go away forever. I was here for her. I had the power.

I AM the power.

She offered me a drink. I said No, thanks. She told me to sit down. Then she went upstairs and came down with a tape recorder. Put it on the coffee table, turned it on and said So tell me what you're not telling me. Suddenly acting tough. And I said Huh? And she said You followed me all the way to Bergdorf's from Madison. You picked me up for a reason. You got something you wanna dish, go ahead and dish. You want it off the record we'll make it off the record. My word is gold. I didn't get to where I am by boning my sources. Go on, dish me, do me, c'mon.

Friend E, I just sat there staring at her like a fool. Because she was like this whole different person. Nasty and hard in that New York kind of way. Finally, I said You've got me all wrong, baby. I just want to get to know you. She said You're wasting my time with this bullshit. You want to talk about Him and we both know it. So let's talk about Him. And I said Talk about who? And she said The answer man, who else?

Whoa, trip on this a second, will you, E? She KNEW who I was. She'd HEARD of me. But she didn't know she was sitting there TALKING to me!

Damn, talk about a player being a step slow going to the hoop.

She eased off a little now. Tried the gentle approach, which went something like this . . . Cassandra: Is he a friend of yours? Is that what it is? Me: Yes, that's what it is. He's a friend. A real close friend. Cassandra: He's really something, isn't he? Me: That he is. I have a huge amount of respect for him. Cassandra: Gawd, so do I. Wanna tell me his name, cookie? Me: Actually, I can do better than that.

What I did, E, is I got up and sat down right next to her on the sofa and said You have to turn off the tape first. And she said Why? And I said Because that's the way it has to be. Just turn it off. Turn it off and I'll tell you the answer man's name. She said Promise? I said Promise. So she reached over and turned it off.

And that's when I gave her the special something I'd brought for her. The gift that would take her out of that lonely misery of hers. I had it tight around her throat before she could even react. She let go much easier than the others did, which surprised me. Her being so tough and all. I think I must have crushed her windpipe, because she made this gagging noise and right away pitched over onto the floor, her eyes rolling back in her head. Twitched once and was still. I put my brand on her, grabbed that tape recorder and got out of there, my deed done.

It was a good deed, too. A happy deed. I had a real spring in my step all the way home. I felt fulfilled. I felt useful. That's one of the nicest things about my work, E. That feeling of being able to give something back to the community. It does almost as much for me as it does for them, you know. It's especially nice to find out that others have heard about my work and are responding to it in a positive way. My hope, just between us boys, is that I can inspire people to join me. Just trip on this a minute, E. Think about what a world it would be if each one of us performed a small, random act of kindness every day. That's not so much to ask of people. A few minutes. That's all it takes—a few minutes. But what a difference you can make. Think about what a difference I've made in this big, cold, heartless city in just a few short days. Think about what a world it could be if we ALL gave something back. Think about that.

Damn, I'm starting to carry on. I just feel so good I may have to go out and party. I miss you, man. See if you can slip out the back way. We'll make us a weekend of it. I know I can get you laid. No problem meeting beautiful honeys in this town. There are more than you can shake your big ugly stick at.

Your pal, T

p.s. Money helps. Bring some, the more the better

Fourteen

THE NEWS was wall-to-wall answer man for some time after that. The no-brain supermodels and no-game slam dunkers and no-nothing politicians could pretty much forget about getting any ink or airtime. People wanted to know about the answer man, period. They wanted to know about his unmasking as Tuttle Cash, the former Heisman trophy winner and Rhodes scholar and close personal friend of Stewart Hoag, that dashing one-time It Boy of contemporary American literature. They wanted to know about Tuttle's incredible gridiron feats. About his long and painful fall. About his dramatic suicide on the field where he had known his greatest triumphs. They wanted to know it all. Every detail. There was, believe it or not, a high road here. *Sports Illustrated* put its best people to work on an insightful cover story that took over most of that week's issue. ESPN threw together an instant one-hour special, *From Heisman to Madman*. Pretty thorough work, actually, considering that they didn't have Tuttle as a source. Or me.

Of course, this being America in the nineties, there was a broad, four-lane low road, too. No speed limit here. The tabloids dug up a seemingly endless bevy of women who'd once had violent, kinky sex with Tuttle—going all the way back to the ex-wife of his geometry teacher at Choate. Not surprisingly, the hottest figure to emerge from obscurity was Luz Santana, exotic dancer, who got six figures from one of the TV shows to tell all and another six figures from *Playboy* to bare all. Luz also got her own worldwide web site and a recurring role on *Baywatch*. I don't know if she and her new boyfriend ever got hitched. We lost touch somehow, Luz and I.

Naturally, the whole Tansy thing came out again—in painstaking, ugly detail. Not that Tansy would go anywhere near it. She wasn't talking, no matter how much money they offered her. Me, I didn't stop to think for a moment how much I could get for that awful photo album. It didn't occur to me. Not once.

Cassandra Dee, the answer man's fifth victim, went from rising TV tabloid glam princess to media martyr overnight. Her emotional on-air plea—"Call me, fax me, E-mail me, I'm yours"—became one of those phrases that catch on. Everyone in the one-name sphere started saying it. Newt. Deion. Batman. Whitney Houston even put it to music—if you call what she does music. I call it breathing. In death, Cassandra got her second *People* cover and a degree of respectability that had eluded her in life. There was even talk of setting up a scholarship fund in her name at the staid Columbia Graduate School of Journalism, which would have made her shriek with laughter. I can practically hear her now.

Inspector Dante Feldman started shopping a proposal for his story, *The Hunt for the answer man,* around town almost immediately. Those publishers who lost out on the big book ended up bidding on his, and one of them overpaid dearly for it. The big book, of course, was my book. Or I guess I should say *our* book—for it was to be a collaboration of sorts. Part of it would be the five chapters that Tuttle had sent me, including his cover letters. Part of it would be my account of my life and times with him, an intimate biography climaxing with my blow-by-blow reenactment of those harrowing last days. My involvement with the police. My friendship with Cassandra. What it was like discovering her body. What it was like discovering his body.

Damn, there were a lot of bodies.

Three publishers stayed in on the final bidding. And in case you're wondering, the answer is yes, the answer man *was* worth more than Colin Powell. Of course, there were some legal hurdles to jump. Technically, those five chapters weren't mine to sell. They belonged to Tuttle's estate—his mother in Pennsylvania, where his body was being sent for burial. And then there was the Son of Sam law, which says that no one who has been found guilty of a crime may be allowed to profit from that crime. This one was a bit thornier, since Tuttle had never actually been convicted or even so much as charged with any of the killings. One publisher's lawyer was even floating the theory that the Son of Sam law didn't apply here. Not that any publisher would care to test this particular theory out by getting sued by the victims' families. Me neither. I hate going to court. I never know what to wear, and no one ever smiles. Still, these hurdles could be and would be cleared, given enough lawyers and money. And there was no shortage of either of those. There would be a book. A major movie, too. I could even write the screenplay if I chose to. The money was huge. All of it was huge.

The trouble was, I wasn't sure if I wanted any of it. I was deeply torn. Part of me wanted to get Tuttle's sorry life story down on paper myself, and get it right. Part of me wanted to turn my back on the whole goddamned thing. Because I didn't want to live with it any longer. And because, to be honest, I still hadn't figured out what it all meant. What the so-called moral of this twisted and violent story was. Or if there even was a moral.

So I let the faxes from my agent pile up on my dresser. Didn't respond to them. Just brooded, which happens to be one of the things I'm best at.

"Maybe I should bail out, Merilee," I said as I lolled in the tub with my martini, Lulu sprawled mournfully on the tile floor next to me. She still had not gotten over Cassandra's death. Wouldn't eat. Wouldn't even touch Pam's kippers and eggs, which for Lulu is akin to the Reverend Al Sharpton walking away from a live microphone. "Maybe I should just forget it."

"Maybe you should at that, darling."

She was in the bedroom, dressing for dinner. A rare evening off—her director was in the hospital passing a kidney stone, news of which had prompted her to remark, "There is a God." Opening night of *Wait Until Dark* had been pushed back a week.

"Then again," I said, "maybe I won't be able to forget it. If only I hadn't waited. If only I'd turned him in right away. Cassandra would still be alive. He'd still be alive. . . ."

"I want you to stop that this instant, mister," Merilee commanded me, padding into the bathroom in her stockings and white silk camisole. She was searching for her hairbrush. She was always searching for her hairbrush. "You cannot blame yourself for what Tuttle Cash did."

"Easier said than done, Merilee. I was involved. I was his accomplice. He made me into his accomplice."

She stood there in the doorway studying me, her golden hair a mass of tangles. "Hate him for it, darling?"

"I don't love him for it, that's for damned sure. And now he's bailed out and left me here to live with the consequences of what he did."

"Tuttle Cash was not a nice man, darling. You must have figured that out by now."

I said nothing, just lay there in the hot water feeling limp.

She settled on a comb and went to work with it there in

the mirror. "If it's all of that money that's bothering you . . ."

"The money's no problem. I can set up a fund for the families of the victims. No, the money's the easy part." I took a sip of my martini. "Possibly it was the roar of the crowd, Merilee."

"The roar of the crowd, darling?"

"Possibly he missed it so much he'd do *anything* to get it back. Even try to walk on water. Maybe that explains it." I was silent a moment. "What am I saying? Nothing explains it. Nothing explains why anyone would do anything that sick."

Merilee lingered there, watching me in the mirror. "I phoned Tansy this afternoon."

"So did I. She wouldn't take my call."

"She took mine."

"Really?" I glanced up at her. "How did she sound?"

"Hollow and empty, poor thing. I invited her to dinner. She said dinner would be very difficult right now. I do wish there was something we could do for her."

"I'm afraid she'll have to do that for herself, Merilee." I pulled the plug in the tub and climbed out. She handed me a towel. "He wasn't out of her life. Not really. So there's a great big empty space there now. It's up to her to figure out how to fill it. Her and Malachi both." I was surprised at just how low a profile Malachi had been keeping the past couple of days. He'd shuttered the restaurant, given no interviews. Wouldn't return my phone calls. I wondered how he was doing.

There was a tap at the bedroom door. Merilee went and opened it.

It was Pam. "Are we decent?"

"Not if we can help it," I answered, climbing into my shawl-collared silk dressing gown.

"Yes, yes, dear boy. Now then, I was wondering . . ." She stopped herself, her cheeks flushing a rosy shade of pink. "That is, *we* were wondering—Victor and I—if it might be convenient for the two of us to drive out to the farm tomorrow. Begin making those *arrangements* of which we spoke."

"Arrangements? What arrangements."

"I've offered them the farm, darling," Merilee explained. "They're getting married there."

"Ah. Excellent idea."

"Isn't it, though?" Pam agreed breathlessly. "It's so romantic there over the holidays."

"Tomorrow will be fine, Pam," Merilee told her. "The three of us will join you as soon as we can."

"Oh, good, good," she exclaimed, fluttering girlishly. "We'll, ah, leave first thing in the morning. Dinner will be ready shortly. I assume that will be satisfactory?"

"That will be perfect," Merilee said.

And with that Pam headed off. I dressed—the navy-blue suit, white broadcloth shirt, red and yellow silk polka-dot bow tie. Merilee already was. Dressed, that is. That silk camisole she'd been modeling was in fact an evening dress. This all became splendidly and erotically clear the second she stepped into her three-inch heels. Which, by the way, did her long shapely calves no harm.

"What do we think of this rather surprising romantic development?" I asked, working on my bow tie in the mirror over the dresser.

"It's not in the least bit surprising, darling." Now she was pawing through her jewelry box for her diamond earrings. "They enjoy each other's company. They're comfortable with each other. I, for one, am thrilled that it has blossomed into something more."

"Their age difference doesn't bother you?"

"Don't be so Bumsteadian, darling. Cheese Louise."

"I've been missing your quaint little expressions."

"Evidently that's not all you've been missing," she said tartly, nudging me out of the mirror so she could put her earrings on.

I nudged her back. "How is it you knew this was going on and I didn't?"

"Because I'm a woman. Women *sense* things."

"Things? What things?"

"Feelings, of course. Men don't. You're too busy clomp-ing around the house—"

"I do not clomp. I stride purposefully."

"—Thinking about how wonderful you are. Frankly, dar-ling, it was as plain as the nose on your face. Or at least the nose on mine." She stood shoulder to shoulder with me in the mirror, examining hers critically. "Is mine getting larger as my face sags or is that just my imagination?"

"Maybe we should invite her out, Merilee."

"Invite who out, darling?"

"Tansy. For the holidays. It might be good for her to get away for a few days. And I need to talk to her about this book. I won't do it if she's against it. I want her to be comfortable with the idea."

"That's an excellent idea, darling. She won't come, but I'll try. I'll call her in the morning."

The doorbell rang now. I heard footsteps. Clomping, if you must know. Followed by a knock at the bedroom door.

"It's Inspector Feldman and Lieutenant Very, Hoag," Vic called to me.

"Turn on the lights in the living room, Vic. I'll be right there."

Merilee joined me. Lulu did not. Merely moved from the bathroom floor to the bed, whimpering softly. Possibly a dose of cod liver oil was in order.

Merilee and Romaine Very were old friends by now. The lieutenant got a kiss on the cheek, not to mention some highly tactful words about his haircut. As for the Human Hemorrhoid, he got the full star treatment. First the dazzling smile. Then the firm handshake. Then the modest, the just-plain-folks: "Hi, I'm Merilee."

As if he wouldn't know. The poor man was pie-eyed and speechless. Her outfit certainly didn't hurt. "A fan," he was finally able to croak. "I'm a huge one."

"Why, thank you, Inspector," she said graciously, folding

herself and her long, silken legs onto the leather settee. "I do hope you'll come see my new show. Bring a friend. Bring the whole department."

"Wouldn't miss it," he assured her. He was regaining his cool. The shooting and smoothing thing was happening. Shooting and smoothing. Shooting and smoothing . . .

We sat, neither Feldman nor Very so much as noticing me there on the settee next to Merilee. I was used to this. It happens whenever I go anywhere with Merilee. Especially when she's three-fourths naked.

"May I offer you gentlemen a martini?" I said. Merilee and I were still working our way through our pitcher.

"A scotch would go down pretty good," said Feldman.

"I heard that," Very chimed in.

I poured them each two fingers of the Singleton. We drank, the smell of Pam's braised pork tenderloin with fresh sage wafting toward us from the kitchen.

"We turned up the typewriter, dude," Very announced into his glass.

"Where was it, Lieutenant?"

"His place," Feldman answered sharply. "Where else?"

"I had assumed . . . I thought you searched his place right away."

"Oh, we searched it, all right." Feldman's voice was heavy with sarcasm. "Same day the Cassandra Dee killing went down. We went over it fiber by fiber. Came up empty. No typewriter on the premises."

Merilee and I exchanged a confused look. I said, "I'm afraid I don't understand. Where did you—?"

"Typewriter wasn't *in* the house," Very explained. "It was in that woodshed out in the garden."

"We missed it first time around," Feldman said, biting the words off angrily.

I guess I knew how the man felt. I had missed it, too. Hadn't even thought to look out in the woodshed when I searched the place. True, I'm an amateur, but why split hairs? It made sense—that part did, anyway. "What I can't figure out is where he wrote it. The last chapter, I mean."

Now it was Very and Feldman who exchanged a look.

"What are you talking about, dude?"

"He killed Cassandra at about three in the afternoon. He stole Luz's car at around eight for that final drive to Cambridge. That means he must have written it some time in between, right?"

"Right . . ." Feldman said doubtfully.

"Where did he write it? He didn't go home. He didn't go to the restaurant. He couldn't have—you were watching both places."

"What about Luz's place?" Merilee wondered.

"She says no," Very replied.

"She could be lying," Feldman said.

"She could be," I conceded. "Only *how* did he write it? He only had a few short hours. I'm a professional writer, gentlemen. I couldn't have banged out something that good that fast. Especially under such extreme circumstances. Plus it's so clean. Not so much as a single typo. And here's another question: Say he did write it before he drove to Cambridge—"

"He *did,*" Feldman interrupted. "That's a fact."

"Okay, then how did he get the typewriter back in the woodshed?" I asked. "You were watching the place. You had men stationed there. How did he do it?"

Very and Feldman both froze. This hadn't occurred to them.

"Dig, there must be a simple explanation." Very tugged at his little tuft of beard. "If we trip on it a minute, I'm sure it'll come to us."

"Aw, Christ," Feldman said disgustedly. "Here you two pineapples go again, circling over this thing in your helicopter. Pay attention to the facts, will you? The man's dead. The man won't kill anymore. The man won't—"

"Wait, I know what he did!" Merilee broke in excitedly.

"He had already written it—*before* he killed Cassandra. It's all a work of fiction. None of it actually happened the way he described it."

"That's a promising theory, Miss Nash." Feldman spoke politely, trying not to stare at her legs. "Only it did go down the way he described it. Cassandra Dee *was* in Bergdorf that day. Sales clerk in the Prada boutique, salty old broad named Madelyn Horowitz, recognized her right off, even with her hair tied back. Lots of the ladies did. One of them even asked her for her autograph."

"What time was this?" I asked.

"Noon, maybe," he replied.

"Did she spot Tuttle, too?" I asked.

"That's a negative. He must have hit on her out front when she came out."

Very said, "Except, he distinctly mentions seeing her in a designer boutique with only one name. How would the man know that unless he was inside?"

"It's tres chic to go by one name these days, Lieutenant," Merilee said. "There's Prada. There's Fendi, Kenzo, Krizia . . ."

"Safe guess on his part, in other words." Feldman took a sip of his scotch. "I figure he was playing with her. Pretending to give himself up to her. And she played right along."

"If only she'd called us," Very said glumly. "She'd still be alive if she'd called us."

I said, "She was picturing banner headlines, Lieutenant. Not herself dead. No reporter thinks that way. Not if they're any good." I stared down into my empty glass. "Odd how Tuttle didn't say good-bye, don't you think? Here he was, hours from his own suicide, yet there's nothing in his final chapter reflecting that. Or in his letter. It's all very upbeat and enthusiastic. Not so much as a hint that he was about to blow his brains out."

"There wouldn't be," Feldman said, going into his lecture mode. "Serials typically experience a sense of exhilaration after they do their victims. When Cash sat down to write that, he was on a temporary high. But then that euphoria wore off, and up popped his demons all over again."

"I understand that, Inspector," I said. "It's just that he was so obsessed about making a big splash. All he talked about in his letters was the publicity, the money. Who was going to play him in the movie, who was going to play me, you—"

"I forget, darling," Merilee said. "Who was he talking about for the role of me?"

"He wasn't. He didn't mention you."

She drew herself up at this, outraged. "What?"

"Okay, I lied. He wanted Anna Nicole Smith."

"How *dare* he write me out of the picture? That son of a sea cook *never* liked me."

"You never liked him, Merilee."

"Harrumph."

"You were saying, Hoagy?" Feldman said.

"I just find it hard to accept that Tuttle would end it like he did without putting that part down on paper, too. I mean, he went out with a kaboom. Literally. But in terms of his final chapter, he went out with a whimper. Do you gentlemen understand what I'm saying?"

They didn't. They were both staring at me blankly across the coffee table.

Very cleared his throat uncomfortably. "You been close to this since day one, dude. Closer than any of us. Maybe you ought to do some serious chillin'. Try to remember what life was like when it was normal."

"My memory doesn't go back that far, Lieutenant."

Merilee took my hand. "I'll do what I can to jog it for you, darling."

Very grinned at her. "I'm down to that."

Pamela started making discreet noises at the dining table.

"Will you gentlemen stay for dinner?" Merilee offered. "I'm sure we can throw another potato in the stew."

Feldman let out a guffaw. "Christ, I haven't heard that expression in thirty years."

I said, "Stick around, Inspector. She's just getting warmed up."

For which I got a swift, hard elbow in the ribs.

"Thanks, but we have to be going." Feldman got wearily to his feet and stuck his hand out to me. We shook. "Sorry it had to end the way it did. You finding your friend dead."

"I found two friends dead, Inspector."

"They never make it easy for us, do they?"

"No, Inspector. They do not."

"But it's over. That's the bottom line, Hoagy. You just stick to the bottom line, that's my advice. Sometimes we lose sight of the bottom line when we're trying to get over something like this. It's happened to me. It's happened to all of us." He managed a grim, sympathetic smile. The effort seemed to pain him. "You're still not my kind of guy, you know. You're not a team player. But I'll tell you one thing— you made one helluva choice in a wife."

"Ex-wife," Merilee and I both said.

"Whatever," he said. "You got lucky, my friend."

"It's true, Inspector. I'm a lucky man."

"Ride easy, dude," said Very.

Then they said their good-byes to Merilee and were gone.

We had asparagus with our pork tenderloin, also Pam's world-renowned macaroni and cheese. She uses just under one metric ton of two different grated cheeses, Italian fontina and Pecorino Romano. Pam's macaroni and cheese is ordinarily a major event in my life. But I barely touched it or the moist, fragrant slices of pork. I just sat there at the table, listening to the tall clock tick in the entry hall.

"What is it, darling?" Merilee asked fretfully, her green eyes shimmering at me in the candlelight.

"I have no idea, Merilee."

"Well, I have. You've gotten less than two hours of sleep

in the past four days. Why don't you pop into bed with Lulu and a good book? I'll join you as soon as I've helped Pam with the dinner things."

"You know, I think that's exactly what I'll do."

So I undressed and climbed into bed with B. Traven and Lulu, who climbed right up onto my chest, her paws on my shoulders, and started whimpering at me woefully. She truly was not herself. I felt her large black nose. Cold and wet. She wasn't sick. But something was definitely bothering her. I scrunched her chin, wishing she could tell me what it was. I lay there under the down comforter with the lights of the city sparkling outside the window.

Romaine Very was right, of course. I was too close to it. Too full of hurt and loss and confusion. But chillin' was no answer. Because the hows and whens still wouldn't add up. How and when Tuttle wrote that final chapter. How and when he got the typewriter into his woodshed. How and when he chose to die. They didn't add up. No one could make them add up.

And there was something else. Something that had bothered me several days ago about one of those chapters. An odd feeling I couldn't put my finger on. It was in the third chapter, "the answer man takes a plunge." The Bridget Healey murder.

I climbed out from under my glum chum and fetched my copy and got back into bed with it. I read the pages over again carefully. Read all about him finding her there in the pool, swimming laps . . . *She had on a string bikini, the kind they wear when they're advertising* . . . Joining her in the whirlpool. Hearing her story. Walking her to her dark, cramped apartment. Performing his random act of kindness . . . *She just sort of went away, snap, like some bug on the kitchen floor* . . . That empty feeling he was left with. I read it all over again. And I re-read it.

And then I found it. It wasn't much. It was just a word. One word. But it was wrong. And now the pieces started to fit together. Almost. One piece was missing. I needed the missing piece.

I looked at the clock on the nightstand. It wasn't yet ten. I pulled out the Manhattan phone book and started working the phone, seated there on the edge of the bed. Merilee came in after awhile. When she saw me there, saw the look on my face, she went into the living room to read. I had no luck in Manhattan, so I tried calling information. I worked my way through Brooklyn, Queens, Staten Island. Then I started in on Long Island, working my way outward from the city, town by town. Luckily, I had to go only as far as Mineola. It was after midnight by then. But I got what I needed. I got the missing piece.

And then I knew. I knew why it didn't add up. Oh, yeah, I knew all right.

Fifteen

THOSE TWO wacky lovebirds, Pam and Vic, went chugging off to Lyme in the Land Rover shortly after dawn. The morning weather forecast called for snow changing to sleet, followed by high winds, hailstones and lemmings. They wanted to beat the worst of it out there, get the kitchen stocked, the firewood chopped, the hurricane lamps filled. Pam served us our breakfast in bed before they left, which happens to be one of Merilee's two or three favorite things in the whole world, right up there with shopping for clothes in Milan and boycotting the Oscars. I don't hate it myself. There was fresh-squeezed orange juice. There were waffles, sausages, poached eggs.

Tracy joined us in the big bed, chock full of giggles and gurgles. She wasn't old enough yet to wake up in a shitty mood. How nice that must be, I thought. Lulu just lay there on my feet, sulky and morose. Still wouldn't so much as sniff at her kippers and eggs. During the night I had even heard her prowling the apartment restlessly, which she almost never does. I was really getting worried about her.

After breakfast, Merilee climbed into her gray silk loung-
ing pajamas and went around closing her blackout curtains
and turning off all the lights in the apartment. Time for a
little blindness practice, bless her. Tracy got a one-way ticket
back to her crib in the nursery. Me, I put in a call to Very.
Came up empty—the lieutenant was in court that morning.
I left word for him to call me as soon as he could. I went in
the bathroom and showered and shaved and doused myself
with Floris. When I came out Lulu was standing in the
bedroom doorway barking at me. Her way of informing me
she was ready for her morning constitutional in Central
Park. I told her to hold her horses. She started barking
louder. I told her to shut up. She wouldn't shut up. And
then a heavy thud came from the direction of the living
room. Shook the whole apartment. A definite 6.3 on the
Richter scale.

"What did you bump into this time, Merilee?"

She didn't answer me. More barking from Lulu.

"Was that you, Merilee?" I called out, louder this time.
"Are you all right?"

Still no response. She was, possibly, out cold. Actresses.
Stay away from them if you can help it. And if you can't,
make sure you have good health insurance. I threw on my
dressing gown and went searching for her, stopping first in
the nursery just to make absolutely sure that Tracy hadn't
somehow managed to tumble out of her crib and hit the
deck. She hadn't. She was in there, all right, inspecting her
toes. Lulu elected to hang there with her, commandeering
the rocker. Not one of her usual haunts, but I didn't press it.
I was just happy she'd stopped barking.

"Merilee?" I started down the hallway toward the dining
room, plunging headlong into the complete and total blackness she had created. "Merilee, are you all right? Hellooo?"

"Psst, in here, Hoagy," she whispered at me from the
dark, her strong hand grabbing mine, tugging at me urgently.

It was to be the powder room again, near as I could tell.

"Merilee, I have this really kinky idea. There's a large, soft bed in the master bedroom. Just for the sake of variety why don't we—?"

"Shhh!"

And then we were in there with the door closed and her breath hot on my face and her lips on mine. Hands flinging my dressing gown open. Legs wrapping around me tightly.

"Oh, God, Hoagy," she moaned. "This is so *right.*"

Only it wasn't right. Not the lips. Not the legs. Not the voice. I pushed her away, violently. I groped for the light and flicked it on.

It was Tansy Smollet who was in there with me. It was Tansy Smollet who was up on that bathroom sink with her bare white legs clutching me, her shapeless designer smock flung half off her, her eyes bright and cunning as a wild animal's in the firelight.

It was Tansy Smollet who had a Smith & Wesson Ladysmith pointed directly at my stomach.

It was Tansy.

"What have you done with Merilee?" I gasped, my chest heaving.

"Tied her up to a dining chair," she replied, her voice incredibly calm. Eerily calm. "Stuffed a sock in her mouth so she couldn't scream. I'm very good at doing that sort of thing in the dark. I've had a lot of experience, you know. The doorman let me up. I told him I was Merilee's long lost sister and it was a surprise and would he please not spoil it. When she opened the door—"

"She got a surprise." That explained why Lulu had started barking. To alert me. And that was why she had stayed behind in the nursery. To guard her baby sister. Protecting Tracy was her job.

"We're almost there now, Hoagy," Tansy said softly, letting the gun fall casually to her side. "She's all that's stopping us now. *He's* not here anymore. We made sure of that."

"We did?"

She nodded her head slowly, like a good, obedient child. "Now we just have to take care of Merilee. Once she's gone we'll have what we've always wanted." Her hand reached inside my dressing gown, playing with what she found in there.

I grabbed her hand and held it. "Which is what, Tansy?"

Her eyes widened. "Why, to be together, of course. We've been pretending for too long, Hoagy. We won't have to pretend any longer. Oh, God, this is going to be so good. And I swear I'll be a good mother to Tracy. You'll see."

My eyes were on the gun. The Ladysmith has a slimmer grip than the standard issue. Not that she needed one. The hand that gripped mine was big and strong. *Someone with strong hands.* That's what Mrs. Adelman had said about the typing sample. She never said a *man* with strong hands. Just *someone.*

I thought about lunging for it, wrestling with her for it. But there was no telling what might happen. She might shoot me. And there was my family to think of. Merilee, who was tied to a chair out there in the dark somewhere. Tracy . . .

"We'll make it look like a break-in, Hoagy. Before we go we'll make it look like she was the tragic victim of a random break-in."

"We're not going anywhere, Tansy. You've killed five women. You've driven Tuttle to suicide. You're sick, Tansy. You're very, very sick."

She shrugged this off, her smock falling to her waist. I looked at her small, firm breasts, the nipples rosy and taut. There was a time when the sight of Tansy Smollet's naked breasts would have stirred me to a frenzy. There was a time. Now there was no time. She looked at me looking at her. "Listen to you," she said. "You make it sound like I did all of this for no reason. I did it for *us.*"

"Lulu knew it was you," I said. "It was your hand cream.

She smelled your hand cream at Cassandra's apartment. That's why she was howling—not because Cassandra was dead, but because she realized that you were her killer. She adores you, and this meant she'd be losing you."

Tansy let out a laugh. "Losing me? She'll be *gaining* me." She glanced down at the gun in her hand. "All we have to do is finish what we started."

I said, "Feldman was so wrong. He insisted serial killers are never women. He had all the statistics and the facts and the case studies. He had everything but the exception to the rule—*you*. And it all makes so much more sense this way, too. How the answer man was able to pick up bright, attractive single women so easily. How he was able to convince them to take him home—even in the midst of a citywide scare. How come no one ever spotted any of the victims with a man shortly before they died. How come he didn't sexually assault them. Because the answer man *wasn't* a man. He was *you*. No reason for a woman to be worried about *you*. *You* with your concentration-camp haircut, the better to leave no samples behind. *You* with your short, unpainted nails, the better to leave no scratches or traces of polish behind. . . . Madelyn Horowitz, the sales clerk at Bergdorf, spotted you, you know. She saw a woman ask Cassandra for her autograph. Madelyn lives in Mineola. I spoke to her late last night. She described the autograph seeker as a tall, leggy Amazon type wearing a Zoran." I smiled at Tansy. "That's what Cassandra was trying to tell me on the phone when she was dying. She wasn't saying, 'It's raining.' She was saying, 'Zoranian.' You told her you knew something about the answer man's identity, I suppose. That's how you convinced her to take you home."

"I could have sworn she was dead when I left," Tansy said blithely. "I guess she just had more fight in her than the others."

"She was desperate to be the one to break this story. That's what kept her alive long enough to dial that phone.

She was a reporter to the end, always a terrific eye for detail. Of course, that's true of you as well, isn't it? You filled those chapters with one incriminating detail after another—*E* as in Ezra, *T* as in Tuttle. Ring Lardner, Yushies, Tuttle's penchant for leggy, toothy women. His loathing of computers. His old sign-off—'Just think how much fun I'd be having if I didn't have to work.' You used all of those things. You *knew* all of those things."

"And I know you," she added, gazing deeply into my eyes. Hers burned as if there were a fever inside of her. "I knew you'd figure out that the answer man and Tuttle were one and the same. I knew you'd agonize over it for a few days. And I knew that when push came to shove you'd turn Tuttle in."

"I'm glad I'm so predictable."

"You're not predictable. You're a dear, sweet man who is way too decent to ever hurt Merilee, even though she's been tormenting you for years. Throwing you out. Taking you back. Putting you through that awful pregnancy scandal in the tabloids. You deserve better, Hoagy. You've always deserved better. And now you're going to get what you deserve, only we have to move fast."

I gripped her hand tighter, holding her there. I didn't want any of what she had in mind for outside of this room. "What about the novel, Tansy? The auction, the movie sale—was all of that just pretend or was it for real?"

"Why, of course it was for real," she replied, her manner turning bright and cheerful. "Because I also knew you'd never, ever be content to live on my money. You're too proud. You'd have to have your own. That's why I made up the answer man. I'll have you know I made a thorough study of the matter. *Nothing* sells better these days than books about serial killers. Especially when the victims are young and pretty. Especially when the killer is a cold, merciless stalker who hunts down his innocent victims and numbers them. That's why I put the question marks on their foreheads. Because I knew the New York tabloids would have a field day with it. Just as I knew New York book publishers would be reading about him every single day and growing more and more desperate to buy the book. Nothing gets them more excited than a hot story in their own backyard. That's why I did it the way I did, Hoagy. That's why I put the city through all of this. I did it so you'd have a best-seller." She raised my hand to her lips and kissed the knuckles softly, one by one by one. "I did it for you."

"Tansy?"

"Yes, Hoagy?" Now she was rubbing her unfeeling cheek against my hand, rather like a cat.

"Why didn't you just kill Tuttle?"

"No fucking way," she snarled savagely. "That wouldn't do. No, no. I wanted him to *know* what public humiliation feels like. I wanted him to lose his restaurant, lose his name. I wanted him to go to jail for life. And find out for himself what it means to lie in fear, night after night, waiting to be violated and abused and tortured. This was my revenge, Hoagy, for what he did to me. Thirty-one. That's how many bones he broke in my face. All because I committed the unpardonable sin of getting upset that he was fucking other women behind my back. I went through months and months of unbearable pain. The operations. The healing. This was how I got through it. I lay awake, night after night, planning my revenge. I planned it and I took it. I pursued the kind of women he always liked to fuck, the ones with the big smiles and the good legs and the pretty hair. I befriended them. I killed them. And I framed him. He wanted to be a writer. I made it look like he was one. I still had his typewriter—never did throw it out. I constructed the perfect frame, in my opinion. Of course, I wasn't figuring he'd commit suicide. Men like Tuttle, men who beat up on women, they generally don't have the nerve to take their own lives. But I'm okay with that. Because it's over now. And because I was getting tired."

"So you said in your last letter."

"It took so much work, Hoagy. The planning, the doing, the writing. I had to be so careful. No slips, not one. I left no fingerprints, no hair samples, no fibers, no nothing. Do you have any idea how hard that is?"

"Something of an idea."

"The first one was the hardest, you know."

"Diane," I said. "Her name was Diane."

"I-I almost blew it. I actually brought her back to my own apartment, which was just so stupid. Only, well, I needed a safe place to hide her body while I wrote the first chapter."

"You kept her in your apartment? How cozy."

"I *had* to," she insisted. "I wanted to make sure you got Chapter One before the body was found. You know, for maximum effect. The downside was that they might find something on her body that they could somehow trace back to me."

"Only they didn't, your apartment is so spotless. No rugs. No pets. Nothing but bare surfaces. Plus you have the perfect setup for disposing a body. Your own private elevator down to your own private garage. So you stuffed Diane in a blue garment bag, knowing Tuttle had one just like it—"

"They were ours, from when we were married."

"—and you put her in one of your Garden Lady vans, took her to the park in the middle of the night and dumped her there. Diane was little. You had no problem carrying her."

"I was such a nervous wreck," she said with a shy laugh, as if she were an ingenue talking about her opening night performance. She seemed relieved to be talking about it. She hadn't been able to talk about it. Possibly she'd even be smiling, too. If only she could smile. "That's how come I bashed her head in. I panicked. But I got better at it after that. Went to their place, not mine. And I did it neat and tidy. It got easier after that. It gets easier."

"Score one for Inspector Feldman," I said. "Next came Laurie . . ."

Tansy was growing impatient again, pulling away from me. "What about her?"

"You made such a big deal about that Band-Aid on her foot. You even took it with you. Why? How did that point to Tuttle?"

"That was just me getting into it. This guy I used to work with was always staring at my feet. Drove me nuts."

"I'll say. But you knew what you wanted to do. You were cool. You were calculating. You were everywhere. You followed me from the outset—that first time I met Lieutenant Very at Barney Greengrass."

"I felt closer to you that way."

"How long did you follow Luz? She thought it was Tuttle. Tuttle swore it wasn't him. And it wasn't. It was you."

"Tuttle had written me all about her," Tansy said. "How she'd dumped him. I intended to make her one of the answer man's victims. I figured this would tighten the noose around Tuttle's neck for sure. He was a jilted lover, violent past. My problem was opportunity. The stupid bitch slept all day, had an attentive new boyfriend. The cow was never alone."

"Lucky her. So you played it safe and you moved on. But then you panicked all over again with Francie, the flute player. It got ugly between you two in Riverside Park. *You* got ugly. What happened, Tansy? Why did you do that to her?"

"She kissed me," Tansy replied simply.

I considered this a moment. "Francie was gay?"

She nodded her head in that little girl way of hers again. "She came on to me, big-time. And it threw me, big-time. Believe me, Hoagy, this was not something I was expecting. And she was *so* insistent. W-We struggled. I hit her with a rock and . . . It happened just the way I wrote it, really. Only, she *scratched* me."

"I saw scratches on your hands that night I visited you. They were from *her?*"

"Yes. My skin was under her nails. And she bit my lip

when she was kissing me. Not terribly. Not so anyone would notice. But what might they find in her mouth when they did their DNA tests? Would they find a trace of my blood? My saliva? I didn't know."

"Score one for Lieutenant Very. So you went back and you hacked off her head and her hands with one of your Garden Lady axes before you buried her. Thus making the story ten times hotter than it had been."

"The publicity wasn't in my thoughts at all when I did it," she confessed. "Although I was glad about it, for your sake."

"What did you do with Francie's head and hands, by the way?"

"I stopped off in Central Park on my way home and buried them there. I improvised."

"Like the way you improvised when you found out Tuttle had gone and ended it," I said. "The police had sealed his apartment. Only, there was one vital piece of evidence missing—the typewriter. It was nowhere to be found. Because *you* had it. A troubling loose end. So, once again, you improvised. After the police had searched the place from top to bottom you slipped over the garden wall in the night and you planted it in the woodshed. You knew about the back way in from Sixty-sixth Street. You did live there once, after all. No one saw you. And of course no one suspected that the typewriter had been put there *after* the search. They had no reason to. They had their man and he was dead. They just figured they did a sloppy job first time around. You're smart, Tansy. And you're a gifted writer."

This seemed to startle her. "W-Why, thank you, Hoagy. That means a lot, coming from you. I always kept a journal. At Miss Porter's, at Vassar, at Cornell. I got in the habit of scribbling. I'd fill notebook after notebook lying on my bed at night. I guess that's how I was able to do it—just kind of churned it out." This was vintage Tansy. She always had been modest about her many accomplishments, no matter how remarkable they seemed.

"Well, you caught your character's voice perfectly. Who was he, anyway?"

"Just someone lonely and angry and hurting. He was me, I guess."

"I loved that whole random-act-of-kindness thing. It was so convincing. You had everyone believing that this guy actually existed. You even fooled a panel of shrinks."

"Shrinks believe what they want to believe." She said it bitterly. "I've been fooling them for years."

"You fooled me, too, Tansy. Almost."

She stiffened. "What do you mean, *almost?*"

"You made one mistake. It was in the third chapter, when you were watching Bridget swim laps at the health club. A small detail, really. But it gave you away."

"What was it?" she demanded angrily. "What did I say?"

"You said, and I quote, 'I just stood there in my own swimsuit watching for a minute, transfixed.' "

"What's so wrong with that?"

"Not a thing. Except that there isn't a man alive who would have written it. Men say *swimming trunks* or *swim trunks* or just plain *trunks.* Men never, ever say *swimsuit.* Only a woman would use that word. But don't get down on yourself about it. Writers always nitpick each other's work."

She was edging toward the door now. Time was running out.

"You put me through hell, Tansy. You do know that, don't you?"

"I do, Hoagy. But I couldn't let you know the truth. That would have spoiled everything. You understand that, don't you? It's going to be worth it, I swear. I'll make it worth it."

She reached over and flicked off the bathroom light. I didn't know why. Now there was only blackness. And silence. I could hear her breathing. It was warm in there. I could smell her, a humid, pungent scent that tweaked my nostrils.

"Hoagy?" she whispered at me in the darkness. "Are you feeling the way I'm feeling right now?"

"I doubt it, Tansy. How are you feeling?"

She showed me how. Guided my hand down between her legs, gasping when my fingers made contact with the wetness that they found there. "It's the anticipation, Hoagy. I always feel this way when I'm about to do it. Afterward— you won't believe how it feels afterward. And now that we're together, God, it's going to be *so* good." Now she was in the bathroom doorway, tugging me out into the great sea of blackness. "Come on, darling. Let's go for it."

So I did. I went for the hand with the gun, groping for it blindly in the dark, grappling with her, wrestling her for it. She fought back savagely, a hissing sound coming from between her teeth. God, she was strong. And then suddenly there was this tremendous explosion and my shoulder, my right shoulder, went completely dead.

"Now look what you've done, Hoagy," she scolded me.

"Stupid me," I said. The sound of the gunshot was still crackling in my ears. My arm felt like I'd been sleeping on it all night. No sensation. None.

"It's very important to keep your cool. Come on, we have to scoot. The neighbors. We've made a noise."

"Stupid us," I said, the fingers of my right hand turning cold. My ears were ringing. And I felt dizzy. Couldn't get my bearings in that darkness. Couldn't tell if I was standing up or lying down or . . .

She flicked on the bathroom light again, blinking at me in the brightness. "Oh, dear, look at your shoulder."

"I'd really rather not, thank you."

"Here." She pressed a hand towel over it, grabbed my other hand and held it there. "Just keep pressure on it. We'll take care of it afterward." She pulled me out into the entry hall, the light from the powder room illuminating our path. There was a light switch on the wall next to the front door. A pair of them actually—one to the entry hall ceiling fixture, one to the dining room chandelier. She flicked them both on. Nothing happened. "What's wrong with your lights?" she wondered, flicking them on and off repeatedly.

I just stood there dumbly. I had no idea. I was too busy losing blood.

"Oh, shit, never mind. Come on, Merilee's this way."

Now we were heading toward the dining room, which meant we were back in the blackness again.

"Is there a lamp in here, Hoagy?" Tansy sounded very businesslike now. "Turn on a lamp."

There was a Frank Lloyd Wright prairie lamp on the sideboard. I staggered blindly over in the direction of it. "It's okay, Merilee," I said, raising my voice. "We'll be okay." I listened for a muffled moan in response, for the sound of her body straining and heaving against the ropes that bound her to one of the dining chairs. I listened for a sound, any sound. All I heard was my own breathing. I was panting, shallow and quick, like Lulu did on a hot summer day. Lulu . . . Where was Lulu? Luluuuu . . .

I found the prairie lamp. I flicked it on. Nothing.

"Turn it on, damn it!" Tansy cried, her voice shrill and insistent.

"I'm trying, Tansy. This one's dead, too."

I heard the floorboards creak under her feet as Tansy moved closer to the dining table. "Where are you, Merilee?" she called out. "Let us know where you are. Give us a signal, dearest."

"How's this, Tansy?" Merilee replied in a loud, clear voice. A voice that was nowhere near the dining table.

A voice that was *behind* Tansy.

Tansy let out a startled yelp and a curse. And then things happened really, really fast. Thrashing in the darkness. Groans of pain. Chairs kicked over. And then a truck ran into me and I went down hard, my head smacking into something sharp. And I thought I heard gunfire but I couldn't be sure because it might just have been inside my own head and I couldn't see anything or hear anything and then I was out.

❑ ❑ ❑ ❑

Someone was waving ammonia under my nose.

Merilee. She was crouched over me, looking terribly concerned. Also terribly pale. She had a gash on her forehead and one of her silk sleeves was torn. I could see her quite clearly. All of the lights were on now. I could see Tansy quite clearly, too. She lay in a pool of blood on the floor right next to me, staring at me. In death, she looked like a marionette, her long legs crumpled awkwardly, her neck twisted, her blue eyes frozen and unblinking. All that was missing were the puppet strings. There were no strings. She'd been shot twice—in the neck and in the stomach. Merilee was still gripping the gun, her knuckles white.

I took the gun from her. She let me take it from her.

My head was swimming. My right arm was throbbing and not available for use any time soon. But I wanted to stand up. It was extremely important to me to stand up.

Merilee helped me. "I'm so sorry about that bump on your head, darling. You hit it against the dining table when I shoved you aside. You were terribly in my way, you see."

"I'll try to be more careful next time." I put my good arm around her to steady myself. My legs were made of Silly Putty.

"She got here when you were in the shower, Hoagy," Merilee informed me. She herself seemed quite steady. It amazed me how steady Merilee seemed after killing her oldest friend.

"I know that, Merilee, but—"

"She tied me up to a chair at gunpoint and gagged me."

"I know that, too, but—"

"I kicked over Tracy's high chair," she went on. "That was the thud you heard. I heard you call out my name. I heard you come looking for me. I tried to warn you, darling. Oh, how I tried. But I couldn't. It was like in a nightmare when you're trying to yell and you're trying and you can't . . . and then she intercepted you in the dark and dragged you away. She told me you were in on the whole thing with her. That you two planned it together as a way of getting rid of Tuttle."

"Merilee?"

"Yes, darling?"

"How did you get loose?"

"Oh, that was easy. Tansy was never very clever with knots. Not like I am. I used to sail with Father in Maine every summer, remember?"

"Okay, but then what?"

"I did precisely what I've been training myself to do for the past six weeks. Thanks to Susy I am ten times more resourceful in the dark than I ever was. I know where every doorway and stick of furniture in this apartment is. I simply did what Susy would do."

"You leveled the playing field."

"I had to move fast," Merilee explained. "I didn't know how much time I had. I went straight for the fuse box in the kitchen. Pulled out all the fuses except the one that runs the powder room—I didn't want her to suspect anything. When you two came looking for me in the dark, you had no way of knowing where I was. But I knew precisely where you were. I could hear you, smell you, *sense* you. That's how I was able to sneak up behind her. I jumped her. We fought. The gun went off by accident. . . . And now you know the whole story."

I thought about this a moment: "You'll have to do better than that, Merilee."

She gazed at me, puzzled. "Whatever do you mean, darling?"

"I mean, the police won't buy it if you tell it to them that way. When a gun goes off by accident, it goes off once, not twice. Never twice. Tansy has two bullets in her. That means it wasn't an accident. Lieutenant Very will know it the second he walks in." I looked deeply into her eyes. Or at least I tried to. She wouldn't look at me. I reached for her chin with my good hand and turned it toward me. "Merilee, you don't have to hide anything. No one will prosecute you. No one will think less of you. I know I won't."

Her mouth tightened, her chest rising and falling. I thought the tears would come now, but they didn't. She remained calm and strong. "You're absolutely right, of course. I took the gun away from her and I shot her the way you'd shoot a rabid animal. She came into my home. She was going to kill me, take my baby away, take my man away . . . I wasn't going to stand for that. I'm sorry."

"You don't have to be sorry," I said, stroking her high forehead. It was a nasty gash she had there. I wondered if it would leave a scar. I wondered if the camera would see it.

Now Merilee was gazing down at her friend. "Poor Tansy. I've known her since we were fifteen and she had Jim Morrison posters in her room and . . ." She trailed off, shuddering. "My God, Hoagy. Who was she? *What* was she?"

"She was the mess that Tuttle Cash left behind. Are you going to be all right, Merilee?"

"Of course, darling. I'm fine."

Because it still didn't seem real to her. She was still into her performance, still into being strong, being resourceful, being Susy. Later, when the reality hit her, she would sob and tremble and hold on to me tight. For right now, I was the one who was holding on to her.

"Merilee?"

"Yes, darling?"

"Where's our daughter?"

"Oh, I hid her—somewhere Tansy wouldn't find her. She's, um, she's in the kitchen."

"Good Lord, Merilee, you didn't stuff her in the oven, did you?"

"I did not."

Actually, Tracy was in the broom closet. Seemed quite merry in there, too, curled up on the floor playing with a rubber glove. Merilee picked her up and hugged her to her chest and cooed and laughed and started singing her favorite lullaby to her, which happens to be "Eve of Destruction." As for Lulu, she was still standing guard there outside the closet door. Her mommy had told her to stay put there, even though it had been terribly, terribly dark. And she had stayed put there. Although now she was whimpering and snuffling, tail going thumpety-thump-thumpety. Maybe just the teensiest bit happy to find me semi-alive and well. I told her she was a very brave girl. She stood on my foot and let out a war whoop and allowed as how she wouldn't mind an anchovy. I managed to get the refrigerator open. I found her jar. I gave her one.

"So what do you intend to do with me, Merilee?"

"Do with you, darling?"

"You've saved my life. In some cultures, that means you own me."

"I've always owned you, mister. It's just that now you know it."

"I see," I said. At least I think I said it. I can't be sure. That ringing in my ears was back. And Merilee seemed uncommonly tall all of a sudden. And the kitchen had a peculiar tilt to it. "Would you mind doing one more thing for me?"

"Of course, darling. What is it?"

"Could you call 911?"

I didn't hear her answer. I was out cold on the floor by then.

Sixteen

A PARK AVENUE orthopedic surgeon spent four hours putting the blown shreds of my old javelin shoulder back together again. Afterward, he told me he couldn't remember the last time he'd had so much fun. It was just like building a model airplane, is what he said. Surgeons are weird people. Necessary but weird. After it healed, there would be three visits a week with a no-nonsense sadist who called herself a physical therapist. For the time being I had to carry my right arm around in a sling, my coat thrown over my shoulders like one of those pieces of Eurotrash you see floating around town.

When I felt up to it I went out looking for Malachi Medvedev. Found him holed up with Coochie in his roost on East Fifty-eighth Street. It was a newish high-rise. They had a one-bedroom on the eighteenth floor with a terrace overlooking the Roosevelt Island tram. The decor was from straight out of the Mr. Goodbar days. Lots of kidney-shaped chrome and glass. A fake leopard skin on the floor. There was even a mirror ball on the ceiling. Malachi greeted me wearing a caftan and bedroom slippers. Coochie had on a sleeveless terry-cloth top, black leather hot pants and way too much eye makeup. And if she was more than thirteen years old, then I'm T. Coraghessan Boyle. But that was Mal's business.

Besides, she got on well with Tracy, who happened to be in my care that day. They played on the living-room floor together while Lulu shopped around in vain for a comfortable place to lie down. Malachi fixed him and me hot tea with lemon and honey and brandy, conversing with me over the counter while he waddled around in the kitchen, forever a bartender.

"How's the flipper?" he asked, slicing up a lemon.

"Better than new. In fact, I'm thinking about making a comeback."

"Oh, yeah? What as?"

"And you, Mal?" I growled. "How are you?"

"Place may not reopen, is how I am. Partners may just shut it, now that The King's gone."

"What will you do, Mal?"

"A good bartender can always find himself a spot."

"I'm well aware of that, but what will *you* do?"

"Always the kidder, huh?" he said, grinning at me. "I've had a million calls from the newspapers and the TV shows. A book publisher even. But between you and me, I ain't up for it. Man's dead, you know what I'm saying? I dunno, I may just give it up. Got my other business interests, three apartment houses in Queens earning me rentals, the condo down in Boca . . . I'll be fine." He ran a hand over his face, his doughy features scrunching up in sorrow. "About that gun, Hoagy. The one he used on himself. I hid it good, just like you told me to. Only, he found it. I-I don't know how. I just don't."

"Don't blame yourself, Mal. He wanted to go. If he hadn't found that gun he would have just bought himself another one. Or thrown himself off the top of the Empire State Building. It wasn't your fault." Although I must admit that part of me did wonder whether Malachi Medvedev had performed his own little random act of kindness—by leaving that Smith & Wesson lying around for Tuttle to find and to use. But I would leave that one alone, I decided. Like he said, the man was dead.

He pushed my hot tea over the counter to me and took a noisy slurp of his. From the living room came cascades of juvenile laughter, Tracy and her new playmate.

"Exactly how old is she, Mal?"

"What difference does that make? She's fan-fucking-tastic."

"And Muriel?"

"I love my wife," he said, simply and sincerely.

"I envy you, Mal."

"You do? Why?"

"Because you have an answer for everything. And you believe those answers. That must be a wonderful way to go through life."

He stood there across the counter studying my face a moment with those moist brown eyes of his. "Something you want to spill, Hoagy?"

I reached for my mug with my good hand and took a sip. "Not today."

"Sure, sure. Anytime. You know where to find me." He took another slurp. "I'll miss the action, Hoagy."

"You'll miss Tuttle."

"He was like a son to me," Malachi conceded, shoving his wet lower lip in and out. "Fathers ain't supposed to bury their sons. Violates the laws of nature. Leaves me feeling kind of empty." He paused, pondering this. "How does it leave you feeling?"

I smiled and said, "Like celebrating."

❑ ❑ ❑ ❑

So I went to the Oyster Bar for some bluepoints. Not a dozen, not six, *nine*. Seemed like the thing to do. This was where I had been on that crisp early December afternoon when the first chapter arrived. Besides which, a bowl of Tony's pan roast seemed like the least I could do for Lulu. I'd put her through a lot, and now that Tuttle was gone she was my best friend in the whole world. Please don't tell her I said that.

I asked Tony to mix me a Bloody Mary for openers, extra spicy. When he brought it I raised it in silent tribute to my gallant, departed friend and my gallant, departed youth. I was about to take my first sip when someone slid onto the stool next to mine.

It was Detective Lieutenant Romaine Very. He knows my haunts.

"How's the shoulder, dude?" he asked, patting Lulu hello. Tracy got a goofy face.

"Better than new. In fact, I'm thinking about making a comeback."

"Oh, yeah? What as?"

"Where's the Human Hemorrhoid?" I growled. "Shooting and smoothing in seclusion?"

"Say what?"

"Never mind."

"Check it out, we found traces of blood from the first victim in one of Miss Smollet's vans."

"Diane, Lieutenant. Her name was Diane."

"Also fibers from a coat of Miss Smollet's match fibers we found on the second . . . on Laurie's sofa. And, dig, I got a message for you from the inspector." Very's knee was starting to quake under the bar, rattling the bowls and silver that were on it. "Said to tell you he would have caught up with her eventually."

I sipped my Bloody Mary in silence.

"He's ultrasure of it, dude. Man believes in his system."

"That's nice, Lieutenant. Only, what if Tansy Smollet

hadn't come after Merilee? What if she'd simply resumed her so-called normal life and never killed anyone ever again—what then? Would Feldman have known what really happened? Would he have even suspected?"

"Man believes in his system," Very said again.

"Well, tell the man from me I'm just pleased as punch that he does. Someone ought to believe in something. It may as well be him." I drained my Bloody Mary and signaled Tony for another. "May I offer you one, Lieutenant?"

"Make mine a virgin."

"By all means."

"At least you found out your boy wasn't no killer," Very pointed out. "By trying to do right by him you didn't cause Cassandra's death. Or anyone else's. It wasn't your fault. That's something you can put in the bank, and it ain't no chump change."

"You're right, Lieutenant. That's no chump change."

Our drinks came. He took a swig of his. He sat there. He seemed terribly depressed all of a sudden.

I said, "Look, if you'd like I'll see if I know anybody who knows somebody who knows her, okay?"

Very frowned. "Knows who, dude?"

"Cokie Roberts, who else?"

He brightened considerably. "You'd do that for me?"

"I would."

"Check it out—does that mean we're friends?"

"Lieutenant, I don't know what we are." I clinked his glass with mine. "Until next time."

"Dude?"

"Yes, Lieutenant?"

"Does there have to be a next time?"

"It would seem so. I'm sorry."

I agreed to go ahead and write the definitive, the authorized, the one-and-only true story of the answer man. I donated most of my whopping advance and all of my royalties to a fund that I set up for the families of the victims. And I would only sign with a publisher that was willing to do the same with *its* share of the proceeds. The contract turned out to be a nightmare. For one thing, the publisher now had to come to terms with Tansy's estate, not Tuttle's. And she left behind many relatives and they all had lawyers who were expensive and annoying. Or am I being redundant?

The other reason the contract got so complicated was that I would only do business with a publisher who was willing to take on Novel No. 3. Package deal, take it or leave it. Hey, proud I am, stupid I am not. I know a buzz ploy when I see it. I also know the meaning of the word *leverage*.

I like to think Cassandra would have been proud of me.

Everyone wanted a piece of Merilee after it came out that she single-handedly slew the fire-breathing she-dragon that had been the answer man. Oprah wanted her. Barbara Wawa wanted her, Jane Pauley, Lesley Stahl . . . Merilee declined them, one and all. Said she was in seclusion, preparing for an upcoming play. Which she was. Although the revival of *Wait Until Dark* turned out to be something less than a major theatrical event. The play closed after three performances in spite of the mountain of publicity that Merilee brought it. Not to mention those unqualified raves that Luke Perry got from the critics. Audiences just stayed away. No one knew why. No one ever knows why. That's show business. Although I must tell you that several critics did find Merilee's performance unconvincing. I agreed with them, actually. I think she left it in our dining room and she never got it back. I think it was all just a little bit too painful for her to relive on stage every night. I think she was grateful when the show folded. I can't say how Luke felt. We were never close.

I was there that morning in our dining room. I was there for her real performance. And it was plenty convincing, believe me.

We fled home after that. Home to the eighteen acres at the end of the twisting lane in Lyme. Home to the 1736 center chimney Colonial with its seven working fireplaces and its post-and-beam carriage barn and the chapel with the stained-glass windows where I did my writing. We made it out two days before Christmas. It snowed the first night we were back. We awoke to eight inches of fresh, white powder. Lulu went romping in it, arfing ebulliently. Tracy, done up like a Russian cosmonaut in her water-resistant Gore-Tex snug suit, ate a handful of it and pronounced it not dissimilar to cheeseboogers. Vic and I tromped deep into the woods and cut down a blue spruce—a great big one like I wanted—and dragged it home. I made a huge fire in the parlor fireplace and Merilee and I drank spiked eggnog and listened to old Nat King Cole records while we decorated the tree. Her old decorations that had been handed down from mother to daughter for the past five generations.

"I'm afraid you're going to be stuck with me for awhile, darling," she announced giddily. Eggnog happens to go straight to her head. "The Brad Pitt movie's not going to happen."

"It fell through?"

"It didn't. I did. They went . . . younger."

"Who?" I demanded.

"Romola."

"The fashion model? They can't be serious."

"She's nineteen and she's gorgeous and the whole world wants to see her naked."

"But she can barely speak."

"They'll dub her."

"You mean like a voice double?"

"Something like that. They offered me the job, actually. I told them to stuff it. I said if they want my voice they have to take my big fat forty-year-old butt with it."

"Good for you, Merilee."

She sighed dejectedly. "Hoagy, I hate the real world."

"It doesn't have much going for it," I agreed.

"What do you say we stay out here until spring and watch the daffodils come up?"

"Okay, but that's not the only thing that comes up in the spring, Miss Nash," I warned.

"Why, Mr. Hoagy. I do believe your shoulder is starting to feel better."

"Better than new. In fact, I'm thinking of making a comeback."

"Oh, yeah? What as?"

'Twas the day before Christmas when the polite young minister from the Congregational Church arrived to perform the ceremony. He has a red beard and keeps bees. Vic Early and his blushing bride, Pam, were married in the parlor next to the Christmas tree with a few close friends standing up for them. Merilee and me and Tracy, of course. Lulu, who blubbered uncontrollably through the whole thing. Mr. Hurlburt, the farmer next door, who Vic fishes with. And Pam's little reading group from the Lyme library. There are ten ladies altogether. Pam, being under eighty, is the baby of the group.

Vic was trembling badly when he handed me the ring before the minister arrived. He'd cut himself shaving so many times that morning it looked like he'd been in a swordfight. I fortified him with a stiff shot of Laphroaig while Merilee and Pam fussed over Pam's dress. Fortified myself as well.

"You d-don't think I'm m-making a mistake, d-do you, Hoag?" Vic asked, his teeth chattering.

"I do not."

"It's n-not too late to make this a d-double wedding, you know."

"Oh, yes it is."

Afterward, we ate red velvet cake and drank champagne and Merilee officially gave them their wedding present from us, which was the deeded rights to the hand-hewn chestnut carriage barn and an acre of land around it to turn into a home of their own.

And then all of that laughter and good cheer started to get

to me so I threw my coat over my shoulders and slipped out the kitchen door and sat by myself on the bench by the pond in the snow. I thought about those three bright and shining young track stars in that photograph and about what twenty years of living had done to each of us. I thought about that scrawled message I'd found in Tuttle's notebook: *Subject for short story—Doof. How does he keep going? Doesn't he fucking KNOW?* I wondered what he meant by that. God, how I wondered. I thought about Tansy and that time I kissed her good-night outside of her building. I thought about how many times over the alone years I'd almost picked up the phone and called her. Almost . . . I thought about a lot of things, sitting there on that bench by myself in the snow, until Merilee came out and got me and led me back inside to my own fine version of a life.